I0739293

FATES
AFLAME

Defy fear and face change bravely

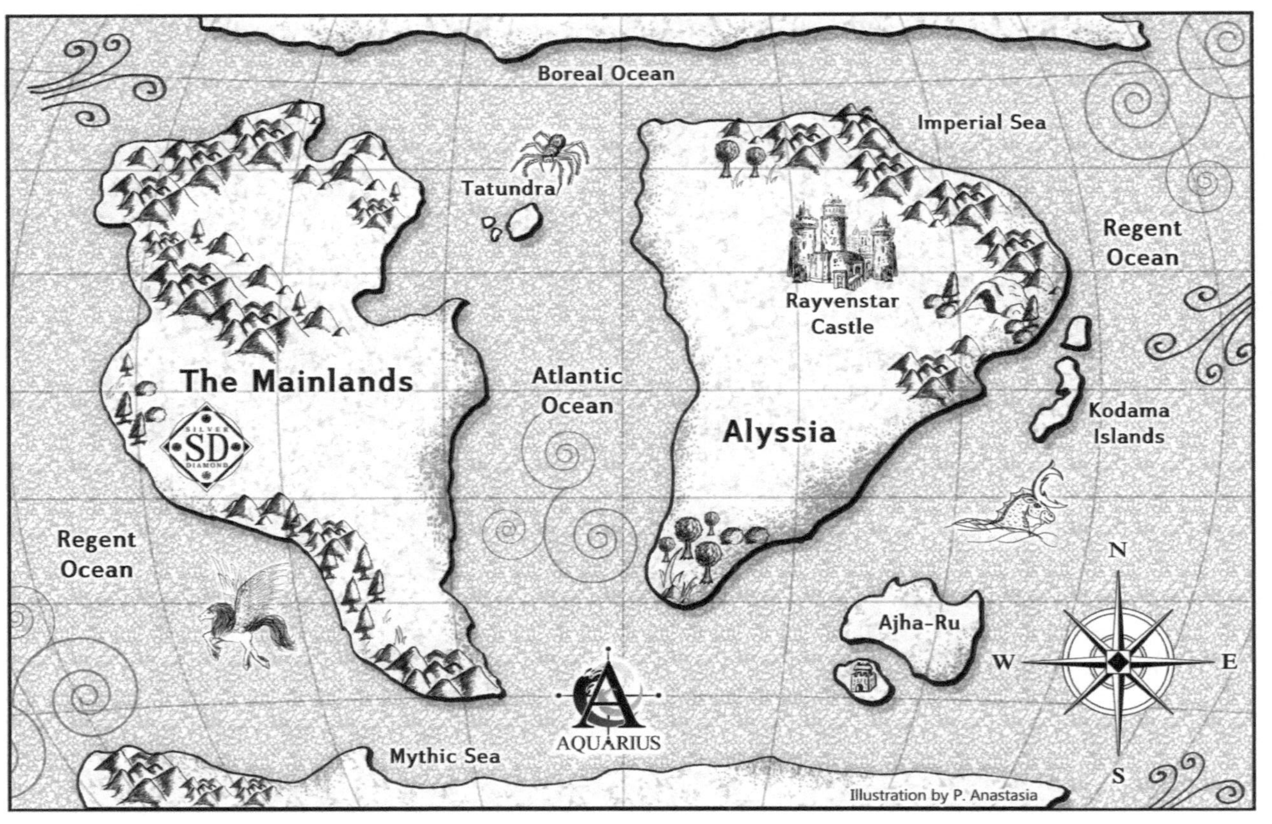

Boreal Ocean
Imperial Sea
Tatundra
Regent
Ocean
The Mainlands
Rayvenstar
Castle
Alyssia
SILVER
SD
DIAMOND
Atlantic
Ocean
Kodama
Islands
Regent
Ocean
Ajha-Ru
N
W
E
S
AQUARIUS
Mythic Sea
Illustration by P. Anastasia

CHARACTERS:

Valhara Hawksford: (val-HAR-uh HAWKS-ferd)
18-year-old Celestial Galaxy Lieutenant. Sister of Major
Atira Hawksford.

Mattheia Draven: (MATH-ee-ay DRAY-ven)
High Commander, Silver Diamond Academy, Mainlands.

Amanda Quill: (uh-MAN-duh kwill)
Private First Class, Silver Diamond Academy.

Jacksiun Ray: (JACK-see-un)
Childhood friend and Celestial Galaxy training partner of
Lieutenant Valhara Hawksford.

Captain Lansfora: (LANS-four-uh)
Captain of Silver Diamond Academy.

Captain Ventresca: (VEN-tress-kuh)
Captain of Celestial Galaxy Academy.

Kinasetsu: (key-nuh-SET-sue)
Kiva: (KEY-vuh)
Malachite: (MAL-uh-kite)
Firagia: (FEAR-ah-jhey)
Tryamour: (TRY-uh-more)
Mahora: (muh-HOR-ah)

Consumed by anger and forced to hide my feelings from the world, I wept behind closed doors. A riveting ache pierced my temples and my face flushed with heat. The captain's decision spurred a bout of nausea to squeeze my stomach, cold sweat beading on my forehead.

I wanted to wake from the nightmarish reality.

I hadn't worked so hard to become a pawn in a political game, and my captain couldn't push me around because his priorities weren't in order anymore.

He'd scheduled me to temporarily transfer to Silver Diamond Academy—the Mainland's most prestigious military school—to tie up "loose" ends. Whatever that meant.

Dirty work, more like it, disguised as formalities to make both academies look good in light of recent, petty power struggles.

Why me? Why now? The two academies have been at each other's throats for at least a decade, each trying to one-up the other in an effort to gain worldwide recognition.

My chair teetered on two legs as my feet pressed against the wall behind my desk and I pushed back. A scream swelled in my chest, clanging at my ribs, banging on my lungs, but I smothered the desire as quickly as I could. Making my discomfort known wouldn't change a thing, and it would only make me look weak and... *unqualified*.

Top of my class. I didn't get here by pouting and questioning orders. I worked hard. I listened. I contributed.

Now there were no contributions to be made, and I had no say in the matter.

As a lower ranking official of Celestial Galaxy, I shouldn't have been given such a prominent assignment, but the captain and my sister—a major—had their own scandal to keep secret.

They assumed I didn't know what they were hiding, like I was a child who wouldn't catch on. I wasn't blind to the odd glances they'd been exchanging lately. The subtle scent of his aftershave, cologne, (whatever it was), wafted from her when she hugged me goodnight. It was so obvious. Atira had always admired our captain, but admiration had evolved into something more.

For their safety, I held my tongue and pretended not to notice, but now I couldn't stop myself from scrutinizing every single order the captain gave. Was he really putting his best judgment forward, or were many of his decisions tainted by his desire to keep his love-interest out of harm's way? Of course, I wanted my sister to be safe, but not at the cost of her integrity.

No one should hide stuff like that. Not from family.

All four chair legs hit the floor again. I tucked my hands behind my elbows, rested my arms on my desk, and then nestled my head upon them, taking in a deep breath and exhaling loudly.

I wanted to deny it, but it wasn't only jealousy sucking the strength from me. Something deeper and more sinister prickled my soul.

I hadn't been home to Earth and the Mainlands for years.

Not since *the accident.*

The switch on my desk clicked and the blinds opened on the far side of my room, flooding the walls with cascading rays of warm, artificial sunlight. I blinked, adjusting to the brightness, and then rubbed my tired eyes with my palms.

I twisted thick locks of my hair together and tied them, as neatly as I could, into a high ponytail at the back of my head. People complimented me a lot on my red hair, but most of the time I didn't know what to do with it. In my line of work, there are few style options.

Some rogue strands on the left side of my face were always too short to tie back, so I clipped them out of the way with a silver, cherry blossom-shaped barrette. It was small, but the gift from my mom meant the world to me.

It was my lucky charm... and all I had left to remember her by.

I'd decided to stay at Celestial Galaxy year-round because I didn't want to return to Earth and tear open old wounds—the scars I carried from my parents' untimely, tragic deaths. Captain Ventresca's assignment meant I *had* to go back, whether I wanted to or not.

"Hey, Sis," Atira's voice resonated from the callbox on my door. *"Can I come in?"*

"Sure." I tapped a button on my desk and the door whooshed open.

My sister entered and the door closed behind her.

"Feeling lucky today?" she asked with a smile, eying the hair clip already.

I sighed and shrugged. "Not really."

"Mom's flower." She pointed to it and flopped down on the edge of my bed beside me, draping an arm across my shoulders. "You're worried about this thing, aren't you?"

"Who wouldn't be? The captain should have picked someone else, and you know it." I crossed my arms and looked away.

"You're strong, Sis." She squeezed me closer and nudged me encouragingly. "He trusts you because he knows you can do this. Why else would he have sent you?"

Because he didn't want to send you...

Trust had very little to do with it. I shifted my weight. "Atira, Silver Diamond is a *very* different academy, and I'm scared they won't take me seriously. I didn't work my butt off here to be dropped off at a school that basically hates us for existing."

"Sis," Atira turned me toward her and looked me in the eye, "I don't think that's the real reason why you're so upset. You're not one to back down from a challenge. You never have been."

My throat tightened.

She was right.

I felt tears creeping back up and I squeezed my eyes shut tightly to force them down.

"All things happen for a reason," she said. "Think of this as an opportunity to branch out. You'll pick up some stuff there you probably never could have learned here. Try to make some friends. Just don't let what happened years ago stop you from living today."

"Do you miss them?" I looked her square in the face.

Atira's smile melted away and she took a deep breath. "Every day."

"Me, too."

She rubbed my shoulder and worked up a fresh smile. "But being afraid to return to Earth isn't going to bring them back. Nothing will. Not fear. Not hate. You just have to find the courage to move forward."

"Have you?"

"Have I what?"

"Found the courage? Have you let it go?"

"Well, no, but..."

"Then how do you expect me to?"

"I..." She paused and looked away, nibbling her lip. "I don't expect you to let it go and I'd be lying if I told you *I* had. But I *do* expect you to push forward with your life. Find your place, Valhara. Reach as far as you can and make a difference in this world. Mom and Dad would have wanted you to, and they would have been proud to see how far you've already come."

She leaned in closer and lovingly traced Mom's hair clip with the tip of her index finger.

"I know it's cliché to say this, but I'll be up here, watching over you while you're there. In any way I can." Her fingers grasped my shoulder. "I love ya, Sis. I want you to be happy, okay? Do great things. For me. For *them*."

It didn't really make me feel much better, but I knew she'd meant every word of it. Her sweet, encouraging smile lifted some of the anger from my heart and I grinned back.

"I'll do my best. For you and for Mom and Dad."

"Lieutenant, we need to leave soon."

I pressed the intercom button on my desk to reply. "I know. Come in, Ray."

The door slid open and Lieutenant Jacksiun Ray entered my room.

"Are you ready to go?" He looked at the pile of paperwork scattered across my desk and then grazed over the laundry sprawled out on my bed. He tipped his head down and narrowed his eyes.

"Almost." I folded a pair of dark-green slacks and tucked them into my suitcase while he watched.

"Do you need any help?" He lifted his gaze and pressed

a finger along the bridge of his slender nose to slide his glasses back up his face.

"No, thanks." I unplugged my laptop and tossed it on top of the folded clothes, then I reached for a stack of paper—admission forms—on my desk.

Jacksiun stretched an arm out to me. "Don't forget the—"

"Thanks!" I snatched the charging cable from his hand and threw it into the outside pocket of the luggage.

"What else do I need?" I muttered as I shoved past him to grab a shirt out of my dresser. "I hate traveling. I don't want to forget anything."

I hadn't packed a suitcase in years and I didn't want to be unprepared. It wasn't like I was going for a week. I was going to be there for an entire semester—*six months.*

Six months is a long time to be stuck in a place where you don't know anyone.

What if they hate me?

What if everyone thinks I'm too young to be—

A hand pressed against my forearm and I veered my head.

"Valhara, please." Jacksiun looked me firmly in the eye. "Calm down." His voice was comforting.

I dropped the pair of shoes I was holding and huffed. "How? How do I calm down wh-when all of *this* is happening to me right now?"

"Breathe," he said in a soft, patient tone.

I looked at his fingers as they squeezed my arm gently, wanting to raise my voice at him and tell him to let go, but...

I hugged him instead.

"I don't want to go," I grumbled against his chest. He released my arm and hugged me.

"I know. I know, Valhara," he said, his embrace tightening. "But you have to. It's for the best. Really, it is."

He was so much taller than me that his hugs were kind of all encompassing. They made me feel safe, as if he were my big brother. Who was I kidding? He practically was.

Accomplice. Peacemaker. Best friend in *literally* the entire galaxy. Jacksiun wore a lot of hats, and I was grateful for that.

"You're going to be fine." He let go and then playfully tapped the tip of my nose with his finger. I laughed and shook my head, trying to fake a scowl. *As if I cared.* Anyone else would have gotten a swift kick in the shin for a move like that, but his calming blue eyes and good nature had never given me a reason to be upset. "It's only going to be for one term. Six months. That's all." He smiled reassuringly. "You'll be back here before you know it. Maybe you'll make some new friends while you're there."

"Why does everyone want me to *make friends* there?" I cocked an eyebrow. "Are you guys planning on replacing me while I'm gone?"

"Of course not!" He chuckled. "Don't be silly, Valhara."

"Do boyfriends count?" I snickered. *Touché!*

"What?" He scowled and shook his head adamantly. "No. No, they don't. I said *friends*." He did air quotes. "Not *boyfriends*. I'm not going to be there to look out for you."

I laughed and patted him on the shoulder before he could get any more flustered. "I was *joking*." I did air quotes back. "Don't worry. I won't parade around like I'm Celestial Galaxy's most eligible Lieutenant." I sighed. "I know the rules around here, unlike *some* people."

"She'll tell you when she feels the time is right." He sat on the chair beside my desk and clasped his hands together in his lap.

I tried not to roll my eyes as I folded my last shirt and stuffed it into the bag with a good shove. Jacksiun was an observant guy, but... "You know about *them*?" I asked, zipping the luggage closed.

"Yes."

I groaned.

"I won't tell anyone," he said.

I believed him, but he wasn't the one I was concerned with. How many other people knew? Or... suspected something?

"I don't think anyone else knows, Valhara," he added, as if he'd just read my mind. "If that makes you feel better. We're close, us three. It's more obvious to us than it is to other people. Atira and the captain aren't fools. They'll keep quiet about it."

I froze in place and shook my head. "I wish she'd tell me. Why does she have to hide it from her own sister?"

"She loves you, Valhara. Maybe she doesn't want you to worry about them. It could be a lot of things. I can't really say I understand, either, but she's smart. She has her reasons."

"Do they have swords there?" I carefully lifted the Azure Phoenix from its mount on the wall behind my desk and held it.

"At Silver Diamond? I'm not sure. They're well known for their artillery classes, but I don't know if they do sword training. You could bring it anyway. Just in case."

I balanced the light-weight, deeply serrated-edged, brass-colored blade in my hands and then set it on my desk. There was a polishing cloth in the top drawer. I used it to wipe some fingerprints off the four talons protruding from the pommel and then swept over the crimson orb embedded in the center of them. The blade granted a cold welcome to anyone who dared attack from behind. Misused or misheld, however, it came with a risk to the bearer, too.

There wasn't another blade like it in the world. It was said to have been forged with a blend of platinum and molten phoenix blood, attributing to its dark, brassy sheen. It was called the Azure Phoenix because of the blue-white heat created while tempering it into the unbreakable blade it was rumored to be.

"Will they get worried if I show up with a sword like this? Wouldn't it be safer here with you?"

"It's yours, Valhara." Jacksiun stood. "You earned it because you're a great, intelligent warrior. Ancient treasures like it don't pop up every day. They'll take notice, and if they have any sense at all, they'll respect you for your prowess."

My stupid eyes were getting all watery again. I sucked in a deep breath and blinked, trying to resist my emotions.

"Well, that's everything, I think." I looped my leather scabbard over my head, dropped it down to my waist, and buckled the second strap near my hip. I reached behind my head and carefully snapped the sword against the custom-made, hybrid magnet attached to the back.

Jacksiun reached for my suitcase and dragged it off my bed. It hit the floor with a loud thud, catching him off-guard with its deceptive heft.

"Let's go. The captain's waiting." His brow furrowed and he looked down. "Did you put bricks in here while I wasn't looking?"

"Only a few," I replied with an innocent smirk.

He laughed.

I glanced around my room at my barren desk, empty dresser, and freshly-made bed.

"Goodbye for now," I whispered and then sighed.

I had no choice but to face my fears. I had to do what

Captain Ventresca had requested of me. It was my responsibility as Lieutenant.

"Valhara?" A hand pressed against my shoulder again and I flinched.

"It will be here when you get back," Jacksiun said with a confident grin. "I can promise you that."

"I know." He was right, as always.

We walked down the main station corridor toward the docking bay. Bright fluorescent lights leading the way stretched on for seemingly ever. We passed half a dozen classrooms, each filled with students sitting at their desks with tablet screens glowing beneath their fingers as they listened intently to the lecturer at the head of the room.

I had been in those very same classrooms less than two years ago. Writing essays. Cramming. Trying to pass final exams so I could keep rank and make my sister proud. They'd thrown me into advanced classes when I was only fourteen—only two years after enlisting—and most of the kids there were much older than I was.

Except Jacksiun. He was a prodigy child whose inherited wit had landed him grades he'd never seemed like he had studied hard enough to earn. I was so jealous of him then. He'd be reclining in a chair reading some book, while I was working my rear end off trying to get a passing grade.

Jacksiun was intelligent by nature, but I've always been

a fast learner, and talent like that will get you noticed here.

The elevator door chimed and Jacksiun wheeled my suitcase inside. He typed in the docking bay floor code and the elevator doors closed. We began to descend. There were exactly one hundred floors in the academy and all lieutenants were assigned rooms on the ninety-eighth, so the ride down to the first floor took several moments. I kept my head down and tried not to breathe too loudly. My heartbeat raced and the intense anxiety coursing through me made me feel like I was lucid dreaming. Only, I had no control over the outcome, or my captain's orders.

I sensed Jacksiun watching me, but didn't open my mouth, for fear I'd say something unfitting of my rank. I was already beginning to miss him and we hadn't even stepped foot in Silver Diamond. A jittery, sick feeling made my chest hurt and I had to keep sucking in deep breaths and squeezing my eyes closed to keep from bursting into tears.

Maybe it was stupid and immature of me to be freaking out like a child, but I couldn't help it.

The elevator came to a halt with a faint ding and the doors slid open. He allowed me to exit first and then came out behind me with the baggage.

The docking bay bustled with people. Personnel hauled boxes and unknown spacecraft parts between various rooms. We passed a team of mechanics discussing something about "stabilizers" and "supersonic inlets." Whatever those were. I could have asked Jacksiun and he'd have been able to tell me, but I wasn't in the mood for spacecraft talk. Ships were his thing, not mine.

"Where to?" I asked, scanning the massive room. Most of the ships had been tucked away in their respective garages, but a few were out in the open and being tinkered with by the maintenance crew. I didn't recognize any of them, but I'd heard a new fleet had been commissioned recently, so the designs were still fairly new.

"To your left," he replied with a nod in the direction. "You can't miss it."

I turned and gasped.

It was huge.

"Meet the Goliath." Jacksiun propped my suitcase up on its wheels and pointed toward the enormous, beast of a ship.

Gunmetal in color, square and boxy around the sides—vaguely reminiscent of a large four-legged animal (a lion?) sitting at attention. It was sleek and sharp toward the front and, from what I could see, both sides were flanked with elaborate, wing-like motifs. I couldn't tell if it was aerodynamic or just meant to look intimidating. Both, perhaps.

"So this is where all that flight training has gotten you?" I asked. "It's giant. It never looked *that* big on a screen."

Although he hadn't been an officially delegated academy pilot, Jacksiun had been studying flight and ship construction and repair since his first semester. It was more of a hobby and passion than a work requirement. For years, he'd rambled on about how he'd someday pilot the rare and legendary thing that was Celestial Galaxy's elite Goliath. I used to laugh at him and tell him they were pipe dreams.

The joke was on me now.

He took the handle of my suitcase again and started wheeling it toward the loading ramp. My neck craned back as I swept over the intricate underbelly of the monstrous ship. Rows of hypnotic green and gold lights sparkled on and off in rhythmic patterns. Large orbs of some kind radiated red pulsations of light and a whoosh of hot air gushed past us from whirring exhaust fans as we approached the large metal bridge that would take us inside.

"Isn't it incredible?" Jacksiun asked, closing his eyes as the gust of warmth made locks of his kept, black hair dance across his brow. He hastily swept them back into place with a brush of his hand. "You're lucky, Valhara," he said, turning to look at me. "The Goliath can get us to Earth in hours instead of days. Have you ever seen a more remarkable ship in the entire galaxy?" There was a huge grin across his lips and an intense sparkle of awe in his sky-blue eyes.

Today was his day, even if it wasn't mine.

The complex procedures that had to occur before we could depart baffled me, and all I could do was watch as personnel readied the Goliath for flight. Jacksiun helped me get situated in my seat, first securing my sword and luggage in a special lockbox in a large side panel of the main bridge, and next showing me how to properly use the safety restraints on my chair. He did it all in a way that didn't make me feel like a child, though, and I appreciated that.

Afterward, he left me alone for several minutes and went to discuss flight plans with some of the others on board. Although programmed to be self-sufficient overall, the Goliath required a small crew to assure everything ran as programmed. This dedicated group of trained experts supervised ship functions in the rare case something may have an error and require manual control.

Jacksiun had been assigned to captain the ship for my flight, and I couldn't have asked for a more reliable person to trust with my life. This was a very exclusive and rare opportunity our captain had given him, and he took it very seriously. It wasn't like him to strap himself into a hyper jet and go exploring the universe, but if weird noises starting coming from the thrusters, he'd know how to troubleshoot the problem better than any standard issue academy pilot.

I tangled my fingers around the thick nylon seatbelt strapped across my lap and stared up at the ceiling. The grey interior had olive green filigree and metallic gold accents along the perimeter of the walls as well as on all the control consoles in the room. Green and gold were Celestial Galaxy's emblem colors and I'd become accustomed to seeing them on *literally everything*. But the delicate, intricate designs swirling around corners and edges of the nearby chairs and control panels had regal flair, and I felt honored to be surrounded by such exquisite craftsmanship. The Goliath was the golden chariot of our academy, and I was privileged to be riding in it.

"Is it everything you thought it would be?" Jacksiun asked, approaching me from behind and patting my shoulder.

"Shouldn't I be asking you that?" I shifted in my chair; the belt constricted my movement.

He took his seat in the large, rounded Commander's chair a few feet across from mine and spun it around to face me. "Everything and more," he answered, beaming. "The simulations have nothing on the real thing." He caught me tugging my seatbelt and furrowed his brow. "It's going to be a five-and-a-half-hour flight. Are you comfortable?"

"As comfortable as I can be." I shrugged. "It's my nerves more than anything."

"Ah. I figured that. You'll be fine." He swerved back around and punched some colorful keys on the long, arched keypad in front of him. The floor rumbled softly beneath my feet as the engines kicked on and the thrusters propelled us out of the docking bay. I watched on a monitor to my left as the bright lights of the academy vanished from sight, consumed by inky blackness and endless space.

"There won't be much to see from this point forward," Jacksiun spoke to me over his shoulder. "We'll be there soon and you'll be back here before you know it. Why don't you rest your eyes a bit?"

My eyes didn't need resting.

"I would if I could." I glanced forward at the glass viewing panel spanning the length of the front of the room. He was right. Nothing much to look at.

"I'm sorry. I know you can't sleep when you're anxious."

He leaned forward, reading a long strip of dialog text appearing on a screen at the front of the bridge. "Let me know if you need anything, Lieutenant."

"Will do." I tried to smile but couldn't. It wasn't like he could see me with his back turned, anyway.

A sharp beeping sound jolted me to attention. I lifted my face up from my computer, leaned to the side, stretched my neck, and squinted to try to get a better look at Jacksiun's screen.

"Is that supposed to happen?" I asked, my heartbeat spiking.

"Yes. Everything's fine. It's a transmission from Silver Diamond. I'll patch it through to the main projector."

A beam of light poured from a projection system overhead and an image appeared on the far wall. It flashed an animation of the Silver Diamond logo—a black globe containing four colored gem-like accents representing the cardinal points and a diamond-shape overlapping the design. The initials 'S' and 'D' rotated in the center in elegant black serif font.

A stout, middle-aged man with a shaved head and black uniform with green trim along the collar came on screen.

"This is Sergeant Joe Shunckly of Silver Diamond Academy.

State your flight jurisdiction code, please."

Jacksiun didn't miss a beat, and before I could tuck my laptop away, he'd already rattled off a dozen seemingly random numbers and letters to the sergeant.

A moment of silence passed and Sergeant Shunckly gave a nod of approval. "Cleared. Captain Lansfora is expecting you. You have been granted permission to enter the academy flight zone. We will have the tarmac cleared for your landing momentarily."

"Thank you, Sergeant," Jacksiun replied.

The light beam faded and the image went away. The sooty grey showing through the main window across from us slowly changed color and brightened as we entered Earth's atmosphere. A series of buttons flashed on Jacksiun's control panel and I panicked again as turbulence caused the floor beneath my feet to quake. Reality set in once again.

This is really happening.

I took a deep breath and exhaled.

We landed safely and Jacksiun stood from his chair and came over to me. He ordered a crew member to retrieve my personal items and then bent over to look me in the eye.

"We've arrived. Let's go," he said. Now that everyone was out of earshot, his voice softened. "I'll be at your side for as long as I can, Valhara. I know you still don't want to do this, but I promise you, it's for the best."

"I know." I relieved myself of my seatbelt and stood, wobbling a moment on tingling legs. "My things?" I noticed someone removing them from the locker.

"The security office needs to inspect them first, so I'm sending them ahead of us to speed up the process."

I feared for the Azure Phoenix, unjustifiably, perhaps, but I couldn't help but worry about being separated from the priceless sword. I'd almost gotten killed trying to acquire it years ago and it meant a lot to me. "You're sure that—"

"It will be fine," Jacksiun said with an air of confidence. "Trust me. I've never steered you wrong before, have I?"

Never. I shook my head.

I polished the small golden sun emblems on my left and right lapels and then brushed both hands down my shirt to smooth some of the wrinkles.

"Captain Lansfora is waiting." Jacksiun escorted me to the main elevator which took us back down to the loading bridge.

I stepped onto the tarmac and took in a deep breath of crisp, fresh air. Grass. Sea water. Concrete. Jet fuel. So many smells hit me all at once that I was taken aback. Back to my last day on Earth—the day Jacksiun and I boarded the Celestial Galaxy recruitment ship and left for what I thought would be forever. Six years ago. Six years I'd been running away from this place only for it to chase me down and drag me back on its own.

"Lieutenant Hawksford. Lieutenant Ray." A brunette girl with a tight, high ponytail, accented with two perfect braids on each side of her head, saluted us with her hand flat and rigid above her brow and then brought it down in a sweeping, arcing movement to her heart, palm up.

"I am Private First Class Amanda Quill and I will be your personal escort from this point forward." It surprised me how young Private Quill looked; she appeared to be a few years my junior.

Her thigh-length, jet-black uniform had royal-purple piping trimming the high-collar, chest pockets, epaulets, and in a band around each cuff. Large, white diamond outlines were on the bicep of each sleeve and she wore a matching decorative belt at her waist. The uniforms were much more elaborate than my own forest green and grey with simple, notched lapels, but Silver Diamond had been well known for its elegance and intricacies in every detail of their organization.

"Here." Private Quill handed the two of us laminated visitor cards which we then clipped to our left chest pockets. "I will take you through security and then to meet with our captain. Come this way." She turned, with precision, and we followed her across the tarmac to the academy entrance.

Matte-coated glass walls flanked the entire building on

all sides. I could barely see our muddled reflections as we approached the entrance gate. A motion sensor beeped and the tall glass sliding doors pulled apart. We were shuttled through security scanners by two screening personnel and then rejoined by Private Quill moments later.

I was quick to notice how different personnel had different colored trims. I recalled Sergeant Shunckly's had been green and securities' were orange. It must have been part of Diamond's elaborate ranking system. I'd heard about it—among other things—and it sounded so confusing at first. Now that I was actually seeing it in action, it made perfect sense.

"This way, please," Private Quill announced, directing us down a long hallway of classrooms. As we walked, I saw several students at their desks through the windows. They, too, had purple trim on their uniforms, but many also had light blue or yellow. "Lieutenant Hawksford," the private started, "should you ever—on the rare occasion—find yourself lost in our academy, always know that the colored lines on the floor will lead you to wherever it is you wish to go." She slowed down and pointed at the grey marble tile floor. Small lines of color ran along the length near the walls, some branching off in other directions up ahead. "Orange will always lead back to the tarmac and loading areas. Blue is for the offices of all professors and student staff. Ruby is elite housing. Purple is the student dormitory. Those are all the ones you'll need to know for now. You'll catch on as you make your way around our academy. I believe the captain has assigned you with an advisor for your time here, as well."

An advisor?

I glanced at Jacksiun and he shrugged as if he'd had no idea what she was talking about. No one had said anything about having to have a babysitter while I was there. They did realize I was *one* promotion away from becoming a major, right? Or did no one tell them that?

I shook it off and continued behind the private as she pointed at a set of black doors in the distance. "The meeting hall is down there."

We approached the heavy black steel doors and a guard at the entrance made one quick pass up and down each of our sides with a portable security scanner. He gave Private Quill a nod of approval.

The guard pressed his hand onto a square of black glass beside the doorframe and a red light flashed beneath his fingers. The double-doors opened automatically.

The meeting space was large and well-lit. A long, oblong table that sat around twenty (with a quick chair count) took precedence in the center of the room. At the far end sat the academy captain.

"The lieutenants from C.G. are here to see you, Sir," said Private Quill, walking ahead of us.

Upon our entrance, he stood at attention.

"Thank you, Private," he said. "Thank you for coming, Lieutenants. Please have a seat." He gestured to his side.

Jacksiun was quick to pull out a chair for me and then, after I sat, took a seat beside me.

Captain Lansfora's uniform was also jet-black, but his trim and belt buckle were bright, metallic gold. His high collar had a matching gold diamond pinned on the left side and, unlike other personnel there, his cuffs had three gold bands around them instead of one or two. Just above his right shirt pocket, a gold starburst badge with an engraving of the academy logo surrounded by four colored crystals shined. The diamond outlines on his biceps matched the stripes on his sleeves.

"Let me be the first to say how very honored we are to have you here," he said, smiling warmly at us and tipping his head. It *seemed* genuine. "Welcome to Silver Diamond Academy. I do hope it is all you had imagined it would be."

"It is a very beautiful school, Sir," I said, clasping my hands on top of the table to stop myself from fidgeting. "I am honored to be here." Really, though, I was freaking out inside again. Any minute now, Jacksiun would get up and leave and I'd be stuck for six months in some strange place I'd never been before, on a planet where my last memories were despicable ones.

"I understand there may be some tension in you right

now because all this is so very new and different," Captain Lansfora continued. "I'm sure you're feeling a little overwhelmed at this point, Lieutenant, and that's very normal."

Was my face bright red? It didn't feel that way.

"But your participation in the formulation and execution of an academy treaty is imperative, and your work here will be significant. Captain Ventresca told me a lot about you and sent you here with high recommendations. I've read up on your records and past accomplishments and I agree with his decision to choose you. For this reason, I've assigned my second-in-command to work with you during your stay. Excuse me for one moment." At the head of the table was a flat, black intercom box with various colored tabs. He pressed a blue one down until it lit. "Commander Draven? I requested your presence at the conference hall this morning." He released the button.

Silence.

He pressed again. "Commander?"

"I'll be right there, Sir," someone finally responded. The intercom clicked off.

"He will be here momentarily. Did you have any questions for me, Lieutenants?" Captain Lansfora looked at me and then to Jacksiun.

"Just one, Sir," Jacksiun said, lifting a hand. "If I may."

"You are welcome to speak freely in this room, Lieutenant Ray."

"I mean no disrespect, and I am only asking to settle my own curiosity. Has Commander Draven been here long? Our captain has not spoken of him before."

"I understand your concern," Lansfora replied. "Commander Draven has been a student here since he was enlisted at age ten. Before I became Captain several years back, I was one of his trainers and I worked closely with him throughout his studies. He's highly versatile and extremely intelligent. He was promoted to my second-in-command two years ago, which may be why your captain is not too familiar with him yet. I can assure you, personally, that Lieutenant Hawksford will be in capable hands with his guidance."

A beep sounded from the far side of the room.

"Sir." Private Quill saluted the man who entered.

He stopped in the doorway to acknowledge her and then approached us. He was a lot younger than I'd imagined him to be. Light, golden blonde hair—uncommon on Celestial Galaxy. He couldn't have been much older than my sister, and yet, he was second-in-command?

"Sorry to keep you waiting, Captain," he said, clearing his throat and tugging at the cuffs of his sleeves. "I lost track of time and—"

"No need to apologize, Commander," the captain cut him off. "This is Lieutenant Valhara Hawksford. She is the student I've assigned to you while she works with us on the academy partnership agreement."

He looked me in the eye and flinched. Briefly, but he did, and I noticed. It made me uncomfortable. Was he expecting someone else? Maybe he didn't want anything to do with me—another reason why he had been late to the meeting. He *did* appear flustered...

"Would you take a seat, please?"

Commander Draven pulled out a chair across from me and sat. He messed with the high collar of his jacket. His uniform mirrored the captain's, only all the trim and accents were metallic platinum instead of gold.

"This is her traveling companion, Lieutenant Jacksiun Ray," the captain continued. "Commander Mattheia Draven will be your main contact during your stay, should you require anything at all, Lieutenant."

The commander looked over at me, this time, with less tension in his gaze. His eyes were such a striking and unique blue color; they reminded me of Jacksiun's.

"It's a pleasure to meet you, Lieutenant," he said, standing from his seat to reach a hand across the table to me. I hesitated, catching on his friendly smile. Jacksiun nudged me lightly and conspicuously in the elbow.

"Uh, yes. Thank you." I stood and reached out to shake his hand. "Pleasure to meet you, too, Sir." His grasp was firm and *surprisingly* cordial.

We reviewed the paperwork; I signed the temporary transfer agreement tying me to Silver Diamond for the next six months, and then returned one copy of the article to Captain Lansfora. Jacksiun took the other. Captain Lansfora dismissed himself from the meeting and left me with Jacksiun, Commander Draven, and Private Quill.

"Can I get you anything?" Commander Draven asked me. His demeanor had softened significantly over the past hour. "A glass of water, perhaps?" He glanced at Jacksiun. "How about you, Lieutenant?"

"I'm fine, thank you," Jacksiun replied and then looked at me.

"Water would be nice," I answered. "Thanks. I can get it myself if you tell me where to—"

"No need," Draven interrupted. "You are our guest."

He got up and crossed the room to retrieve a glass of water from a dispenser on the other side. He brought it back and gingerly handed it to me.

Despite the brisk meeting room, his fingers felt warm when I brushed them accidentally during the exchange. "Thank you." I grinned, noticing now that his blue eyes were a shade fairer than my friend's.

"I apologize again, to both of you, for being late," he said, taking a seat beside me. He took a deep breath and exhaled, forking a hand through his golden hair. There was an awkward moment of silence. "Lieutenant Ray, may I congratulate you on your accomplishments at C.G. You must have done some incredible things to have been given permission to captain the famed Goliath."

"Thank you." He perked up with the change of topic. "I've been training many years for the opportunity."

"Well," Commander Draven started enthusiastically, "I don't want to brag, but my father was a squadron leader during the Atlantic Strike about twenty years ago. President Alexander gave him a Silver Crest badge for his accomplishments. I wanted to follow in his footsteps. That's why I'm one of the head pilots here today."

Oh, great. Boy talk. Maybe Jacksiun should have been

the one staying.

"The Atlantic Strike?" Jacksiun was immediately enthralled. "That's astounding! I'd love to talk to him about it sometime. Where is your father now? Retired?"

Draven's smile twisted down glumly. "Unfortunately... he was taken from us by a jet malfunction several years ago."

A twinge of sorrow squeezed my gut.

"Oh. I'm... sorry." Discomforted, Jacksiun looked away. "I'm sure he accomplished great things with his time. You're here and I'm certain you will be a great mentor to Lieutenant Hawksford during her stay." He grinned awkwardly at me. "Our academies need you both right now."

"I agree." Commander Draven glanced down and polished one of his cufflinks anxiously. He cleared his throat.

"I... suppose I should take my leave." Jacksiun stood and straightened his jacket. "May I have a word with Lieutenant Hawksford before I go?"

"Of course," Draven replied. "I'll wait in the hall with Private Quill. She will see you to your ship when you're ready."

"He seems nice," Jacksiun said quietly once the others had vacated.

"Yes." I didn't know how else to respond.

"Couldn't tell if he was your type or not."

"Hey!" I jabbed him in the arm and he laughed. He was

only trying to make me smile. It worked.

"I'm sorry. I'm going to miss you. Take care of yourself, Valhara." He reached his arms out toward me and we hugged tightly but briefly.

"Going to miss you, too, Jacksiun." I mustered every ounce of courage to stop a stray tear from escaping my eye.

"Before we part, Atira asked me to give you this." He pulled a lump of black cloth from his side pocket and held it out to me. He unfolded the fabric and revealed Atira's prized sunstone amulet. "She's wanted to give it to you for a while, but time slipped by too quickly and... well, here I am, delivering it to you as promised."

I stood there, staring at it. Atira's fire-red sunstone had been in our family for generations. Why would she give it to me?

"Just take it, please," Jacksiun said, gesturing to his hand. "Take it, or I'll never hear the end of it from her. I'm the one who has to go back there."

I chuckled because I completely understood. Atira was stubborn. When she wanted something done, she got it done one way or another. "Okay. Okay." I carefully took the amulet from his hand and gently rolled it back up in the cloth. I tucked it into my side pocket. "I don't want you getting into any trouble with my sister. I know how fiery she can be when things don't go her way. Thank you, my friend. I'll miss you."

"I'll miss you, too." He wrapped his arm around my shoulders, pulled me into a quick side hug, and then we walked together toward the exit. The door opened automatically; Private Quill and Commander Draven awaited us just on the other side.

"I will see you to your ship now, Lieutenant," Private Quill said, motioning for Jacksiun to follow.

We exchanged brief goodbye smiles and I watched as he walked down the hall and seemingly out of my life.

Commander Draven stepped beside me. "I can tell you two are very good friends. Silver Diamond may be new to you and our customs might not all coincide with Celestial Galaxy's, but I assure you you'll feel at home soon enough. I'll do whatever I can to make you comfortable during your stay."

I turned to look up into his blue eyes, and a small, sincere grin curled his lips. There was warmth and honesty in his eyes and that actually did make me feel less anxious.

"I've already had your things transferred to your room," he said. "I'm not sure if they told you, but all your weapons will be confiscated and held for a minimum of thirty days."

"Understood." Security was top priority, though if anything happened to the Azure Phoenix, I'd—

"Would you like me to give you a tour of the academy?"

I glanced down the hall again. Jacksiun had disappeared from sight. "I'm actually quite tired right now from the flight. Would you mind showing me to my room so I can rest a bit?"

"Of course, Lieutenant. Right this way." He slid a folded pamphlet from his side pocket and opened it. "Here," he said, pointing to a legend in the corner of the map. "Purple leads to the dormitory. Dark red leads to Ruby Hall—elite housing." He slid his finger up the map toward a colored box on the far side of the school. "This is the dormitory, marked by purple. Elite housing," he slid his finger down toward the center of the map, "is right here. This is where I and many of the instructors stay."

"So I'm over here, then?" I pointed to the purple area.

"No. You've actually been assigned a room in Ruby Hall."

"What?" I narrowed my eyes. "Why am I getting special treatment?"

"Because we want you to feel comfortable and safe while you're here. If you need anything at all, there are plenty of high-ranking officials and professors there who can help you—along with myself."

I found it peculiar that a high commander would want to live on academy grounds and not have a house some-where off the military base. But I didn't know how things worked here, so maybe he had his reasons.

"You can have this." He handed me the map. "I'll show you to your room."

We walked down a series of halls, the flooring beneath our feet marked by thin, high visibility lines of color, until we came to a pathway with only a line of red.

"This is my room," he said, pointing to the brass number plate near the top of the door.

It read '007.' I laughed. "Double-oh-seven? Is that a joke or did you lose a bet?"

He rolled his eyes and looked away as if he'd been asked the question a hundred times. "It was funny at the time, okay? Don't judge me by it, please. And yes, it was a joke."

"I'm sorry," I apologized, feeling like an idiot for calling him out on something so silly. I didn't need to start something with my mentor on my first day. "I think it's funny, actually. In a *not* stupid sort of way."

"Really?"

"Yes." I smiled, meaning it. "Really."

"Thanks." He pointed ahead and started walking again. "Your room is down here." He crossed the hall and approached another door. Room 23. Then he pointed at a room across from mine. "Make a note of room 26 just over there, as well. That's where our head recruitment officer, Angela Meadows stays. She's in charge of all new recruits. I recommend you meet up with her first thing tomorrow to get your class schedule."

I nodded.

"Uh." He looked around blankly and bit his lip. "I'm trying

to remember what else I needed to tell you." He paused and then took a sharp breath. "Ah! Before I forget." He reached into his shirt pocket and pulled out a metallic silver keycard. "This is yours. Whatever you do, *don't* lose it." He emphasized the 'don't' sternly, as if he, himself had misplaced a card once before and the repercussions had been highly unpleasant. "It's your I.D., room key, and academy access card." He held it out and I plucked it from his fingers. It was cold, real metal.

"If you need anything at all, I'm always on call. Don't hesitate to ask me or any faculty with ruby or sapphire trim on their uniforms. Other personnel here will know who you are but not why you're here, so I recommend sticking to the higher ranks if you have questions. If no one is around, ask any desk worker and they'll direct you to the right people."

He rested a hand on his belt and smiled at me warmly. "Anything else I can help you with before I go?"

"I think that's all. Thank you, Commander."

I looked down at the shiny keycard and turned it over, unable to tell which end went into the slot on my door. "Okay," I muttered. My eyes narrowed and I flipped it over again. Both sides were identical.

"You, just... uh." Commander Draven reached for my hand but hesitated. "If I may. Turn it this way." He gently rotated the card until it was face up in my fingers. "There's a faint etching on that side." His index finger traced a subtle design on one end of the card. "Right there. The logo. That's the top."

"Oh. I see." It was more obvious than I had realized, but the shimmer of overhead lights against the metal had distorted it at first. "Thank you." I pinched the card at the top and pressed it into the slot on the door. A soft beep sounded and a light turned from red to green. The door clicked.

"There you go," Draven said with a nod. "Perfect. Anything else, you know where to find me."

I entered the room and as the door began to close behind me, paused.

"Commander?" I backed up and caught the door with my foot. He had just turned away.

"Yes, Lieutenant?" He swerved around and his brow rose.

"In... my things... I brought a sword." His expression shifted into one of intrigue. I carefully formed my words so I wouldn't offend him or make any unwarranted accusations. "It means a lot to me and it's very rare."

He took a step closer. "You understand you can't have it back before the confiscation term has ended, right?"

"Yes. I understand completely. I wasn't insinuating that I wanted to retrieve it prematurely. I had meant..." I swallowed hard and then cleared my throat. "I've had it for a while and it's the only one in the world like it. Could you..."

He cocked his head to the side and then a small smile

twisted his lips and he nodded. "If it makes you feel better, I'll personally assure you of its safety in our security hold. Nothing will happen to it, and as soon as the thirty days have passed, I'll make sure it's delivered to you without so much as a scratch." He laughed to himself and shrugged. "Well, without any *new* scratches, at least. How does that sound?"

I grinned. "Thank you. I meant no disrespect, I only—"

"No need to explain yourself, Lieutenant. Have a good evening."

"You, too, Sir."

I closed my door.

The room was huge compared to the one I had back on C.G. A walk-in closet. A full-size bed in the center of the room. A dresser beside that and a large, flat-screen television suspended from the opposite wall. It was comfortable, had a clean scent, and was definitely more spacious than my previous room. My suitcase had been left for me just inside.

I flopped onto the bed and kicked off my shoes. The mattress was soft but firm and the comforter made of wonderfully fluffy fleece. I rolled over and grunted as something hard poked me in the chest. I reached into my pocket and pulled out the ball of black cloth—Atira's necklace.

The amulet was large but fit snuggly in my palm, the polished rose-gold flame-like setting forked out from the inner stone in various directions and pressed against my skin with sharp points. The bright-red, octagonal carved sun-stone had been passed down through our family for generations. We didn't even know where it had come from or who had made it, only that it was there—in our family.

Following the accident, Atira had decided to take it and I had no quarrels with her about that decision. She was the eldest child; she deserved it. But now, she was passing it on to me. Already? Why? Jacksiun didn't tell me her reasoning behind it, only that I had to take it or she would be upset with him.

I lifted it up by its thick chain and over my head. The pendant fell just below my collar, so I tucked it behind the front buttons. We weren't typically allowed to wear jewelry on duty, but I wasn't about to let it out of my sight.

I lay back down on the bed and rolled onto my side. My eyes closed and my head sunk into the crisp, fluffy pillow.

My stomach grumbled. I rolled onto my back and groaned. My shoulders were stiff from how I'd slept—sprawled out from exhaustion in a completely unnatural position. I sat up and glanced at my reflection in the mirror across from the bed. My uniform was a wrinkled mess. I stood and tugged it down, flattening my hand and brushing it firmly to try to smooth some of the crinkles out. It looked *a little* better. I didn't have the time or ability to steam them out and I really needed to get something to eat.

My eyes still blurry from sleep, I squinted to see the nearby clock. Past nine. Probably too late for dinner, but until I got my bearings, I had to do something. My belly rumbled like an angry troll; I hadn't had a decent meal all day.

I adjusted my pony tail and my cherry blossom barrette, made another quick pass over my uniform (which proved useless), checked in the mirror, and then grabbed my I.D. card from the dresser and left my room.

It was dead quiet in the hall. Not one person in sight. Most classes ended at six at C.G., so I guessed Diamond was about the same.

I walked down the hall and then stopped in front of Commander Draven's room. I could barely hear muffled words and odd noises coming from within. I reached my hand up.

KNOCK.

KNOCK.

KNOCK.

The noises silenced.

"Just a minute," he said, raising his voice so I'd hear him.

The door opened a crack and I noticed him quickly working to button the top button of his collar. "Lieutenant Hawksford, can I help you?" He slid a headset down off his head and slung it around his neck.

"Am I interrupting something?" I peeked into his room. Stacks of video game boxes and books were spread across the floor and a bright white glow emanated from a television set just out of sight.

"No. No. Nothing at all. I'm on call 24/7 anyway. Rather be interrupted by you than a fire alarm or... worse. What did you need?" He held his door open with his elbow.

"I'm really hungry and I didn't bring much to—"

"Say no more." He held up a flattened hand and grinned to soften the playful gesture. "I figured this would happen. Just give me a minute to wrap this up and I'll help you out."

"Take your time," I said, smiling gratefully.

He popped back into his room and left the door propped open slightly with a nearby shoe. He threw the headset back over his ear and adjusted it. I couldn't hear the entire conversation from where I stood, and I didn't want to enter his room as he'd not invited me to, but I listened anyway because I couldn't help it.

"I have to sign off now, guys," he said, via the headset mic. "I know. Yes, I'm sorry, but you know I have things to deal with. Work and stuff. Yes. I know you can't survive that dungeon without a healer." He paused to listen and then hit a few buttons on his console controller. "I'll be back on later, okay?" He pulled off the headset, tossed it onto his couch, and then the room became dark once the T.V. went off. "Sorry about all of that," he said, returning to the door and kicking his shoe out of the way. "I'd invite you in, but," he peered over his shoulder and then back at me, "my place looks like a bomb hit it. No pun intended."

"Don't worry about it." I was the one interrupting him, after all.

He shot a glance at the clock across the room and grimaced. "Eh... It's a little late. Cafeteria closed several hours ago, but the chef will be in for another hour or so. It *should* be okay."

"I don't want to be trouble."

"It's no trouble. I'll explain along the way. But really, it's not a problem so don't feel bad. I just need to find my..." He patted his shirt pocket briefly. "Okay. Got my card."

I stepped back and he exited the room, closing the door quietly and waiting for the lock to click.

We walked together down the empty halls and passed a handful of security guards who didn't give me a second look. I guessed that being with the commander was enough information for them.

"Are you sure the chef won't be upset with us showing up this late?" I asked, looking down at the remaining wrinkles in my uniform and scowling. I should have tried harder to get them out.

"No. Let's just say this won't be the first time I've shown up after hours."

"Oh?"

"But they do have a limited menu right now. Is pizza alright with you?" He turned to me and cocked an eyebrow, walking backward as he spoke. "You *do* eat pizza in space, right?"

"Yes." I laughed. "Of course we do."

"Good." He smirked and turned back around to walk alongside me. "Because if you didn't, that would be numero uno on the docket for the academy treaty. Menu changes. Seriously."

I chuckled and shook my head. He pressed open the cafeteria door and let me in ahead of him. A bell chimed near the back of the room and a chef poked her head out of the kitchen and then came toward us.

"Good evening, Commander Draven," she said with a brief salute. "Who's your friend?" She grinned at me inquisitively.

I opened my mouth to reply but he answered first.

"Chef Amelia, this is Lieutenant Valhara Hawksford from Celestial Galaxy. She's going to be with us for one term and will be under my care for the duration of her stay."

"Nice to meet you, Lieutenant," Chef Amelia replied. "That means you'll be under my care, as well, and I won't let you go hungry." She beamed. "I'd... well, shake your hand," she held out her gloved hand and shrugged, "but I'm in the middle of preparations right now. I hope you understand. Don't mean to be rude."

"Of course. Nice to meet you, Chef."

She turned to Draven. "So would you like the usual or something special for the lieutenant?"

"The usual is fine." He glanced at me and cleared his throat. "You aren't, by chance, a vegetarian, are you?"

"No."

"Pizza is a vegetable anyway, right?" He chuckled, flashed a charming grin, and then motioned for me to sit down in a nearby booth. I plopped onto the soft vinyl seat and scooted in. He made a short walk to a drink machine nearby and returned with two glasses of ice water.

"The usual?" I raised an eyebrow. "So you weren't joking when you said it wouldn't be the first time you've eaten here after hours."

"Nope." He slid into the booth and sat across from me. "Unfortunately, I was not. I work crazy shifts sometimes and have to eat when I get the chance. That's what it takes to be the Second Commanding Officer here, though. No regrets." He leaned over the table and lowered his voice. "Just don't tell the other students about this. Okay? I'm not exactly supposed to be here, either, but I do what I must to get by and I wasn't about to let you go hungry in the meantime."

I felt bad for making a joke about it, especially since he was doing *me* a favor. "I didn't mean to be trouble. I'm sorry. I—"

"No need to apologize, Lieutenant. Just keep this between us. That's all I ask."

"Sure. Thank you, by the way, for bringing me here.

What do I owe you for the pizza?"

"Don't worry about it."

"Thanks."

"You worry about getting situated here and I'll take care of the rest."

Chef Amelia came by and set a still-sizzling pizza down between us on the table along with a few plates and napkins. "Careful! It's hot." She looked at the commander and then at me. "Anything else I can get you two?"

"Not for me. Lieutenant?"

I shook my head. "No, thank you."

"Enjoy." The chef left our table.

The cafeteria was completely empty except for the two of us and it was a bit surreal. I took a sip of my water and sat back in my seat, hesitating to take the first piece of fresh, hot pizza.

Draven passed me a plate. "Don't wait for me. Take whatever you want." He began prying a cheesy, pepperoni-topped slice from the pan and then I did the same. I folded it in half long-ways and took a bite. The cheese was incredibly sharp and delicious. The sauce had a subtle tangy-sweetness to it, and the crust was pleasantly crisp. Much better than anything I'd ever gotten back on C.G.

"Is the pizza always this good here?" I took a closer look at my slice and then sniffed it briefly, hoping I didn't look like a weirdo in front of the commander. My teeth sunk into a second bite and the flavor explosion hit my taste buds again. It really was *that* good.

"Yes. As far as I know, but I don't have much to compare it to. Is it different from what you're used to?"

I nodded and widened my eyes slightly as I chewed.

"Hmm. Well, we could always squeeze that back onto the list then." He smirked and I started to giggle, imagining my captain's face if I pointed out how terrible our pizza was in comparison to the stuff at Silver Diamond.

Then I coughed.

"Hey. Careful!" The commander set down his food. "Are you okay?" He started to stand from his seat.

The piece of crust dislodged from my throat and I took in a breath. "I'm fine." I rested the slice back onto my plate and wiped some grease from my fingertips onto a napkin.

"Alright. I promised to get you back to your academy in one piece after the semester." He sat back down and took a drink of water. "Care to share with the class what was so funny?"

I cleared my throat and the tickle finally went away. "I was just imagining the look on Captain Ventresca's face when I tell him our pizza isn't up to code."

Draven shrugged. "Hey, you gotta eat, right?" He cracked a smile and took a bite out of the crust of his pizza slice.

I liked his smile. It was real, or at least I believed it was.

I needed to talk to someone who could laugh and act down to Earth despite all the uncertainty brewing inside me.

"Yes." Food played an important role in academy life, but it wasn't the reason I was at Silver Diamond.

If only things were so simple.

A shrill beep shook me from my slumber and I rolled over in bed. The orange light on the intercom box atop my dresser blinked rapidly. I reached across the bed and whacked the thing with my hand. It clicked on.

"Yes?" I asked hoarsely.

"*Good morning, Lieutenant Hawksford!*" a female voice (which was way too perky in the morning) responded.

"Good morning." I cleared my throat and sat up, putting my feet onto the cold floor.

"*This is Officer Meadows, in charge of recruitment and student counseling. I do hope Commander Draven mentioned me yesterday. I apologize for not being able to greet you upon your arrival, but I had a full schedule yesterday and couldn't get away from my office."*

"I understand, Officer," I replied, rubbing my shoulder. It was a little sore from the way I'd slept. My hand tingled, so I shook it out to try to get the numbness to fade. I'd get used to the new bed eventually. Hopefully sooner rather than later. I didn't want to spend the next six months exhausted.

"I'd like to see you in my office this morning. Will 6 o'clock work for you?"

I glanced at my clock. In an hour? What time did this school start? Celestial Galaxy started classes at 8AM. Worst case scenario, we would have training exercises at 7AM. Silver Diamond must have been full of morning people.

Or at least one that I knew of already...

I didn't think I had much of a choice in the matter, so I mustered up a more cheerful tone and replied, "Yes, that will work for me."

"Great! I wasn't sure if it was too early, but I'm glad to hear it's not. Do you know where my office is?"

"No. I'm sorry."

"I believe the commander gave you a grounds map yesterday. Could you retrieve that, please?"

"Just a moment." I walked across the room to the writing desk at the other side and snagged the folded map. "I've got it," I replied as I walked back over to the bed and sat closer to the intercom.

"Open it and take a look at the floor plan. If you follow the Ruby Hall toward the entrance and continue straight, you'll see a little bridge walkway that leads to the second building of the academy: the office sector. Do you see that?"

I followed along with my finger. "Yes. I see it."

"My office is on the first floor and it's the fourth on the right when you enter the building. Room 1008. If you have any trouble finding it, just ask any student or staff member."

"Alright. I'll do that."

"Thank you, Lieutenant. I can't wait to meet you. I'll see you shortly."

CLICK.

With less than an hour to spare, I cleaned up, changed my clothes, grabbed a snack from the handful I'd packed in my things, and then headed out. With the map in hand, I made my way to the second building of the school.

There were some students and professors gathered in the halls along the way from whom I received more than a few curious glances. My forest-green uniform (which was a completely different cut and style than everyone else's) drew attention. I tried to shake my discomfort, but it was awkward to have people randomly gawking at me.

Stay calm. They're just curious. That's all.

I needed to focus on the real reason I was at Silver Diamond—to help make things better for our academies. Being part of Celestial Galaxy made me different and they'd chosen me for a reason, so I needed to suck it up and be proud of where I'd come from. They weren't staring at me because I was doing something wrong; they were staring at me because I was doing something *right*.

The entrance area and bridge weren't hard to find, as each area of the academy was clearly marked with floor lines, as well as colored wall trim confirming each specific section. A large lighted yellow sign hung above the connecting walkway and was impossible to miss. The school was laid out in a way that made everything very easy to locate. Celestial Galaxy was huge, so getting around required you to navigate several elevators or winding concourses.

The bridge took me outside to a long, covered walkway which stretched between the two facilities. I entered the office sector and counted the rooms as I passed them.

One. Two. Three. I stopped at the fourth room, which had the door propped open, and confirmed with the number plate beside the doorframe that I was in the right place. 1008. I poked my head in. A black-haired woman sat at the desk in the back of the room, her face buried in what appeared to be a scheduling book.

"Excuse me." I knocked on the door and Officer Meadow's face came up.

"Oh! Lieutenant Hawksford!" She stood and came out from behind her desk to shake my hand vigorously, smiling enthusiastically. She was quite dainty, looked to be in her mid-thirties, and (to my surprise) was a tad shorter than me.

I always thought I was short compared to other girls.

She had a delicate curve to her eyes, long, jet-black hair held out of her face with small barrettes, and unlike many other female professors I'd seen thus far, she wore an ankle-length black skirt and boots with a black, high-collar blouse with dark red trim. On her left lapel was a red-colored, diamond-shaped embroidery design.

"Wonderful to meet you!" She released my hand. Finally. "Allow me to introduce myself properly. I'm Officer Angela Meadows, the lead recruitment officer and head counselor here. It is an absolute pleasure to have you with us. Please, take a seat. Anywhere you like is fine." She pointed to a row of seats in front of her desk and a soft-looking couch beside it.

I chose one of the chairs in front of her desk just to be consistent and professional. Officer Meadows returned to her desk, sat, and scooted her chair in. Several photo frames rested on her immaculate tabletop and on the surrounding bookshelves. They contained photos of her with various groups of students around the base.

She pulled open a drawer by her leg and took out a large,

black folder with a metallic Silver Diamond logo embossed on the cover.

"Here is your orientation packet," she said, sliding it over to me. "Everything you need to know is in here. Important contacts. Special events. Et cetera."

I took the folder up into my hands and flipped through some of the pages tucked inside.

"Is everything okay?" the officer asked.

I must have unintentionally been making a weird face.

"Yes." I closed the folder and smiled. "It's just been a long time since I've been given anything in paper form. At Celestial Galaxy, everything we record is digital and all records are kept on our tablets or on the main network server."

Meadows leaned closer to me and her brow wrinkled with worry. "Is... that a problem? The folder?" Her voice was very soft with genuine concern.

"No. No. I'm so sorry," I replied. "I don't mean to seem ungrateful. I suppose it's because we don't have a lot of outlets for trash or the ability to create paper on-demand in space. We need to cut back on any excess supplies we can." But then I realized that our way of doing things could probably save Silver Diamond a lot of money and resources, too. "Perhaps it is something we could add to the list of possible suggestions for this academy to consider. Digital formats make things quicker and easier to update and share amongst personnel."

"That sounds fantastic!" Meadows clapped her hands happily, her voice rising to the same overly perky pitch I'd heard on the intercom earlier this morning. "It's only your first day here and you're working already! I know you're going to be a fabulous asset to our academy, Lieutenant."

She was so energetic, it was unreal; she emitted a friendly, earnest energy and it was obvious she loved her job.

"Let me know if you have any questions whatsoever about the orientation information." She smiled. "My contact number and office hours are both listed inside, and you are always welcome to reach out to me if you have any concerns. My door is always open, but I also offer private and confidential counseling if you should require it."

She swiveled in her chair to face her computer, which was just off to her side, and then pushed the flat screen monitor around so I could see it, too. "Let's get down to business, Lieutenant. We'd like to enroll you in at least one or two advanced classes while you're here. I understand you're already on your way to becoming a major, but this will allow you to interact with other students and staff and give you a better sense of how our academy works. What are your interests?" She gave me her full attention. "Do you like mechanics? Ecology? Anything of that nature?"

"Not particularly," I replied. I was good with computers. Not so good with mechanical stuff. I knew how to do a little of everything and had a passion for ancient weaponry and the history of combat techniques. Neither of which were helpful on an average day of being a lieutenant. Maybe for my next promotion, but right now...

"Okay. Let's try this." Meadows opened her desk drawer again and slid another folder out. It had my name in the corner. She cracked it open and skimmed over a few pages inside. "Here!" She pointed to a paragraph on one of the pages. "It says here you are an excellent markswoman!" Her voice perked up again. "We have an exemplary shooting range. I don't like to boast, but it's been rated the best in the country for seven years in a row."

"That could work," I muttered, still feeling groggy.

"You've excelled in historical studies. And it says you are skilled with a sword, as well." She brought a hand to her chin and narrowed her eyes. "That's incredibly unusual nowadays. Did they teach you that at Celestial Galaxy?"

I nodded. "Yes, but much of it is self-taught from my own personal research. The sword I have is ancient and there's very little information on it in existence."

"Lovely. Then, perhaps, this would be a great opportunity for you to share some of your skills with others. Do you mind if I enroll you in the Advanced Firearms course?"

I straightened up in my chair once I realized I'd been slouching. "That's fine."

Officer Meadows went back to her computer and started typing some things I couldn't see. "I also read in your file that you are training to be a major. May I recommend a Proactive Management course? We do suggest those to anyone pursuing a high-level position. It's designed for students and faculty of various age groups, so you won't feel out of place."

I nodded in agreement again.

A few mouse clicks and keystrokes later, something was being spat out of the printer behind the officer's desk. Meadows spun around, yanked out the sheets, and then swiveled back toward me. "Here you go. The firearms class is held in the outdoor range and, on days of poor weather, it takes place in the Green District. Management will be in the Silver Hall. Both sectors are on your map."

"Thank you, Officer." I slid the pages into my black folder and tucked the entire thing under my arm. Then I stood from my seat and saluted her absentmindedly with the C.G. salute—my right fist over my heart. She paused for a moment and then grinned in understanding. Luckily, I hadn't offended her.

"If you don't mind, Lieutenant," she added just before I could turn to go, "I'd like to see if Commander Draven is available to show you to your firearms class today." She tapped some buttons on her desk intercom and waited.

"This is Draven."

Officer Meadows' face lit up. "Good morning, Commander! How are you?"

"Fine... Thank you. Is something the matter?"

"Oh, no, Commander. Everything is perfect as peaches over here. Oh! But I did have a request, if you're not too terribly busy this morning. You're not too terribly busy, are you?"

There was a brief moment of silence before he responded.

"I don't have anything scheduled at the moment. What do you need?"

Meadows beamed. "I'm here with Ms. Lieutenant Hawksford right now and I was hoping you might be able to escort her to her first class today and help get her a firearm assigned."

We waited for a reply, but it took a while this time.

"Commander?"

"I'm here. Just thinking. When is her first class?"

Meadows glanced at the clock perched above her doorframe. "In about an hour."

"I can do that. Is she currently in your office?"

"Yes, Sir."

"I'll be over shortly."

CLICK.

I appreciate everything you've been doing for me, Commander." I walked alongside Draven in the hall.

"You're very welcome, Lieutenant." His voice had a pleasant quality to it.

"I'm sorry they've assigned you to babysit me while I'm here." I laughed.

"Babysit you?" Draven halted, turned toward me, and then scoffed, his forehead wrinkling. "Is that what you think this is?" He looked me right in the eye and I froze.

"Well, I—"

"That's the last thing I'd call it," he said. "It's my duty to handle whatever responsibilities Captain Lansfora assigns to me, and working with you is for the good of our entire academy. It isn't a chore, if that's what you're insinuating."

"No. I'm sorry." I smiled awkwardly back at him and then looked away, clearing my throat. He started walking again and I continued alongside him.

We approached a pair of metal, sliding doors and he swiped his keycard through a panel on the right side of the frame to open them.

"I... uh... apologize if that came off harsh," he said, glancing over at me with a softened expression. "I didn't mean for it to."

The comment about babysitting? I'd already let it go. "It's fine. I didn't take it that way, Sir."

"Good." A look of relief swept over his face.

The building had been segregated into several long glass rooms with dark grey, sound-proof paneling all around and various targets suspended at the far end of each row. Lockers and a small office with see-through walls were located at the far end. Racks of tactical earmuffs and goggles hung inside the office.

"You'll check out your gear back there," Draven said, pointing to the room with the supplies. "You can keep all assigned weapons in your locker along the back wall." He reached up a hand to direct my attention to a huge metal door. "That door will take you to the outdoor range. It's really nice outside, so you'll likely be there today. It's about the same setup, except with better airflow... and grass." He chuckled.

"Is this where you trained, too?"

"Yes. It's changed a lot since then, though."

"Commander? You mentioned we can check out weapons for our class. I already have a gun. Would it be possible for me to use my own instead of borrowing one from the academy, or is that against rules?"

"It's not against rules, but what model is it?"

"A Platinum Galaxy 53."

"Whoa! What!?" Commander Draven's eyes widened. "The one with the titanium grip and engraved slide?"

"Yes." I nodded proudly.

"That was a limited edition. Where in the world did you get that? They're impossible to find nowadays."

He was much more excited about my gun than I'd thought he'd be, and that was okay. I'd always been considered the Celestial Galaxy geek-girl who preferred to study weapons instead of boys. Weaponry and historical artifacts were my interests and those weren't bad interests to have in a military academy.

"My sister got it for me a few years ago for my sixteenth birthday and for my promotion to Lieutenant. It was sort of a congratulatory-birthday present."

"You must have an awesome sister."

Yes, and she's taken...

The words just sounded weird coming from him, but maybe I was assuming something I shouldn't have. What was I thinking?

"Yes. She's great. Always taken good care of me." I lifted my hand toward my collar, remembering the heirloom necklace I had now, because of her. I looked down and sighed as a sudden wave of homesickness unsettled me.

"I'd love to meet her someday," Draven said. "Perhaps when your term is finished here, the four of us can get together for a meal or something like that."

"Four?"

"You, me, your sister, and your friend, Lieutenant Ray."

I'd assumed he'd forgotten about him by now. The commander must have had a lot of friends at Silver Diamond. Perhaps all the pilot talk stuck with him.

I smiled. "That would be nice." Atira probably wouldn't be returning to Earth for many years, but it was a nice gesture on his behalf.

"We should pick up your gun if you want it in time for class today," he said, motioning to the door. "I'll go sign it out for you."

"What about the thirty-day mandatory confiscation rule? I thought I couldn't get it back until then."

"Officer Meadows signed off on your firearms class, and her decision means you'll have a gun in your hands no matter what we do with your personal firearm. As high commander, I decide whether that firearm is your own or school property."

"I appreciate the exception."

"I'm sorry to say, you will not be getting your sword back just yet, however. That remains in lockdown until the holding period has passed."

"Understood, Sir."

He walked me down the hall to the large desk area near the tarmac where we had entered upon our arrival. He spoke with a man at the desk, swiped his I.D. card in a slot on the table, and was then handed another keycard.

"Please wait here, Lieutenant," the commander said to me. "I'll be right back." He entered the room of lockboxes just behind the desk. I could watch him from where I was because the room had a huge glass window making up one entire side. Not to be funny, but Silver Diamond *was* very transparent—lots of glass.

I watched him use the new card to access the metal drawer containing my weapons. One look at my firearm and he was stunned. He lifted it carefully from the drawer and examined it, flipping it over to inspect the engraved designs along the muzzle. His fingers drifted over the frame and a smile drifted across his lips.

He removed the magazine and slid the ammo out, round-by-round, then racked the slide and emptied the cartridge from the chamber. He poured them all into the drawer and then shoved the magazine back into the gun.

His gaze caught on my sword, which had been lying beside the gun in the long drawer. He tipped his head to the side and his eyes narrowed. His hand reached across to touch something, though I couldn't tell what, and then he shook his head and pushed the drawer closed.

He left the lockbox room and returned to the front desk.

"Here you are," he said, handing the Platinum Galaxy to me with both hands. "Beautiful piece. I removed the rounds that were in it as you'll be given special ones at the range. What were those, by the way? Kinetic?"

I nodded.

Kinetic rounds contained a high-powered accelerant that caused a chemical reaction when fired, making bullets burst into flames while electrical pulsations surged in the shell, waiting to discharge a powerful shock in the target.

They were good for only two things—stunt shows and clean kills. It made sense for the commander to keep them in lockdown.

"The sword is incredible, too, by the way," he added as we began our trek back down to the Green District. "I've never seen anything like it."

"It's one of a kind," I replied, tucking the unloaded gun into a side-pocket.

"I vaguely remember reading something in your file about you having an affinity for weaponry studies and Old-World and ancient artifacts. Is that sword one of them?"

"Phoenixes have been extinct for centuries, but my sword was forged with the blood of a phoenix mixed with platinum excavated from the Amber Vale."

"You know a lot." Draven grinned with approval. "The question is, how does it handle?"

"Cuts through anything and is light as a feather," I said with a quiet laugh. "Really. It's incredibly lightweight. It's also rumored to be indestructible."

"That's an awful lot to ask of a sword."

"Not *my* sword."

We reached the shooting range and, this time, the doors were open. We went inside and were immediately approached by the instructor. She was a tall, lanky woman with dark blue trim on her high-collar and a tight pony-tail of rich golden-brown hair pulled back and up high on her head. Above her left pocket was a badge or medal of some kind—an embroidered diamond outline filled in with silver and scarlet stripes with a shiny metal diamond pin affixed in the center.

She forced a somewhat mechanical grin. "Commander," she said flatly, barely parting her lips. She saluted him briskly and then cleared her throat and squinted. "Can I help you?" Her words were drenched in cynicism and it made me uncomfortable. Had we arrived at a bad time?

"Lieutenant Hawksford," he began, his voice noticeably tense, "this is Gunnery Sergeant, Shakira Vlain. Sergeant

Vlain, this is the student from Celestial Galaxy who is staying with us for the term. She's been enlisted in your class per the recommendation of Officer Meadows. She also has her own firearm, which you'll need to—"

"Yes. Yes. I understand," Vlain interrupted. She held out a hand. "Gun and I.D., please, Lieutenant."

Her piercing brown eyes cut through mine.

I reached into my pocket, withdrew my card, and then my firearm.

"Thank you." The sergeant snatched both from me, turned, and marched off toward the lockers in the back of the room. She slid my I.D. through one of the locker security panels to open it and then set my gun inside and shut the door.

"I will keep your card until class begins," she said, tucking my I.D. into her shirt pocket as she marched back over to us. Draven stiffened awkwardly as she approached. "I can take it from here, Commander," Vlain said, glancing at him with a sharp, near condescending look. "I'm sure you have more important matters to deal with."

Why are you letting her talk to you like that!?

I couldn't believe a high commander would let a sergeant address him with such malice in her tone. Maybe there was something going on I didn't know about or bad blood between them.

"I've got some things to take care of, Lieutenant," Draven

said to me. An uncomfortable grin coiled his lips. "Have fun. We can catch up later." He backed away and then hastily left.

"Hawksford," the sergeant addressed me sternly. "I assume you are a seasoned markswoman, else you would not have been put into my class."

I nodded.

"At Silver Diamond, we say there is always more to learn. I am quite certain no matter how many classes you've taken or how much experience you may have thus far, that you still have a long way to go before you will truly master any of your skills. In this course, you will not only learn to better your techniques on the battle field, but also how to trust your intuition, defend yourself with whatever weapons the situation provides, and react with speed and accuracy.

You brought a very nice firearm with you, but it's an older model that only takes standard or kinetic rounds. Are you familiar with a modern Sparkbow or shard gauntlet?"

"I'm very skilled with a sword, but have never had the opportunity to get either of those weapons into my hands yet. I've read a lot about them, though, and I'd love to get the chance to work with them."

"You will," Vlain replied, crossing her arms. "Please take a seat, Lieutenant. The rest of the class will arrive shortly."

Okay, then...

I sat in the front row, near the instructor's desk so I

could hear easily. Other than the clear tension I noticed between her and the commander, I couldn't tell much about Sergeant Vlain. She came across as intelligent and focused, albeit a little intimidating. I'd had instructors like her before, though. I kept my head down, did my work, and never let a bad attitude pull me off course in my studies.

A few students came trickling into the room. Each of them took a second look at me upon entering (my unfamiliar green uniform demanded it), and then quickly took their seats. A handful introduced themselves, but most seemed preoccupied with their own thoughts.

"I didn't expect to find you here," a soft, feminine voice said from beside me. I turned to see the private who had greeted me upon my arrival at the academy yesterday. "Good morning!" She smiled with her eyes and stretched out a hand toward me. "Private Amanda Quill. We met yesterday."

"I remember." I shook her hand for the first time. "Lieutenant Valhara—"

"Hawksford." The private sat next to me and tossed a canvas messenger bag onto the floor by her feet. "Which is an awesome name, by the way. I mean really. Quill. *Hawks*-ford. Birds of a feather. Am I right?" She beamed and giggled girlishly as she reached down into her bag to rummage around for something. She pulled out a pad of paper and slapped it onto her desk. "So you're good with a gun?" There was a pen tucked into the bun of hair at the back of her head that she slid out.

"I guess." Okay, I was actually one of the best markswomen in all of Celestial Galaxy, but I didn't want to turn off a possible new friend by saying so.

"You *guess*." She lifted an eyebrow and shook her head. "You wouldn't be in Sergeant Vlain's class if you 'guessed' you were good. She only takes the best, so don't go being modest about your skills here, unless you want her to kick you out."

"Oh. Well, Officer Meadows enrolled me, so..."

Private Quill leaned on her elbows and rested her head in her hands. "She's great, right? The nicest person ever, I think."

"She seemed nice," I replied, though I wasn't comfortable talking about other officials in public places.

"She *is* nice. Stay on her good side. Last year, I had some family stuff going on and was late to enroll in one of my major classes. Meadows managed to get me in by calling the instructor and asking him to make an exception for me even though the class was a really small one and already full." Quill glanced at my desk with a look of surprise. All I had in front of me was my orientation folder. "Oooh. You've got a shiny folder. They broke out the good stuff for you." She chuckled. "So, where are the rest of your things? Can't take notes on that collector's item."

"Um... things? I didn't bring anything else to take notes with and hadn't had a chance to get anything new yet."

"You're so needy!" Quill exaggerated a scowl and then transformed it into a grin. "No problem." She reached into her bag and fished around, then pulled out another notebook. There was a pen in the side pocket of her bag. "Here you go. Brand new one I just picked up a few days ago."

It was dark brown with white and red calligraphy letters decorating the cover.

"Thanks. I'll pay you back." I felt bad taking stuff from her. "Let me know what I owe you."

"Hmm." She nibbled on the back of her pen; I started wondering if the one she'd given me had been in her mouth before, too. "Maybe I'll think of something later." She shrugged and snickered quietly to herself.

Quill apparently liked to laugh. It was sort of cute, but would take some getting used to if it turned out to be a regular thing. Jacksiun and I had a lot of running jokes between us, but we didn't make waves in class. The private didn't seem to care who was watching.

"So you don't get tablets for note-taking, either?" I whispered as Sergeant Vlain made her way back to her desk at the front of the class.

"We might be smart, but we aren't all rich," Quill replied.

"Seems like so much wasted paper to not go digital, nowadays. At C.G., they're academy issued. We don't pay for them."

"I see. But still a big nope. Sorry. Did they spoil you up there? Hanging out with all us Silver Diamond lowlifes is going to be rough, huh?"

She was joking; I could tell from her exaggerated expression.

"No. And I wouldn't call it being spoiled."

Sergeant Vlain cleared her throat and my gaze shot up at her. She narrowed her eyes at me and then came out from behind her desk.

"There will be plenty of time for chatter later." She sneered.

"Apologies, Sergeant." I lowered my head.

"You may or may not already have met our new transfer student from Celestial Galaxy—Lieutenant Valhara Hawksford. I like to make introductions brief, so if you would like to know more about her, please speak with her after class. I expect you to treat her with the same level of respect as is expected of a Silver Diamond recruit. Anything less is unacceptable."

After pressing her hand against a small black panel on the side of her desk, Sergeant Vlain popped the top panel open, much like the hood of an Old-World car. They didn't make them anymore, but my dad had some little toy ones I'd gotten into at a small age.

Sergeant Vlain lifted a compact crossbow from the

compartment in her desk and abruptly aimed it toward the class. "Rule number one. Never. Ever. Point a charged Sparkbow at someone you don't want to execute." She lowered the weapon to her side. It wasn't anything like crossbows of the olden days—the ones with cocking stirrups and strings you had to hold on the ground and pull back with both hands. Sparkbows didn't need strings because they relied on condensed, manipulated energy to discharge. They were highly evolved weapons created by assimilating long bows and standard crossbows with technology not unlike that used in kinetic ammunition.

There was a row of targets in the distance just behind her and a starting line a few feet in front of me where one could stand and aim. The sergeant approached it, stretched out her arm toward a target, and—with her other hand—swiftly drew two fingers over the center groove toward the trigger, as if pulling an imaginary string back. A bolt of white-hot light formed in the groove. I didn't stare at it because it was so bright, it could damage my eyes.

Without seemingly even trying to focus, Vlain pulled the trigger, a sparking sound echoed around the room, and she made her mark in the center of the target at the other side of the range. A video feed from the target came through on a tiny monitor embedded in the upper corners of our desks.

"This had yet to be activated," she said, turning to face us. "This is only one of many precautions you must keep in mind at all times when handling a Sparkbow. You must also remember that once you activate the bolt, you cannot return the pulse wave to the battery chamber and the shot *must* be discharged promptly. Where you choose to discharge the shot is your own choice. Make the decision carefully or you risk harm or death."

She set the weapon on her desk and turned to us again, this time clasping her hands together. "I will show you all how to load the battery into the chamber before we begin. When on the battlefield, keep in mind a Sparkbow will cause interference with certain types of electrical units in the area, so be sure your acting superior knows you are armed with one. They will assign to you an insulated intercom and tracking particle for the duration of your mission. That being said, if you have any electrical devices with you at this time, I suggest you leave them on your desk or in your locker while we move forward with the trial lesson."

I was starting to understand why tablets weren't popular here. They had some very high-tech artillery, even though some of their other practices seemed outdated.

One by one, Sergeant Vlain called each of us up to the front. She showed us how to handle the Sparkbow, how to draw it, and how to load the battery pack into the chamber. The piece was durable but lightweight, owing to its titanium casing. Scratch and corrosion resistant, titanium is also a poor conductor of electricity, so it was well-suited for a battlefield.

I watched other students take practice shots at the target until it was my turn. Most came within inches of the target—not bad for first tries. Private Quill and I were within *centimeters* of it, something the sergeant was quick to praise us for. That made me feel good. My first day of class at the new academy and an instructor who came off cold, at first, had already given me a pat on the back (figuratively).

I couldn't believe how seasoned Amanda was, though. She had to have been a few years younger than me if she was a private (and she looked it, too), but she handled the Sparkbow like a pro. She said it was her first time, but I could hardly believe that.

"So, where are you staying?" Quill asked, tossing her notebook into her bag and carefully sliding her pen back into her hair bun.

"I'm in room 23 in Ruby Hall." I tucked my I.D. card into my chest pocket and buttoned it securely. The sergeant had returned it to me at the end of class. "Here's your notebook and pen, by the way." I handed them to Amanda, but she gave me this look like I was crazy.

"Keep them. I have plenty. I buy them by the case.

They… uh… have a bad habit of walking away." She snorted. "Anyway, Ruby Hall!? Dragons! You are so lucky!"

Dragons? Was that the word kids used for it nowadays? I'd been away from Earth for too long.

I stacked the orientation folder and notebook together and shoved them under my arm as we walked out of the classroom and started off down the hall.

"I'm not *that* lucky," I said, hoping she wouldn't be jealous. "I think they only put me there to keep an eye on me."

"Oh." Her voice lowered. "Ew. Forget that." She stuck out her tongue. "I don't need people 'keeping an eye on me' all the time."

"That's not what he's doing!" The defense came out before I could stop it.

"He? He, who?"

Ah! I didn't really want to answer that. I thought she knew.

"Wait. Wait. Are you talking about Commander Draven?" A toothy grin cracked across her lips. "Is that why he's been hanging around with you? I saw you two earlier in the hall. I thought you'd gotten in trouble for something already."

"No. He was showing me around. He told me they put me in Ruby Hall in case I needed any help during my stay."

"Oh. Okay then. Between you and me, what do you think of the commander, anyway?"

"He's... nice."

"Nice... looking? Or just *nice*?"

What!? I wasn't sure what to say. Why was she putting me on the spot like this?

"Eh, nevermind," she said, shaking her head. "Not my type. But..." She stopped walking and turned to me, her index finger raised. "That lieutenant you came down here with yesterday..."

"Jacksiun? Uh... I mean, Lieutenant Ray?"

"First name basis? Ouch." She screwed her lips up to the side. "I guess I can forget him."

"We're not *together*," I corrected her quickly. "He's my friend. As in, my best friend since I was a kid and I'm not going out with him." My face was burning up now.

"I see. How old is he?"

This isn't hallway talk!

"He's not, like, twenty-five or anything crazy, right?" she continued. "He looks around seventeen or so. Am I warm?"

"He's... eighteen."

"Oh, good!" She chewed her lip a moment. "Might have to cash in that favor you owe me for the notebook."

"What?"

"Don't worry about it. We'll talk boys later. I have to go to my next class. Take care, Val! Uh... can I call you Val?"

I just shrugged.

"Catch up soon!"

Amanda entered the nearby classroom and left me by myself in the empty hallway. I looked around, not recognizing this particular part of the academy at all—the Green District. I shuffled the grounds map out of my folder and flipped it open. I used my finger to trace the map as I skimmed over the buildings. Green to White. White to Ruby and other sections. It was color-coded clearly, but I hadn't memorized it yet.

I followed the map back to the covered bridge and the main building. There, I stopped and put my nose back into the map again to try to get my bearings.

"Where'd you go?"

I lifted my face from the map. Ocean-blue eyes looked back into mine—Commander Draven's.

"I came back to look for you, but you were already gone," he said, crossing his arms. "Is everything okay?"

"I was walking with Private Quill to her other class." I shied away from his concerned look. "I didn't mean to wander off."

"It's fine. You're welcome to explore the academy."

I brought my face back toward his and our eyes met again. He had an inviting smile on his face.

"I came back to find you to ask if you'd like to have lunch in my office. That is, if you don't mind some company."

Company?

Immediately, I assumed it had to be either his girlfriend or the captain. Both possibilities put me on edge.

We passed the cafeteria, grabbed lunches to go, and then headed off toward what I was then told was called Sapphire Hall. Draven mentioned he preferred to eat in his office because it was quieter, despite the fact that the cafeteria actually had a separate room for administrators.

There was a gold nameplate perched just to the side of his office doors and a polished metal Silver Diamond emblem set prestigiously above that. He swiped his keycard through a reader outside the door and pressed his hand onto a familiar black glass panel until a red light flashed and a note chimed. The doors slid apart and we entered his office.

It was a large room with bookshelves surrounding the desk on three sides, all filled with color-coded folders, books, and documents stacked in rows between pieces of fighter jet memorabilia, model planes, and a few photographs. Piles of paperwork littered his workspace and lay scattered across his keyboard.

I didn't see anyone else in the room.

"Where's the company you—"

A deep growl reverberated from his desk and I stepped back, startled. It sounded like a bear or a huge—

"Whoa! I'm so sorry," Draven said, embarrassed. "Wait here a minute."

Easy. I had zero plans to move until I knew exactly what the ferocious-sounding thing was.

He trotted behind his desk and bent down, muttering something I couldn't hear to someone or *something* I couldn't see. The growling ceased and a moment later, the commander came out from behind his desk with a massive black, longhaired shepherd dog. It was leashed with a long leather strap and had a heavy metal choke-chain collar dangling around its neck. The animal was so tall, its head came up to Draven's hip.

"Oh!" I staggered back as the enormous beast headed toward me, still close by the commander's side.

"Don't be afraid," he said, patting the dog on the head. "This is Wolf. He's one of our tracking dogs. He won't hurt you, I promise. Are you... okay with dogs?" One of his eyebrows rose.

I'd been around dogs a lot growing up, and we did have a few at Celestial Galaxy, but none quite so large and intimidating. Maybe it was because he was solid black, or maybe it was because he was the size of a timber wolf on steroids.

"I'm fine with dogs," I replied, my voice cracking. "He's beautiful." My experience with animals taught me not to approach them without being instructed to, so I simply raised my hand, knelt down a little, and slowly lifted it, palm-up.

"Okay, Wolf," the commander said in a firm voice. "Go to them." He gave Wolf some slack on the leash and the colossal black dog neared me to investigate my hand.

"Is he yours?" I asked quietly as the dog sniffed my hand.

"No. His handler is on leave and I've been given permission to work with him until he returns."

"He's a gorgeous animal." The dog's rich brown eyes met mine and a breath caught in my throat. The sheer presence of the dog made me feel so small.

"He's very smart, too," Draven boasted. "He stays in the academy kennel at night, but I keep him here or take him outside when I can. I... really hope you don't mind him being here. I should have told you first, but—"

"I don't mind at all." I stood slowly. Wolf sniffed around my shoes and then lifted his head and nudged my hand with his powerful muzzle. He snorted and wagged his tail as I looked down at him again. "He seems sweet."

The commander pointed to the center of the room, in front of his desk. "Leave it," he commanded. Immediately, Wolf lost interest in me and scampered off. "Down. Stay." Draven made subtle hand gestures I didn't understand, and then Wolf lay down in the center of the room and lowered his head onto his paws. "Good boy."

Draven pulled a chair out for me and motioned for me to sit. Then he wheeled the chair out from behind his desk and sat across from me.

I crossed my legs, leaned back in my chair, and began unwrapping the paper from the sandwich I'd brought. I felt naive for making assumptions about who would be joining us.

"For some reason, I thought maybe Captain Lansfora would be meeting with us for lunch." I chuckled nervously and took a small bite of my sandwich.

"Really?" Draven tilted his head. "Oh, well, I guess that's not too far fetched, considering I'm his high commander, but... really, he's too busy for that kind of stuff."

"It's okay. I was getting a little anxious anyway because of that."

"Why?" He slipped a slice of meat from his sandwich

and tossed it to Wolf, who practically inhaled it as soon as it reached his mouth. "Captain Lansfora is friendlier than most people think. I know he can seem a bit abrasive, but he's got a heart of gold and an entire shelf full of medals on top of that." He laughed and then bit into his sandwich.

"So do you and the captain get along well?"

"Yes. To be honest, though, I don't hang out with many people. I game a lot in the evenings with some of the students here and some people from other cities—anonymously, of course. That's what I was doing last night when you came by." He made hand gestures like he was putting on earphones. "That's what the headset and all was for. But I don't do stuff like *this* too often."

"Have lunch with people?" I pulled my head back, surprised. A guy like him should have been fairly popular, considering how outgoing he was. Maybe his rank intimidated others? I couldn't wrap my brain around that, though.

"Yes." He nodded and sighed. "Sad, right?"

"Well, I think you're a nice person. From what I've seen so far, at least." I chewed on a bite of bread.

He smiled gratefully. "Really? That's what my mom keeps telling me, but..."

"Oh, does she live near here?"

"Yes. Our house is within walking distance."

"You... live with your mother?"

His eyes widened. "Uh... no. Not exactly. Well..." He

straightened up in his chair and struggled to put his words together. I felt a little bad for putting him on the spot like that.

"I didn't mean to assume—"

"My mom lives with me, actually. I only go home on the weekends, and since my dad passed away, I thought it would be nice for her to have company sometimes. Please, don't think it's weird. It's not really—"

"No. It's not weird at all. Why would I think it was weird?"

"Because the second-in-command at an elite military academy is still living with his mom."

"You mean your mom is living with you." I smiled. "And there's nothing wrong with it. You're a good son to do something like that."

The look of discomfort on his face melted into a more comforted, serene grin. I wondered how many other people had made fun of his situation without even thinking. "Thank you, Lieutenant. Thank you for understanding."

A few moments of silence passed and then he rolled his paper wrapper up into a ball and tossed it into a nearby trashcan. I would have done the same with my own, but I knew I couldn't make the shot, and I didn't want to embarrass myself.

"Oh, before I forget." He wheeled his chair back behind his desk, leaned to the side, and pulled open a bottom drawer on his desk. He dug something out and then slammed the drawer closed. Wolf perked up from the thunderous sound and Draven cringed as if he hadn't meant to push it in so forcefully. "You should have one of these," he said, scooting his chair closer to mine and holding out an open hand. There was a small silver button in it. "It's an intercom link. Anyone here can use it to contact you if they have your link code."

I took the small thing from his hand and then realized he, too, wore one—on his right pocket.

"And, full disclosure, it contains a tracking particle. I highly recommend you keep it on you at all times for your own safety. In case of an emergency, you can press it and it will patch you through to the primary transmission line."

"Of course. Thank you." I nodded. "Does it matter where I affix it?" I unclasped my silver hair pin and turned it over. There was just enough space on the underside to tuck the tiny chip securely.

"Yes. That's perfect. That amount of silver won't deflect the satellite signals. Be sure to keep it on you at all times, please."

That would be easy.

"So how did your class go today?" he asked. "I meant to ask earlier, but I think everything got off course accidentally."

Draven whistled sharply. Wolf jumped to attention and

dashed over to his side, shoving his face against his lap to get petted while his tail wagged excitedly. The commander scratched him behind the ears and smiled, lowering his face and mumbling something to the dog as he tried his absolute best to lick him.

"It went well, I think," I replied. "Sergeant Vlain said I was doing great, so that's a plus."

"That's good." He roughed up the fur on the back of Wolf's neck and then scratched his chin. The dog's tongue hung out of the side of his mouth and his whole body swayed back and forth happily. "She can come off as a little cross sometimes, but she's a great sergeant and she does, indeed, know her stuff."

A personal question popped into my head and, while I thought it might be rude to ask, I felt very at ease with the commander. I decided to phrase it as delicately as possible.

"Commander?"

He looked up at me. "Yes?"

"I noticed you seemed to be in quite a hurry to leave Vlain's class this morning. Was something wrong?"

"Uh..." He looked down at the dog again and patted his head. "I probably shouldn't be telling you this but, off the record, we aren't on the best terms. Sergeant Vlain and I."

"May I ask why? You are the high commander here. I believe she should respect you for that, at the very least."

"Yes, but that's also part of the issue." He pressed his

lips thin and shot me a stern glance. "This conversation stays in my office, understood?"

"Yes, Commander."

"The sergeant and I were *sort of* going out."

"Sort of?"

"Sort of, as in, literally a few hours and she'd had it with me. I don't even think you can call a few hours an actual date. Can you?"

I shrugged.

"Anyway, that didn't bother me and I thought she was okay with the fact that our personalities just clashed too much, but it turned out there was a much larger issue at hand. I eventually learned that she was under the impression I had stolen the position of high commander away from her when, in fact, she wasn't remotely qualified at the time to be considered for the job. But people believe what they want to believe and she's still angry with me over that."

"That's terrible. I'm sorry she still holds a grudge. Sometimes you have to let things go."

"I respect her job. I do. She's great at what she does and I wouldn't feel comfortable appointing anyone else to gunnery sergeant. I only wish she'd understand that and stop hating me for something that could never have been."

"Can you talk to her about it?" I leaned forward in my seat and reached a hand out, unconsciously brushing it against his knee. "Maybe that would help?"

He exhaled loudly and looked away, shaking his head. I took my hand back and entwined my fingers in my lap.

A few moments of silence passed. Wolf sat patiently at his feet. I bit my lip and wondered if what I had said was helping or hurting.

"We should get going." He stood and swept his hands down his slacks to smooth the wrinkles and brush away some of Wolf's hairs. "I've got things to do and Wolf needs to go out for a run." He picked up the dog's leash in both hands and pulled it taut. "You can do as you please today. We've got a lot of resources to take advantage of."

"Thank you for inviting me to have lunch with you, Commander." I walked over to the trashcan and threw my wrapper in. "I appreciate it." I scooped my belongings up off the chair and held them in my folded arms.

Draven tipped his head. "I'm here if you need anything." He gestured for me to go ahead of him and then he and Wolf followed me to the door.

I flipped open my laptop and launched a chat application, pressing a preset button so it would begin to dial the communications hub at Celestial Galaxy. My screen flickered and, after a brief pause, a communications agent dressed in a familiar green uniform appeared on screen.

"Please state your rank and the party you wish to reach," he said.

"Lieutenant Valhara Hawksford, requesting Major Atira Hawksford."

"I'll patch you through right away, Lieutenant. Please hold."

"Thank you."

There were several moments of silence and black on screen until Atira picked up the call. Video began streaming in and my sister appeared, donning a big, toothy grin.

"Hey, Sis!" She waved at the camera. "How was your first day?" She carried her computer over to the bed, the shaky footage almost making me dizzy, and then put it down and sat in front of it.

"Well, it's technically still my first day, but everything has been fine thus far." I leaned out of the frame so she could see the bright red clock behind me. It was only mid-afternoon on the Mainlands. C.G. ran on Noble Time—six hours ahead.

"Ah. I forgot about the time difference. Jacksiun reminded me before, but..." She shrugged. "I have so much stuff to do around here."

"Oh! Thank you for the necklace, by the way." I tugged it out of hiding and dropped it in front of my collar. "I still don't know why you decided to give it to me, but—"

"You're welcome. I wanted you to have it. Now don't be stubborn about it."

"Sorry."

"Anyway, are you getting along okay with everyone?"

"Yes. I think so. There's a very nice student in my firearms class. Her name's Amanda Quill and she's a private first class. She's also the same private who showed Jacksiun and me around when we arrived."

"A private?" Atira scooted closer to the laptop and rear-ranged her cross-legged position. "They put you in a class with a private? How old is she?"

"I don't know, actually. I think she's younger than me. She was asking about Jacksiun's age, so I'm assuming sixteen or seventeen. She's amazing with a Sparkbow, though."

"A Sparkbow? They let you handle a Sparkbow on your first day?"

"Apparently, they get straight to business here." I chuckled.

"Nice. I don't even remember when they let me handle one. It was an old model at the time, anyway; a water-gun compared to what they have today."

"Yes. They're much more powerful now."

"Oh, I forgot to ask you about the advisor they assigned to you. How's that working out?"

"Did Jacksiun tell you who it was?"

Her brow furrowed and she narrowed her eyes. "No... Should he have?"

"Yes. Because my advisor is only the second commanding officer of Silver Diamond."

Atira's jaw dropped. "What!? The high commander? How the—? Why would they—"

"He's nice," I interrupted. "I don't think you need to be worried."

"I don't know if whether or not he's a nice guy is what I

was going to ask, but... that's crazy. Doesn't he have other, more important things to do? They aren't using him to keep an eye on you, are they? Surely, they don't think you're a spy. That would be ridiculous, not to mention it would go against the entire reason you're there—to establish trust."

"You're freaking out about something you shouldn't, Atira. Commander Draven has been nothing but welcoming to me since I've stepped foot in here. We had lunch together today and dinner the first night I got here. I... kind of like him."

"Like him? As in... *like* him?"

I hadn't meant it like that exactly, but... "No. I mean... well, I think he's kind. Okay?"

"Oh, alright. I'll let it go, then. I was going to say, he's probably old enough to be your dad, so I was getting a little concerned."

"No, he's not, actually. He's really young for a high commander. You'd be surprised, I think. He must be smart to have advanced so quickly. His dad received a Silver Crest Badge from President Alexander for his service in the Atlantic Strike, too."

"You're kidding me? Those are very rare honors. He must have done something outstanding."

"I haven't had a chance to ask him about the details. His dad's... um..."

Atira frowned. She knew exactly what my solemn face

implied.

"Did you... tell him about our parents?"

"No. I haven't known him long, and talking about that... hurts, you know?"

"Of course I know, Sis. I'm sorry." Atira lowered her head and looked away.

There was a long pause and I couldn't think of anything else to say.

"Tell Jacksiun I said 'hello,' please," I added. Atira's face came back up. "I'm sure he's worrying about me already."

"Oh, you know how he is."

"Well, you can tell him I'm doing just fine here and I think I'll be okay."

"Do you want me to tell him about your commander friend?" She cocked an eyebrow and smirked, insinuating something she shouldn't have been.

"No!" I scowled at her and all she did was start laughing.

"Why do you take everything so seriously, Sis? You know I'm only kidding. Jacksiun is overprotective enough."

Lately, it seemed like everyone was 'only kidding' about things they shouldn't have been. Maybe I was just really tired and still a bit jet-lagged from the trip.

I chuckled nervously, embarrassed by my outburst. "Sorry. I'm a little fatigued, still, and not really thinking clearly. Tell Jacksiun not to worry about anything. I'm going to go for now, alright? You take care. I'll talk with you again when I can."

"You, too, Valhara. Love you." She grinned and then saluted me with a clenched fist over her heart. I did the same.

Our salute meant more than honor and loyalty; it represented our bond as leaders in an organization united to serve mankind by advancing studies in technology, medicine, and economics. Our salute meant we fought for the same cause, and that we looked to the same star for inspiration and hope.

"Love you, too."

We waved goodbye and I shut down the chat application.

Mid-afternoon and the time difference toyed with my internal clock. It was too early in the day to go to bed, and I needed to keep my mind occupied so it would begin adjusting to the schedule change.

My room at Silver Diamond was much larger than the one at C.G., and I didn't feel quite as closed off from the outside world as I did there. Still, it was probably better if I didn't stay cooped up in my dorm all day. I needed to get out and try to make friends, or at least get a better feel for where everything was at Silver Diamond.

Commander Draven had mentioned a library and I vaguely recalled seeing it on the academy map. Surely, I could find something there to keep me busy for a while.

I ventured out, map in hand and academy pride on my sleeve. Literally and figuratively. I had to keep my wits about me as I sifted my way through the halls toward what I hoped would be the school library. People kept glancing at me. Some surprised. Some unaffected but curious, I think. A small number of students couldn't keep subtle gazes of contempt from crossing their faces. I felt out of place in my green C.G. uniform, but I also kept telling myself that I needed to wear it with honor and respect. If they had a problem with my academy, they had a problem with me, and I had been chosen to attend Silver Diamond to address that very issue.

I brushed off the awkward stares and made an effort to introduce myself to students who seemed receptive and curious about me, hoping it would spread the idea that I wasn't an alien from outer space who had six eyes and extra limbs hidden under my uniform. Alien, yes. Human, also yes.

I only lost my way once, and a professor was nice enough to point me in the correct direction. Light blue lines led me to the library and the bright blue trim around the colossal door frame was a dead giveaway that I had found the right place.

With my I.D., I could access any of the research computers inside and peruse the massive catalog of books, both digital and hardcopies. The library at Celestial Galaxy was all digital. This was a great way of conserving space, while maximizing the number of titles available to personnel. This also meant the majority of books on file had been written and digitized within the last decade, limiting our selection to newer, more pertinent books, but leaving out some of the more interesting historical works that were only available in the Presidential Archives on the Mainlands and the esteemed Alyssian library in Alyssia (which was owned by the king and inaccessible to the general public).

"Do you have anything on the Atlantic Strike?" I approached the front desk where a librarian sat, his eyes set on the computer screen in front of him.

"Oh, hello." He looked up at me and smiled.

His name was Brent, according to his nametag. Senior Librarian. Though he was anything but a senior, looking to be in his mid-thirties.

"The Atlantic Strike," he repeated. "Is that what you asked for?"

"Yes."

"Give me just a moment. I know we have at least one compendium. I'm not sure if we archived it or if it's still out in the main catalog, so please allow me to go check on that for you."

He typed some things in on his computer and nodded, his lips moving to form silent words as he skimmed over the text on his screen.

"Yes. We do have one in the archive. I'll have to get it out for you." He stood and came out from behind the large, half circle desk. "Come with me... um..." He squinted at the brass nameplate above my left pocket. "Lieutenant Hawksford."

He escorted me to the back of the library into a large round room with massive, open shelves reaching up several floors and ladders with wheels on them placed intermittently. The smell of old paper hit me like a wave, crashing into my nostrils and making my nose itch. The room was a cooler temperature than the rest of the building and quiet, aside from a soft whirring sound from overhead. All the books were locked behind metal grating with little locked latches every few feet.

"I didn't mean to be a burden," I muttered, feeling bad about how much extra work I was putting Brent through to get me a single book.

"It's no trouble at all, Lieutenant," he replied. "Honestly, this is my favorite room in the entire building, and rarely do I have an opportunity to crack open a door or two and handle some of our rarer editions."

So this was fun for him? What a relief.

"It should be on the third tier. Row 19. Section S." He raised a finger and pointed to a location on one of the upper levels of shelving. "Over there. Somewhere." He stepped away, took one of the ladders by the railings, and began pushing it around the perimeter of the room until he reached the general vicinity he had gestured. "Let the scavenger hunt begin," he said, chuckling to himself. He looked at me. "Really, though, everything here is organized down to the letter, so it's not hard to find and no one misplaces anything here. Not on my watch." He put one foot onto a rung and then the other, climbing slowly to the mid-center of the room. There, he stretched out an arm to the side and began tapping across a line of spines until his finger stopped at what appeared to be a massive, navy-blue book. "Here we go." He pointed and looked down at me. "I've found it!" Then he reached into his pocket, removed a key, and unlocked the nearest latch so he could access the book.

He closed the door, juggling his key and the book so he wouldn't fall backward or drop either one. With the book securely tucked under his arm, Brent began backing down the ladder.

"I'll require your keycard, please," he said, holding out his empty hand toward me. "This book cannot leave the library, but you're welcome to sit anywhere you like and read, and if you require excerpts or copies of anything from inside it, please let me know. We can scan any article and have it uploaded to your school account for access whenever you need it."

"Thank you, Brent," I said, handing him my metallic card. It was strange surrendering something so important, especially after the commander had been so adamant about me keeping it on me at all times, but I couldn't assume a librarian would use it for nefarious purposes.

He pulled a small plastic folder out of his pocket, flipped it open with his thumb (while still holding my card), inserted my I.D. inside, and then clapped it closed and put it away. "Safe and sound," he said with another grin. "Here you are." He finagled the book out from under his arm and handed it to me with both hands. "Careful. It's a hefty one."

By "hefty" he really meant "weighs as much as an armload of bricks, hefty." When he handed it to me, I almost lost my balance. The book was heavier than any computer or tablet I've ever held and it had me laughing internally about the idea that librarians must have incredibly strong arms—at least those on Earth.

I hugged the heavy thing tightly to my chest and tried to compose myself quickly. *Who would have thought paper could be so heavy?*

"Let me know if you need anything else," Brent added and then turned to head back to his desk near the front of the building.

I staggered over to a nearby table just outside the archive and carefully set the book down. There was a small desk lamp perched there, though the overhead lights were more than adequate for reading.

The front of the book had a large academy emblem embossed with silver metallic ink. The pages were gilded with silver, too, and the entire thing had been case-wrapped in navy-blue fabric. It was about the size of two and a half vintage textbooks placed end to end and about three inches thick. A weighty book, for sure, like most war documentaries.

I lifted open the book's heavy cover and the spine let out a subtle crack. I grimaced, fearing I'd damaged the rare book, but it was only the sound of stiff paper and, as I flipped through the pages carefully, I realized it was in pristine condition.

I didn't know exactly what I was looking for in the book, but I did know who and when. I located the chapter on the Atlantic Strike and began skimming the pages. A separate section had been dedicated to those wounded or killed in the fight, and an even smaller segment to those who had received a Silver Crest badge. I turned one more page and my jaw fell open. There was a photograph of a pilot who bore a striking resemblance to Commander Draven (with much shorter hair), wearing a fully-decorated dress uniform, shaking hands with President Alexander. The caption below the image read:

"Presidential Squadron Commander, Lieutenant Colonel Anthony Draven graciously accepted the coveted Silver Crest Badge at last night's Excellence In Service banquet presented by President Alexander at the Mainlands capital. Lieutenant Colonel Draven received the award to commend his incredible, life-saving decision and his ability to act quickly and precisely in the face of imminent danger. During an evacuation, President Alexander's private plane came under fire, sustaining major damage to the left wing and engine, causing the aircraft to destabilize.

Lt. Col. Draven orchestrated an incredible sequence of flight maneuvers with his squadron which guided the president's plane to a safe landing. The Lt. Col. sustained only minor injuries from a shattered metal side panel that came loose inside the cockpit during the flight, but was released from the hospital to recover at his home. President Alexander thanked the Lt. Col. for his service and quick thinking, and cordially invited him and his family (his wife and three-year-old son) to attend a formal dinner at the presidential house, once fully recovered."

I sat back in my chair and sighed, shaking my head in disbelief. Commander Draven's father was a presidential squadron leader. That is an incredibly difficult position to acquire. And to earn a Silver Crest Badge on top of that was an even greater accomplishment. I'd heard only one or two are given out per year, and that they are reserved for only the most prominent and outstanding acts of courage and military prowess.

It's quite a legacy to try to live up to, but Commander Draven seemed to be following in his dad's footsteps. He had been promoted at such a young age that he'd already made it into the books as the youngest high commander in the history of Silver Diamond academy.

I slowly closed the book and pried it up off the table with both hands, bringing it close to my chest so I wouldn't lose my grasp on the monster. Then I lugged it to the front desk where Brent noticed me coming and shot out of his seat.

"Let me help," he said, rushing over and holding out his hands. I happily surrendered the book to him and he asked me to wait by his desk to receive my I.D. back. Brent disappeared into the archive and reappeared a few minutes later without the book. He handed me my I.D. and then resumed whatever he had been doing on his computer.

Now that my nagging curiosity (or perhaps, just plain nosiness) had quieted, I decided to check out a few books that would actually help me in my classes. Most of the modern catalog had gone digital, even at Silver Diamond; titles could be checked out with my I.D. and then sent to my account for viewing on either my personal computer or any academy kiosk. I was a fast reader, so I chose six titles ranging in topics from modern firearm mechanics to military leadership tactics and team building and then went back to my room to study.

KNOCK. KNOCK. KNOCK.

I gasped, startled from my sleep by an abrupt rapping at my door. I'd fallen asleep on my laptop and woke with a computer key-shaped motif stamped in pink on my cheek. Proactive Management class had ended early in the afternoon, and I had gone back to my room to read. Apparently, the time difference continued to mess with my head, even on my third day there.

It was past dusk and classes had ended a few hours ago. Who was knocking at this time of night?

I dragged my feet to my door and pressed the blue button on the intercom box. "Who is it?"

"It's Draven. I'm sorry if this is a bad time."

"No. It's fine!" I answered more quickly than I thought I could. "Just give me a moment, please." With my ponytail disheveled and my hair frizzed and out of place, I pulled the tie out of my hair and grabbed my brush from the bathroom. I quickly brushed it into submission and then gathered it up into my hands and tied the pony tail up once more. A subtle imprint still remained on my cheek, but I patted on some foundation and it masked most of the excess color.

"Yes, Commander?" I cracked open the door, keeping some of my face hidden behind it.

My heartbeat quickened.

Stop it. Why are you freaking out? My body didn't want to listen to my brain, but I tried to compose myself and smiled sheepishly.

"How have you been doing with the time difference?" he asked, grinning awkwardly himself. He seemed unsettled.

"I'm okay. Still not quite situated, but I think I will be in a few more days. I hope."

"Ah. Well, um... you've probably eaten dinner already, I take it?" He brushed a stray lock of blonde out of his face and over his ear.

I came out from behind the door. "Kind of. Why?"

"Since I didn't have time to check up on you today, I thought I'd see if you cared to join me again for a late din- ner. If not, I understand."

"Sure." I had nothing else to do, and... he was nice company.

"You would?" His smile brightened and his blue eyes met mine.

"Yes, but I thought this wasn't supposed to be a regular thing—eating this late."

He looked away and shrugged.

"I'm sorry," I said, reaching out as if I might brush a hand to his arm, but I caught myself and pulled back. "I *am* actually kind of hungry and, like I said, the time difference still has my stomach and internal clock confused. Please let me shut down my computer."

"Go right ahead, Lieutenant."

I closed the door softly and went back to my desk to turn off my laptop and pick up my I.D. Then I shoved on my shoes and double-checked my face in the mirror. The redness had completely subsided, or the makeup had made it invisible. Either way, I felt less embarrassed.

"Thank you for waiting," I said to the commander.

"Do you have your I.D.?" he asked.

"Yes. Of course," I scoffed jestingly. "It's not like you don't know who I am." My door closed and the lock clicked.

"True, but I don't want to have to get the master key card to let you back into your room after hours. That and you are required to have it with you at *all* times. Rules are rules."

"Most of them, right?" I chuckled, thinking about how ironic it was for him to say that while we were heading out to have dinner together after hours at the cafeteria which was technically now closed.

"Excuse me?" His smile went straight and his gaze intensified with narrowing eyes.

Oh...

"I'm sorry. I didn't mean to—"

"Lieutenant, don't *ever assume* I would do anything to jeopardize the integrity of this school." The tone of his voice was stern and unlike it had been since we'd met. "I believe in this academy and I will do whatever it takes to uphold its values and rules. Maybe... maybe I bend them a little now and then, but only because I have to. Only because I have a completely different schedule than most personnel and I can't clock out whenever I feel like it."

"I'm really sorry," I whispered, humiliated.

"It's okay, but you need to understand how much I care about Silver Diamond and its regulations. I always have. Academy life is in my blood, and I would never break or bend a rule that might put anyone in danger."

I looked away, feeling like an idiot for challenging his honor. I'd never meant to upset him.

"Lieutenant," he said quietly, cocking his head and leaning down a bit to look me in the eye. The expression on his face was much softer now—almost apologetic, though it shouldn't have been. "Don't worry about it. Let's go eat."

After dinner, we left the cafeteria and headed back to Ruby Hall together. My eyes kept wandering and I continued to find myself staring out the windows as we walked. Looking through matte-black glass was like looking through nothing at all. The stars sparkled, vying for my attention as we passed. I meandered closer to the windows, raising a hand to drag my fingers over the cool, smooth surface. Then I stopped, without thinking, and pressed my nose to the glass, peering toward the sky.

"What are you looking for?" Commander Draven asked, halting beside me.

I took a deep breath and sighed, the exhalation leaving a fleeting puff of condensation on the glass. He probably thought I was crazy by now, stopping in the middle of the hallway in the wee hours of night just to stick my face up to the glass and stare outside. The truth was, I was looking for Celestial Galaxy. I'd been told we could see it from the Mainlands and I recalled moments spent searching for it with my mom when I was very little. It was a small, golden dot in the vast blackness of space. Somewhere. I'd forgotten where, exactly.

"Home," I whispered.

I think it took him a moment to understand what I had meant by that, but a moment later, he stepped closer and touched me on the shoulder. "I... don't think you can see it from here. I'm sorry. These halls face west and it's probably..." He lifted a finger to point in the opposite direction.

"Oh." I sighed. "Well." It was stupid of me to ask, but I was going to ask anyway. "Could we... go outside? Just for a few minutes?" I glanced down the hall at a security guard standing by one of the main exit doors and then chewed my lip, waiting for a response.

"What? No." Draven shook his head with certainty. "Of course not. Not after hours. Wh-why would you even ask that?"

"Are you familiar with the structural design of Celestial Galaxy?" I looked him in the eye. Calm and intrigued sky-blue gazed back. He shook his head. "The two central floors make up a completely transparent hallway around the perimeter." I raised my hands to better illustrate. "Imagine an orange cut in half horizontally with a slice of glass placed between the halves. You can walk through the hallway around the school and, although it takes a long time to walk the entire circumference, the view is surreal after hours when the halls are lit with soft, strip lights of orange and white. You can look out at the stars and it's like being suspended in nothingness. Walking through space. It makes you feel so small in such a vast universe."

Draven's expression was one of admiration and understanding. "What you described sounds beautiful." Then he subtly shook his head again. "I'm sorry our academy isn't quite built like that, but I can't let you go outside. It's a matter of security. I thought we already discussed the 'rules are rules' thing?"

"We did." I glanced out the window again and then looked ahead down the hall. "I didn't realize it was against school policy to go outside after dark. I won't bring it up again." I hung my head low and started walking.

"Sorry, Lieutenant."

Homesickness kicked in. Three days, and I felt the effects of being alone in a big new world creeping through me. Routines were changing, more quickly than I had hoped. What was I really supposed to be doing here? How would taking a few classes and talking with the commander actually change anything between our schools? Why was I the only one carrying the burden of this massive assignment, while Silver Diamond got away without sending one of their own in exchange? Perhaps my captain hadn't disclosed everything to me yet. Maybe he would in time, or something new would happen soon which would put my mission into a better light.

Right now, though, I was scared, and the fears bubbling up inside made me feel isolated. Things were different here. I had more freedom at C.G., and I didn't feel like I was trapped, despite living on a giant military station floating in space. Trapped might be too strong of a word, but something was out of place. I couldn't stop anxious thoughts from wracking my brain.

"Keep up, Lieutenant," Commander Draven said. I'd been lagging behind him.

I lifted my face and gasped.

We'd gone down a grey hallway without windows... I didn't recognize it. I looked around but saw no colored markings.

"Wh-where are we going?" Preoccupied with my thoughts, I hadn't been watching where we'd been heading.

"There." He pointed to the dead end, narrow, unfamiliar hall not far ahead. It appeared to be a maintenance access point of some sort, but I couldn't tell for sure. "It..." He cleared his throat. "Leads to the roof." He lowered his voice substantially so only I could hear him.

"What?" I mouthed the word, unsure of his intentions but somehow trusting him enough to continue following him to the end of the hall.

There was a small monitor on a panel there, dimly lit by a few tiny, off-white lights. The commander typed in a code and a series of motors churned noisily behind the wall. I veered around and looked up to see a hatch opening in the ceiling and a metal ladder unfolding from a hidden panel overhead.

"All of the main exits will sound an alarm if we try to

leave," Draven said softly. "This one... won't."

I froze.

Was he actually letting me go outside? But... he was breaking the rules, right?

For... me?

He looked back at me with one eyebrow slightly lifted. "You do still want to go outside, right?"

I nodded and smiled. It was hard to see his face in the dim light, but he seemed relieved at my response.

"Then after you, Lieutenant." He gestured for me to go ahead up the ladder.

I stepped up onto the first rung and then grasped the one above me tightly, pulling myself up each step, one by one, until I poked my head up through the hatch in the ceiling and felt a wisp of cool breeze caress my face. The smell of foliage and the ocean tickled my nostrils.

I pulled myself up onto the roof and turned to offer a hand to the commander; he declined.

The roof went on for seemingly ever, and I could barely see anything in the darkness as my eyes adjusted to the subtle lighting cast from the bright moon and distant walkway lights below. Shakiness came over me, so I found a flat spot not far from the maintenance hatch and sat down. Commander Draven sat beside me.

I pulled my knees up to my chest and took a deep breath of the quiet night air. Looking straight up, I could now see the tiny amber glow which was Celestial Galaxy.

I smiled.

"There," I said, pointing. My eyes had adjusted and I could actually see the commander's face and outline fairly well. His line of sight followed my hand. "That's it. That's been my home for six years."

He only sat a few inches away, and when the breeze blew, I could smell the very subtle scent of him—crisp and clean. It reminded me of snow, though it had been years since I had smelled that. Brisk. New. I couldn't explain it, but it was nice and... I didn't mind it. But then he glanced over and my pulse began to race.

The feelings brewing inside me were ones I didn't want. Commander Draven was nice. What he'd done and... the rules he'd broken for me... made me grateful for his kindness. But uncomfortable feelings began racing through my head.

Stop. Just stop. There was no place for them.

I struggled with the sudden anxiety shooting through my veins.

"If you need to talk, I'm here," Commander Draven said softly, pale moonlight illuminating his face. His voice was honest and assuring. "I know we've just met, and maybe you're not comfortable with me, but I'm always available if you need an ear. I've noticed you seem a little uncomfortable here. I want you to feel like you belong."

"Thank you," I replied, looking back up at the stars. "I'm trying to fit in. I know I need to, but it's going to take time."

"Are you missing your friends?"

"Yes. My sister and Lieutenant Ray. I can't remember a day that's gone by without them in it. It's strange. I keep telling myself this is real, but it feels so dreamlike."

He fidgeted with the cuff of his sleeve. "Is Lieutenant Ray your..." He paused. "I'm sorry. I shouldn't be prying like this."

"It's fine," I said, turning back to him. We seemed to be sitting nearer to each other than I had realized, but my heartbeat had calmed. "He's my best friend and we've known each other for years. We enlisted together. We're close, but... not *that* kind of close, if you're wondering."

I should have been a little put off by his inquiry, but I wasn't.

In the past few days, I'd never been under the impression that he was being nice to me because he was attracted to me. Maybe he was simply trying to start a conversation.

"Ah," he replied with a nod. "And your parents? Where do they live?"

I sucked in a breath and my heart plummeted. As quickly as I'd felt some small relief, a wave of dread now consumed me.

"Lieutenant?"

"Um..."

I didn't want to reply. I refused to validate the nightmare.

"Are you alright, Lieutenant?" He pressed his hand over mine and I jolted, pulling it out from under his.

"My parents... are..." I tried to get the words out, but my throat tightened. I gasped and fought back the tears welling in my eyes. "Are..."

"Ugh, I'm sorry!" Draven clenched his teeth and looked off to the side, huffing angrily. "It was probably in your file and I-I didn't read it all."

I sniffled and wiped my cheeks with my palms. "My file?"

"C.G. transferred your personnel file to me before you arrived. I should have read it thoroughly. I really should have, but... things got hectic and I only had a chance to skim it. I didn't know something had happened to your family. I didn't mean to ask anything that would hurt you."

"It's okay, Commander. You're very busy here." I sniffed in a congested breath and wiped my face again with the back of my sleeve, my face growing warm. "It's understandable that a silly file like that could be overlooked with everything else you've got going on."

"No. It was selfish of me to dismiss it. I should have made time to look everything over, but... well..." He heaved a sigh. "I-I really didn't think it was that important at the time."

I felt a little bad for him as he stumbled through his words. Yes, my parents were gone and their absence left a deep rift in my heart, but it wasn't his responsibility to be aware of that.

He took a deep breath and looked at me. "I know this has been coming out of my mouth a lot since you've arrived but, this time, I truly am sorry, Lieutenant."

"Valhara."

"What?"

"Up here... it's just Valhara." I smiled at him, hoping he'd notice beneath the faint moonlight.

He did, and a grateful grin curled on his lips. Then he scooted yet another inch closer to me and placed his hand atop mine again.

"Then I'm sorry... *Valhara*," he whispered, looking me right in the eye.

His touch comforted me.

I didn't know what to say.

All I could think about was how my thigh had begun to hurt from the hard concrete beneath me, and how *next time*, we'd have to bring something soft to sit on.

Hopefully, there'd be a next time.

Days didn't seem as long, now that I'd made some friends.

Within a few weeks, I could find my way around the academy without help. I met Amanda for lunch every other day and had dinner with Commander Draven a couple of times a week. I made small talk with other students but found myself spending much of my free time with either the private or the commander.

Amanda always had something funny to say or some academy gossip to tell, and being around her was like spending time with a sister. Only Amanda didn't know when to stop talking about boys, while I couldn't squeeze an ounce of truth out of Atira about her current relationship status. A younger sister, maybe...

And then there was the commander. We had continued to arrange periodic meetings on the roof after dark, and the excuse he'd made for himself was that we were not, in fact, leaving the academy grounds. Not that we had ever been caught or questioned. Yet.

I found peace in those talks, because it was as if we were on equal ground, and the things we talked about up there weren't school- or work-related, they were just *things*.

Someone knocked. I knew who it was.

"Good evening, Commander," I said, opening the door.

He had a weird, twisted smile on his face, as if he were hiding something. Then I saw that one of his arms was craned behind his back, confirming my suspicion.

"What do you have there?" I bent to the side and tried to see what it was.

"Only this," he said, grinning, backing away and bringing his hand out from behind his back to reveal my sword, the Azure Phoenix.

"Yes!" I must have beamed like an idiot when I saw it; I was so excited. I reached for it and he took another step back, raising a flattened hand toward me.

"Ah ah ah! Not yet."

"What? Why can't I have it back? It's been thirty days, right?"

"Yes. But, I have two conditions."

"Go ahead." I propped a hand on my hip and leaned against the door to hold it open.

"First, you have to tell me *exactly* how you got it. Where. How. When. Everything."

"Deal." I nodded. "And the second one?"

"The second condition is..." He paused and chewed his lip as if he were debating whether or not to tell me. "Hmm."

"Is?" I prodded.

"Well, okay. Number two is probably not so legal, so..." He chuckled playfully.

Was he serious? Probably not. Still, my face caught on fire from all the awkward (and unlikely) assumptions zipping through my head.

"I'd like you to help me find a sword like that for myself," he said. "Can you do that?"

"Well..." I wrinkled my lips to one side and thought hard for a moment.

"Well, what?" He held up my sword, just to tease me.

"I can help you find something *like* it, but there's no way it's going to be exactly like mine. There's only one Azure Phoenix in the entire world and... right now, you're holding it hostage."

"Oh, I see. Well, then it's not fair of me to keep this from you, is it?" He lifted the blade up into both hands and carefully handed it to me. The weight of the dark, brassy platinum felt good in my hands again. I'd missed it...

"Lieutenant, do keep in mind that the thirty-day rule is merely a minimum. The decision to return it to you was my own. I hope I made the right one."

"You did." I smiled. "Let me put it away and then we can go." I turned and carried my sword back into the room. The commander held open the door with his foot while he waited. I laid the Azure Phoenix down on my bed and swept my fingers over the cold blade, my distorted reflection rippling back at me. I'd never seen a sword so beautiful in my life, and while I would try my best to find one for the commander, I knew it couldn't be as gorgeous as my own treasured artifact.

I double-checked my pocket for my I.D. and then shut my door behind me as I exited the room. We took our usual stroll down the quiet, nearly vacant halls, to the maintenance ladder, and then climbed up to the rooftop. There were two off-white mats on the floor, right where we'd left them. They were much more comfortable than cold, hard concrete.

"So, I've got a few business matters to discuss with you tonight," Mattheia said, sitting down on one of the mats. I sat beside him.

"Business matters?" I tilted my head. We didn't talk about work-related stuff on the roof. It was sort of an unspoken rule.

"I meant 'business matters' figuratively," he said, making air quotes.

"Oh. Like what?"

"Let's start with the deal we made about your sword. I really do want to have something like it if I can. I'm willing to work for it. It's not like I got where I am today by sitting on my butt playing video games." He laughed quietly at the irony. From what I had learned, he played *a lot* of FPS war games. "Though I don't let my job keep me from that, either. Got to have priorities."

I wasn't as much of a gamer, but I'd dabbled in video games when I was younger. Until work and studies got in the way.

"My priorities are with my academy," I replied. "Though we aren't supposed to talk about that kind of stuff here, right?"

He shrugged and nodded in agreement.

"As for the sword, I may have some ideas."

He perked up.

"You have to remember, these are ancient and sometimes mythical artifacts. They don't always exist in real life, even when maps and landmarks make you believe they do. It took months for Jacksiun and me to locate the Azure

Phoenix and several days after that to actually find it once we'd begun the hunt. Sometimes, you do all the work and when you get where you're going, you find out it was all just a crazy fireside story told to mislead explorers."

"We still have five months together here. Is that not enough time?"

"It should be, but..."

"Yes?"

"I was keeping this one idea under wraps for a while, hoping my sister would come with me to find it."

"I wouldn't ask you to give that up for me, Valhara," he said, leaning a little closer. "Really."

"She's so busy with work and... the captain." My voice trailed off.

"Your captain?"

"Never mind. It's fine. We can start a new search if she ever finds the time to go with me."

"Are you sure?"

I turned and gazed into his eyes. They were full of anticipation and enthusiasm and I knew in my heart that he cared about the adventure much more than Atira did, at this point. "Yes. I'm sure," I replied firmly.

"I appreciate your willingness to do this for me."

"I know," I said.

"Can you tell me anything about this particular sword you're thinking of? How did you find it? Or, better yet, where do you think *we'll* find it?"

"It's called the Pegasus Sword and my research leads me to Tatundra Island off the eastern coast of—"

"I've heard of it," he interrupted. "Because of its central location, it had been caught in a power struggle for a while—the island, not the sword. Alyssia surrendered it to the Mainlands a few decades back, but since then, word is we've abandoned it, too, because of the major overgrowth and dangerous terrain. And... that's where this sword is?"

"Could be. There's no guarantee it's even there anymore, but I'm confident it's our best chance."

"The Pegasus Sword. Sounds impressive. Do you know why it's called that?"

"There aren't a lot of texts remaining about its origin, but it was supposedly fashioned from sandstone combined with an unknown white metal. That made it lightweight, but still a viable weapon. It was also rumored to have been wielded by the last Pegasus Knight—a leading warrior in an ancient cult sworn to protect the winged beasts. When the pegasus went extinct, like many ancient creatures, the knights died with them. The sword was believed to have been a burial marker for the last knight."

"So we're not only searching for a rare sword, we're also going to be robbing a grave if we actually find it?"

"It's not like that." There had to be a better way to explain this to him. "Mattheia, have you ever held a really old antique in your hands? Something made before you or even your grandfather had been born?"

"Yes. What does that have to do with the sword?"

"Humor me a moment, please. When I was little, I used to go to the local history museum and stare at the exhibits for hours and hours. It didn't even matter how long I stood or how often I returned, there was always something different about the pieces each time I saw them. Sometimes, I'd just put my hand up against a glass case and think about where the pieces came from. How long ago they'd been created. Who lived and who died during that time and who has passed ever since. And I swear I could feel this energy exuding from the displays—calling to me, if you will. Life. History. These treasures were created as a means of showing the future what the past was like. People don't make things with the expectation that no one will ever see them."

"You're losing me a little here."

"The Azure Phoenix has the same type of energy inside. I felt it when I first clasped it between my hands. It is history and life imbued in cold metal. If we find the Pegasus Sword, we wouldn't be grave robbing, we'd be breathing new life and appreciation into a part of our timeline that had been forgotten for years. I believe it's a form of respect and resurrection. And unless you're planning to melt it into something new, I don't see anything wrong with finding it."

Mattheia sat there silently. It made me feel awkward. I

hadn't meant to get into such a profound conversation about ancient artifacts, and hopefully I hadn't alienated one of the few friends I'd made at Silver Diamond.

"I didn't mean to go that deep with all of it, I just—"

"It was fine, Valhara. I actually kind of like how you put it. How the things we create aren't meant to be kept out of the hands of future generations and that they retain a small part of the life-force of their era in them."

"Exactly!" I felt better knowing I hadn't lost him completely.

"Then it's settled! We'll leave as soon as you're ready. We can take my jet and—"

"Your... *jet*?" My voice cracked.

Despite living in a space station for years and traveling to and from there via spacecraft, I had an innate fear of flying.

"Okay, so it is technically academy property at the moment and it's not mine yet, but I plan on buying it when I retire, or when it gets put out of commission, whichever occurs first."

"I didn't mean it like that."

"Then what did you mean?"

"I don't like flying."

"Then you're lucky you'll be with the best pilot in all of Silver Diamond," he said confidently. "If you're afraid of flight, then I'll do whatever I can to make you comfortable and talk you through it. Trust me, Valhara, I've been doing this for years, and before that, my dad took me on flights every weekend. I may be grounded most of the time nowadays, but this is what I live and breathe for."

He looked at me and the intense assuredness in his eyes made me slightly less distraught. True, I needed to get to the island somehow, but I hadn't really thought about it before because I knew it was far in the future. Now it had caught up with me unexpectedly.

Mattheia chuckled. "How exactly do you literally live in a big ball of metal and cement floating out in space, with glass hallways going completely around the center, your best friend studies aircraft mechanics, and you're afraid of flying?"

He was right. It was dumb.

"I don't know." I shrugged. "I guess I don't feel like I'm going to fall if I can't see the ground."

"Then you'll be fine with me," he added, grinning. "There's no ground up there, only clear blue skies and pure white clouds. If anything, it's like gliding through an endless sea of light and color. Especially at dusk. Orange. Violet. Indigo. You won't think about the ground when you're surrounded by nothing but spellbinding, ever-changing hues of sunset."

The breeze whipped by and I closed my eyes, imagining myself there—encircled by warm, brilliant color.

It was nice.

"See?" Mattheia whispered.

I gasped and opened my eyes, startled I'd let my down my guard so quickly.

"Yes. I think so. But I'm still afraid of flying." I laughed and he nodded in understanding. "Anyway." I cleared my throat. "What's the second business matter you wanted to discuss?" I adjusted the flower barrette above my ear; the wind had swept it out of place.

"Oh, *that...*" He inhaled deeply and then exhaled, puffing out his cheeks. "You're probably going to think this is silly."

"I'm sure I won't. What is it? Don't feel weird about asking me anything, please. I'd like to think we're... *friends* now."

His face came up with a look of surprise. "Me, too... I-I guess you're right."

I smiled.

"I'm going home this weekend to help my mom with some chores and other things I've been meaning to get to and... well, my mom kind of invited you to join us for dinner on Sunday. If you want to, that is. I'd walk you back to the academy that evening."

"That's very sweet of her to ask. She doesn't even know me, though. Why would she invite me over for dinner?"

"My mom's really friendly and I may have mentioned

something about mentoring a student from Celestial Galaxy. One thing led to another and she wanted me to ask you to come for dinner. Uh... you *can* say no if you want."

"No."

"Okay. I'm sorry I asked. I didn't mean to—"

"No! I meant I wouldn't say *no*. I would be honored to have dinner with you and your mother this weekend. It would be great to get out of the academy for a little while."

"Great. I'll let her know. She'll be ecstatic to have someone over. It's been a long time since we've had company. She'll appreciate it and... so will I."

His voice lowered a little when he said that and I could hear the gratitude in his tone.

"I appreciate it, too," I said, entwining my fingers together in my lap. "I'm trying really hard to fit in and I-I want people to like me. With all of the arguments and discrimination that's been going on between our academies over the years, it's amazing that so many people here have taken me in with open arms. That means a lot to me. Thank you, Mattheia, for making me feel welcome here."

He looked away and adjusted the silver cufflinks on his sleeves. Then he looked back at me and a little smile curled his lips. "To be honest, Valhara... liking you isn't so hard."

I walked alone down the hall toward the front entrance. No one looked at me funny or stared at my foreign, green uniform. It was Sunday, and many students—including me—were in civilian clothes as they came and went on their day off. The sliding glass doors of the entrance whooshed open and I walked outside, keeping my head down while trying to tell myself everything would be okay.

It had been years since I had stepped foot outside an academy. Years since I'd had a sit-down dinner in someone's house. I couldn't stop twisting my fingers together nervously even though it shouldn't have been such a worrisome thing.

There was a bench just outside the entrance that looked inviting. I sat and waited for the commander. The breeze licked past, sweeping the edge of my ankle-length black skirt up against my legs. I brushed it down with my hands.

It wasn't supposed to be windy today.

Maybe I should have worn something more casual and less dressy, but I wanted to look nice for the commander's mother. Or... maybe I wanted to look nice for...

"There you are!"

I jerked my head up to see Mattheia walking toward me. I hardly recognized him without his uniform. He wore a dark grey t-shirt layered beneath a slate-blue, short-sleeved button-up and dark-wash jeans. A gust of air tousled his hair, making him sweep it back from his brow with his hand. The sunlight peeking in below the overhang made it shimmer with different shades of gold and brass. He looked me in the eye and a hint of sunlight glimmered in his irises, making them appear bluer than usual.

"Hi," I said, having more trouble than I should have just getting the one word out of my mouth.

"Hey. I hope I didn't make you wait long." There was a long, flat metallic object pressed under his other arm, but I couldn't tell what it was. "I went back for this, though, I guess I really didn't need it today." He gestured to the thing under his arm as he started walking.

"What is it?" I'd never seen anything like it.

He pointed toward one of the streets up ahead so I'd know where we were heading. "This?" He withdrew the item and held it between both hands. It looked like a metallic, ice-blue colored Old-World skateboard, but it didn't have any wheels. "It's my jet-board. The Supernova-X. I usually bring it because it's faster than walking, but since you're here, I don't really need it. Habit, I guess."

I vaguely remember seeing some information about the brand at some point. Jet-boards weren't exactly within my field of interest.

"Can I?" I raised a hand toward it.

"Go ahead." He held it out to me. I didn't want to take it. I just wanted to touch it.

"No, it's fine. I just..." I stroked a finger over the surface. It was cool to touch and extremely polished, surprisingly. The topside had a slightly raised texture, which probably helped riders keep their footing.

"Aren't they dangerous?" I asked.

"Not any more dangerous than doing stunts in an actual jet. Besides, you never leave the ground."

"I beg to differ." I glanced at the thin line of bright red LED lights racing around the perimeter. "I don't think it would be called a jet-board if it never left the ground. It would just be a metal board." I laughed a little and he flashed me a look of disappointment.

"I can teach you how to use it." He smiled confidently at

me. "I'd be *more* than happy to teach you."

"No, thanks. I'll keep my feet on the ground, for now."

He rolled his eyes. "In space."

"Hey!" I prodded him in the elbow jokingly.

"What? You keep mentioning how you're afraid of flying and 'leaving the ground,' but you literally *live in a metal ball floating in space.*" He tucked the board beneath his arm. "I'm just saying, it's a little ironic, don't you think?"

"I think it's the reason you're a pilot and I'm not." I sighed and looked up ahead as we turned a block and passed a row of houses.

"Didn't intend to be mean. Sorry. But if you change your mind, let me know."

"Okay." I had *no* intention of changing my mind.

He pointed to an intersection and we crossed a street. "Just another block and a half," he said.

As we walked, I felt his eyes on me but didn't look up for fear I'd meet them and the uncomfortable twinge of anxiety might rear its ugly head again.

"You... look really nice, by the way," he said quietly. "I meant to say something earlier but—"

"Thank you." I couldn't bring myself to say it, but he looked nice, too.

"You didn't have to dress up for me and my mom," he said, referring to my purple, lace-trimmed blouse and black skirt. "Not that I mind. I mean... not that *she'll* mind." He grinned sheepishly. "You know what I'm trying to say, right?"

"Yes."

I wanted to look presentable to his mother. Who knew what preconceived notions she might have about a girl from Celestial Galaxy. The least I could do was try to look my best.

"There," Mattheia announced, pointing up ahead at the next house.

It wasn't a very large house; not something I'd imagine a high commander having, but it was pretty on the outside and friendly-looking. It had a black roof, wooden, covered porch, dark-blue shutters, and light-blue siding. It was all surrounded by a short, white picket-fence and raised rose beds on each side of the steps leading to the front door. A quiet, peaceful little home reminiscent of simpler times.

I nearly jumped out of my skin as a sharp, loud yapping sound came at me from behind the fence. I looked down, but the yellow ball of fur moved so quickly, I could hardly tell what it was.

"Is that your dog?" I asked, raising my voice against the high-pitched barks. The thing was bouncing up and down like a basketball, stuffing its muzzle through cracks between the fence and snorting and sniffing as if its hairy little life depended on it.

"No." Mattheia shook his head and rolled his eyes. "That's Daisy, my mom's dog." He waved a hand up over the fence. "Come on, Dais' get down. No." The dog continued to yap. "Daisy!" He opened the gate to their yard and held out a hand, folding his fingers into a fist high above the dog's head. She immediately quieted and sat down, at attention. "Good girl," he said, leaning down to pat her on the head. "Now stay." He flattened the same hand and took me gently by the arm with his other. "She'll wait. Come on."

We walked up the stairs and I briefly veered my head. Daisy was still sitting in the yard by the fence, anxiously awaiting his next command.

"You're good with dogs, aren't you?" I asked.

"Eh. I'm alright. I learned some things from the other handlers because of Wolf, but I like bigger dogs. Not a fan of the little, yappy ones." He lowered his voice and leaned closer. "Don't tell my mom I said that." He raised his brow and glared at me in all seriousness. "Daisy keeps Mom company and let's her know when people are at the door, so I tolerate her." He stopped on the top step and turned to me. "You don't mind big dogs, do you?"

"No. Why?" I wasn't against any well-behaved animal, really.

"Just wondering." He shrugged and then rummaged through his pockets for a keycard. "Mom, I'm home," he said as he opened the door. He held it ajar for me and I entered ahead of him. Framed photos hung on both sides of the entryway. Most of them were of Mattheia and his father, the blonde-haired man whom he resembled quite a lot.

"Aw. You were such a cute little boy," I said, pointing at a photo of him and his dad with fishing rods, holding up a large catch. He was a bit older there than he was in the book I'd read at the academy archives. Then I laughed at the next photo of him playing with a toy jet on his living room floor. "Started early, huh?"

"He was cute back then," a small voice piped from the next room. "But he's a handsome young man now."

"Whatever you say, Mom," he replied with a chuckle, directing me into the kitchen where his mother was hunched over a cutting board. Her face turned to me as we entered.

Mattheia's mom was short and dainty; she had curly brown hair, light brown eyes, and a big, welcoming grin.

"Hello, dear," she said in a soft voice, a sparkle of joy lighting up her eyes as she reached out to hug me.

I didn't like being touched by strangers, but I wasn't going to make her feel bad by pulling away.

"Mom, this is Lieutenant Valhara Hawksford," Mattheia announced promptly. "Valhara, this is my mom, Kathleen."

"Nice to meet you, Mrs. Draven."

"Please, make yourself at home, dear, while I finish dinner," his mom said, and then turned to get back to work on whatever it was she had been preparing.

"So," Mattheia continued, "what would you like to do while we wait? Sit on the porch? Go for a walk. Watch T.V.? Your call."

I really wanted to know more about him and his father, but I didn't want to act too forward or nosey, either.

"Would you mind showing me around your house first?" I tried to say it as sweetly and inquisitively as I could.

"Oh!" He popped his forehead with his palm. "What was I thinking? Sorry. It didn't even cross my mind. I don't have people over often." He chuckled nervously. "Come with me."

I learned his mother lived upstairs and that the house also had a basement, guestroom, and large living room. The guest room on the second floor, according to Mattheia, hadn't been used in years. I assumed it may have been used for storage or knick knacks. He didn't seem interested in showing me and I wasn't all that worried about seeing it.

His bedroom—on the first floor—was remarkably clean and organized, compared to the fleeting glimpse I'd gotten of his room back at the academy. He had a long, glass, eye-level shelf running along the perimeter of the room on two sides which had different jets and military aircraft models perched on it, backlit by strips of soft, off-white lights.

"Did you build all of these?" I asked, reaching up, tempted to touch one but then realizing how rude that might have been.

"Uh huh." He nodded proudly. "You can... touch them if you want to, just be gentle, please. I mean... they aren't *that* fragile, but—"

"I understand." I tucked my hands behind my back and

clasped them together so I wouldn't be tempted again. "They are so detailed." I leaned closer to get a better look at one. The paint work was amazing on the miniature, electric-yellow jet with black tiger stripes decorating the hull and wings. The tiny brass sign sitting in front of it read "JTA-XI Fighter." The cockpit canopy glass was bright orange and it didn't look anything like a JTA I'd seen before. "This one is..." I removed a hand from behind my back to carefully prod the nose of the piece.

"That's mine," he said softly, a hint of joy in his voice.

"Yes, I figured that, but..."

"No. I mean, it's my *personal* jet in real life. That's what my actual jet looks like at Silver Diamond."

"What?" I stood and veered my head toward him. "Th-this is *your* jet?"

"Well, mine's a lot bigger, but..." He laughed. "Anyway, yes. Custom paint job."

I scowled sarcastically at his making fun of me. "Wow! Okay, now I really need to see it."

"It's called the Tetra-Haizon, and it's the same one we'll be flying when we go on that quest you promised me—for the Pegasus Sword."

I must have clammed up or made a weird face uncon-sciously because the next thing I knew, he was leaning against one of the shelves, staring at me with concern.

"Valhara?"

My gaze broke from the Tetra-Haizon model and met his. There was a great sense of confidence in his rich blue eyes.

"I will take care of you," he said. "I'm a good pilot. I've trained for years and I know what I'm doing. You can trust me on this, Valhara."

As much as I wanted to pretend his words didn't affect me, they did. I hadn't known Mattheia for long, but I felt like he was the kind of man who wore his heart on his sleeve—who told the truth, always. Maybe I was being sentimental (or gullible), but when he'd told me that I could trust him, I... started to.

"Thank you," I said beneath my breath. Then I turned away from the shelf with the models spanning it and to the opposite wall. There hung a portrait of a middle-aged, blonde-haired man in a navy-blue trimmed Silver Diamond dress uniform decorated with a hefty array of medals. The portrait was framed in ornate gold and a plaque listing his accomplishments had been affixed at the bottom.

"I read about your dad and the Atlantic Strike in a book at the archives. He saved President Alexander's life."

Mattheia remained silent but nodded in acknowledgment.

"It must have been hard on your mom when she found out you wanted to be a pilot, too." I looked at him and noticed his face getting a little flush and a frown tugging at his lips. I tried to quickly follow up with something less saddening. "I'm sure she's very proud of you and that your dad would have been pleased to know you made high commander."

"I... like to think so." He polished his sleeve across the metal plaque on the bottom of the portrait and swept a thin layer of dust from the inside edge of the frame.

T hank you for dinner, Mrs. Draven." The from-scratch lasagna she'd served was delicious. Although we have hydroponic gardens and fresh produce, the food at Celestial Galaxy typically lacked that special, home-made taste. "Do you cook a lot?" I asked. There were many spice jars and utensils organized around the kitchen, within easy access of the stove.

"I only cook for myself during the week or when we have company," she replied and then gestured to her son. "Mattheia's the cook around here."

"Really?" I probably shouldn't have been surprised. "Where did you learn?"

"Military classes and... weekends at home," he said, shrugging as if he were trying to downplay the skill set. "I'm sure C.G. made you take a few cooking courses, right?"

Yes. Though, *learning* to cook and *being able to create something edible* were very different things. My sister and I had learned that the hard way.

"Cooking isn't really my strong suit," I said, embarrassed.

"Oh. I see. I think I made a bit of a hobby out of it, I suppose. Maybe I can cook something for *you* next time."

Next time? It had become a common phrase between us, not that I minded.

We were friends, right?

I crumpled a napkin and set it on my plate. Mattheia's mother shot up from her chair and started to scoop up dirty dishes.

"Mom." Mattheia stood and reached across to try to take them from her. "I'll get them."

"No." She got into a brief struggle with her son over the dish in her hands. "Worry about your friend. I'll take care of things."

"Okay, Mom." He released the plate and sighed, defeated. I'd never seen someone so offended about losing dish duty, but maybe he felt awkward letting his mother do it for him with me around.

Mrs. Draven shuffled over to the sink with an armful of

dishes and twisted on the faucet.

"What would you like to do before we head back?" Mattheia asked, walking with me into the living room.

An onslaught of voracious barking sounded from just outside on the back patio. I looked to find Daisy with her muzzle plastered against the glass sliding doors, her beady black eyes focused intently on me.

"Yikes," I mumbled, grimacing. "She really doesn't want me here at all."

"Dais'? Naw. Don't worry about her." Mattheia walked toward the door and then pointed to the nearby couch. "You can sit if you want." I plopped onto it and sunk in comfortably; it was softer than I'd expected. "She's a lot of bark and not much else. Don't get scared, okay? She won't bite you, I promise."

Bite me?

A second after he'd said it, the glass door slid open and a furry gold rocket launched toward me. I cringed and froze, clenching my knees together as the fluffy thing sniffed and huffed fervently around my shoes.

"Just let her go," Mattheia said, coming back over. The couch gently sunk in as he sat beside me.

One final sniff and then a brief lick of her intimidating lips, and Daisy looked up at me, straight in the eye, and snorted. She perked her tail up and trotted off upstairs, disappearing into Mrs. Draven's room.

"What was that?" My muscles relaxed.

"*That* means she approves," he said with a nod.

"Oh? Well, I'm glad to hear that." I rubbed my forearms to chase away the goose bumps.

Mattheia leaned closer. "Between you and me, she's a little brat who hates *everyone*," he said in a hushed tone. "But I knew she'd like you."

"I'm glad someone knew because I was a little... worried."

"I wouldn't put you in any danger, Valhara," he reassured me, a stern look on his face.

I took a deep breath and pressed my back farther into the couch cushion, nestling up against plush textile fabric we certainly didn't have at C.G.

He sat back and entwined his hands in his lap.

We remained there for a few minutes not saying a word. It was comfortable and homey. It was nice to get out of the academy and have a change of scenery. It was nice to feel like I belonged in some small way.

"Today went by fast. Didn't it?" he asked.

"Yes. It doesn't feel like I've been here long at all."

"Same. At least you got to sit down and have dinner someplace other than Silver Diamond. Free, crazy dog theatrics included."

"Can't say I've seen that before. Wolf was so well-behaved."

"He's a working dog. Daisy likes to think she's working. On what, I don't know." He reached toward a nearby end table and switched on a small lamp. It filled the room with soft, warm light. "When would you like to head back?" He glanced over at me.

I was situated in the snuggly couch and it took me a moment to respond.

"I don't know." I shrugged lazily.

"You're just going to highjack my couch then?"

"It is very nice."

"I'll make a note of it." He pretended to write on his palm with an imaginary pen. "Celestial... Galaxy... needs... Wait." He pretended to tap the invisible pen against his chin. "Do you even *have* couches there? Never mind. Dumb question." Before I could answer him he went back to it. "Needs... *better*... couches." He dotted the period and then shoved the pretend note into his pocket.

I laughed a bit too heartily at the gesture, I think, but it felt good to laugh.

Mrs. Draven popped her head into the room. "I'm heading to bed. You two be safe on your walk back."

"Will do," Mattheia assured her.

"Goodnight. It was nice meeting you, Valhara. Don't be a stranger."

I leaned forward on the couch. "Nice meeting you, too. Thank you for the lovely dinner."

"Goodnight, Mom."

She went up the stairs and disappeared into her bedroom, shutting the door.

"We should be getting back," I said quietly.

"Sure. We won't be the only personnel returning on a Sunday night, so you don't have to worry about getting in too late." He got up and went off toward his room. "Let me grab my jet board before we go," he said over his shoulder. It was propped up against the doorframe. He scooped it up and we headed for the front door.

Dusk. The sun set quickly, cloaking the sky in dark purples and vibrant blues. Bright amber streetlamps switched on and lit our way back to the academy, a faint buzzing sound filling the air.

Night didn't bother me like I had thought it would. Perhaps it was the well-lit streets that made me feel at ease, or maybe it was having Mattheia close by. It was wonderful to see the sunset again; I hadn't seen it in years. I'd forgotten what a menagerie of hues would saturate the sky in such a short period of time.

We were less than a block away from the academy now.

There was a question festering in my brain and the desire to ask it made my pulse race.

"Mattheia?" I slowed my pace and looked at him. "What

was the second requirement to get my sword back? The *original* one, I mean?" Maybe it was stupid to ask, but I *was* curious.

"Uh... Heh." He forked a hand through his hair and laughed awkwardly. "I was joking about that one."

"You were?"

"Yes." He shrugged. "Didn't mean for it to come across wrong."

I'd been around enough men to know their jokes mirrored their feelings more than anything else. I didn't know exactly what he'd meant by it, in particular, but there was fondness for me glistening in his eyes and he'd been unable to hide it lately.

Okay, to give him the benefit of the doubt, there was something growing in me, too, but I wasn't going to let it get the best of me.

But then Mattheia stopped abruptly and faced me. "Valhara, I-I... like you too much to disrespect you like that. I'm sorry if what I insinuated offended you."

Offended was a strong word for what was probably a vaguely suggestive comment.

"Thank you for dinner and for having me over," I said, changing the subject. I smiled with my eyes, though I couldn't tell how well he could see me in the fading light.

"It was nothing, but you're welcome."

"Mattheia?"

"Yes?"

"I know there may be consequences for spending time on the roof at night, but I appreciate the risks you've taken in an effort to make me comfortable here. You're kind and your mom is lucky to have you." I brushed my fingers against his hand.

"Th-thank you for saying that." He smiled. "That means a lot to me."

Eagerness clawed at me, and it provoked me to take one step closer to him. I didn't know what I wanted to do, but I wanted to thank him in some small way that might mean something.

I shuffled another inch closer and came off my heels just enough to kiss him on the cheek. A breath caught in his throat when I did, and as my face slid away, I opened my mouth and whispered, "Thank you."

My heels touched the ground and his hand rose toward my face. A soft gasp of surprise escaped my lips.

He paused, his open hand inches away, waiting for me to decide what to do. Only half his face was lit by overhead lamps; the other half was in shadow. Still, I could see his clear, blue irises as he carefully contemplated his next action. His brow furrowed, his eyes narrowing while they searched mine.

Then my heartbeat quickened as his palm came close enough to cup my cheek.

My instincts pushed me to give in, but I fought them. *No. I wouldn't set the wheels in motion. I wouldn't be responsible for that.*

But then I did something crazy. I closed my eyes and rested my face against his hand. His thumb brushed across my skin and my mind raced as I struggled to weigh the pros and cons of my recklessness.

It was the most inopportune moment to be having second thoughts.

I couldn't let him think I...

How did everything change so quickly?

I'd been swept up into a whirlwind of new and exciting emotions, and I didn't want to escape the soft, warm stroke of his fingertips down my hairline.

I felt his eyes on me even while mine were closed. I could hear the flutter of his anxious breaths.

What was I thinking? I didn't actually want him to...

I flinched.

His hand slipped from my chin and he took a deep breath, exhaling loudly.

My eyes fluttered opened and I caught a fleeting, solemn glance, the usual charm in his expression suddenly gone.

My heart sank.

It came and went so quickly. I didn't want him to get the wrong idea, but the moment his fingers graced my cheek, my mind emptied and my entire being just wanted to let whatever was about to occur happen.

What made him pull away?

Had he sensed my hesitation?

Perhaps, I shouldn't have kissed him at all, even if it was only a gesture of gratitude—or at least, I had thought it was.

I wasn't going to be at Silver Diamond for long. Even he knew that. We couldn't start something like this. It wasn't our business to... get involved.

He was smart. He knew better. Right? I owed it to my academy to return without reservations.

Keeping my promise, I continued researching the location of the Pegasus Sword, attempting to update the information I'd had on file. Over the course of several weeks, I had located information that would help us find the lost treasure. It was still on Tatundra Island—according to my research, but due to severe weather shifts, the island terrain had changed drastically in the last decade. The only maps I could find were outdated—none matched the current satellite images. Lush, tropical forests had transformed into scorching desert wastelands, likely inhabited by little more than poisonous serpents and scavengers who had survived the drought.

It was possible the sandy terrain had consumed the sword

long ago and that we would have no way of finding it beneath impenetrable, rock-hard earth.

"What's the plan?" Mattheia leaned over my shoulder, peering at my laptop screen.

"It's... complicated." I pulled the chair out beside me. "Here. Sit down and I'll show you."

"How so?" He sat and scooted his chair close to mine.

I opened an image of a map and traced an area with my index finger. "This area here—the desert—used to be a rainforest."

Mattheia's brow wrinkled. "Oh. That's a problem, isn't it?"

"Yes. Back when Jacksiun and I had begun our search, this area was still alive and green. Now, it's changed and it's going to be very difficult to find any of the landmarks we'd tagged before. If the terrain has evolved this much, it's possible the entire topography may have been altered by wind or rainstorms. We won't be able to tell one end of the island from the other even with a map."

"Hmm." Mattheia scratched his chin. "What if we used archived maps and cross analyzed the differences? It's possible these changes happened once before."

"It's a start, but I'm worried about what else has changed since the drought. From the readings I'm finding, there's still wildlife on the island. I can't imagine anything that could survive that harsh of an environment being... an herbivore."

"We'll have our weapons. We'll be fine."

"Hopefully we won't need them."

Mattheia glanced at the large stack of papers spread out around my desk.

"Would it help if I went through some of the info with you?"

"Sure." I grabbed a pile and straightened it neatly before dropping it into his lap. He lifted the first page and cocked an eye brow at the small print. "I have not had this much homework in a long time."

"I said you'll be fine, Lieutenant." We walked across the hangar.

I'd brought both my gun (per special permission granted to me by the commander) and my sword, and Mattheia had armed himself with his own personal firearm. Still, I didn't feel assured. Tatundra Island was huge, covered in rocks and sand, and it rose to scorching temperatures during the afternoon.

A sergeant stopped us and saluted the commander. "Sir, your gear has been loaded. I'll open the doors to the runway momentarily."

"Thank you, Sergeant," Mattheia replied. The man jogged back to the nearby control office.

"You're sure Captain Lansfora is okay with us doing this in the middle of my term?" I was stalling.

"I've cleared it with him. No need to worry."

"Okay." The word barely made it out of my mouth.

"There," he said. I looked up, caught off guard by how soon we'd come upon the beast. It was exactly like the model version he'd had in his bedroom. The Tetra-Haizon—a bright, metallic yellow fighter jet with thick black tiger stripes across the wings and body. The cockpit canopy was a striking, deep orange color, exactly like on the model.

"Catch!"

I veered around just as Mattheia tossed a helmet my way. I had to grapple it quickly, before it slipped away. It, too, was metallic yellow with three bold, black stripes down the center.

"Let me help. If you don't mind." He came up to me and set his helmet down at his feet. His fingers gently swept my ponytail over my shoulder and then I pulled the helmet down over my head. Mattheia adjusted the chin strap until it was taut, but not too tight. Then he smiled and reached down to retrieve his own helmet. He shoved it on, adjusted the buckles on the straps, securing it in place, and then motioned toward the ladder heading up to the cockpit.

"Ladies first."

I took a deep breath and forced myself to inch closer to the beautiful but intimidating metal aircraft. My entire body began to quake with fear and anticipation as I reached up a hand to grasp one of the rails.

I felt a hand on my shoulder and turned, my peripheral vision slightly altered by the sides of the helmet.

"Valhara." Mattheia waited for my gaze to meet his. "It's just another rooftop," he said, confidence in his smile.

He was right. New adventures waited beyond the Mainlands.

I climbed up the ladder and situated myself in the cockpit, my seat right behind his. He came up after me, helped adjust my oxygen mask, and then slipped into the seat in front.

"Are you going to be okay?" His voice emanated from a speaker inside my helmet.

"Yes."

We slowly pulled out of the hangar and I braced myself as the engines rumbled. We received the go ahead and Mattheia began steering the jet toward one of the runways. We sped up, accelerating down the tarmac until the vibrations in my seat dampened and we ascended. Earth swiftly vanished out from under us, disappearing beneath a thick layer of white.

We touched down on Tatundra Island and climbed out of the jet. My head spun and I felt a squeezing sensation in my temples.

"Are you okay?" Mattheia asked, hopping off the ladder. He looped his leather shoulder holster straps over his arms and then tucked his head down as he pulled it on so it fit snugly across his back. My gun, the Platinum Galaxy, was secured in the holster at my lower waist, comfortably within reach at my hip.

"Yes. Just... a little queasy." I worked to adjust the straps of the scabbard on my back, but the swirling continued in my gut and my legs became shaky. I staggered another step and then my knees hit the sand.

"Valhara?" Mattheia neared, but I held a hand out to the side to signal for him to stop.

"I-I'm just..." And the tightness kept squeezing. Everything around me blurred and my head felt heavy. My hands trembled and, as much as I hoped I could push the sickness away, I couldn't stop the nausea from mounting.

The insignificant meal I'd ingested too soon before my flight resurfaced with a vengeance, sending me reeling forward.

I coughed violently and tried to suck in air as a second wave struck.

The last thing I needed was for the commander to see me like this—hunched over on flattened palms on the desert sand, my face sunburn-red and sweat dripping off my forehead like a towel being wrung.

"Are you okay?" he asked, standing behind me.

Nodding was the only thing I had enough energy to do.

"Here." He handed me a bottle of water.

I took a drink and coughed again, the sour taste making me retch and causing my eyes to water. My stomach felt a little better, though. Only a little.

"Take these, too," Mattheia added, kneeling down to hand me a strip of anti-nausea tablets. "I'm sorry I didn't warn you about not eating before the flight. The Gs hit you harder than I'd anticipated."

"It's... okay." I peeled two of the tablets out of the foil package and popped them into my mouth. They fizzed and melted on contact with my tongue, releasing equally bitter flavor along with the medicine. Another swig of water washed them away for good. "I'm sorry you have to see me like this." I sipped some water, swished it around in my mouth, and spat it onto the ground.

"There's nothing to be sorry about," he replied, lending me an arm to help me up. "Everyone gets sick once in a while." I pulled myself to my feet, wobbling. He helped steady me. "How are you feeling right now? The tablets take a few minutes to start working, sometimes."

"Better." I cleared my throat and took a deep breath. "I feel much better now. Thanks to your quick thinking. I wish I'd thought to bring some of those myself, but I thought I'd be fine."

"Don't worry about it. Do you mind if I take a look at the

map?"

"Go ahead."

Mattheia reached into his pocket for his phone and launched a GPS application. "We're right in the center of the island," he announced, leaning over to show me the screen and the flashing location point. "I've got both the co-ordinates you suggested preloaded. South or west?"

I'd given him two points of interest because I had found mixed information about each of them in my research. To the west stood a tall, rocky cliff and treacherous overhang. I turned toward the south and lifted a flattened hand above my brow to shield my eyes from the white-hot afternoon sun. In that direction lay long, flat tracts of dead brush and trees, along with remnants of the shrines and dwellings of ancient civilizations peeking through the debris. We had to choose whether we were going to tackle a mountain range, or a mess of brambles and possible predators or other dangerous wildlife—not that the cliffside would be free of either.

"I vote south," said Mattheia. "I didn't bring my climbing gear." He chuckled. "Besides, who would leave something that important on top of a cliff?"

"I agree with starting out to the south, but only because it would be quicker to traverse the brush than climb up that cliff and back down again, should we find nothing there. But, it *is* called the Pegasus Sword, not the Dead-Trees-And-Shrubbery

Sword. But who knows, right?"

"Good point," he said.

"South, it is. Can I see your map for a moment?"

He handed me his phone and I looked over the exact coordinates again.

"That way." I pointed, and we headed off.

The heat beat down and the sun was high. I wiped sweat from my forehead and took a drink of water from the bottle Mattheia had given me earlier. It was warm, too, but better than nothing in my dry throat. The air on Tatundra was so very dry. Even my eyes felt dry. I flexed my fingers and the skin felt tighter and rougher.

"How much farther should we go?" Mattheia asked, pushing a thick patch of gnarled branches from my path.

"I'm not sure. Until we find something that tells us we're on the right... or wrong path."

"That might be awhile." He stamped the prickly brush down so I could get over more easily.

We'd trekked about three or four miles thus far and found nothing but old, demolished statues of shrines long gone and dead foliage for as far as the eye could see. The special threading weaved into Mattheia's black jacket helped reflect some of the heat, but my own (made primarily for indoor space adventures) did little to prevent or alleviate a build-up of warmth and sweat on my skin. I wasn't going to give up, but—

A rustle of leaves caught my attention and I drew my gun.

I listened.

Another shuffling noise and then the cracking of a branch. I swerved around and aimed...

A large, furry creature—some kind of hare—leapt from the brush with a terrified squeal and then darted off in the opposite direction.

"False alarm," I whispered, exhaling, tucking my gun back into its holster.

"Good thing, too," Mattheia said. "I definitely don't want to go down in history as the high commander whose last stand was against a desert hare."

He was joking...

"Alright there, Commander," I jeered. "You'd have been praising me had that been a starving bush jackal."

"A what?" He stamped down another entangle of bramble.

"You're kidding." I squeezed through and then side stepped a dead tree. "You don't know what a bush jackal is? What do they teach you at—"

I swung my arm out to stop Mattheia.

Something moved in the distance. "Shh!" I ducked down behind the branches and he did the same.

"What is it?" he whispered. "What did you hear?"

I flattened my hand and pointed in the direction of the sound.

We held our breaths and waited. There was a powerful snorting sound, followed by a loud flap. We ducked down as the sounds neared, and then a massive beast soared straight over our heads, the wind flitting through our hair as the creature's powerful wings sliced through the air.

I stood as soon as it had cleared us.

"A pegasus!" Mattheia's jaw dropped.

The buckskin coat and shimmering black mane and tail danced in the wind, the dark stripe down its back barely visible as the pegasus gained altitude.

"Go after it!" I yelled and took off, dead sticks and debris not nearly as difficult to get through the second pass.

"We aren't going to be able to keep up!" Mattheia yelled from behind me.

The pegasus flew as fast as the wind, sunlight sparkling off iridescent sheen flecking the tips of its feathers. He *was* right, but I wasn't going to let the obvious fact stop me. We hadn't come all this way for nothing.

"We have to try! Where there's a pegasus, there might be a Pegasus Sword!" I leapt over a broken altar stone and pointed it out to Mattheia. "Watch out!"

I picked up speed and ran as fast as I could through the remaining brush, twisting down the path as the creature navigated through part of the island we hadn't yet traversed—a massive forest of greenery and one of the only places not yet ravaged by drought.

"I... can't... keep this up," Mattheia huffed, bending over to rest his hands on his knees and catch his breath. "We're not fast enough."

"We don't have to be," I said, my heart throbbing against my ribcage as I slowed. "We know where it is now." I pointed, exhaling loudly. "In there." The winged horse shot into the woods and disappeared from sight.

"Why do you think it will lead us to the sword, Valhara?" Mattheia came up beside me. "It's an animal."

"In fairy tales, the pegasus is said to be a collector of rare, metallic objects. If it's true, then perhaps it has the sword. If it ever existed on this island at all, I'm sure it would have found it by now."

"I thought pegasi went extinct?"

"Me, too. We don't have time to worry about that right now. There's one here and it might have the sword."

Having caught my breath, I gestured for Mattheia to follow as I picked up speed to the entrance of the forest. "Step lightly," I whispered, passing under and weaving through the first line of monstrous conifer trees. We walked quietly until we came upon a clearing covered in white sand with branches scattered everywhere.

We hadn't seen or heard the animal since entering the forest, but I heard movement in the distance. I ducked down behind some bushes and Mattheia followed. We peered over the brush and waited until the pegasus entered the clearing, rooting and digging around in a pile of leaves. Sparkles of gold and silver reflected back at us as the stallion pushed things around, then it turned and I noticed a bright red gemstone clasped between its teeth.

I was right! They did collect treasures.

We crouched down and crept along the inner edge of the clearing, trying to get closer to the nest without startling the horse. It was busy at work trying to find a proper place for its newest prize and didn't seem to be paying any attention to us.

We were halfway there when the beast lifted its head and let out a thunderous snort, pounding its feet on the ground and twitching its tail nervously, its ears perked forward and its head turning toward different directions as it listened.

Mattheia reached for his firearm, but I stopped him and looked him in the eye, shaking my head and mouthing the word, "No." The horse didn't have a quarrel with us. It was a prey animal—more likely to run than fight.

The pegasus huffed loudly one more time, as if it thought the threat had gone, and kicked a pile of sand into the wind before going back to shuffling around in the heap.

We took a few steps closer so I could better see what its nest of artifacts contained. At least, I had thought it was a nest, until I followed a mound of dirt up to find a sparkling, silver rapier piercing the ground at the head of the pile.

"There." I pointed. It was the Pegasus Sword, protruding from the ground. The blade had a guard made of three twisted sculpted silver wings and a bright yellow topaz in the center of the cross guard. The knuckle guard was also made of a curved wing shape. The entire thing radiated with a supernatural white glow.

The pegasus released the gemstone from its mouth and then bent one leg and bowed down in front of the sword as if it were making some kind of offering. It remained bent down to the ground for several moments before coming back up. It used its tail to gently sweep a scatter of leaves away from the base of the sword, and then turned and headed back to the larger pile of twigs and feathers nearby. The pegasus slowly bent down, pulled its tail in close, and came onto its knees to rest. Its feathered feet looked soft and lush and the long, furry beard on its chin flickered in the gentle breeze. It lay there watching its surroundings intently, its ears cocked two different directions. Spots of sunlight broke through the trees and dappled its glossy black mane with ivory sparkles.

A twinge of guilt twisted my stomach for wanting to steal it away from the poor beast. It wasn't just a mythical weapon, it was a sacred relic. I glanced over at Mattheia, whose expression was one of discontent and hesitance. He frowned and shook his head, his lips pressing thin.

We hadn't come all this way for nothing, but...

I looked over at the horse again. Its wings were pulled in close as if it were a delicate swan. The gentle colt wasn't bothering a soul while it rested its beautiful blue eyes. Taking the sword away might destroy its nest, or worse, break its will to live in this harsh place. It had found a small, viable patch of greenery amongst the treacherous desert to call home, and there we were, about to take away its sacred relic.

"We don't have to," Mattheia whispered close to my ear.

I nodded, reluctantly, but in agreement, and backed away slowly, still captivated by the ethereal white-blue aura pulsating around the blade, hoping the image would remain etched in my memory.

He was right. It wasn't worth it to disturb the poor thing. At least we knew now that it wasn't a hoax. The Pegasus Sword existed.

A few more steps away from the scene and the ground rumbled beneath our feet. I froze and looked down, then my gaze shot up to meet Mattheia's. His eyes were wide and his mouth gaped.

"What was that?" he asked, afraid to budge as the tremor distanced itself from us and moved toward the clearing.

"I... don't know." I turned to look over at the stallion that had risen to attention on all fours. It began stamping its hooves against the ground and snorting anxiously. The earth cracked open on the opposite side of the sandy pit and a monstrous hissing noise seeped from the chasm.

Desperate to protect its nest, the pegasus trotted closer to the hole to investigate, pushed out its enormous wings with a forceful flap, and reared up on its hind legs, letting out a furious, roar-like neigh that echoed through the trees.

The vibration rippled below us again and I gasped. The ground sunk down beneath the stallion, making it stagger to regain its balance. Two huge, spiny black hooks came up out of the hole, ensnared the horse, and raked it forward, dragging the flailing and screaming animal into the earth. A plume of sand and tan feathers puffed up into the air and the noises ceased.

I swallowed hard, my throat dry from desert air.

"What... was that?" I asked, reaching for my sword.

Mattheia had already drawn his gun. "I don't know," he said in a hushed voice. "I don't want to stick around to find out."

"But the sword? It's unguarded." It was now lying in the sand. "Should we—"

"I wouldn't call it *unguarded*, seeing how whatever lies beneath the sand just devoured that pegasus like a potato chip."

"Right. Forget it."

We escaped the scene and left the forest to head back.

"Where to?" Mattheia asked, looking over the map on his phone.

"Back to the ship, I suppose."

He still hadn't holstered his gun and I couldn't blame him for being cautious. I'd only put my sword back because it was wasn't very aerodynamic and made jogging through brush difficult as the barbs kept snagging.

I could see the rocky cliffs from where we were, but we had several miles of terrain to cover before we'd be back on the central path. We picked up pace and I watched as our GPS icon followed us across the island.

"Valhara!?" Mattheia grabbed my arm and I gasped.

The earth shook beneath us, sand and rocks settling into the ground.

We froze in place and I held my breath, hoping whatever it was would pass us by, but the tremors continued in short bursts all around.

Everything quieted and Mattheia shot a piercing glare my way. "Run," he mouthed, his gaze intensifying.

I launched off toward where we'd left the ship and Mattheia followed alongside me. Sticks cracked beneath my feet and loose, thorny branches swiped toward my face and caught on my sleeves, breaking my momentum. I raised an arm to shield my eyes, but stray brambles nicked my cheeks.

A boom erupted and the ground in front of us caved in. A massive, bony black appendage came tearing out of the dusty hole. Then a second. And then a third. The things were long and craggy like dead branches, but the tips came to sharp, dagger-like points. They flailed around until they grasped firmly onto the ground and pulled up, five more legs coming up with them. A prickly, elephant-sized black ball of legs and spines dragged its body from the hole. Bushy black and brown splashes of quills covered the creature, and when the sunlight hit it, it sparkled with random glints of gold, silver, and gemstone.

The hulking spider brought the dead pegasus up with it—the poor, bloodied creature lodged in the thing's pedipalps. It tossed the horse onto the ground and stood there crunching and clicking while scooting the carcass out of its path.

"What is that!?" Mattheia stumbled back.

I drew my sword again, my hands shaking.

I knew exactly what it was, but it wasn't possible. Mahora spiders had gone extinct hundreds of years ago.

This one was clearly alive, and it had dozens of glittering gems and old weapons dangling off its body like family photos in a grandparent's foyer. Like the pegasus, mahoras were collectors of rare, shiny things.

It looked over at us and hissed.

Mattheia dashed off to the side to draw its attention away from me. A shot rang out and one of the spider's middle legs shattered, sending the bottom half of the black spire flying to the ground like a dart. Fluorescent red blood poured out over the ground, sizzling and fuming with toxicity.

I readied my sword and tried to plot in my head how the thing might attack. Eight legs. Okay, seven. Fast. Poisonous. Big. No, GIANT.

Other than lopping off limbs, what were we supposed to do?

"Heads up!" Mattheia yelled.

The spider had caught the brassy gleam of the Azure Phoenix and veered away from him; its bright red eyes zeroed in on me and the thing came charging, its polished, gold mandibles flexing with excitement.

It lifted a leg and jabbed at me, trying to knock the sword from my hands. I dodged, swung hard, and chopped into its front leg. My sword lodged in the thick exoskeleton and I jerked back on it to release it before a second leg came swiping toward my face frantically. Mattheia's gun rang out a second time and the beast fell backward as a hind leg came out from under it. Priceless treasures fell from its body as if it were a piñata being struck by children.

Only we weren't children. And it *definitely* wasn't a piñata.

The piercing hiss made my ears ache, but I mustered the courage to run, regrouping with Mattheia.

"My sword can't cut through the legs," I said, breathing heavily.

"Your gun?" He gestured to my hip.

I reached for it with my other hand, but...

My face hit the dirt and a buzzing sound swirled through my skull. The gun had flown out of my hand. I lifted my head to see the mahora reared up, assaulting Mattheia, flailing its legs at him like scythes. I could have sworn I saw the silver sparkle of the Pegasus Sword gleaming on its underbelly as it reared, or maybe I'd bumped my head in the fall.

The spider jabbed and sideswiped, trying to sweep him, too, off his feet, but Mattheia was agile, and dodged several blows in a row. A long leg came down on him like a knife, tearing open a gash across his chest and sending him stumbling back, howling in pain. A line of blood drizzled down the fresh injury, but I couldn't tell how deep the wound was.

"Mattheia?" I called out, but my voice wouldn't manifest. I'd hit the ground hard and the blow had me fatigued and disoriented.

A sparkle of light drew my attention.

The Azure Phoenix. Within arm's reach. Right to my side.

I stretched out my arm and wriggled closer. Crawling as fast as I could. My elbows dug into the fragile ground.

Only another few inches.

I wrapped my fingers around the grip, the warm metal sliding into my hand. Then I dragged the sword over to me and used it to steady myself as I came to my feet.

Mattheia kept the creature at bay with carefully-timed gunshots, and the mahora struggled to get the upper hand. He'd run out of ammo soon, though, and we hadn't carried enough with us to withstand a full-blown ambush. The thing thrashed its remaining limbs and punctured the ground repeatedly.

Another shot rang out just as Mattheia tripped and tumbled backward.

"Mattheia!" I yelled. I couldn't see him anymore.

It would kill him...

I grasped the Azure Phoenix with both hands and lifted it up.

"Hey!" I hacked at the brush in front of me and waved the sword around so it caught the light. The spider quickly noticed the sparkling metal and reacted by switching its focus.

Mattheia had done some damage, but my sword was no match for the hulking, black death machine.

I continued twisting the weapon in my hands so the blade would reflect the sun back at the creature's excited red-orb eyes, stepping back to lead it away from Mattheia. It crouched down on its remaining legs and lunged forward, making the ground shake as it landed with a thud, dangerously closer. Its golden fangs glittered in the light as it tromped nearer, limping along on severed legs in a swift, wobbly jog.

I glanced at Mattheia. He was still on the ground, fighting to stand but cringing as blood oozed from his chest while he pressed a hand across the lengthy wound. At that rate, he'd bleed to death.

The stomping beast lurched after me, now reaching out with one of its legs to try to knock my sword from my grasp.

"No!" I swung, making contact with a weak spot and hacking the leg off at the lowest joint.

"SHEEEYYAAA!!!"

It let out a deafening screech.

The spider reeled back, its blood showering through the air. I lowered my face and covered it with my sleeve; splashes of red singed my shirt.

The leg slammed down, pulverizing stone remnants into shards and sending treasures from its back flashing through the air like gilded shrapnel.

I held my breath and tightened my grasp on my sword until my palms ached.

This was my idea. Mattheia would die because of me! No. I won't let it happen. I won't let some... thing tear him away from me.

It came at me again, stumping nearer and nearer until its blood-red, glassy eyes were mere inches from mine. It lifted a leg and readied to strike.

Heat poured through me, an unusual sensation of hot and cold sweeping over my flesh until my hairs stood on end.

Yellow-orange light filtered through my vision, tinting my surroundings. The beast's eyes reflected flickers of gold that shifted and danced across its face.

The warmth intensified until every part of my body felt as though it had been injected with liquid fire. It stung, burning so deeply that my stomach twisted and my heart throbbed with pain and adrenaline simultaneously. The Azure Phoenix became feather-light in my hands and I lifted it up high just as the mahora charged.

The ground disappeared from beneath my feet and the sword came down on the beast, splicing it in two as it plowed into me. Shreds of black, prickly spines, crackling legs and shimmering gemstones and treasures went flying in all directions. Blood sprayed through the air as pieces of the thing crashed to the ground, and the moist touch of poison tickled my face.

Searing pain ripped through my eyes and I squeezed them shut. My feet hit the ground and I tumbled to my knees, a gritty, stinging sensation roiling through my corneas. Blood had hit my face, and my eyes burned from a hundred thousand microscopic, venomous fibers tearing through delicate tissue.

I screamed, piercing the sky with a cry of pain.

"Valhara!" Mattheia called.

I opened my mouth to reply but clamped down involuntarily, gritting my teeth while another wave of shredding ache paralyzed me.

"Valhara!" His voice was much closer now. A shuffling noise neared and I veered my head, trying to decipher the direction of the sound.

I couldn't stop shaking, not even once Mattheia came down to the ground and pulled me into his arms.

"I sent for help, Valhara," he said, straining, embracing me tightly. "Are you okay?"

His clothes were damp with his own warm blood, and mine were soaked with the beast's. Every touch was a razor-thin cut, the mahora's toxic blood sharp against my fragile human skin. My jaw clenched and I grunted, tears overflowing as the insurmountable poison surged through my bloodstream.

Valhara may die...

And for what?

This wasn't worth it.

I held the Pegasus Sword in my weary, trembling hands and used the edge of my sleeve to polish a splash of red glaze—blood—off the blade. The sword had fallen from the mahora during battle and I barely had the strength to ask someone to retrieve it before being whisked away with Valhara by a Silver Diamond Field Rescue team.

Valhara had been in the intensive care unit for almost a day, and no one would update me on her condition. All I knew was that she was in so much pain, they had to sedate her heavily in order to get her to rest while they fought for her life.

Was she going to survive? What were the lasting effects of being contaminated with mahora spider blood?

I needed to know how she was doing and I couldn't concentrate on anything else as I waited anxiously in my room for that call.

They told me to rest.

In fact, Captain Lansfora commanded me to.

And I tried... but couldn't. I lay on my bed, staring up at the ceiling, thinking about the previous afternoon.

How could I rest while Valhara's life hung in the balance?

The spider got a good hit on me, too, leaving a nasty, aching gash across my chest that required several stitches, but I'd survive—without question. A doctor bandaged me, administered some antibiotic injections and pain killers, and then discharged me in the morning.

Sure, I was uncomfortable, but Valhara...

I owed it to her friend, Lieutenant Ray, as well as her sister and captain, to tell them what had happened, but I was afraid.

There was no way I'd admit defeat this early in the game. Valhara wouldn't slip away. Not like this.

Not because of something *I* had asked her to do.

The intercom on my desk beeped; I jolted to attention,

cringing in pain as the stitches across my torso flexed. I took in a deep breath and exhaled, then staggered over to the intercom box, lifted an unsteady hand, and pressed down the reception button.

"Yes?"

"Commander Draven, we have an update on Lieutenant Hawksford's condition. She's currently conscious and responsive."

A wave of relief crashed through me. "Can I come see her?"

"Yes. The doctors are still working to treat her condition, but you may visit now while she is awake, if you'd like."

"I'll be right over."

I clicked off the intercom.

Being responsive was good news, right?

I leaned down to reach for my black dress shoes and grimaced, grunting again as the sting of my wound taunted me. With teeth clenched, I slowly brought my torso down and reached again, carefully sliding the shoes closer until I could shove my feet into them one by one. I staggered back toward my bed and lifted a leg up so I could balance while tying the laces. I lowered that foot and then raised the other to do the same, every movement excruciating. Tying my shoes had never been so difficult.

I straightened up and left my room to head to the

infirmary.

"Hello, Commander," the receptionist said cheerfully, though her grim expression didn't reflect the tone. "I'll have the nurse take you to the lieutenant's room."

"Thank you."

"You're welcome to sit," she added.

I glanced around the waiting room at the chairs and vinyl-covered couches. Putting on my shoes had been enough of an ordeal. "I'm fine standing, thank you."

"Commander?" A nurse came in and gestured for me to follow her. She guided me down a hallway into a dimly lit hospital room and allowed me inside.

"Why are the lights down?" I asked quietly. One might assume it was for her to rest, but if she had just now begun to come around...

"Her vision is impaired," the nurse replied, "and the doctor thought best to lower the lights in the room to reduce eyestrain."

Impaired!?

I nodded in understanding and approached Valhara's bedside. She appeared to be asleep, or perhaps only her eyes were closed.

"Valhara?" I leaned closer to her and laid a hand over hers. "It's Mattheia. They told me you were—"

"Hi." Her head turned slightly toward me and she opened her eyes. The hazel green had become muted by a ghostly haze of white. She swallowed, took a deep breath, and exhaled as if it were painful to do so. "Did you... get the sword?"

Valhara had nearly been killed by that *thing*. The sword hardly seemed important anymore, but...

"Yes. I did. Barely. They found it near the dead mahora when they were gathering tissue samples. I asked them to bring it back with them. I have it in my room."

"Good," she said beneath her breath, groaning slightly. "Not a total loss, then." Her lips curled up slightly and then she whimpered and sucked in a gasp of pain. She clenched my fingers tightly.

"Don't waste energy talking." I squeezed back gently. "You need to recover."

"There isn't..." she strained. "I won't."

"What? What do you mean?" My pulse shot through me, rattling my body with quickened thumps.

"I won't recover from this," she whispered. "They won't be able to create an antidote in time to save my eyes. Mahoras have been dead for centuries. I... messed up. We should have run and kept on running, but instead I..." Her breath quivered.

"Shh. You need to rest, Valhara." I stroked a hand across her brow and swept some hair away from her face. She looked a little different with the fiery-red locks framing her features instead of being tied up in the usual ponytail. Her silver hair clip had been set in a bowl at the side of her bed. Part of me wanted to take it as a means of being connected with her even when I had to leave her room, but the other part of me knew she needed every shred of luck she could get right now. She'd told me the thing was a lucky charm from her mom and... I would never dare to take that from her.

"I'll be back to check on you soon. Okay?" I cupped her hand in both of mine. "I'll do everything I can to help you fight this. I promise."

"Thanks," she murmured, closing her eyes. "I'm tired."

I released her hand, backed away from her bedside, and then strained to lower myself down into the nearby chair. My own pain medications were wearing off and the extent of my injuries became more apparent. I heaved a sigh. Even that hurt.

There had to be something I could do to help.

Anything.

I sat there for a good hour thinking about it—wondering what on earth I might do to assist in her recovery. If she returned to Celestial Galaxy blind, they'd discharge her immediately. She hadn't worked this hard in her career for that to happen at such a young age. Her life had barely begun and already...

I forked my hands through my hair and my jaw tightened.

High commander, next in line for the captain's position,

should he fall, and I could do nothing but sit there and—

Wait.

I stood, gradually, so I wouldn't tear a stitch, and returned to the receptionist's desk.

"I was just about to come get you, Commander," she said, standing at attention. "You need your next dose of antibiotics and your pain injection."

"I'll be fine," I replied with a flattened hand. "Thank you." The pain shot they'd given me earlier had made me incredibly groggy. I didn't have time to deal with those side effects. "Is there a computer around here I can use?"

The receptionist seemed taken aback by my question and blinked a few times as if she were processing the request again.

"A computer?" I repeated, this time sternly. "I need to make an emergency conference call. Now."

"Yes, Commander," she replied with a vigorous nod. "Ju-just a moment." She disappeared into a back room off to the side of her desk and then I heard metal drawers being opened and closed multiple times.

She returned with a laptop and power cord in her hands and held them out to me. "Here you go, Sir. It should have everything installed already, but if you need help, please let me know."

"I appreciate it, Tabitha." Her nametag had three gold stars above it and a small sticker of a kitten on the corner. I took the laptop from her hands. "Is there an office I can use to make this call privately?"

"Oh, of course." She pointed toward the hall. "Room 12, on the left. Doctor Chance is on extended leave. You can use her office."

"Thanks." I turned away.

"Sir?"

I looked over my shoulder at Tabitha. "Yes?"

"I understand you're concerned about the lieutenant, but you should rest, as well. That wound won't heal if you keep moving about. Your body needs time to recover."

"I know. Don't worry about me. Worry about Hawksford. I'll take of myself." I went across the hallway and into office 12, closing the door behind me, then plugging the computer into the nearby outlet.

"High Commander Mattheia Draven of Silver Diamond," I blurted before the communications post personnel could even ask me for my name.

"Thank you, Sir. How may we direct your transmission?"

"I need to speak with Lieutenant Jacksiun Ray. It's extremely urgent."

"Yes, Sir. I will get him on the line immediately. Please wait while I contact him and request he take the call." The screen went black and an animated version of the Celestial Galaxy logo flashed in the center.

The few moments that passed felt like eternity.

Finally, the screen changed and a video feed came in of the black-haired, vaguely familiar lieutenant whom I'd been told was also Valhara's best friend. There was a glint of worry in his eyes, but he looked like he was trying to remain composed.

"Greetings, Commander. May I ask why this call is so urgent?" His eyes narrowed. "Has something happened to the lieutenant?"

I didn't know how to begin. Stalling wouldn't help.

"Yes."

His blue eyes widened and he leaned closer to the camera.

"No. Wait," I added. "Let me explain, please."

"Go on." He leaned back, but only slightly, his anxiety quickly becoming apparent on his face.

"She's stable for now."

"For now!? What happened? Where is she?" His expression turned accusatory.

"She's okay at the moment, but I need your help. I also want to be frank with you and I'd like to keep this off the record for the time being. Please give me your word that you'll honor that?"

Ray's lips pressed thin and he looked away for a moment. He exhaled and his jaw tightened as he adjusted the temple of his glasses. "For the time being, Commander. Please tell me what happened."

I took a deep breath in through my nose and exhaled, puffing out my cheeks. "Okay. The Pegasus Sword. Does that sound familiar?"

Lieutenant Ray nodded and furrowed his brow.

"The lieutenant and I went to Tatundra Island to search for it. And, yes, I know she and her sister were going to do it, but she decided to go with me instead. It was on a whim because I asked her about the Azure Phoenix and one thing led to another before... Anyway, we encountered a..." I cleared my throat, visions of the sickeningly large, spiny black beast still haunting my memories. "A mahora spider."

Ray's expression turned fouler. "The mahora spider has been extinct for centuries. Commander, is there a point to this charade or are you—"

"It's the truth." I unbuttoned the top two buttons on my jacket and pried it apart just enough for him to see the tip of the bandaged, bloody gash peeking out near the base of my neck. "No charade. And that's the problem."

The lieutenant's focus softened and he looked off to the side without saying another word.

"We were attacked. I was hit hard, but I'll be okay, save a few—a lot—of stitches. Hawksford sustained the brunt of it, however, as she had blood splashed in her face and now she's—"

"Going blind."

"How did you know?"

"We've studied many myths and legends while growing up. That's how we found our weapons to begin with. Not all myths are made up. Unfortunately, there are worse things to come."

"Worse things?" I shifted in my seat, the movement sending a sharp pain up my chest. "But she said she'd lose her eyesight, she didn't say anything else."

"Then I'm afraid she may have been too ill or her mind too affected by trauma to comprehend the severity of her condition, Commander."

"Wh-what!?"

"The blood of the mahora spider is not only poisonous, it's also lethal when presented into the bloodstream. Blindness is only a symptom of contamination. It's not the end result."

My entire body stiffened and I pulled the laptop closer. "What do I do!? I have to help her. I won't let Valhara..." I cleared my throat, "the lieutenant, suffer."

Ray looked back up at the screen and sternly into the camera, as if he were staring straight into me, his eyes piercing my soul from light-years away.

"Commander, I'm going to make myself very clear here," he started. "You said you wanted this off the record, and so it shall remain as such, for now. That being said, I feel the need to tell you that I consider myself a very good judge of character and that my intuition has always been a defining factor in the decisions I have made throughout my life." He sighed. "I may not know much about you, Commander, but I know you care about her, else you would not have risked consulting me over such a pertinent matter. Not when you have so very many dignified officials there to confer with. The question is, what are you willing to do for her?"

"Anything." The word came out of my mouth without a second thought.

"I need a few hours to do research. I will contact you as soon as I learn something."

"Thank you. If you need me to help, please just tell me how."

Ray's lips twisted to the side with concern. "You can help by getting some rest. You look terribly fatigued and it will do you little good tomorrow when your services may be needed the most."

"I'll try, but I don't want to miss any updates on her health. I will keep you posted, I promise."

"I would appreciate that. Now I must hurry and see what I can find in our old notes and databases. I should also inform her sister."

"Will she tell the captain?"

"It is likely, yes."

"Please wait. I... I don't want to anger him or her sister. I understand this is a terrible thing to ask, but please give me some time. Please. I swear, if her condition changes or worsens, you'll be the first to know and then you can tell her sister and her captain. But please give me a chance before the entire purpose behind her stay here shatters to pieces."

The lieutenant shook his head and fell silent.

"Thank you for understanding."

"I did not agree to anything," he said.

"You said it yourself, I care about her. I do. You tell me how to save her life and I'll do it."

"Rest, Commander. I'll be in touch."

"Thank you, Lieutenant."

The screen went black and our call disconnected. I closed the laptop lid and rested my arms on the desk. I slowly lowered my head into them and closed my eyes. I had to relax, if even for a short while.

There was no telling how much or how little time Valhara had left, but I trusted her friend and I had faith in his ability to help me save her. I tried to relive the incident just to better understand what exactly had happened, but it was all so blurred and distorted by adrenaline and a rush of pain. Valhara had destroyed the mahora somehow. I hadn't seen it happen, but the thing lie in pieces on the ground like it had gone through a blender. I couldn't stop it with my gun and her sword had been unable to cut into its rock-hard exoskeleton in earlier attempts. Something had happened between my being injured and her getting blood in her eyes.

But what?

I sucked in a painful breath. The effects of the pain medication had worn off. The ache was throbbing through my system, a riveting twinge shaking every nerve.

My chest burned—stitched skin and overexerted muscles—but it went much deeper than that. My heart hurt, too, throbbing with the unsettling fear that I might lose Valhara to the vile poison caught inside her bloodstream.

When we'd had dinner with my mom and we walked back to the academy together, she stopped and thanked me with a kiss on my cheek. A spark of something ignited in me then, and I felt a sudden urge to pull her in closer. She even closed her eyes.

The sight of her trust and beauty pushed me to try.

But, I stopped myself.

I made the difficult decision to not kiss the girl I knew would leave me behind—the girl whose fealty to her own academy meant more to her than a romance with someone like me.

Now I despised myself for not taking that risk.

Now I was threatened by the possibility of losing her to a fate much worse than that.

I jolted to attention, awakened by the distinct jingle of an incoming intercom transmission. I flipped open the laptop and blinked several times to try to get my eyes to focus on the screen. The Celestial Galaxy emblem flashed in and out, awaiting my pickup. My arm tingled from being slept on, but I quickly worked my fingers to click and accept the incoming call.

Lieutenant Ray appeared on screen and my pulse picked up speed as I feared the news.

"Have you found anything?" I asked, rubbing some of the numbness out of my other arm. The movements made my chest throb with pain; the stitched skin was very tender.

"I've learned quite a bit, thanks to a very old archive Valhara had saved in her personal files."

"Good news?"

"Good and bad, I'm afraid."

"Let's start with the bad and get it over with."

"From my research, it seems the mahora spider's blood works quickly to desecrate a host. I've spoken briefly with one of our academy biologists and he told me it is highly unlikely that an antidote could be created within enough time to reverse the damage—even if you do have proper skin and tissue samples to work from."

"So relying on the doctors here isn't going to do us any good, is it?"

"No." Ray's expression turned grim and he shook his head.

"Okay. What's the good news, then?"

"For the good news, I'm going to require a certain amount of trust, Commander, as this is all going to sound a tad bizarre. I need you to listen."

"I'm at your mercy, quite honestly, right now."

"I've done additional research and found what I believe may be our only option. It's a gamble, though."

"A gamble? With Valhara's life? Or mine?"

"Both... perhaps."

"I'm only willing to risk my own in this matter, but I want to hear your suggestion, regardless."

"I hope, by now, that you have opened your mind to the possibility that not all myths are made up. The Azure Phoenix. The Pegasus Sword. The mahora spider that never should have been. There is true magic in this world, cleverly disguised as fantasy and fiction. I hope you are willing to suspend your disbelief a little longer."

"I am if *you* are."

"Ajha-Ru Island can be found in the South-Eastern Ocean. It's a small landmass blanketed in desert."

He sent through a satellite image and series of maps showing me the location and coordinates.

"I've had about enough deserts for one lifetime, but continue."

"One document contained stories about an ancient race of apothecaries who were once a center for counsel on deadly poisons and disease. Some called them miracle workers because of how quickly they were able to create cures for various aliments. This was several hundred years ago, mind you, but it's very possible the apprentices of these apothecaries may still reside on the island, although science and medical advancements in our own societies have made their counsel obsolete to most."

I zoomed in on the images he'd sent me. "There doesn't appear to be any buildings on this island. I see remnants of something but..."

"We must have faith, Commander," he said flatly. "This

may be our only chance."

It was crazy of him to ask me to go exploring a deserted island in hopes of finding people who were likely long gone by now, but what other option did I have? Sit around and wait for a doctor to tell me they can't fix her, or take a chance and go looking for someone who possibly could? Honestly, I thought Valhara was kidding when she had laid out the travel itinerary for the Pegasus Sword. I didn't believe it was real, and I certainly didn't believe mahora spiders were alive, either. But I saw that sword glowing with an aura of energy and light—as if it contained some magic power. The glow had faded now, but I was sure I'd seen it earlier, back at the island.

"You're right, Lieutenant. I'll do whatever it takes and explore every possibility I can as long as she's still breathing."

"We don't know what else may reside on Ajha-Ru Island. There's no telling if another feral creature might be lurking there." He tipped his head down and looked at me over the rim of his glasses. "You're willing to do this even if it means putting yourself in harm's way?"

"Yes. Even if it means putting myself in danger. You asked me earlier what I was willing to do for her and I said anything. I meant it, Ray. Now, assuming I find one of these apothecaries, what do I do? Demand an antidote? That doesn't sound polite."

"Bring a tissue sample from the mahora with you. Other than that, I don't know what to say. Let's just hope you can communicate with them."

I hadn't thought about that.

We had translators for some languages, but they required satellite signals to work properly and most likely didn't include Ajha-Ruvian in the database.

"I'm going to prepare for the flight now," I said, moving just enough in my seat that I was coldly reminded of the terrible patch of open flesh recently closed on my chest. I tried not to flinch in front of the lieutenant. "Forward me the rest of the information. Anything you have would be helpful. I'd rather be prepared. I'll head out as soon as I can get my captain's approval. Thank you for your help, Lieutenant. Sincerely."

Lieutenant Ray forced a small grin. "Thank you, Commander. I... apologize for underestimating your concern for my friend. Not being there for her right now hurts more than you can imagine."

"I *can* imagine, Lieutenant. I certainly can. You have my word that I will do whatever I can to help her. Let me know if you learn anything new in the meantime, please."

"Of course, Commander. Take care of yourself and have a safe flight."

I ended the call and immediately began filtering through the series of messages I received from him in regards to the coordinates and land maps of Ajha-Ru Island. It was a fairly small island, which might make my investigation easier, but it could still take days to traverse the entire place alone. Valhara probably didn't have that kind of time. Neither did I.

My career focused on my reliance on fact and science both on the field and in the office. What Ray had told me about the ancient apothecaries had come directly from old mythology—bedtime stories, basically. It didn't make any sense, but neither did what had happened to us on Tatundra Island. That thing shouldn't have even been there.

But did I have time to be skeptical? No. No, I didn't.

I got up from the desk, tucked the laptop under my arm, and unplugged the computer, coiling the cord around my hand as I exited the office.

"Commander?" The receptionist stood. "I didn't realize you were still here! I'm so sorry I didn't come to check in on you and see if you needed anything. I—"

"At ease," I replied with a friendly smile. "I didn't expect you to and I'm not bothered at all. Here." I handed the computer back to her. "Thank you for lending me this."

"You're very welcome, Sir. Is there anything else you need?"

I glanced back toward the hall and sighed.

"She's sleeping, Sir, if you're wondering."

Tabitha set down the computer and came out from behind

the desk. She pressed a hand onto my forearm and looked me in the eye. "We're doing everything we can for her, Sir. The rest will slow damage from the poison while we search for a cure. She's a very strong young woman and she's putting up quite a fight. There just may be hope for her yet."

"Thank you," I replied, appreciating her kind words. "I'm going to do some of my own research, as well, and see what I can find out."

"Good luck, Sir. You've been an asset to Silver Diamond. I have faith in you."

I left the infirmary with those last few words drifting through my mind. Faith. It would take a lot more than that to get through this.

"You have 12 hours," Captain Lansfora said, his jaw tightening in response to my request. "After that, I can offer no more protection. I cannot have the lieutenant's blood on our hands, and hiding the truth from her academy will only make us appear negligent in our involvement in the unfortunate event. Celestial Galaxy and Silver Diamond are on turbulent waters as it stands."

"If anything happens to her, I will take full responsibility for it, Captain. I got her into this mess and I'll deal with it."

"No, Commander. You are a part of this academy. We stand together, or we fall." Captain Lansfora looked me square in the eye. "As your superior, I think your judgment here has been terribly reckless. But... as your friend and a teacher who watched you grow into the intelligent, sensible man you are today, I understand why you've made these choices. I respect your confidence and beliefs, and if there is any possibility at all that a cure exists, I know you'll find it." He looked away from me and frowned. "May you find it before it's too late."

"I will," I replied assuredly. I could hope for nothing less. "Thank you."

"Go. Good luck, Commander."

I tried to appear grateful but couldn't force the expression to come to my face. So much sorrow and fear weighed me down. My mind raced. My heart pulsed like I'd just run a marathon. Every vein thumped with adrenaline.

I hurried back to my room, the pain of my stitches haunting me with every step, and then grabbed the Pegasus Sword. Intuition nagged me to bring it along. Maybe it was because it held some rare value, or maybe it's because I had a childish belief that some magic resided in the immaculate, silver blade.

I needed magic right now.

The struggle to get my gun holster and black flight jacket on was difficult and painful, but I managed with some help. Then I had to climb the ladder to get into the cockpit of the Tetra-Haizon, careful not to tear any stitches while I worked to situate myself in the seat and put on my helmet and oxygen mask. The only thing that kept me going was knowing no matter what kind of superficial pain I was in, Valhara fought a much greater beast. My own discomfort couldn't compare to whatever vile things were working to destroy her from the inside out.

With Lieutenant Ray's help, I located Ajha-Ru Island. As my ship came down onto the desert terrain, a plume of sand kicked up all around, distorting my vision and likely leaving micro-scratches on the entire hull of the jet. I waited for the cloud to subside before climbing out, armed with both my gun and the gleaming Pegasus Sword, which was set firmly in a scabbard near my hip. I didn't know how to use it yet, but I felt better having it with me.

It had gotten us into this mess, after all.

Rocks. Sand. Desiccated animal carcasses. That was all I saw on the island.

But I kept walking, following the coordinates Ray had

given me while keeping an eye on my surroundings. That was easy to do, considering the entire island was nothing but sand. And more sand. If there was a village on the island, it was invisible, or underground. I saw no signs of life of any kind.

I continued on, shuffling my way through sand and bone fragments, shielding my eyes periodically from gusts of wind that swept particles up toward my face. The flat land went on for miles, but I was determined to keep looking.

Suddenly, my foot hit something hard. I bent down to take a look and used a hand to brush away the sand. It shimmered in the light, clear as glass, sparkling with a faint iridescent glimmer. Crystal? I dug deeper. The obelisk went down so far, I couldn't find the end of it with my bare hands alone.

I walked a few more feet and bent down again, sweeping my hand through the sand until I uncovered another bump of the smooth, clear stone. Off in the distance, I saw something else catch the light and jogged over to it. In a straight line, far from the first piece, was another crystal fixture. I kicked at it and it didn't budge, then I knelt and dug the sand away from the base until I could go no further.

The stone pillars were remnants from a building of some kind. A building that once was, but that had been consumed by sand and time.

Great! They were already gone.

It was hopeless. My search had been completely in vain. I clenched a fist and slammed it against the stone, gritting my teeth as a wave of pain shot through my chest and knuckles. A splash of blood colored the crystal.

Defeated and angry, I sat in the sand and pulled out my phone. The map was empty. The satellite showed nothing but desert and more desert covering the entire island.

"How am I supposed to find someone who doesn't exist?" I said out loud, though no one would hear me. I wiped sweat from my forehead and huffed an agitated breath.

Valhara didn't deserve this. Maybe it had been her idea, originally, to look for the Pegasus Sword with her sister, but the plans had fallen through. What if fate had steered her in another direction back then so she *wouldn't* end up this way—with her life hanging in the balance?

But then I came along and prodded her into going on the expedition anyway. A selfish request, but one made only by a selfish heart. All I *really* wanted was to spend time with her while she was still on Earth, before she went back to C.G. and vanished from my life forever.

All this... for a sword?

I slid the thing out of the scabbard and squinted as the high sun reflected back at me, blasting my eyes with white-hot light. The rapier was lightweight but sturdy. The crossbars were intricately woven with detailed feather metalwork pieces curved up around the base of the blade, and the knuckle guard matched in craftsmanship. I couldn't tell what kind of stone it was exactly, but a large yellow diamond-cut crystal had been set in the center of the crossbars. Topaz, perhaps. Citrine?

My mouth was dry. Swallowing made it feel like there were grains of sand in my throat. I gently touched my chest—it ached and the stitches itched and burned. A punishment justly deserved for what I'd done. Maybe I should have called Lieutenant Ray and asked for his advice, but as I looked onward toward the vast emptiness surrounding me, the truth of the matter overshadowed reason.

The island was dead.

Empty.

Abandoned.

If there ever was a race of people on it, they were long gone.

"Agh!" I flung the sword into the air and it spiraled several feet away, piercing the sand at an angle and sinking down several inches.

Maybe it was rare and ancient, but that didn't matter anymore.

I only knew I didn't need the accursed thing. It'd only haunt me—torture me with my mistakes and rub the tragedy brought on by my ignorance further into my already salted wounds.

I looked away and tried to muster up the strength to

stand and head back to my ship. I pressed a hand against the ground and strained as the cut in my chest flexed with each movement. I was halfway up when I noticed it—a glisten of light out of the corner of my eye. I looked up at the sword. It pulsed with the same bluish-white light I had seen before.

"What?" I muttered beneath my breath, resisting the pain of stressed stitches.

Then the ground began to shake and I lost my footing, tumbling onto my back side and flailing my arms to try to escape the vibrations that jostled me around.

I scrambled to my feet and distanced myself just as the desert sand devoured the Pegasus Sword in one gulp. A sparkle caught my attention and I turned my head and shielded my eyes with my hand. The crystal pillars began to rise from the ground, towering high over my head and bringing a massive glass wall up with them. The sun shot through it like a prism, reflecting blinding rainbows in every direction.

The rumbling stopped and I was able to get a better look, careful not to let the light catch at just the right angle where it would pierce my vision again.

A castle!?

What kind of mechanics or... sorcery had it taken to hide an entire castle beneath the ground?

Though terrified by the sight, I needed to know who... or

what lived inside.

I approached the hulking, cathedral-style doors that were split down the center and investigated them. Metal of some kind. Beveled edges with intricately carved flourishes at each corner, encrusted with scarlet and lavender gemstones. Astounding details, but no handles.

I grazed over it, hovering flattened palms across the length to feel for hidden knobs or buttons. Nothing.

So I did what any *normal* person might do—I knocked.

Knuckles against cold, hard metal made a surprisingly tinny sound, as if a small bell were being rung far in the distance. I took a step back and waited. The crack between them expanded and the two doors opened outward, silently, and as if by some unseen force.

It was pitch black inside, so I pulled out my phone and carried on, stepping past the threshold into the inky darkness.

BANG!

The doors slammed closed behind me and I gasped. My other hand reached for my gun.

"Not a wise idea," a low voice croaked from all directions.

"Who are you!?" I slid my gun from the holster and clicked on my phone, using the light to try to see in front of me.

"You are trespassing on my island. I shall ask the

questions."

Was the voice that of an apothecary? Or someone with dark intentions?

Both?

I was trapped and, even with my phone, could see little beyond my own feet and shaking hands.

"I need your help!" I yelled, my voice booming as it echoed off walls I couldn't see. "Please. I didn't know I was trespassing on anyone's land. I swear. I'm..." My voice began to crack from the dry air, but I persisted. "I'm looking for an apothecary. I have a friend who is very sick and—"

"What will you give in exchange for my services?"

"Anything."

"I see."

The room came alive with candles catching fire in a long row on both sides of what I could now see was a stone hallway embedded with chunks of clear crystal. I moved ahead, following the hallway until it opened up into a great throne room. At the very far end sat a large, cloaked figure.

"Approach me, boy," he said in a craggy, unwelcoming voice.

I did as I was told and stepped closer, realizing immediately that the huge man was no man at all, but a creature with yellow-green skin and matte, serpent-like scales. He was bulky and covered in dark brown cloth with silver embroidery trimming all the hemlines. Deep olive-colored eyes the size of baseballs stared back at me, glistening with eerie specks of what appeared to be silver dust twinkling like stars in the night sky. And he did not blink once as he stared into my soul, sending a wave of fear gushing through my veins. The thing could gobble me up whole if he'd wanted to. Like some kind of toad or lizard, his mouth stretched across his face.

The fireplace behind the marble throne cast shadows on the walls, its soft light supplemented by candles burning at all corners. I followed the flickering lights down until I saw a familiar sparkle. The Pegasus Sword! It was in his hand, dangling from one of his armrests.

"How did you?" I pointed. "How did you get that!?"

"You did say *anything*. Did you not?"

"Yes, but—"

"This sword is legendary and much more valuable than a frail mortal life. It belonged to a great prince—Eolias, lord of the Order of Pegasus Knights." The creature made a sound reminiscent of a scoff and laid the sword across its lap. "You are foolish to part with it."

"I don't care about the sword. It's what got us hurt to begin with. She's more valuable to me than a hunk of metal, but now she's dying because of it." I took another step toward the creature. "I was told a race of esteemed apothecaries lived on this island. I don't know if you're one of them or not, but if you can't help me, I want the sword back. If it really is that valuable, then I'll save it for someone who might actually help."

"You are a bold one," the thing growled, placing the sword off to the side. "Calm yourself. I am the one you seek." He wrapped his wrinkly hands around the ends of the armrests and leaned forward in his throne, his bulbous eyes gleaming with curiosity. "What is it you face? A plague? Virus?" He lifted a hand. "A curse, perhaps?"

"A mahora spider."

"A... what?" The pitch of his voice sharpened. "Those are extinct, boy. They have been for cen—"

"We were attacked on Tatundra Island. It's... dead now, but she—the solider who fought it with me—was exposed to its blood and now she's..." I couldn't bring myself to say it.

"Dying." The apothecary filled in the blank.

I looked away and nodded.

"It has been centuries since I have concocted such an antidote."

"Is it too late then? I have a tissue sample." I reached into my pocket. "Is there no way you can—"

"Quiet. I am a master at my craft. I shall mix it once more. My mind is not so feeble that I have forgotten such simple things."

Simple? I tried not to get excited, but his words were promising.

"Wait here," he said, and then strained like an elderly

man to push himself up from his throne, a low, airy grunt reverberating in his throat.

I'd thought about offering my assistance, but he intimidated me.

"How do I know you won't disappear with the sword?" I said as he bent over just far enough to grab hold of it with his lengthy hand.

"A cleric speaks only truth. We hide nothing." He turned his back. "Besides, I do not need a human wandering about in my castle." He disappeared behind the throne into a room or passageway I couldn't see from where I stood.

"Okay, then…" The words came out muffled. I shrugged and decided to look around for a few moments while I waited for his return.

I didn't even know the cleric's name.

Hundreds of candles lined the perimeter of the room, perched in sconces along the walls. The fireplace flared and dimmed with bright gold and sienna embers, but the room was surprisingly cool and comfortable compared to the scorching heat outside.

In each of the four corners of the room stood a small wooden statue depicting a rare and mythical creature. A winged dragon, a rearing unicorn, a scaly, deer-like horned horse, known as a kirin, and a pegasus. They stood to about my waist, were polished to a rich, glossy sheen, and had eyes made of faceted gemstones. I reached out a hand to gently stroke the muzzle of the fierce-looking dragon. The carved scales were smooth beneath my fingers. I'd never seen such intricate wood craftsmanship.

"Do you like my work?" the cleric asked, startling me. I veered my head; he stood beside his throne.

I jerked my arm back and clasped my hands together, feeling very rude for touching the cleric's sculpture without permission. "I'm sorry. I..."

"No need to apologize," he replied in a soft, neutral tone. "They are not so fragile. They can withstand admiration."

I smiled awkwardly and scooted away from the statue. "Were you able to make something?"

"Of course," he said, lowering himself—with some difficulty—back onto his throne. He held out a hand. In his scaly palm was a tiny glass vial filled with shimmering blue and green particles suspended in clear liquid. He gave it a brief swirl and the mixture came together into an effervescent teal fluid. "This will neutralize the effects of the mahora's toxins."

I reached out to take it from him, my fingers trembling as they grasped onto the bottle.

"Put a drop in each affected eye and then have her take the remaining via ingestion, or the bloodstream. Improvement shall occur swiftly."

"Thank you," I said, feeling a massive weight lift from

my heart as I carefully tucked the precious antidote into the front pocket of my shirt. Now I could only hope Valhara would still be alive by the time I returned.

A beam of light peeked into the throne room, pouring in from the main doors at the entrance as they eased opened.

"Wait," the cleric called as I turned to leave. "Your wound." He gestured to my shirt. "It has been compromised. You will not fare well on your journey back in this condition."

I looked down. Wet patches darkened my shirt. I tucked two fingers into my collar and drew them out. Fresh blood.

I'd torn a stitch.

He was right. The flight back would accelerate the blood loss.

A scaly hand lifted and its fingers folded inward. "Come here, boy."

My nerves kicked in again, but I did as he requested, staggering toward his throne, pressing a hand against the open gash to slow the bleeding.

He brought his index and middle fingers together on one hand and then reached out to touch them to my collar. A sharp shock of painful heat pierced me and I stumbled backward, grunting from the impact of what felt like electricity.

I pried open my collar and looked down at the wound; it had been cauterized, and the swelling was substantially less apparent.

"Th-thank you." The pain had nearly vanished, too. "You really are a miracle worker. What do I call you? Er... what's your name?"

"As you have noticed, this island is destitute and barren. I am the last of the Ajha-Ruvian clerics. I am called Kinasetsu."

"I'm sorry for the loss of your people, but I hope you can find some peace knowing you've done a great thing for a brilliant young woman who deserves to live."

"Speaking of living..." Kinasetsu leaned forward. "How ever did you survive the battle with the mahora?"

"I... I don't know, actually. I was knocked back with this wound, and *she* fought it without me. Before I knew it, it had been slaughtered and she was covered in blood. I didn't see exactly what had happened."

"I see." Kinasetsu tilted his head and flexed his reptilian fingers. "Bring the girl to me once she is healed. One week from today should be more than sufficient."

"Why? I thought our trade was for the sword."

"Our transaction for the antidote has been satisfied. This is purely to settle my own curiosities. I ask you to please return with her. I can promise no harm will come to either of you, and that you need not fear the island when you return."

All I wanted to do was leave Ajha-Ru and *never* lay foot on the searing fire pit again. But the cleric had a stern look in his mystical, starry eyes, and if the antidote really did work, it was likely Valhara would want to thank him in person.

"I'll return with her when she is well." I bowed my head slightly and then left the castle.

I landed the Tetra-Haizon with less finesse than usual and pulled in disturbingly close to the hangar, sending the landing crew into a frenzy.

Another second could mean the end for her. I had no time to waste. The cockpit canopy lifted and I climbed out. I'd secured the antidote in a small leather pouch and tucked it away in my heavy flight jacket for safe keeping.

"May I help you, Commander?" The receptionist stood upon my arrival to the infirmary. The woman I'd spoken with earlier, Tabitha, was no longer there.

"Yes. The... Lieutenant... from Celestial Galaxy." I was

out of breath from the rush over. "Hawksford. How is she?"

"She's still in Intensive Care, Sir. I believe her condition has declined and they moved her to another room in case she had to be placed on life support."

"What!?" A chill swept over my skin and a sickening feeling of dread made my stomach turn. "I need to see her. Now." I marched down the hall toward the room she was in before.

"She's not there anymore, Sir!" The woman trotted after me. "She's at the end of the hall, but—"

I picked up speed, glancing through the glass windows in the last few doors of the strip, hoping to find the room they'd put Valhara in.

There!

"You can't be in here!" a man wearing a long white coat said, alarmed by my sudden bursting into the room. Valhara was there, hooked up to half a dozen machines, her skin an unnaturally ashen shade, resembling a color I'd seen before, but not on anyone still breathing.

"Doctor, I have something you need to give her." I reached into my jacket for the satchel and carefully slid out the vial of colored liquid. "This is the only thing that can save her right now."

The doctor scowled, looking at me as if I had lost my mind. "You expect me to give her that?" He scoffed. "I don't even know what it is."

"Nothing you've done for her thus far has helped, has it?"

The doctor's lips thinned, but he fought the urge to validate my question.

"*This* is the cure. You have to give it to her. Now. Before it's too late." My hands shook, but I held firmly to the priceless bottle of life-saving liquid. "Please. Trust me, Doctor."

"Commander, do you know how many hospital policies you're violating right now, and how many *I'll* violate if I administer an untested, unknown compound to my patient?"

I glanced at her. Her skin was so pale.

She was slipping away right in front of me, and there I was trying to convince her caretaker that I had the *one* and *only* thing that would give her a chance.

I flexed my fingers and took a deep breath, contemplating the ignorance of the dangerous thought flitting through my mind. It would, without a doubt, get me court-martialed.

But it was my first reaction.

Valhara was going to die.

"Give it to her." A sneer wrinkled my lips. I parted the flaps of my jacket and slid my hand in, wrapping my fingers around the grip and sliding my gun out just far enough for him to see it.

"Commander!? What are you—" He staggered back and lifted both hands in surrender.

"Please, Doctor. You *have* to trust me on this." I spoke

through gritted teeth. "If you don't, Valhara *will die*. Do you want her death on your conscience?"

"No. Of course not!" His voice cracked.

"And I don't want yours on mine. So, please..." I lifted my other hand up and unwrapped my fingers from around the potion. "Give it to her."

"O-okay, Commander," he said, shuddering. "I'll do it." His wavering hands came up to retrieve the antidote from my palm, and I narrowed my eyes as he took it.

"The cleric who made it said to put a drop in each of her eyes, and have her ingest the rest or give it intravenously."

"Alright," the doctor replied, cupping the glass vial gently in both hands as he took a closer look. "I'll get a syringe and an eyedropper." He moved across the room toward a desk. "They're right over here." He slid open a drawer and reached in to retrieve a sealed hypodermic needle and syringe. Then he rustled around in the drawer another moment and pulled out a small, plastic-sealed item. He was still shaking with fear, though I honestly had no intention of hurting him or anyone else.

My fingers slipped from my gun and I pressed the retention strap back into place before withdrawing my hand from the inside of my jacket. "I won't hurt you, Doctor. I only wanted you to listen to me. Is there anything I can do to help?"

He shook his head. "I can take care of this." He tore

open the eyedropper and then twisted open the lid of the vial. The dropper filled with some of the teal liquid and he walked it carefully over to Valhara's bedside.

"Actually, could you come here—to the other side, please?" He looked up at me and I quickly walked around to the opposite side of the bed. "Just press your hand gently on her forehead so she doesn't squirm around in case this mixture stings."

I did as he asked, pressing my fingers gently, but firmly against her ice-cold forehead. I gestured for him to go ahead and he carefully pried open one of her eyes, released a droplet into it, and then did the same on the other side. Her back arched slightly and a nearly inaudible groan of discomfort welled in her throat.

He ripped open the needle and syringe next and used it to withdraw the remaining fluid from the bottle. I watched as he discharged it into a tube connected to her I.V. and held my breath the entire time as the color flowed from the needle into her arm. Thinking about how close she was to death made me lightheaded, but I fought the ill feeling, determined to keep my focus. The heart monitor barely beeped as each slow, subtle pulse of her heart struggled to force the digital line.

"All we can do now is wait," the doctor said, capping the needle and disposing of the entire syringe in a nearby sharps container.

"Then I'll wait," I said, taking her frigid hand into mine.

The doctor wheeled a chair over and gestured for me to sit.

"You look exhausted, Commander," he said with a solemn gaze. "Your own wounds haven't even begun to heal."

"If she dies, they never will." I swallowed hard and brushed my thumb across her hand.

✦

"Commander."

Someone nudged me in the shoulder.

"Wha—?" I pried my eyes open and suddenly remembered where I was. "Is she!?" I stood and clasped Valhara's hand, looking toward the doctor for a reply.

"Ask her yourself, Commander," he said with a small smile and a nod toward her. I turned my head and heaved a sigh of relief.

The white haze had cleared from her eyes and enchanting, mossy green hazel looked back at me.

"Hi," Valhara uttered. "How long have I been..."

"Three days," I answered, massaging her hand with my fingers. Her skin had warmth and color to it again.

"Can you... help me?" She strained to sit up and I quickly moved to assist her.

"Slowly. Be careful, Valhara." I helped support her

216

weight as she pushed up off the bed. The doctor came around to put a firm pillow behind her and then she lay back against it.

"Th-thank you," she said weakly. "My body hurts." She pressed her palm to her forehead.

"Mine, too," I said with a smirk, trying to hide the discomfort twisting my face because of all the emotions swirling inside. "I think you're going to be okay, though. We weren't so sure for a while there." The doctor returned with a glass of water and helped her take a sip from it.

"I can see again," she said, looking up into my eyes. "And I'm so grateful for that. Thank you, Doctor, for helping me."

"You should thank him," the doctor said. "He did most of the work, even though he's still recovering from a serious injury."

Her brow wrinkled and she reached for my hand.

"Thank you, Mattheia." She smiled with her eyes.

"You're welcome. You should take it easy today. Rest and recover. I'll stay close by."

"You need rest, too." Valhara settled into the pillows and released my hand. "I'll be okay. I... feel myself getting stronger already."

"I'll send in a nurse to give her some pain medication and to observe her," said the doctor. "Come, Commander." He propped open the door for me.

I glanced at Valhara once more and felt better knowing

the warm glow was quickly returning to her skin, subtle pink coloring her cheeks again.

The doctor escorted me into a room across the hall and closed the door.

"You can stay here if you'd like. There's a washroom down the hall with a shower. Keep your stitches clean. You don't want to get an infection."

I plopped down in the padded chair beside a small desk against the wall and rested my head in my hands. The room also had a futon and a rollaway bed. He probably wanted me to stay somewhere he could keep an eye on me until he made *the call.*

"Thank you for everything you did to help her and... for administering the antidote I brought," I muttered through my hands. My forehead was sticky with perspiration. "And thank you for stitching me up, too." I tried to chuckle, but the humor wasn't there.

The clock ticked; as soon as the doctor gave the word, I would be escorted off the premises and detained for my actions. Valhara's lieutenant friend was probably going stark mad worrying about her; I'd never get the chance to tell him what really happened.

I pulled my I.D. from my pocket and set it on the side table, and then I reached up and released the silver diamond emblem from my collar and placed it beside the card. "I'm sorry for what I did to you, Doctor," I said, looking over at him. "But I don't regret fighting to save her life." I took a deep breath and exhaled, hanging my head down. "I did what I needed to do."

The doctor pulled a chair up beside me and sat. He entwined his hands together in his lap and remained quietly beside me for several moments.

"As a man of science and medicine," he began, "I must be open to considering any option that might help a patient, especially one in such dire need. I should have listened to you; if I hadn't, she would be dead, I'm sure of it."

He lifted my lapel insignia up from the table and polished it on his sleeve.

"You're very brave, Commander," he continued, speaking softly. Then he leaned closer, reached up, and tacked the silver pin back onto my collar. "You made the right call when I didn't. I'm the one who should be handing over my badge."

My sorry expression turned into a smile; a bittersweet one, perhaps, but a smile all the same. "You did what you could," I said. "It wasn't your fault this was an unusual case."

"I think we can both agree our choices and actions were *unconventional*, at best."

I nodded.

"The most important fant thing here is that the lieutenant will live, thanks to you." He patted me on the shoulder and stood. "Take care of yourself." He slid my I.D. over to me and tapped it. "Oh, and don't forget your card, Commander."

I squeezed my hand through the cuff of my sleeve and tugged my uniform on over my shirt, wincing as tender, stiff muscles made every movement an endeavor. I buttoned it one by one until I reached the collar, then scooped up my gold lapel badges and pinned them into place. The silver cherry-blossom barrette held my loose hair out of my face as I bent over to brush my hands down my slacks, sweeping out some faint wrinkles. My necklace had been kept in a tiny lockbox beside my bed. I looped it around my neck and carefully tucked it beneath the collar of my shirt.

"I'm finished," I said in a raised voice.

The hospital room door opened slowly and Commander

Draven entered.

"Good as new?" He smiled.

"Hardly," I said with a scoff, rubbing my arm. "My muscles ache."

"Your vision is back to normal, though. Right?"

"Yes." The doctor had examined my eyes earlier and given me a vision test.

"Good. I was... uh... worried about you."

"Worried about me? You're saying that like I was on my deathbed."

I couldn't remember anything that had happened after the mahora attack, but certainly my sister and Jacksiun would have gotten involved had it become severe.

"You..." Mattheia squinted. "Wait, you don't remember *anything*?"

I shrugged. "Not really." What was there to remember? I got hurt. An infection maybe? A high fever or something else that obscured my memories. Trauma? But... I didn't remember anything about actually being sick. Only the aftermath now paining me—making every stretch of skin sting when I moved the wrong way or too quickly.

Or when I moved at all.

"All I remember is watching that pegasus be devoured by a horrible monster and that the spider came after us and then... wait..." I did remember something. "Mattheia?" I inched closer and lifted my hand toward his collar, vaguely recalling a brief, vivid image of blood across his chest. "Are you..." My fingers pressed against the top button of his shirt and my gaze met his.

"I'm fine," he replied, glancing down at my hand.

"Sorry." I pulled it away, embarrassed. "I thought I remembered something... but—"

"Everything's okay, Valhara. As much as I would have liked to have come only to check up on you, I actually came here on Captain's orders."

"Oh?"

"He's ordered me to suspend you from classes until next week—to give you ample time to recover."

"What? I'm feeling better. Why do I need to miss classes?"

"They are the captain's orders, Lieutenant." His tone darkened. "You must oblige."

"Yes, Sir." I lowered my head. "I-I understand."

"Trust me, Valhara, it's for your own good." His expression softened and a small grin curled one side of his lips. "You need the rest." He pressed a hand to my shoulder. "There's one other thing. The cleric, who crafted the medicine we used on you, requested that you visit him in a few days. I know you're not a big fan of flying, but I believe you should thank him for his work. You were in very bad condition until he helped."

Such bad condition I didn't even recall most of it, apparently. Perhaps that was part of why they'd given me the week off.

"Okay." Not really. I had gotten sick once already from the flight in his jet and was not looking forward to an encore, but I'd take some motion-sickness medication beforehand this time. That would make things easier.

"Valhara?"

My gaze reeled up toward his.

He took a step closer and let his hand drift down my arm. A tingling sensation rippled up my spine as he clasped his fingers around mine, making the hair on the back of my neck prickle.

"I *really* need to speak with you tonight," he said. "Please." The stern look on his face and the soft tone of his voice indicated he'd meant on the roof. It had been several days since we'd partaken in an evening conversation.

"Of... course," I whispered. The intense blue of his eyes, more entrancing than usual, left me scrambling to find my words.

"Thank you," he said.

His fingers held mine; I couldn't bring myself to pull away from the warmth.

My computer screen flashed with an unread message dialog box. It was from Jacksiun from earlier today.

It read: *Checking in. Call as soon as you can. I don't care what time it is.*

It was mid-afternoon, so he'd still be awake if I called now, albeit a little late in the day at C.G.

I pressed the bold yellow button beside his avatar on my chat application and waited for the call to be patched through.

"Where's the fire?" I said jokingly after he came on screen.

He scowled—something I'd *rarely* (okay, *never*) seen him do. "That's a bit inappropriate right now, don't you think?"

"Inappropriate? Why? I thought it was funny." I crossed my arms and sat back in my chair. "You're the one who messaged me while I was out, asking for me to call. I thought it was something important."

Jacksiun narrowed his eyes at the screen and shook his head. "I know you well enough to know you don't take things this lightly. Are you feeling okay, Valhara? We can talk about it if you want to. I'll do whatever I can to help."

"Help what? Wait... you're not talking about the commander, are you? He and I aren't really... um..."

"That's not what I meant. Do you have any idea what's been going on for the past few days?" he asked very matter-of-factly, a hint of impatience in his voice.

"I was sick. Jacksiun, I'm sorry, but I don't remember

much of what happened after I got attacked on that island. Is there something you need to tell me?"

"Commander Draven didn't say anything to you about it?"

I shook my head.

"Hmm. Then we have some catching up to do."

Jacksiun explained to me what had occurred once I'd been taken to the infirmary. He told me how Mattheia had called him and asked for his advice and how they had worked together to find me a cure. He also told me Mattheia had sacrificed the legendary Pegasus Sword—the sword I didn't even know he'd acquired—in order to pay the cleric for my antidote. And that he had taken on the entire journey while heavily injured and in pain from his own battle with the mahora. That he had refused painkillers in order to keep a clear mind during the flight.

He also told me that I had almost died.

DIED...

There I was thinking I'd gotten a few scrapes and bruises, only to realize the traumatic event had somehow been wiped clean from my memory.

Mattheia had risked infection and even death by venturing to Ajha-Ru Island to find me that antidote.

I felt like a fool for not so much as thanking him for everything he'd done, but I didn't know.

"Does my sister know?" I asked, biting my lip anxiously. Atira didn't like secrets being kept from her, despite how she sometimes kept them from me.

"Yes," Jacksiun replied. "She knows, and I think she wanted to strangle me for hiding it from her, but I had to. Full disclosure, I also informed Captain Ventresca since some documents will be forwarded to us after your term is completed. Better to answer to it now than later."

"How did he take it?"

"He nearly withdrew you from the academy. He threatened to, at least, but I talked him out of it. It wasn't negligence that caused you to get hurt and, well, even if you had gone with your sister to the island, there still could have been the possibility of being attacked by the same creature. I don't believe the commander had any intention of putting you in danger."

"I'm sure he didn't know or we wouldn't have gone. He had been hurt badly, too, after all. I vaguely remember that—him bleeding everywhere. The thing hit him really hard across the chest and..." A brief glimpse of the gash and peeled skin and blood flashed across my mind. "I'm glad he's okay." I spoke more quietly as my chest tightened painfully.

He'd tried to hide his discomfort from me even when I had confronted him about it in the infirmary room.

Why?

Mattheia waited for me at the base of the maintenance ladder, as he always had. We climbed up to the roof and I unfolded two fluffy white mats before sitting down. I crossed my legs and set my hands in my lap, expecting him to sit beside me.

He didn't.

He just stood there, staring off into the night sky. I wondered if he was looking for Celestial Galaxy, as he appeared to be gazing in that general direction.

"Mattheia?"

He took in a big breath and then exhaled, remaining there with his back turned to me.

"Matth—"

"I'm not afraid of anything, Valhara," he said, flexing his hands. "I've never been afraid of anything. That's why I'm able to do the things I do, and have the job I have. The possibility of war breaking out and my mom losing another man she cares about has crossed my mind in the past, but it's never stopped me from doing what I love or protecting my country." He paced in front of me, still not looking at me even as he walked.

"My dad died in a crash because his jet malfunctioned. Do I worry about the same thing happening to me? No. No, I don't, because I don't have time for that. I have a job to do and other people rely on me to do that job." He paused and turned toward me. "But when you ended up in the infirmary... and all signs pointed to your death, for once in my life, I felt fear. True fear. For once in my life, I was afraid of something—losing you. And do you know why that frightened me so much, Valhara? Do you know why the thought of your death was the only thing that's ever been able to break my nerves?"

He came closer and knelt.

I shook my head as he searched my face for the reply.

"Because I couldn't control it," he continued. "For that moment in time I had absolutely no control over whether you lived or died. I couldn't choose where or how to steer my jet. I couldn't choose which ammo to load or when to fire a round."

He hung his head and sighed.

I didn't know what to say. He *had* been able to do something—make a decision that saved my life.

"Thank you," I said softly, reaching up to take his hands. I squeezed his trembling fingers gently and looked him in the eye. Moonlight reflected off the side of his face just enough for me to see him dimly.

His breaths were shaky and he opened his mouth as if he were about to reply, but didn't. He swallowed hard, his eyes locked onto mine.

"Thank you for what you did for me, Mattheia. For

sacrificing the sword and your welfare to do whatever it took to keep me alive. I can't thank you enough and I'm sorry I didn't say anything earlier, but I didn't know what had happened. I forgot everything somehow. Maybe it was the medication, or the trauma. All I recalled was..." I took away a hand to brush my fingers over his collar. "You were hurt. I remember you bleeding. I remember thinking I'd gotten you into this mess and wondering how was I going to get you out of it alive. Guilt and fear crushed me then. We didn't need that sword and you didn't need to get hurt." I pressed my hand against his chest and shuddered. "You're going to have that scar forever. And I'm sorry for that." My throat tightened.

"Don't be," he said reaching up to cup his hand over the one below his collar. "I'd do it again if I had to. I'd do it again because we're friends and... because I care about you."

You don't risk your life for someone you simply *care* about.

"I like you, Mattheia," I said, smiling a little as I strained to get the words out. It felt really awkward, but I had to say it. "I do." His expression seemed to brighten even in the darkness. "But I don't want to start something I can't finish."

He laughed lightly, moonlight sparkling off the silver trim on his epaulets. "Who said anything about having to finish it? If it's meant to be, it will be. Easy as that."

Nothing is easy.

"When we walked home from your house after having dinner with your mom the first time, I saw passion and desire building upon your lips. And for some reason, I closed my eyes and, for a moment, imagined what it might be like to let that passion into my life. But you changed your mind, too, and that has to mean something. I know you've been trying very hard to remain professional about all this, but I can tell it's becoming difficult. Especially after everything that happened. I don't know how this could change for the better. I have to go back to Celestial Galaxy in a few months. It's just not possible for us to have a relationship."

His brow crinkled, but it wasn't a judgmental look. "If you like me at all in *that way*, and I think you do—in fact, you just said it—then give it a chance. Give *us* a chance. I'm willing to fight for something that's worth keeping, but how are we going to know if this will work if we don't at least try? You can't make up excuses for something you haven't even attempted."

"I don't want to regret anything," I said, looking away. "What if this is a mistake?"

"A mistake? If there's one thing I've learned from the people I grew up around, it's that sometimes it's the things we *don't* do that we end up regretting. Sometimes it's the opportunities we turn away from that leave the biggest scars."

He neared and the scent of his skin charmed me when a gust of air fluttered past. Brisk. Clean. Comforting. I did like being around Mattheia. He made me feel safe and... happy. What else could I ask for in a friend or... something more?

My heart thumped against my ribcage. I glanced at his collar again, trying to envision the ugly mark the mahora had left on his chest that would likely become a scar—a ridge of darkened color on his fair, sun-kissed skin.

I leaned toward him as if being compelled by some invisible force and I didn't fight it this time. I didn't want to.

His words rang true. I had to give it a chance. Maybe it would fail. Or maybe—

Mattheia's hand came up to cup my cheek and his intense gaze captivated me, bright moonlight shimmering off crystal blue. His fingers felt warm against my skin and his breaths shallow and soft amidst the quiet backdrop of night.

"Valhara, would you regret it if I...?" The words slid off his tongue like velvet.

I shook my head without giving it a second thought, and then he pressed a kiss to my lips.

A wave of comfort consumed me and my eyes closed.

Fear dissipated, following a wave of goose bumps and tiny hairs standing on my skin as his fingers slid toward the back of my neck.

Anxiety subsided, blanketed in the new, fervent sensation electrifying my heartbeat.

The taste of his breath. The feel of his own pulse, thumping through my fingertips as my other hand remained against his chest. It was new and riveting—more potent than I had imagined it could be.

I thought about pulling away... but I didn't want to be released from the spell of peace and elation he'd cast upon me as my fingers nestled against the folds of his shirt.

I didn't know what it was supposed to feel like to be kissed, but it felt like I was the only person in the world who mattered in his life right then and there, and I liked that.

The brush of his thumb across my cheek as he held my face. The overwhelming thoughts coursing through my mind at breakneck speed. A hint of dizziness swirling through me while a pitter patter of tiny wings made my stomach tingle with what must have been the thing people called butter-flies.

I know he'd hesitated to try to kiss me before and, back then, I was glad he had; I didn't want to be heartbroken and I didn't want to break his heart, either. I'd tried so hard to resist something deep down I truly wanted to experience.

It was the first time I'd ever been kissed, and the won-drous sensation had me questioning why I hadn't pursued it sooner.

From him.

It was perfect. Warm and gentle—and for the time be-ing, he was mine alone. Like two stars aglow in an endless sea of black.

That's what was going through my head at the time.

That and a few other... *little* things.

Like how I was top of my class. Always making the right decisions and doing what was in my best interest and the best interest of my academy. How I'd promised myself I'd never have any regrets—that I wouldn't harbor my mistakes or dwell on things I couldn't change.

And now all I could think about was how I was making one of the biggest mistakes I'd ever make in my life.

I was falling in love.

KNOCK. KNOCK. KNOCK.

I rolled over in bed and groaned. I didn't have classes today. Who was bothering me?

"*Hello!?*" Amanda's voice chirped from the intercom. "*Are you in there, Valhara?*"

"Yes!" I roared, but my voice broke, coming out as a weak, congested grumble. I slid off the bed and tossed on a robe and slippers.

"What's up?" I opened the door a crack and rubbed my tired, crusty eyelids.

"Have you seen the time?" she said, pointing behind me. I turned my head.

Lunchtime. Already?

How the?

Oh.

"Pain meds," I growled. "They've got me on stuff that could knock out a grumble puff."

"Well, I haven't seen you in, like, four days. Dragons! *FOUR* DAYS. That's 96 hours if you didn't do the math." She lowered her voice to an exasperated whisper. "96 hours of gossip that is tearing at my seams. But." She crossed her arms and frowned. "I can leave if you're toooo busy."

"Oh, Amanda, no." I backed away from the door and opened it farther. "Please come in for a bit. I haven't even had breakfast yet."

"Haven't brushed your teeth yet either, huh?" She chuckled, scowling sarcastically as she passed the threshold.

"Sorry," I muttered from behind my cupped mouth. "I've been through a lot this week. Give me a break."

"What's that supposed to mean?" Amanda sat on the corner of my unmade bed and kicked off her shoes. She bent down to rub her ankles. "These shoes. Ugh."

I went into the bathroom. "Didn't anyone tell you?" I asked, my voice dampened by the wall separating us now.

"Tell me what?"

I twisted on the faucet. "Wull... I waz en duh enfirmary." My mouth was full of toothpaste foam.

"What!?" Amanda poked her head into the bathroom.

"The infirmary!?"

I spat water back into the sink and wiped my face with a towel. "Yes. I figured everyone knew about it already."

"Uh. No."

"I'm sorry I worried you," I added, pressing a hot washcloth against my face. "But since no one else knows about it yet, please don't say anything to anyone."

"I won't," she said with an honest smile. "I'm your friend. Gossip is one thing, but secrets are another. You can trust me, Val."

I'd never officially given her permission to call me that, but it was sort of endearing. Only when Amanda said it, though.

"So when did you get discharged from the infirmary?"

I left the bathroom and took a seat in the chair at my desk across from my bed. "Yesterday afternoon."

"Oh? I didn't see you at all then. Were you here?" She flopped back onto the edge of my bed.

"For a little while, just to call Lieutenant Ray, and then... um..."

"Yes?" Amanda cocked an eyebrow.

"I..." My cheeks grew warm and I was too embarrassed to say anything else.

"Oh, I know where this is going," Amanda said with a giggle. "Scandalous." She pressed her hands against her cheeks and puckered her lips, making an exaggerated look of shock.

"Hey... don't..." I looked down at the floor sheepishly. There was no hiding it from her.

"You're too cute for your own good," she said with a laugh and a nudge against my elbow. "He probably has no clue how lucky he is."

"Actually..." I shrugged. "If it weren't for him, I'd be dead right now."

"Dragons! You're kidding me!" She latched onto my arm. "It was *that* serious?"

"Yes."

"Well, I hope you at least showed him some gratitude for whatever he did for you. Kiss him yet?" She leaned closer to me. "You can tell me."

"You said you were my friend!"

"And a friend can't ask you a question like that? It's not like you two are twelve."

I sighed and crossed my arms. "There's such thing as privacy."

"Hah!" She jabbed me in the arm with her elbow. "You waived your right to that when you became my friend." She flashed a toothy, mischievous grin my way. "*Friend.*"

"You're weird."

"As long as your other *friend* appreciates a girl like that." She winked, referring to Jacksiun, as always.

Amanda was boy crazy and it seemed to get worse over

time, or perhaps it was in anticipation of the next time she'd see *him*.

"You're not letting up on that, are you?" I said.

"Nope. I keep your secret; you put in a good word about me with the lieutenant. All's fair in love and war. Right?" She snickered.

Her attitude and playful threats didn't worry me at all. Getting on my bad side was no way to get on Jacksiun's good side. Amanda knew that.

Mattheia sat quietly at his desk while we had lunch in his office, munching (almost daintily) on his sandwich while I did the same. We'd crossed the boundary beyond friendship and things couldn't be the same from here forward.

He asked if I'd regret it if he kissed me and all I did was shake my head no and move in closer, leading him to assume that my answer was, in fact, no.

"Are you alright with what happened last night?" he asked, setting his sandwich down and looking at me. "You haven't been very talkative today."

"Yes. I'm alright." I reached a hand up to adjust Mom's silver hairclip.

Could Mattheia really be there for me no matter what distance separated us? How?

I wanted to believe him and give him the chance he requested, but I also felt like I was setting myself up for heartbreak. Long distance relationships are one thing, but we would be *planets* apart, not continents.

"Whatever you're thinking right now—stop," he said, an earnest smile spreading on his lips.

I dropped my hand into my lap.

"I meant what I said; I'll fight for anything worth fighting for, and if that's *us*, then I'll fight for us."

Mattheia swept his fingers across my brow, tucking the loose hair behind my ear. Then he leaned over and kissed me on the cheek. I closed my eyes and smiled, some of my anxiety lifting as his warm lips pressed to my skin.

"Just because you only have a few months left here doesn't mean we need to rush this." His hand cupped mine and I opened my eyes.

True.

I nodded.

He let go of me and rested back in his chair, clasping his hands together.

"The captain gave us permission to return to Ajha-Ru Island," he said. "I thought it would be best for us to go as soon as possible to reduce further disruptions of your classes. Will tomorrow work for you?"

I thought on it for a moment. It was still very early in the day. I had nothing else to do and if the commander wasn't busy...

"Might we go today?" I asked.

"Today?" He paused and looked away, thinking. "I suppose nothing I have left for today can't be rescheduled for tomorrow. Today it is." He pulled out his phone and began composing a message to Captain Lansfora. "Oh." He pointed at me. "Don't forget to take some motion sickness tabs before we go."

I grinned with embarrassment.

How could I forget?

I did not want to throw up in front of my *not*-boyfriend.

Sweat caused my uniform to stick to my skin and the bone-dry desert air made me swear I'd inhaled some sand. I unscrewed the cap of my canteen and poured water into my parched mouth.

"Where is the castle?" I asked, looking out at the vast array of nothingness. Sand and more sand for as far as I could see. Mattheia had landed his jet not far from where we were, but I couldn't see anything but beige for miles.

"It's here, trust me," he replied, kneeling down to dig at the sand with his hands.

"Are you sure? I don't see anything." I bent down beside him. "What are you looking for?"

He stood and kicked another mound. Then he walked a few feet and went through all the strange motions again.

"Here! Come look!" He waved for me and I sprinted over to him. "There." He pointed excitedly at something small and shiny.

I leaned down to take a closer look at what appeared to be a chunk of crystal sticking up from the sand.

"If that's the castle, we're in trouble," I muttered, looking up at him skeptically.

"It is, but don't think I'm crazy just yet." He nudged the crystal nub with his shoe and backed away, taking me with him by the hand. "Kinasetsu, I brought her back, just like you asked!" he yelled at no one. "Stop hiding and face us, please!"

At this point, I'd begun thinking Mattheia had gotten a little overdone in the desert sun, but I tried to bite my tongue and wait it out. He'd never led me astray before.

The ground began to quake and his grasp tightened.

"*I hide from no one!*" a formidable voice boomed from out of nowhere. I gasped and staggered back. Mattheia jerked me closer.

"Don't be scared," he whispered.

A tower of sand rose up out of the ground, gleaming and catching rays of sunlight as grains tumbled off the smooth, crystalline surface. I shielded my eyes from the reflection.

"Come with me," Mattheia said, tugging me along gently.

I followed him, still covering my eyes from the painful glow searing my retinas, shaking from the subtle tremors still rippling beneath my feet.

The ground changed from soft sand to hard, solid flooring and I opened my eyes. A huge pair of double-doors stood before us, silver, encrusted with various crystals and decorated with detailed filigree engravings. I followed the door frame up several feet and my jaw dropped. They must have weighed a thousand pounds; there'd be no way we could—

The monstrous doors began to move on their own, opening toward us with surprising grace and silence. It was black as coal inside.

"It's okay, Valhara," Mattheia said, smiling confidently as he touched me softly on the back, nudging me to go ahead.

I took a step into the darkness and the unforgiving desert heat dissipated, giving way to a cooler, more comfortable temperature. The doors closed behind us and our surroundings came to life, aglow with the dancing light from at least a hundred candles set aflame on sconces at both sides of a stone hallway.

"Where are we?" I said, my breath fluttering anxiously.

"*You are in my castle,*" the mysterious voice sounded from up ahead this time.

I walked slowly, clinging to Mattheia's hand as he coaxed me through the dim hall and into a large foyer with a fireplace and enormous throne at the back. A creature cloaked in dark brown sat upon the throne, reaching a thick, greenish-yellow hand out toward us.

"Come here, child," it said in a craggy, throaty voice. "I must see you in better light."

I held my breath as I neared the thing, my heart thumping like mad against my chest and sweat beading on my forehead.

It lifted its big, round face and looked at me with glassy, bulbous eyes the size of my fist. Tiny flecks of white light sparkled from them as if they were formed of glass with swirls of iridescent dust mixed in. Scales covered the creature's face and hands and it appeared vaguely toad-like in structure. At least, that was the only thing I could think to relate it to. Toads were much less intimidating.

"I will not harm you," it said. "I gave your companion my word as a master cleric."

It was safe to assume this was the cleric who had saved my life.

Another step closer and I could see that he held a wooden box in his lap, cracked open, one hand resting in it. Small colored lights twinkled from between the cleric's long, pointed fingers.

"Are you..." The words came out with a breath.

"I am Kinasetsu, last of the Ajha-Ruvian clerics." He pinched a single, blue light between his scaly fingers and examined it, squinting his giant, reptilian eyes. "My vision is not what it once was," he said. "Now tell me exactly what *you* are." He flicked the glimmering bead of light at Mattheia and it popped in the air like a tiny fire cracker, casting a haze of soft aquamarine fog around him like a bubble. He froze completely in place.

"Mattheia!" I jolted toward him, hesitant to touch the moving particles of color that encompassed him now. I turned back toward the cleric. "What did you do to him!?"

"Tell me what you are and I will set him free," he said, narrowing his eyes. "It is as simple as that."

"What do you mean? I'm human. That's what I am. What do you want to hear!?" I stepped closer, squeezing my hands into fists and clenching my jaw. "Let him go!"

A flicker of amber-red light splashed my vision and the cleric's eyes widened with fear.

"Calm yourself, girl," he said, leaning back in his throne. "I do not need you setting fire to my castle."

"Don't call me girl. My name is Valhara. Lieutenant Valhara Hawksford of Celestial Galaxy Academy. That is who I am. Now let him go, please!" I glanced back at Mattheia.

"Yes, Lieutenant Valhara Hawksford of Celestial Galaxy Academy. I will let him go, but you must answer my question. It is very important that you look deeper inside to find the answer." The cleric stood from his throne and set the box of light beside it, then shuffled over and looked down at me. He stood well more than two feet taller, easily, but I wasn't intimidated anymore. Not by his round, toady features or the giant mouth that stretched across his face and could probably eat a cat whole.

"You fought a mahora spider, did you not?" he asked, lowering his face toward mine.

"Yes."

"How did you kill it?"

"I-I don't remember."

"Do not remember? Or do not wish to remember?"

I really didn't remember anything about the fight, aside from the damage Mattheia had taken.

"Your sword. Show it to me."

I reached behind my back and wrapped my fingers slowly around the grip, then I carefully tugged the blade free of the specially-forged hybrid-magnets. The brassy metal had been discolored by a sooty-black fringe and it left an imprint of ash on my hands as I held it out for the cleric to see.

"A phoenix blade," he said with a nod. "Those are very rare. Are you certain you can remember nothing about the event with the mahora? You should trust in your sword to remind you of the reality of the ordeal. Think carefully about the battle."

I looked at the Azure Phoenix and followed the jagged, deeply serrated edge of the blade up to the guard.

I remembered...

The ground disappearing from beneath my feet.

Bright light—red color flashing through my vision as I squeezed the grip in both hands while facing the beast.

A wave of heat flushing through my body, making me feel sickly hot and cold simultaneously.

I had lifted the sword and brought it down onto the rampaging spider, slicing it in two as it plowed into me.

Then I hit ground and collapsed.

That was all I could remember.

"There is nothing to be ashamed of, Lieutenant Valhara—"

"Call me Valhara."

"Valhara, be proud of what you are," Kinasetsu said. "It is a gift given only to a chosen few."

"I don't know what you're talking about." I sneered, lifted my sword up over my shoulder, and snapped it back into its scabbard. I turned my head; Mattheia was still petrified by light. I walked over to him and ran my fingers through the cool, dusty aura. "What if I ignore this and pretend it never happened?"

"You cannot ignore the fate you have been dealt. You are an Elemental Guardian and you have been granted the gift of flame. I wish only to help you. Some past Guardians abused their gifts and disregarded the true purpose of their abilities. You must allow me to train you before it is too late."

"Too late? What does that mean?"

Kinasetsu waved his hand through the air and revealed a smoky apparition—a row of ornate gemstone amulets of different colors and metals. "There were Guardians before you." His fingers sifted through the image until all but one of the amulets disappeared. "Very few have survived Tryamour's Wrath." The final necklace vanished.

"Come. I will show you more." He turned his back on me and walked around his throne to the wall behind it.

"What about Mattheia?" I glanced at him again. Still as a statue.

"He is in no danger." Kinasetsu placed his hand upon the fireplace mantle and whispered something I could not understand. The fireplace shifted and wrinkled like paint being smudged around a canvas. Kinasetsu stepped forward through the wall and gestured for me to follow.

I held my breath and passed through the masonry as if it were nothing but a curtain of mist. On the other side was a library filled with shelves carved from more crystal.

"You are aware the mahora spider has been extinct for centuries?" the cleric asked while approaching one of the bookshelves. He reached his hand up and trailed his long, snake-like finger along the shelf as he searched for a specific title.

"Yes. I had read about them in books as a child."

"Then you should know it was not a mere coincidence that the beast found you and your companion so easily upon that island." He plucked a small book with a gilded golden spine from the shelf. "They are collectors of rare artifacts, but they also cannot thrive in dry, dusty environments. They are like the chameleon—they require a damp, jungle habitat in order to live." The cleric pried the book open between his fingers and revealed a page full of images to me.

A drawing of someone in the grips of a great battle with an enormous serpent. Splashes of color dotted the sketchy, black-ink design. A ray of blue light was being emitted from the person's hands.

"It was your first test—the test that awakened your power." He turned the page to an image of the same character kneeling on the ground, crumpled over what appeared to be another person lying... dead?

"What does this page mean?" I asked, not really wanting to know the answer.

"Failure," he said flatly, clapping the book closed beneath my nose. "A mistake you cannot make, and how your next encounter will end if you refuse my training."

"*Next* encounter?" I wrinkled my lips skeptically. The cleric had been living alone on the island for far too long. "It was an accident. A freak accident. Everyone knows the president's academies have been experimenting with genetic mutations for years. The island was abandoned by the Mainlands and maybe the government threw one of the accidents there hoping no one would notice. I don't know how to explain it, but that book is wrong. I control my own fate."

"No!" Kinasetsu's voice rose rigidly. "It is not possible. Tryamour has been performing her own *tests* for centuries. I have witnessed too many Guardians die at her vengeful hands. Do not become one of them."

Legendary weapons were one thing, but whatever he was talking about was too far-fetched for my tastes. I'd never even heard about these so-called "Guardians" before today, and I had done a good share of research on ancient mythology.

"Kinasetsu, I don't know exactly what happened to me on that island, but trauma can distort one's memories. So can being alone on a desert island for hundreds of years. We were attacked by a feral creature, I fought it off, and I ended up in the hospital. Nothing more. Nothing less." I wiped remnants of dusty black soot from my hands onto my slacks. "Please let me go." I turned to head back toward the throne room.

"Wait. At least take this," he said, just as I approached the wispy wall between this room and the next. He scuttled over to me and held the book out. "Please."

I turned, reluctantly, and looked down at the old, leather-bound tome balanced in his scaly fingers. I didn't want it, but I knew the cleric was a powerful old one, even if he was a little crazy. Refusing to take the thing may have offended him and I didn't want to do that, not while Mattheia still stood trapped in time and bound by some magic spell in the other room.

"Alright." I reached up and grasped the hefty book with both hands. Flakes of leather came off as my fingers gripped it and I brought it in close to my chest. "Now please let Mattheia go. We have to return to the academy."

Kinasetsu nodded in agreement, and we stepped through the fireplace illusion once more.

With a flick of his long, wiggly fingers, Kinasetsu freed Mattheia from the spell.

"What?" he asked, glancing at me. "What is he talking about?"

I had to think on it a moment to remember the last thing he'd heard us say.

'Tell me what you are,' Kinasetsu had said just before freezing Mattheia.

"I'm a girl who fought a mahora spider and survived because of what you did for me," I said, walking up to him, smiling. "Throughout history, very few people have ever been that lucky."

His brow furrowed and he thought on it for a moment, confused, but unsure what else to say as the cleric had seemingly lost interest in the question, as far as Mattheia could tell.

"Yes," Kinasetsu said. "It seems fate is on her side."

"We can go now." I tucked the book under my arm nonchalantly. It caught Mattheia's attention and he tipped his head to the side.

"Where'd you get that?"

"I gave it to her," Kinasetsu said, lifting his hand from his lap to make a subtle movement through the air. "And I am returning this to you."

Mattheia looked down at his side and gasped. Dangling at his hip was a leather and chain scabbard holding the Pegasus Sword.

I veered my head toward the cleric.

"You were right about her, boy," he said, lifting his large, round head slightly. "She is more valuable than the sword."

The weeks that passed following our visit to Kinasetsu made me stronger; little evidence remained that I had ever been hospitalized. And, although he had not actually shown me it, Mattheia assured me the mahora's mark on his chest had completely healed.

I kept the book Kinasetsu had given me, but I tucked it away in my suitcase that same day and hadn't taken it out since. I'd add it to my collection of antiquities once I was home at Celestial Galaxy.

Home.

I'd be back with my sister and Jacksiun soon, and Mattheia and I would part ways.

While I hadn't necessarily abstained from his company, during the final month of my stay at Silver Diamond, I had done my best to put some distance between us, even if only in my mind.

His mother's dog, Daisy, had stopped barking at me and had even jumped up onto my lap a few times for a scruff behind her fuzzy ears—that says a lot. But despite the pleasant weekend dinners at his house, and the serene moments Mattheia and I spent on the roof of Silver Diamond, I kept telling myself to stay focused on the bigger picture.

I wouldn't go home broken; I wouldn't return to my duties at C.G. with emotional baggage. This wasn't about my happiness. Captain Ventresca had sent me to Silver Diamond to do a job, and that's what I would do.

With the final few weeks of my term fast approaching, I began to work on the proposal to submit to Officer Meadows. She would review the document and then forward it to Captain Lansfora if everything looked good. Amanda helped me arrange everything, offering suggestions on how to better incorporate effective transitions for both academies. Upon completion, Officer Meadows would give me a special packet of proposed terms for me to release to Captain Ventresca upon my return.

We would remain independently governed, but the president of the Mainlands would have the final say in any and all changes either academy chose to undergo.

"I'm leaving next week," I said firmly, glancing over at Mattheia as he sat beside me on the roof, looking up at the sky. He hadn't said a word in several minutes. "Mattheia?" I scooted closer to him and he turned his head to look me in the eye. Without saying anything, he reached up to cup the back of my head. He pulled me forward and kissed my brow, then let up just enough to touch his forehead to mine, closing his eyes as he sighed softly.

"I know," he whispered, his hand sliding down to my neck.

"Then... why aren't you saying anything?" I withdrew and scowled. "Why are you acting as though nothing is going to change?"

"Because nothing has to change."

I stood. "*Everything's* going to change."

He came to his feet and narrowed his eyes at me. "All this time, you've been struggling to pretend you don't have feelings for me, while I have been here from the very beginning, waiting for you to decide what you wanted—whatever that was. And now you're telling me that all has to go away?" He took my hand and grasped it firmly. "I already told you I'm willing to work for this. You and I are good for each other. You've seen that in action. You still haven't made up your mind?"

I'd made up my mind when I'd let him kiss me, but now I couldn't wrap it around how I'd make this work. It scared me to think about how much time we'd spend apart and how long I'd be alone up there in space.

"I have to go back to Celestial Galaxy," I said, my voice breaking as I jerked my hand from his. "You're a pilot, Mattheia; you should know that a standard transport ship takes two days to get here. That's four days of travel, not counting the time I'd stay on Earth. I can't take off that much time whenever I feel like it."

"So we'll see each other between terms, then."

"You're the high commander, next in line to Captain Lansfora if the Mainlands requires your service. You can't leave to come see me, and you know I hate traveling. I don't know when we *can* see other again. I'm going to be stationed at C.G. for a very long time and being separated from you for that long might—"

"Might what, Valhara?" His voice remained soft and comforting. He reached up to caress my cheek with his warm palm. "Might make me forget about *us*? Might make me betray you, or cheat? Is that what you're afraid of? After everything I've done to earn your trust, why would I do anything like that?"

"Distance changes people." I broke eye contact with him and looked off to the side.

"I know you're scared and that this will be hard on you.

It will be hard on us both, but we can work something out. Maybe…" he shrugged, "get you transferred here permanently."

"Transferred!?" I stepped back, escaping his grasp. "You want me to give up my friends and family for you?"

"No! Th-that's not what I meant. I—"

"You've said enough. I get it, you're willing to sacrifice a lot for this, but I don't know if I am. I'm just not strong enough, Mattheia."

Intense sadness washed over his face and his solemn gaze of disbelief made my chest ache. I had to let him go, even if he didn't want to let go of me. I really didn't want to hurt him like that, but it was for the best. We could focus on our jobs, not on how many light-years separated us.

I turned and started walking back toward the maintenance hatch. "Thank you for everything you've done for me. I'm sorry we can't be together," I said. I climbed down to the main floor, gritting my teeth as tears of regret welled in my eyes.

It had been several months since I'd seen the tall, raven-haired young-man with sky-blue eyes behind thin metal frames of glass.

"Nice to see you again, Lieutenant," Jacksiun said with a

familiar smile.

I resisted the unprofessional urge to hug my best friend in front of other personnel. We met on the academy tarmac in front of the Goliath. Private Quill had accompanied me and Commander Draven was supposed to be there, too, but had yet to arrive.

"Nice to see you, too, my friend." I grinned, unable to hide my happiness. "This is Private First Class Amanda Quill," I said, gesturing to her as she stood at attention beside me, much quieter than I'd become accustomed to.

"A pleasure to meet you, Private Quill," he said reaching out a hand. Her firm, eager handshake caught him off-guard. His brow wrinkled briefly, but he brushed it off with a quick smile. "I've heard good things about you from Lieutenant Hawksford."

"Glad to hear it," Amanda said, nudging me in the arm.

"Would you care to join me on a brief walk around the Goliath?" he asked with a flourish of his hand toward the massive gunmetal craft behind us.

"I'd be honored," she replied, beaming. I could only imagine how much excitement bounced around inside her despite her calm outward appearance. They walked off toward the ship and I imagined Jacksiun was quick to begin pointing out the important features of Celestial Galaxy's prestigious craft.

"Lieutenant?"

I turned my head the direction of the voice.

Mattheia.

"Commander, you came?"

"Why wouldn't I have?" he asked, his lips pressing thin. "As high commander, I am obligated to see you off on your departure." His tone was frigid.

Obligated?

I looked into his eyes and he lifted his head slightly as our gazes met.

"I wish you a safe trip back," he said stiffly. Then he raised his hand to his brow and saluted me, something only subordinates typically did to someone of my rank. "We thank you for your work here, Lieutenant. Captain Lansfora sends his regards."

The coldness of his words made me feel terrible, but there was nothing I could do. I'd made my choice and I'd told him we were finished. There wasn't anything else to say. It hurt. Both of us, I assumed, and as much as I wanted to imagine us together, I couldn't dedicate that much of myself to a cause not in line with my academy duties.

"Thank you, Commander," I replied, saluting him in return as I heard Jacksiun and Amanda approaching from behind.

I watched sunlight sparkle off the shimmering silver trim along Mattheia's collar and took in a deep breath of Earth air. The humor and affection had faded from his expression and only unfamiliar sternness remained. It wasn't a good look for him, but it was a mask he now wore because of me. Maybe I shouldn't have shattered his heart the way I had. Maybe I shouldn't have forced him away and convinced myself we couldn't be together, despite his willingness to try.

It wasn't like I would regret the soothing, clean smell of his presence or the way his smile lit up when I came into the room.

It wasn't like I would regret Mattheia's warm fingers on my skin or his careful, patient kiss upon my lips...

We need to talk!" My sister, Atira, watched me exercising in the training hall. It was late in the evening and other students had already come and gone, so it was only the two of us in the large, insulated black and white gymnasium.

"About... what?" I grunted, hacking into the composite mannequin with my sword again, chipping away at the target marks. "Can't you... see... I'm busy?" I jerked my sword free from the dummy and wiped sweat from my forehead with my sleeve. My palms ached from squeezing the grip of my blade.

"Valhara, please," Atira said, infringing upon my training

perimeter, while remaining a safe distance from my sword.

"I don't want to discuss it right now." I raised my sword over my head and struck down at an angle, chopping the plastic head clean off. "Good thing... these are composite." I bent over to catch my breath and heaved a sigh, balancing both hands on the grip of the Azure Phoenix. "You should train with a sword more often, Atira." I glanced up at her. She stood with a hand on her hip and a look of discontent on her face. Eyes narrowed. Lips thinned.

"What?" I straightened up and snapped my sword onto my back.

"We *need* to talk," she repeated, glaring at me like avoiding the conversation further would *not* be an option.

"Okay. What is it?" I scooped up my towel from just outside the training box and dabbed my face. Wishful thinking had me hoping it was about her and the captain, but...

"You haven't been yourself for days. What happened to you at Silver Diamond?"

"Nothing."

"Really? I'm your sister, Valhara, you can tell me anything."

"And I'm yours," I said with an angry huff, glaring at her judgmentally. "I've never kept secrets from you before and I never thought there'd be a time when you'd start keeping them from me. Why didn't you trust me enough to tell me you and the captain were—"

"Oh!" Her eyes widened. "Oh, Valhara!" She grimaced and brought her hands to her mouth. "I didn't know you knew."

"Well, I did. But I'd much rather have had it confirmed by you instead of Jacksiun."

"I-I didn't know he knew, too. I was going to tell you both, I swear." She reached to grasp my shoulders.

"When?"

"Not soon enough, and I'm sorry. I should have told you before you left, but I didn't want it to interfere with your assignment. I wasn't sure how you'd take it."

"I would have felt better knowing. Besides, I like Captain Ventresca—you know that." I shrugged and raised my eyebrows. "Not enough to want to *date* him, but..." I shook off the awkward feeling. In my opinion, the captain was out of my age bracket, but not too old for my sister.

"I see that now, and I apologize again for my mistake. I didn't know it would come to this, but it did."

And to think, I'd been dating the high commander of Silver Diamond and not told her a thing about that, either. This wasn't about me, though.

"Then now's the time to tell you the truth. All of it." She gestured toward the benches along the entrance wall. "You may want to sit for this."

My sister was marrying our captain.

No dates had been set, but he'd already asked her and she'd already said 'yes.' His service term would be over soon and she wanted to move back to the Mainlands with him once he was discharged.

This came on top of other bad news.

"Why didn't you tell me, Jacksiun!?" I crossed my arms and stared at him, adrenaline pumping through me as my heart raced.

"You knew I filed for the transfer to Aquarius before you left for Silver Diamond. I didn't expect them to accept it this quickly, either!" He folded the acceptance letter and tucked it into his shirt pocket. "I wanted to tell you earlier—I was excited about it, even—but I didn't want to disrupt your studies at Silver Diamond."

"Why is everyone afraid to tell me things lately? What's with all the secrets? I'm not a fragile little glass flower."

"I-I didn't know what you were going to do about the commander." He shrugged and tipped his head apologetically.

"What does he have to do with anything?"

"Maybe you might want to transfer, too, or—"

"I broke up with him."

"What?" He scoffed at me, for what I think was the first time ever. "Why would you do that? He cares about you and he..." He paused and wrinkled his brow. "He *loves* you, Valhara."

"I don't need the stress of a long-distance relationship weighing on me."

"So when I get transferred to Aquarius, does that mean it's over for us as friends, too?"

"Don't say that!" I thrust my arms down my sides and clenched my fists.

"You just said you broke up with Commander Draven because you were afraid of the distance. Same thing, right?" His blue irises began to shimmer with worry as warm color flushed his face and the edges of his eyes reddened.

"No. Well, yes, but... no. I can go a few months without seeing you and we can still talk over video chats like always. It's different when you're *involved* with someone. Maybe I can't go months without seeing *him*."

Jacksiun stepped closer to me and wrapped a hand around my forearm. "I understand, Valhara. But I also think Draven isn't the type of man to let go without a fight. He sacrificed a lot for you down there—to save your life. And no, you're not obligated to be in a relationship with him because of something like that, but if you have feelings for him at all, you should *think* about the possibility of finding a way to make it work. He deserves at least that much."

"I already told him I couldn't."

"It may not be too late to take back what you said." He gently squeezed my arm. "People say rash things when they're under pressure."

"I've made my decision, Jacksiun." I cleared my throat to stop my voice from breaking again. "Please don't try to change my mind."

"And I've made mine." He smiled and then reached his other arm up around my shoulders and hugged me tightly. "No amount of distance will stop us from being friends. I'll be here for you no matter what—even if I can't be *here* at Celestial Galaxy."

The people I loved were slipping away from me.

In a matter of hours.

I couldn't sleep. I just lay there in my bed with my eyes squeezed shut, trying to block out the world. My mind raced like a jet engine; every sound kept me awake. The subtle whirring of the ventilation system. The thumping of my own heartbeat through my fingertips as I clutched my pillow.

I opened my eyes and stared at the wall on the opposite side of the room. Why couldn't I stop ruminating? Mattheia didn't deserve to have his heart broken, but I was frightened and I made a decision I thought would be best for us both.

My stomach churned from the sickening thoughts. Had the universe decided to punish me by sending both my sister and best friend away? I closed my eyes again, my body settling more deeply into the bed.

Green color flooded my vision and a forest surrounded me, foliage glistening with dew in the warm light of spring. Beams of golden sun shone down from branches overhead, peeking through vibrant leaves dancing in the breeze.

A rustle in the distance made me turn.

I gasped.

A unicorn!?

The large, muscular draft horse stood regal and tall—his withers barely at eye level. His rich coat was dark teal, and his feathered feet blended up into his strong legs in shades of lighter greenish-blues.

Malachite?

Yes. His name was Malachite. I knew this much to be true.

He approached with caution, each step of his massive hooves making the ground rumble gently beneath my feet. The stallion came face to face with me, his mystical, bright amber-yellow eyes crisp and alert. I fearlessly lifted a hand to fork my fingers through his striking crimson mane. Deep cherry-red strands intertwined with bright red locks and flowed in luxurious waves.

Malachite lowered his head and nudged me with his muzzle, tilting his face to avoid piercing me with the long golden horn protruding from his forehead. I nestled my fingers into the teal softness of his coat and roughed it a bit, releasing a plume of dust into the air as my hand drifted over his neck.

"You have been rolling in the dirt again, my friend." I chuckled, patting him firmly. He snorted and nudged me, flapping his lips playfully at the beaded sash around my waist.

I combed my fingers through his mane again, this time, tugging out some tangles and plucking broken bits of twigs from between the strands.

Then I heard loud voices shouting in the distance, words echoing through the trees from every direction. Malachite nuzzled me again, the fearful whites of his eyes beginning to show. I had to get away from this place. Someone was hunting me. Hunting *us*...

My unicorn knelt before me and I hiked up my dress and climbed onto his back, clutching to his mane with all my strength. We set off into a swift but smooth gallop, gliding over broken trees and bounding past thick forest brush. I trusted his intuition; my Spirit knew where to take me, and I let him run until he felt we were safe.

"Emerald!" a man called.

Malachite's pace slowed to a trot and then he halted at the sight of movement. A knight in a full suit of gleaming silver armor stretched his arm up into the air to signal to us as we neared.

The detail etched in his chest plate was uniquely his and

I recognized my husband instantly.

"Ortainius, you must go!" Malachite brought me closer to him and I reached down to grasp his hand. "They will come for you, too, if you do not leave this place at once."

"They are already searching for me, my love," he said with a solemn glance into the distant woods behind me. "Go as far as you can, Emerald. Do not let them catch you. Use your gift. Use anything at your disposal." He rubbed the bridge of Malachite's snout and reached around to pat him on the neck. "I know we have been at odds in the past, my beastly friend," he said with his forehead pressed to the horse's nose, "but I know you love her as much as I do."

Malachite nodded and snorted loudly in response, stamping a hoof into the dirt. I felt my beloved Spirit's heart swell with confidence and pride as he neighed in agreement.

"Ah! There is the ornery, formidable creature I have come to know," Ortainius said with a bittersweet grin. "Take care of my love, Malachite. Protect her with your life and I will do the same."

Ortainius backed away solemnly and pointed into the distance. "Go! Run like the wind and do not look back!"

I did not want to leave him there, for I knew in my heart that he would perish in his attempt to save me from my fate. A courageous knight would die because he chose to love the wrong woman... because he chose to love the secret half-sister of King Arthur Pendragon of Alyssia. I became the second Elemental Guardian in the bloodline, and one the king assumed to be a threat despite my desire to stay hidden.

I held fast to Malachite's mane, my fingers entangled deep within the crimson waves, as we raced through the forest, vines and branches bending to my will to let us pass and young trees folding over and out of our way. Powerful, feathered hooves pounded the earth, tossing up rocks and detritus with each stride until he leapt into the air and came upon a clearing.

Dirt. Mud. Broken trees. I veered my head around fearfully, realizing a trap had been set.

A row of sharpened wooden spires had been planted around the perimeter of the pit, leaving us with no way out. I looked up. The nearest tree was several feet away and, while I could bend it, it was not growing near enough to reach us. Malachite kicked up dirt and snorted angrily, his rising fears tainting my own sanity.

We turned several times, confronted by more and more pikes pointed our way, surrounding us completely—too tall to scale. I lifted a hand to summon the woods to my aide. It would take time, but I felt the presence of friends nearby.

"You cannot escape," a voice boomed from an overhang above. I craned my neck to look up.

Arthur loomed over me, his sword, Excalibur, glistening in his grasp.

"Brother!?"

"I am no brother to you, witch!" His bright chain mail and breastplate reflected the sun and I had to shield my eyes from the searing light. There were rustling sounds moving through the trees. I glanced up to see an army of fully-armored knights marching our way.

"Coward!" I screamed, still clinging tightly to Malachite's mane, even as he twitched nervously beneath me. "You carry the same burden as I, and yet you abuse your power!" I raised a hand toward him and called upon the roots of a nearby eldertree to steal away his beloved sword. A trio of thick-brown roots sprouted from the ground and ensnared Excalibur, jerking it from his grasp and then pulling it down into the earth.

A knight by Arthur's side plummeted to his knees and began digging frantically in the dirt.

"Do not waste your time searching for the sword," Arthur said. "She will find her way back to me. I can take the witch down without it. You and the others, destroy the beast!" He pointed at us—at Malachite.

"Let me down!" I tugged his mane and he hesitated at first, curving his neck back to look me in the eye and question my request. "Please, my friend," I asked again, gazing at him with determination and confidence.

He huffed angrily and stamped the ground several times before finally lowering his body and allowing me to dismount. I fell to my knees and pressed my hands into the soft, damp earth, closing my eyes as I called to *them* again, speaking in words that were not my mother-tongue—words which came to me as a chant, as if an unseen force guided my lips to speak them.

The ground rumbled and I opened my eyes as a stampede of fur and flesh plowed toward us, a clamor of wild beasts bounding to our aide. A knight crashed into the brush, felled by a powerful wildcat, his companion assailed by a pack of wolves that had erupted from the forest.

I rushed to the edge of the clearing and reached for one of the wood pikes, pulling it with all my strength in an attempt to dislodge it from the ground and make clearance for Malachite to pass through. A hearty roar rang out and a hulking brown bear trampled another knight in an effort to reach me. The bear bent her head and locked onto the spear with her powerful jaws. She tugged with all her might, slowly freeing it from the ground.

"Hurry!" I cried, wrapping my hands around another one. An enormous elk approached, lending his antlers to help catch the stake as it tipped over so it wouldn't crush me.

Arthur stood over us on the cliffside and swirled his hands through the air, sending a flurry of dust and leaves up to block the second oncoming wave of animals. He flicked his hand and launched a large timber wolf into a nearby tree, incapacitating it on impact. He had the upper hand with his armed, armored knights, but my creatures swiftly worked to diminish their numbers.

Another pike dislodged from our path.

We were almost free of the pit!

As the brown bear worked out the final spike that would let us pass, an arrow whistled through the air, striking her in the throat and sending her plummeting to the ground. Arthur leapt from the overhang and coasted gracefully down to the ground with the help of his powers. He landed across from us on the other side of the clearing.

Malachite whinnied with fear and pawed at the dirt, preparing to charge. He whipped his tail, lowered his head, and stormed after him, his gleaming golden horn poised for combat.

A sharp, riveting pain tore through my side and I fell, screaming. My fingers drifted toward the wound; a crossbow arrow had pierced me below the ribs, penetrating my stomach. Malachite neighed in agony and slid across the dirt headfirst, his pain mirroring my own.

"Kill the Guardian," Arthur said with a snarl, "kill the Spirit."

"Malachite!" I coughed, spitting up red.

Humming sounded overhead and I glanced up. A flock of arrows soared through the air and, at Arthur's command, spiraled toward me.

Unable to run, I closed my eyes and held my breath, fearing for my life and the lives of my animal friends.

A thunderous neigh rang out along with the sweeping sound of a thousand arrow fletchings whizzing past.

My eyes reeled opened only to witness my magnificent Spirit crashing down at my feet, a pool of blood quickly accumulating around his body.

"Malachite!" I dropped beside him and ran my fingers across his withers, stroking his trembling flesh as he fought to get in each panicked breath.

There must have been a dozen arrows sticking from his side and no way for me to remove them without bleeding him dry almost instantly. I could heal him with magic, if...

But the dirt pit contained little living earth to call upon and there were no healing plants within reach. Not ones that could sooth such a deep, widespread injury.

I forked my fingers through his curly scarlet mane and bent down to hug him, my own side aching from the arrow still lodged there. I sat back a moment and reached across to grasp the arrow tightly, then I bit down on my sleeve and snapped the arrow off at the entry point. My muffled scream made Malachite lift his head.

His golden amber eyes glistened with fear and pain and I felt sadness and defeat coursing through his veins. He flailed in the dirt, trying to right himself so he could stand, but it was impossible.

"I'm sorry, my friend," I whispered, leaning in close to his head. He rested his face on the dirt and choked on a strained breath. "You did your best to protect me. Thank you." I kissed his brow and pressed my fingers against his golden horn, quieting him.

Arthur watched us from a distance.

"This is why you were never given a Spirit!" I roared, the warmth of Malachite's innocent blood now staining my hands. "You have no honor in your heart! You are not worthy of their companionship."

"Hush, witch!" He swiped his hand through the air and a gush of wind swept up around us, tearing the final breath from Malachite's lungs.

"No!" I came to my feet as my Spirit's life-force drifted away, a great emptiness filling my soul. He froze stiff, and his body turned translucent-white and smooth as if it had been carved of fine stone. "I wanted to live a quiet life. I did not want anything to do with you, your family, or your throne!"

The knights that had survived the onslaught approached, surrounding me from all sides, stepping over fallen beasts that had given themselves to my cause.

"You are a witch, girl! And a liar!" Arthur replied, pointing at me scornfully. "Your powers have no place on this Earth. I am the king, and I am the only one worthy of this gift."

"The Earth has chosen us both." I stumbled closer, holding my fingers across my wound as the blood continued to drain down my side, discoloring my ivory dress. "I am your sister and you know it in your bones."

"You bewitched the forest animals, just as you bewitched my horse to throw my daughter. Murderer!"

Arthur's daughter had died not long ago in a riding accident, but I had nothing to do with it. Still, he sought me out in his thirst for blind vengeance. I only wanted to be left alone with my husband. There was not a shred of contempt in my heart for my brother's tortured soul. Not until now.

"I wanted peace, Brother! I did nothing to harm your family. The animals here... they were coming to my side because they knew I was in the right to defend myself. I am no witch, despite your desire to paint me as such." I stumbled, the arrow head delving deeper into my organs. "If I could," I said, coughing hard, struggling to breathe with the searing ache, "I'd curse you and every one of your kind. You would be the last Guardian to soil this precious Earth with your filth and discord. But, I am no witch... and my magic does not lend itself to the same evil as yours."

I came down onto my hands and knees and pressed my fingers into the dirt, calling upon the strength of the ancient wilderness to guide my actions. "Help me!" I groaned, glancing again at Malachite's lifeless body which was now immortalized in frosted white stone. Perhaps nature would allow me one last chance to avenge her children from the corrupt Wind Guardian. I closed my eyes and surrendered my soul to the request, crouching over dirt and rocks even as the arrowhead continued to bury itself deeper into me.

Then a sudden shock of heat poured through my veins.

My nails stretched beyond my fingertips, changing from clear to black as they curled downward into rigid scythes. Thick reddish fur sprouted between my fingers while my arms and legs elongated, bones twisting and cracking as they shifted. My face widened and stretched outward, growing into a powerful, cat-like muzzle with sharpened, lengthened teeth.

A mane of crimson flecked with white sprouted around my neck, and thousands of tiny, iridescent green scales pushed through my skin, forming a line from my long, wiry tail to the tip of my nose. Like a decorative helmet accent, a downward hook protruded from the end of my snout to protect my nostrils and part of my jaw like a vestigial beak repurposed for impaling prey. Monstrous paws pushed off the dirt, lifting me up onto my hind legs.

I growled and flexed my claws anxiously, eying the remaining knights as the saliva of anticipation saturated my mouth.

Part dragon. Part lion. And a shard of man encased inside a huge, battle-worn beast. I'd been transformed into an ancient bloodmane—named such because of the vivid red splashes staining the creature's mane following a kill.

A riot broke out among the remaining knights and Arthur

worked frantically to quiet them as I lurched closer, injured still, but less aware of it now that the arrow had been suppressed by my stronger form.

I lunged after him, kicking my back feet into the dry terrain to gather the force necessary to make myself airborne. A gust of wind knocked me back into the pit before I could clear the wooden pikes and I thumped onto the dirt on my side, snorting loudly as the breath was knocked from my lungs.

"I will defeat her myself!" Arthur shouted, fanning his hands out to the sides. He levitated off the ground, a spiral of leaves and dust kicking up into a cyclone below his feet as he floated up and over the spikes to drop down into the pit with me.

I pawed at the earth, baring my fangs and wrinkling my lips into a nasty snarl. "I do not want to fight you, Brother." The words came clumsily off my beastly tongue. "But I will defend myself. Let me and my husband live in peace."

"Your husband? The traitor, Ortainius?" He laughed wickedly and sneered. "He will pay for betraying my orders and consorting with a witch."

None of us were safe from the king's misguided rage and his erroneous definition of witchcraft. His mind had been clouded by greed and power and we had both become targets of the vengeful fire fueled evermore by the loss of his daughter at the hands of fate.

My muscular body coiled low to the ground and then I charged. He swept a flight of arrows up from the ground and launched them toward me. I ducked and rolled to dodge a few, too slow to avoid them all. Arrow heads struck me in the back, knocking scales clean off my skin as metal embedded into the furry flesh hidden beneath. I reared, roaring in pain.

"It would be easy to kill you with metal and wood," Arthur growled, stepping back. "But I can deal a more fitting punishment. If you claim to be a Guardian of earth and nature, then may you be buried with the very thing you covet."

The ground shook and my feet sunk into the dirt as a chasm ripped open beneath me. I pawed frantically at the dusty ground but could not grasp on to anything more than tumbling rocks and detritus. I slipped farther and farther down into a hole carved out by a swirl of wind and stone, until it was so deep I could no longer see out of it. I thrust my body at the side and scrambled to grab the ledge but tumbled off and onto my back, the arrows in me shifting in place, causing me to cower in agony.

The abyss deepened and I continued to sink. I looked up and called out to my brother with my last ounce of strength.

He ignored me.

A plume of dirt and rocks fell upon my face and I shook my head, blinking as grit scratched my eyes. A deep, throaty howl poured from my mouth toward the sky, and the earth swallowed me up, blanketing me in eternal darkness.

I reeled out of my sleep and sat up in my bed, panting hard, trying to catch my breath. My throat hurt and the taste of fresh dirt tainted my tongue. I pulled my legs out from under my covers and set my feet on the floor, my entire body aching. Every breath was difficult to get in and it felt like a heavy weight pressed against me. The poor woman—Emerald. She didn't deserve to die like that, buried by her own brother.

Something fluttered on my shelf and I jerked my head toward the commotion.

The book Kinasetsu had given me...

I stood and crept over to the bookshelf, watching the pile of paperwork from Silver Diamond shudder as the book danced beneath it. In an instant, I snatched the book from the shelf, grasping it tightly in my fingers as if it were an animal. The movement ceased and the book remained still within my hands.

Though the images inside were ones that left me unsettled—ghastly visions of sorcery and death—I was compelled to crack open the thing again. My hands trembled as I wrapped my fingers around the edges of the cover and pried it back. A flash of orange erupted from inside and I pulled away, turning my face to avoid the raging burst of fire that rose from the pages, licking violently at the air. I dropped the book onto my bed.

Smoke filled the room and I began choking in the inky blackness.

"You are not worthy," a voice writhed through my ears, twisting into my brain from all around me.

"Who are you?" I asked, stumbling back until I'd cornered myself against a wall. "What do you want from me!?" I batted at the smoke, coughing as I tried to cover my mouth with my shirt.

"You do not deserve your gift," the voice hissed, a wisp of cold breath tickling my ear. I swerved, only to see more nothingness in the cloud of dark consuming my room. Then I felt pressure on my throat—hands wrapping around my neck. I reached up to fight them off but there was nothing there but pressure. I felt it—*someone*—latching onto me and squeezing my airway closed. I tried to cry for help.

Nothing came out.

I was dying at the hands of someone or... something I couldn't even see!

Smoke stung my eyes.

My lips formed words that wouldn't manifest as sounds.

Why couldn't I see them? Why couldn't I see the face of my murderer!?

I jolted awake—again—in my bed at Celestial Galaxy.

Alone.

A throbbing headache pounded in my forehead, but it was a pain I'd rarely experienced. My gaze darted toward my bookshelf. The book was there, buried beneath the pile of paperwork just as it had been in the dream. I sucked in a quick breath, remaining there for several moments, my blanket pulled up to my chest and my fingers clutching a corner of the soft fabric.

It was only a book. Right? And it was only a dream that had frightened me. I was an adult—a lieutenant up for promotion soon—and shouldn't have been shaken by a silly old book.

I slid out of my bed, stood, and then inched closer to my bookshelf, reaching an arm out and shoving my fingers beneath the paperwork to fish out the book. It appeared from the stash, its gilded pages glistening as light shone upon them. I took a deep breath and turned open the cover.

The first page was blank.

I flipped to the next.

Blank.

And the next.

Blank.

I quickly riffled through the entire book.

All the pages were bare.

I released the book into one hand and used the other to cup my forehead. The headache was intensifying, making me cringe.

But the book... its pages... What had happened to them all? There were images—sketches on every page when Kinasetsu had given it to me. Now, the entire tome was empty.

Then the voice from my dream haunted me in my memories.

'You are not worthy,' it had said to me.

Worthy? Of... what?

My powers?

Kinasetsu had warned me of something he called 'Tryamour's Wrath,' but I'd ignored him back then because it had seemed so absurd.

Would I be consumed by my own fire if I didn't learn how to wield it properly, or would the woman in my dream come after me?

I clapped the book closed and took a deep breath.

I had to return to the island.

I must take leave," I said firmly, back straight, knees locked, and feet planted on the floor of the captain's office. It was an audacious move, but I couldn't take no for an answer.

"This is an awfully bold request of you, Lieutenant," Captain Ventresca replied, his brow wrinkling. "It's not a matter of 'yes' or 'no.' I cannot simply let you take leave because you've asked me. You should have put in this request a long time ago; the pre-approval alone can take weeks."

"I apologize, Captain, but this is..." I cleared my throat and heaved a breath. "This is a pertinent matter that cannot wait. I must go." Sickness brewed in my stomach as thoughts of being discharged flitted by. The captain had no reason to say yes and every reason to expel me for my insistence. "If this means the end of my term... then—"

"Granted."

I gasped. *No.* I didn't want my career to end that way. "Captain, I'm sorry, but—"

"No, Lieutenant. Your request is granted. Two weeks. Max. *Including* travel time. That's the best I can do right now."

Standard commute time alone would cost me several days; the Goliath and express transport ships were reserved for official business. I was lucky he granted me any time at all at such short notice.

He moved my proposal folder over on his desk and gestured to it. "I know you put a lot of work into this document and the transition between academies was likely a stressful one. You've handled it with finesse, however, and I am honored and proud to have a person of your caliber in my force."

"Thank you, Captain," I said, smiling like an idiot because of how relieved I was to *not* be getting kicked out of my academy.

"I will waive the pre-authorization process just this once, Lieutenant." The captain narrowed his eyes at me. "Never ask for something like this again," he added sternly.

"Of course not, Sir. I apologize, Sir."

"Your promotion evaluation is coming up shortly, as well.

Do you think you are ready?”

“I hope so.”

“Make sure you are, Lieutenant. I’d like to see you promoted before my service term ends.”

“I will do my best.” My voice was shaky, remembering what my sister had said about her going with him.

Captain Ventresca swiveled his chair toward his computer monitor again and began typing up a document. “Return to your regular duties for the next twenty-four hours. I will alert the flight deck that you will require transportation to whatever your destination will be, and I will see to it that your shift and duties are covered for the duration of your leave.”

“Thank you.” I tipped my head and grinned graciously. Then I turned on my heel and started for his office door.

I paused after only two steps.

“Is something the matter?” he asked, as I slowly turned back around.

“Congratulations, by the way.” I tried to smile; my sentiment sounded more bittersweet than sincere.

“For?”

“Your... *engagement*.”

His eyes grew wide and his mouth eased open. “Th-thank you, but... you know you can’t discuss—”

“It’s safe with me, Sir. But why didn’t you trust me with the information sooner? Before it escalated to this?”

His brow crinkled. "You didn't know? I assumed she'd..." He scowled at the realization and then frowned. "I'm very sorry, Lieutenant. I hadn't realized how incredibly stubborn she would be."

"I knew earlier, but only because I discovered it myself. I guess it's not your fault, Captain. I apologize for assuming it was you who had chosen to keep things quiet." It dawned on me that the man I'd looked up to during my entire time with Celestial Galaxy would soon become my brother-in-law. I wasn't sure how I felt about that. Weird. Anxious. Indifferent. All that mattered to me was Atira's happiness. "Congratulations all the same." I bowed my head slightly.

"Thank you. I promise to make this right. Off the record, we're going to be family and I want to earn your trust outside the call of duty." He smiled sympathetically and I knew he was being earnest. I appreciated that.

He was right. He would become part of my little broken family some day.

"One last thing before you go, Lieutenant," he said, raising his hand just as I looked away. "Participation in certain diplomatic endeavors on behalf of the academy does come with *some* residual perks. While I cannot offer you access to the Goliath, I can extend your leave to three weeks. That way, you won't have to factor in commute time. Does that sound fair?"

"Yes." I nodded. "Thank you very much."

I had no idea what Kinasetsu wanted to train me in or how much time he needed, but most likely a crash course would be in order.

Jacksiun would be gone by the time I returned. I wouldn't have the chance to wish him luck or see him off on the day he'd leave for Aquarius, but I said what I could before I left, and we promised to keep in touch no matter what.

Our paths *would* cross again.

I trudged through sandy terrain, dragging my bag of extra clothes behind me. The crew that had dropped me off in the middle of Ajha-Ru Island probably questioned my sanity as they were firing up the engines to ascend. There were no buildings in sight, but I kept insisting I knew where I was going and that I would be safe on my own once they left me in the seemingly endless wasteland.

I had marked the location of Kinasetsu's castle on my tablet the last time we'd visited, and I knew where I was headed. As the sun beat down, I regretted leaving the calm, temperature-stable safety of Celestial Galaxy behind. But the book had a message for me—one I heard (and saw) loud and clear.

With the book tucked under my arm, I carried on, wiping sweat from my brow every so often and checking my map periodically to be sure I was heading in the right direction.

My tablet chirped, alerting me that I was within the vicinity of the castle. I looked around but saw nothing. No glistening crystal spires peeking up from the ground. Maybe they were buried beneath the sand again. If Kinasetsu wanted me to return, he wasn't making the invitation very... *inviting*.

Should I have called first?

I dropped my bag and walked up ahead, digging my shoes down into the sand to feel for any remnants of the walls. Then I took another step and smacked face-first into something. My head spun for a moment and I groaned out loud, blinking several times and shaking my head as a wave of pain shot up my nose. I lifted a hand and slowly moved it forward until it touched something cool and polished. A shimmer of iridescent color rippled around my fingers and the crystal wall suddenly appeared before me.

The trickery made my jaw tighten.

The castle had been there the *entire* time, hidden right in front of me, and the cleric hadn't had the courtesy to let me know before I'd face-planted into it. Hopefully it wasn't a representation of how the remainder of my visit would go.

A subtle chime rang out and I followed the delicate humming to the entrance doors which were already ajar. I lugged my bag with one arm snaked through the nylon straps, clutched the book beneath my other arm, and made my way inside.

Candles illuminated the shadows up ahead but extinguished as I walked past, as though I were being intentionally led through the winding castle corridors by motion-sensitive lighting. The pathway opened up into a large foyer decorated with what appeared to be old oil paintings of famous figures from ancient Arthurian legends, as though I'd stepped into the pages of an enormous illustrated storybook. I set down my bag and looked around, gazing across the fanciful scenes.

"Hello again," a croaky voice said.

I swerved and pressed my lips together to hold in a startled squeak. Kinasetsu stood with clasped hands hidden beneath the long, floppy sleeves of his cloak, his sparkling, bulbous eyes mere inches from me.

"You seem surprised," he said, his round head tilting in place like an owl's.

"No," I lied. "I just didn't expect to see you behind me, without warning." I let out a nervous chuckle and swallowed hard. "Hello."

"It is good that you have returned," he said, turning his back to me. "I have prepared a room for you. Come." He started walking away, shuffling off much more smoothly and swiftly than I'd expect from such a crotchety old creature.

I scrambled for my bag and made haste to keep up.

We walked through the halls, and I was captivated by how the candles along the walls would glow and die as we passed, revealing flashes of different, elaborate paintings and tapestries with each spark. I shadowed the cleric, his heavy robe dragging along the floor, a soft, rhythmic sweeping sound accompanying each step.

"Here," he said, stopping and turning toward a passageway. I poked my head inside and squinted, unable to see anything through pitch black.

A flicker of yellow ignited and arced across the space, illuminating the room with warm tones. Massive portraits of mythical creatures decorated the walls from corner to corner. A dragon. A pegasus. A unicorn. The fourth wall featured a peculiar violet deer-like creature with sparkly scales, an elongated body and legs, and a single golden antler on its head.

"That is a kirin," Kinasetsu announced, pointing to the wall in question. He must have noticed me gawking at it stupefied.

"Ah," I replied with a nod, not that I had any idea what that was either.

"It is a beast once said to have roamed the Kodama Islands. They carry strong magic in their antlers and each golden scale represents a year of life."

I approached the painting and examined the animal's

back, following the line of scales trailing down its spine. There were hundreds of them.

"That kirin would have been over three-hundred years old."

My eyes widened. I'd never known anything that could live that long, though I had a feeling Kinasetsu had seen his share of centuries pass.

My gaze shifted across the entire room. Plush, crimson rugs covered the floor and an intricately-carved bed frame with tall spiraling posts made of amber-colored wood sat in the center of the room.

I dropped my bag onto the floor and approached the unicorn painting next. The shimmering silver horn captivated me and I lifted a hand to lightly touch the lines with my fingertips, brushing over the ridges of paint.

"Who painted these?" I asked, craning my head back to look toward the colorful matching ceiling.

"I did," Kinasetsu replied.

My hand slipped from the image and I turned. "You made these?"

"As well as the furniture." He gestured toward the bed and then to the writing desk on the other side of the room. The carved wood design matched the details of the bedposts and headboard.

"You're very gifted." I felt so small in such a beautiful room graced by such rich artistry and talent.

"Once you learn to cultivate and master your abilities, your gift will flourish." He turned and passed the threshold back into the main hall.

"Kinasetsu?" I bolted after him. "Wait!"

He stopped. "Take some time to grow accustomed to your new residence," he said without turning to face me. "Dinner will be ready in the dining room when it is convenient for you. The light will show you the way."

"Thank you," I said faintly.

He walked off, disappearing into the shadows of the hall.

I returned to my room and dragged my bag over to the desk. I unzipped the top and pulled out my tablet and laptop. There were no outlets of any kind in the castle but, luckily, I'd brought along a solar charger for my equipment. With no windows in the room, I'd have to place it outside during the day and keep an eye on it. One gust of wind and it might get swallowed up by the desert.

I set the book on the edge of the table and swept my finger across the cover. The visions of Emerald and her unicorn, Malachite, fighting for their lives still rattled me, making my stomach turn at the thought of the bloody fight they'd endured. The sickness made me tired (perhaps it was the motion-sickness tablets) and I felt the need to rest.

I left my things where they were and approached the large bed in the center of the room. The frame was so tall, I had to climb up onto it as if I were a child. The mattress was firm but soft, and the brightly colored embroidered comforter thick and warm inside the surprisingly frigid castle. I flopped onto the fluffy pillows and closed my eyes, taking in a deep breath. The soft ambience from the candles soothed my nerves and the lights began to dim, the peacefulness lulling me to sleep.

I awoke to a raging grumble quaking in my stomach. With no clock in the room, and no windows by which to judge the hour, I couldn't immediately tell how long I'd slept. I sat up and the sconces around my room bloomed to life with soft, yellow flames. My feet touched the floor and I left my room in search of the dining hall.

Though everything was black at first, firelight guided me through the massive hallway, illuminating the pathway up ahead and extinguishing it behind as I walked.

All the candles went out, except for one. I approached it slowly and stared at it, as I did not know where else to go.

The tiny flame shot up over my head toward the ceiling,

raining down like a glimmering firework, igniting a series of wicks atop an elaborate, crystal chandelier.

"I see you have found your way." I heard Kinasetsu from across the room. Could he see in the dark?

Beneath the chandelier was a long, rectangular dining table—also carved of wood. I counted twelve chairs, but only one place setting had been made, and it was at the head of the table. The other seats were ghostly bare.

"Yes," I replied, waiting for him to give me permission to sit. "This castle seems to know exactly where I'm going." I smiled, but his long expression did not change in response. He continued to remind me of an old toad. He did not emote with his face, and yet I was not unsettled by it; his resting expression was neutral, not intimidating. *Luckily*.

"The castle retains much of the ancient world in its veins. It will speak to you if you listen."

I didn't know if I felt prepared to hear the castle '*speak*,' but his words piqued my interest.

"You may sit," he said, gesturing with his large, scaly hand toward the only chair with a place setting.

I pulled out the chair and sat, then scooted in closer to the table. My hands intertwined in my lap.

Kinasetsu took a step back and flicked two fingers toward the table. My place setting shuddered and rippled out of focus, converging into a plate of colorful food.

"I thought you were an apothecary, not a magician," I

said, leaning down to take a closer look at the dish. A warm, savory scent wafted from little semi-curled pink and blue striped morsels I could only liken to what I knew to be shrimp. Small green florets of some kind of vegetable had been artfully arranged around the outside edge, interspersed with another fruit or vegetable I couldn't name.

"Magician? Magic, as you call it, is made of vagrant energy. Magic users are able to summon and bind that energy into forces you humans call spells and curses. Some are very capable of learning the craft of energy manipulation, while others have an inability to bend their own minds to accept it as a viable source of power. You will learn all these things very soon. First, you must eat. Without your strength, you will be fatigued and you cannot be fatigued whilst you train."

A dainty silver tone fork appeared beside my plate. I reached for it and then carefully pricked one of the little curls and lifted it up, taking a sniff. It smelled like shrimp, too.

"Those are sea butterflies," Kinasetsu said. "They are native to this island if you know where to look."

Sea butterflies? That would mean they came from the ocean, but I didn't know he'd even left his castle long enough to reach the shores, which were a considerable trek several miles out.

"The vegetation is from the garden," he continued. "I will introduce you to that place soon enough. Eat." He gestured for me to go ahead.

I opened my mouth and forked in the tiny shrimp. It was warm, and remarkably delicious, tasting of ocean and a hint of salt and some spice I couldn't decipher, but liked already. I pierced a vegetable and shoveled that in next. Not quite broccoli and not quite asparagus, but something in the middle. It tasted good, though.

The things on my plate disappeared quickly; I was hungrier than I'd realized. I set the fork down beside the plate and looked up, ready to compliment Kinasetsu on his work, but he was gone.

I heard only my own breath and the incredibly soft crackling of the candle flames along the walls. I turned in my chair and looked around. Large tapestries decorated the four walls, hung from bronze rods with leaf-shaped finials. The tapestries, like much else in his castle, featured artwork from ancient mythology. Warriors in full suits of armor mounted on hairy four-legged beasts I'd never seen before. The other walls featured constellations and world maps, both new and old.

"Do not be afraid to ask questions," Kinasetsu said, appearing on the other side of the room from out of the shadows of the hallway. He scuttled closer to me and waved a hand over my empty plate, making it vanish. "You must ask questions while you are here. You must learn as much as possible."

"I will," I replied, nodding. "I will ask." I pushed my

chair out and stood at attention. "I'm still learning, but I will grow accustomed to your ways."

"Very well. Your first few days will be filled with many mistakes."

I... hope not.

"You will grow and change rapidly." He tilted his head and looked me in the eye. "Or you will die."

I sucked in a sharp breath and my pulse quickened.

"It is the truth, Valhara. You saw it in your dream, did you not?"

"The dream about Emerald? How did you know about that? I never told you—"

"The book spoke. The castle listened. I listened. Emerald has haunted every Elemental Guardian since King Arthur's death, and her visitation in your dreams confirms you will be next. I knew it would not take long for her to find you after you fought the mahora spider. No doubt, she planted the creature there, herself. She sensed your power and will now hunt you like a quiverthorn fox hunts in a famine."

Quiverthorn foxes were known for crafty, brutal hunting strategies often leading to the demise and extinction of entire prey animal populations. They devastated wildlife for sport.

"What do I do? I only have two weeks. Will that be enough?"

"It must suffice."

"Can you tell me more about Tryamour's Wrath?"

"After Emerald's death, her soul refused to surrender its life force back to the earth. Instead, she awaited the birth of each new Guardian so that she may challenge and destroy those she deemed unworthy. It is sometimes referred to as Emerald Tryamour's Wrath."

"Has anyone ever survived?"

"A few... rarely. A young warrior by the name of Joan survived. Joan of Arc may be the title you have heard used. She survived the wrath of Emerald, only to be smote by her own people because they did not understand her power."

While researching artifacts, I came upon a story about an ancient solider named Joan of Arc and the tale of how she led an entire army when she was only my age. When she was a young girl, she believed she could hear the voices of the earth compelling her to go forth and protect her people. She died at a young age, too, unfortunately.

"She was burned at the stake," I said, recalling the tragic end of Joan's story. "What kind of Guardian was she?"

"An Elemental Guardian of ice. The punishment chosen by her peers was a fitting one, albeit cruel and unjust."

A sick feeling gnarled up my stomach. Might someone try to freeze me to death? Or... drown me?

"Times have changed, Valhara," Kinasetsu said, pressing a hand onto my shoulder as if he had sensed my uneasiness. "You are safe from your own people in this world. Emerald is your only concern for now." He released me. "Now there are matters we must focus on."

He reached into his cloak and withdrew a closed hand. "Before you can begin training, it is imperative you are bound to a Spirit Guardian since you have not yet acquired one on your own. Your Spirit will advise you along your journey and the bond will grant you additional skills you would otherwise be incapable of possessing."

He lowered his large hand and unfurled his pointy fingers. A sparkling gemstone amulet glistened in his palm, the chain chinking softly as he flexed his fingers.

"You must take this," he said, motioning toward the translucent, ruby-red cabochon set in yellow gold. I brought a hand toward my neck and paused, thinking about the one I already wore—the family heirloom Atira had given me.

"Why do you hesitate?" he asked, tilting his head and peering at me with huge, sparkly eyes.

"I... I have one already," I replied quietly, feeling foolish for saying it. Surely the one in his hand was more valuable. "I understand it isn't the same thing, but—"

"Give it to me," he said firmly, reaching up toward my neck.

"But..." I took a step back, shuddering at the idea of losing my precious gift.

"Give yours to me. I will return it to you." His tone softened as he reached his other hand out.

I dug beneath my collar for the chain to my necklace and then tugged it out from beneath the first few buttons of my shirt, coiling the chain around my hand first before releasing the entire clump of metal and gemstone into the cleric's rough-textured hand.

He held each amulet, stone facing out, between his thumbs and index fingers and lifted them to eye level. Light glittered inside the one he had offered me and then he immediately pressed the face of the stone against the face of mine. They crackled loudly and I gasped as the fiery-orange light inside his amulet slowly leached into mine, causing my scarlet sunstone to emit a bright glow.

He separated them and the cabochon faded in color from the once bright-red to a dull, pale rose.

"Here." He handed my necklace back to me. "Your Spirit resides inside it now."

My... *Spirit*? He'd meant something metaphorical, but I still didn't quite understand what it was.

"There is little space here for introductions," Kinasetsu said, his eyes moving in his head to glance about the dining room. "I will show you to the garden. There, you may call upon your Spirit. You will have the remainder of the evening to grow accustomed to one another."

My Spirit was an animal? A person? I vaguely recalled Emerald telling Arthur he didn't have one because he wasn't worthy, and I sort of remember her communicating with her unicorn, Malachite, in some strange, telepathic way.

"How do I call them?" I asked, bustling after Kinasetsu as he began to walk off without warning.

"That is for you to discover on your own," he answered without turning.

I came up beside him with my hands cupping the amulet.

"What are you waiting for? Put it back on." He flicked his hand impatiently.

I looped the chain over my head and tucked two fingers into my collar to pry it open enough to drop the amulet beneath my shirt.

"Do not hide it," Kinasetsu growled. Though he hadn't turned around, he somehow knew what I was doing. "It is highly disrespectful to the Spirit."

"But... my job may not allow me to—"

"If you continue to make excuses for yourself, you will not survive the endeavors that are to come, Valhara."

I released the necklace and let it hang outside my collar.

We walked under an archway and he swept a long curtain of dangling green vines out of the way, holding them back for me to go ahead of him. I ducked and walked out into a large garden. My gaze shot up to see the moon, sparkling high overhead, beaming with a white aura. My feet came down on softness—short, lush grass. Bushes and trees surrounded me, spaced out quite purposefully it would seem, as there was plenty of room to walk between them.

The moon cast diffused, white light on everything, and a sparkle of tiny green fireflies decorated the branches of the trees, throwing brief lime-green sparkles past my line of sight every few moments as they fluttered by.

A gust of wind rushed past, cool and comfortable, contrary to the scorching heat I'd endured in the desert afternoon. I looked around, turning in place as I skimmed over the thriving flora and fauna that had popped up out of seemingly nowhere. This place, too, must have been hidden from view when we'd arrived.

I took a whiff of the air and grinned; it smelled clean and fragrant—like jasmine and honeysuckle—flowers I hadn't smelled in years.

"How did you grow all of this here?" I asked, turning toward the entrance.

Silence.

He was gone, and I could no longer see the archway of vines from where I had entered.

I reached up to fidget with my amulet, feeling alone, but not really frightened in the vast darkness of the garden. I lowered myself down to the ground and sat with my back pressed up against a tree trunk, heaving a sigh as my sight lifted toward the stars.

The tiny yellow sparkle of Celestial Galaxy floated in a sea of endless black. I remembered pointing that yellow star out to Mattheia and telling him what it was.

And then... I remembered Mattheia kissing me for the first time on the roof of Silver Diamond. He had kissed me, and, although I hadn't regretted it necessarily, I hadn't been able to stop hating myself for letting it get that far. He'd sacrificed a lot to save my life, but I had to let him go. It was in our best interest to stay focused on our careers.

Now we were apart, and I'd never see him again.

I'd... *never* see him again.

A tear rolled down my cheek and I wiped it away with the back of my hand, clearing my throat as I took in a deep breath.

Don't regret it. Don't.

I closed my eyes and rested against the tree, dropping my head back and sniffling.

Intense heat swelled in my chest, making my eyes reel open from panic. A beam of amber-crimson light shot from the stone in my amulet, intensifying rapidly as I scrambled to me feet.

I swallowed hard, fighting back a lump in my throat as the surreal fire grew more vibrant, streaks of color shooting through my skin, down to my fingertips. Flames poured from me as if a phoenix were erupting from my chest, jolting the air from my lungs like a violent punch in the back. My body trembled as the last streak of light left me and the heat dissipated.

I bent over to catch my breath, resting my hands on my knees as I huffed and puffed, beads of sweat building on my forehead like a roiling fever flushing across my skin.

Then the garden came alive with dancing lights and I lifted my head, goose bumps prickling as I locked eyes with the thing that had escaped from inside me.

"Do not be frightened," it said; its voice had a distinct, Alyssian accent to it.

It stood on two legs, about a foot taller than me, with an extended neck, fine-boned body, and long sweeping tail coiled near its dainty, clawed feet. From its gently sloped back rose a pair of what appeared to be wings, only they were composed completely of fire and flickered and shifted as if constantly fueled by something. Light refracted off its millions of iridescent blood-red scales, and their color shifted subtly from red to green as the firelight caressed them.

"What... are you?" I asked, my voice cracking as I looked the creature in its vivid green eyes.

It cocked its head and moved nearer. I froze in place.

"I am a dragon," he replied, his voice and facial features somehow appearing more male now. "I see that you are tense, but please do not be frightened of me. I will not harm you, my dear." He took another step closer, walking upright not with the naturalness of a human, but more reminiscent of a kangaroo or other animal suited to balance on either two or four legs.

"I'm not scared," I said quietly, lifting a hand toward him. My fingertips brushed against the tip of his long, narrow snout, avoiding a line of thorns running across the bridge. He slowly lowered his head as I stroked a line past his cheek and down toward his throat. The scales were smooth as silk, warm, and finely textured.

"Why do you touch me like this?" he said softly, closing his eyes to press a little weight against my palm and nudge me gently with his neck.

"I-I don't know." I smiled at how silly that must have sounded coming from my lips. I didn't really know what had compelled me to reach out to him like that, but it felt right.

He opened his eyes and straightened his neck. "My name is Firagia. It is a pleasure to meet you." He bowed his head. A line of short quills poked up from over his eyes like eyebrows, and a jagged, fin-shaped appendage adorned each side of his head—like an ear, but likely more decorative than functional. A row of armor-like golden chevrons ran down his chest from his throat to below his belly. The dragon wore several pieces of jewelry, too: a bangle of various gemstones set in gold, a thick arm band of matching colors, and in one of his hind legs, I spotted a large, emerald stone embedded so that the surface of the stone remained completely visible at skin level.

"Nice to meet you, too." I tipped my head a little, unsure of the proper way to greet a dragon.

The entire length of the back of his neck and all along his spine down to the tip of his tail also had a row of sharp quills sticking up. I wasn't nearly as scared as I should have been. Or perhaps I shouldn't have been scared at all.

"Pardon my ineptness," he said with a chuckle.

I'd never seen a dragon smile before.

I'd never seen a real dragon.

"It has been centuries since I have spoken to another. I hope you can be patient with me as I become reacquainted with the art of conversation."

"Well," I let out a nervous laugh and shrugged, "I've never spoken to a dragon before, either, so please pardon my awkwardness."

"How did you summon me? If I may ask?" He cocked his head to the side and blinked; he blinked so rapidly, I could barely catch it.

"I... don't know."

"Ah. I feel it." He narrowed his eyes. "Your heart is hurting." His voice became like a whisper.

I furrowed my brow, pretending he was wrong. He stared at me, patiently awaiting a response.

"How do you know?" I chewed my lip and looked at the grass, sorry to admit the truth, but too self-conscious to lie to him.

"We are bound together. I sense everything that drifts through your heart. I sense your apprehension to take on the role fate has dealt to you. And..." He pressed his delicate hand onto my shoulder and lowered his head to my eye level. "I know your heart aches because of *him*."

Him?

Mattheia?

"Yes," Firagia replied, though I hadn't said the thought out loud. "Because of the young commander who gained your affections. You must not fret over the past. If things are meant to be, they will be. That is all you need to know, Valhara."

I didn't want to hear anything else about *him* right now. I wanted to put it all behind me and just—

"Ease your mind," he said.

I instantly felt less anxious. Somehow.

Firagia looked toward a shallow clearing nearby. "It has been a long day for you, my dear." He sat on his back legs and slowly lowered his torso to the ground, keeping his head high and his arms loosely crossed. "Please, come sit with me," he said, patting the ground with his hand; his golden bracelet sparkled near the grass, illuminated by glimmering fireflies. "I will not hurt you in any way." His voice was soothing and kind, like a father speaking to a daughter. The tip of his long tail swayed from side to side leisurely.

I approached and crouched down beside him, sitting on the dry grass and pulling my knees in toward my chest. A faint click sounded and all the quills along his back, tail, and arms retracted into his skin, disappearing from sight.

Though his wings did not give off heat, his shimmering red scales emitted pleasant waves of warmth, and as the air turned brisk, I felt the urge to move closer to the friendly dragon, pressing my back up against his side and settling more weight against his smooth scales. Our eyes met and a comforting grin curled on his dragon lips.

My gaze lifted until I could see the faint glint of Celestial Galaxy. I stared up at it, my eyelids growing heavier as the moments passed. The colorful light of Firagia's wings began to fade, and I drifted off, ushered to sleep by the cool evening breeze and twinkling night sky.

Birdsongs fluttered into my ears. My eyes eased open and I found myself alone in Kinasetsu's garden. The dragon—the one from my dreams—seemed so real. His vibrant green eyes gazing thoughtfully into mine with a kindness that was almost human. His soft, comforting voice making me feel safe, though I knew nothing more about him.

I reached up to clasp my necklace, polishing the sunstone with my thumb. The crystal was cold to the touch and the stems of the elaborate setting as sharp as always. The light inside it had vanished, leading me to believe that everything that had occurred after dinner was an aftereffect of the strange new food I'd consumed.

I sat up, stretched my arms over my head, and yawned.

There was a rustling sound in the distance and I veered my head toward it. I couldn't see much from where I sat, so I stood and crept closer to the noise. I heard branches shuffling and leaves being pushed around just behind a large shrub. Squinting, I inched toward the side of the bush, pressing up against it as I peeked around to the other side.

Red scales glistened in the light of dawn, hints of green sparkle rippling over them as the dragon shuffled about in the brush in search of something.

It wasn't a dream, after all.

"Excuse me?" I whispered, not wanting to startle him.

His long neck popped up over the greenery and he twisted around to face me, a look of embarrassment on his very expressive face. He shoved one of his arms behind his back and turned slowly.

"Good morning, Valhara," he said, his voice a pitch higher than I remembered it being last night, but still colored with a dignified, Alyssian accent.

"Good morning, Firagia," I replied, cocking an eyebrow. "What are you hiding there?"

"Oh, this?" He cleared his throat and grinned nervously. "It is nothing. It is..." He heaved a sigh and lowered his head. "I should not keep a secret from you. I simply cannot." He withdrew his hand from behind his back and revealed a large rose. Its apricot-colored petals blended into vivid magenta edges and it took up most of his long, slender hand.

"It is a gift for you," he added, holding it up into the sunlight. Colorful arcs of flame licked up from between the petals, producing an orange aura. "The last of the season. I have enchanted it so that it will never fade away. I would like you to have it, Valhara."

I didn't know what to say or how to react, only that the gesture was a very thoughtful one on his behalf. The rose pulsed with fiery color. I reached out with cupped hands and he dropped it into them. It wasn't hot—as I had expected it to be—considering it was consumed by flames.

"Thank you." I held it securely but gently.

"It is not as brittle as one may assume," he added with a dragon smirk. "Not anymore."

I shifted the rose into one hand and used my other to lightly poke one of the petals. It was firm but flexible. Like soft plastic.

"You're very sweet, Firagia. You must have been very popular with the girl dragons of your time." I chuckled.

Sorrow tore through me from out of nowhere. A wave of sadness swept over him and his cheerful expression faded.

Had I said something I shouldn't have?

He sighed. "I was the last of my kind," he said, the air of happiness abandoning his face. "After centuries of peaceful cohabitation, humans turned on the dragon race. Times changed and the hearts of men grew cold, finding more value in our bones and skin than our company. They hunted and killed all but me. I survived only because I became reclusive and forwent human friendships."

"I'm sorry," I replied, ashamed of the naive comment I'd made. "I didn't mean to—"

"You did not know, Valhara." His forgiving gaze rested on mine. "I cannot be angry with you as your soul is much too pure to say things with vile intent."

"Where did you come from?" I held the rose he'd given me near my chest.

"What do you know of Spirit Guardians?" He clasped his hands together.

"Very little." I shrugged. "Nothing, I suppose."

"Well, then I fear to say that makes two of us," Firagia said with a toothy grin. The way his top two canine teeth peeked out over his lower lip was endearing. "I will tell you what I know, however, if you will listen."

"Of course. Thank you." I wanted to learn anything I could.

"Will you walk with me?" He lifted a hand, palm up and offered it. I'd seen pictures of such a gesture in books about the ancient world, but it was rarely used today, except by members of the royal Alyssian family.

I raised my free hand and rested it lightly atop his and the rich green of his eyes brightened joyfully. We strolled through the garden and I realized how vast it truly was as the light of day shone down upon the lengthy pathway winding between the foliage.

"I was once a flesh and blood creature," Firagia started. His scales were warm and soft beneath my fingertips and his presence was like having a very good friend by my side. "I wanted to continue befriending humans, as I had as a young dragon, but the century had changed, and darkness and greed roiled in the blood of Alyssian men. It was around that time a young sorceress named Morgan Le Fay stumbled upon me in the forest while I scavenged for food. I wanted to scurry away and hide, but she pursued and begged me to hear her out.

"'I can see to it that you live forever,' she had said to me with confidence. 'Let me protect you, dear dragon—last of your remarkable kind.'

"It was not the promise of immortality that led me to agree, but the earnestness of her words and her desire to do good for others in light of how she'd been treated over the years. A vibrant magical aura surrounded her, masking a deep sadness in her heart. She was an outcast, too—tossed aside by her own brother, the king."

"Arthur? The same king who..."

"Betrayed his other half-sister, Emerald, and brutally took her life. The same man whose arrogance incited the Forest Guardian to pursue every Elemental born since.

"It was Morgan who decided to create and enchant various amulets in an effort to protect forthcoming generations from the Forest Elemental. Each Guardian has a Spirit Guardian for a companion, but not all of them are gained by the same means. Emerald's was her pet—a valiant and strong horse changed by her own magic."

"She said something about Arthur not having a Spirit. Was that true?"

"Emerald did not know the truth about her brother," Firagia continued. "Morgan told me otherwise. Her brother did have a Spirit—a wise gold and white owl infused with extensive knowledge of the stars and topography of the world. Because he feared it posed a threat to him, should it be captured by his enemies, Arthur promptly destroyed the poor fledgling creature."

Thinking about Arthur's actions made me grit my teeth. Who could do such a terrible thing?

"And you? How did you become a Spirit?"

"Morgan Le Fay drained my essence and locked it inside the stone on the amulet Kinasetsu offered you last night. Essentially, I cannot die now that I have no physical body to have taken from me. I will, however, feel your pain whenever you are injured, just as Malachite shared Emerald's." He raised a hand and tapped my sunstone lightly with a sharp, dainty claw. "I can return to the amulet whenever you wish. This is something not all Spirits can do, particularly if they are still attached to their skin. Please tell me when to leave you, and I will. I will always respect your privacy."

"No." I shook my head and smiled. "I wouldn't ask you to leave or to stay confined in this little thing." I swept my hand over my necklace and laughed lightly. "I would never do that to you. Not after all the centuries you spent trapped inside it."

"Th-thank you, Valhara." Firagia cocked his head and drew back, surprised. "You are very kind to be so lenient with me."

"We are partners now, and friends."

"Friends?"

"I hope."

"I have not trusted a human since I trusted Morgan, but I am quite fond of you already, you know." He gestured toward the enchanted rose still cupped in my other hand and it grew brighter momentarily.

"Then I will be careful not to betray your trust in me. You're the only dragon I've ever met, and I would hate to lose you."

"I will not stray from your side unless you ask me to," he said with a confident nod. "That is a promise."

I liked that idea. His company made my heart a little less heavy. I hadn't known Firagia for long, but everything he said felt true. Maybe it was the bond Kinasetsu spoke of—the bond between Guardian and Spirit—as I did not doubt a single word that poured from the dragon's mouth.

"Do you know what happened to Morgan after you became part of the amulet?"

We walked beneath an overhang of dark green vines dotted with red flowers and came out facing a wall of the castle. I shielded my eyes from the blinding reflection and turned my face to the side.

"Sadly, I do not."

"Ask Kinasetsu," I suggested. "I believe he collects things from ancient times. Maybe he could tell you more about her." Detailed paintings featuring Arthurian lore hung wall-to-wall in the castle, and dozens of books sat neglected in his hidden library behind the throne room.

"I can tell you anything you wish to know," Kinasetsu's voice boomed behind me. I turned, startled, and squinted as light beamed off the castle wall.

The old cleric clearly had a preference for sudden, dramatic entrances.

Firagia seemed startled, as well, at the abrupt appearance. "Greetings, Great Cleric," he said with a low bow of his head, trying to hide the tremble in his voice.

"If your Guardian permits, you may forage through the library in search of answers to your questions. The library in the north wing will have what you seek." Kinasetsu turned toward me. "We must train today, Valhara."

"Yes. I'm anxious to begin." I glanced at Firagia, who

stared at me imploringly with enlarged, eager pupils and a hopeful smile. "You may go, my friend," I said with a grin. He thanked me with a quick bow and then motioned toward the rose he'd given to me which was still in my hand.

"May I take it back to your room?" he asked.

I handed it over and then he scurried excitedly off toward the castle, his long, scarlet tail whipping from side to side as he scampered away.

"Tell me what you know thus far about summoning your powers," Kinasetsu said, gesturing for me to face away from the castle walls toward a long stretch of grass.

"Nothing."

"That is understandable. Many Guardians scarcely remember using their abilities at all the first time."

That would explain why I couldn't remember how I had defeated the mahora.

"Hold out your hand."

I looked down at them both and narrowed my eyes, trying to decide which to use.

"Either will do," he added.

I chose my right—it felt more natural—and lifted it to mid-chest level.

"To call upon your powers, you must siphon energy from the space around you and channel it into light. Make fire from shadow and make visible the invisible."

That made no sense to me, but I pretended to understand

by nodding.

"Flatten your hand and direct the palm toward that clearing." He pointed and I did as instructed.

"Free all thoughts from your mind and close your eyes."

I squeezed my eyelids down with some difficulty; the excitement racing through my veins gave me jitters.

"Visualize each response as I ask you questions," Kinasetsu stated. "Do not speak. Picture the answer in your mind. Become one with it. We will start with the simplest and expand from there. To begin, you are fire. What quality do you embody at your very core?"

Heat.

"What are you made from?"

Energy and light.

"What colors symbolize life to you?"

Yellow. Orange. Blue?

"Focus on the breath and how air moves in and out of your lungs. Breathe in deeply."

I inhaled fully, my chest expanding.

"Exhale. Slowly. Now take another breath, holding it briefly this time, focusing on your previous responses."

Heat. Light. Energy.

"Why do people fear you?"

Because... I burn.

Answering sent a shockwave of fear through my system and my heart pumped faster.

My eyes remained closed, but I was suddenly in a different place in my mind—a cramped, dark room welling with agonizing heat and vapors that made my eyes sting.

Bright colors exploded all around, and the temperature skyrocketed. I tried over and over to cry out for *them*, but I couldn't. The words wouldn't form. My throat kept seizing. Burning. Twisting.

Smoke drifted overhead, creeping toward the other side of the room in sinister plumes of black. I held my breath and choked on what little oxygen remained as the mounting flames sucked it from me, spewing back air I couldn't breathe. The smoke grew thicker and more opaque until the walls disappeared.

Paralyzed by shock, I could only sit there with knees pulled up to my chest and tears spilling down my cheeks. My feet wouldn't budge.

A hot rush of pain shot through my bones, sending me to my knees as I bit my tongue to suppress a scream. I opened my eyes, but fragments of terrifying imagery lingered. I hunched over on the cool, damp grass, holding myself until the burning sensation—and ultimately, the visions—subsided.

"You have reservations," Kinasetsu said, approaching me.

I was back in his garden...

"What are they?"

I tried to catch my breath, but I was shaking. I slowly lifted myself from the ground and straightened up, swallowing hard to try to push back unpleasant thoughts.

Unpleasant *memories.*

"I don't want to discuss them," I said, looking away from his intrusive stare.

"And I do not want you to die at Tryamour's hands," he grumbled. "Tell me at once, or I will discontinue your training and banish you from this island."

What!?

I gasped. "No!"

"Then speak at once." His tone was firmer than it had ever been and his starry eyes even wider.

"My parents," I blurted, taking a shuddering breath. "My parents... died."

"So is the way of the world, child," he said with indifference, tilting his head. "All children lose their elders."

"In a fire," I added, grimacing. His expression softened only the slightest, but I was sure it *did* soften. "They died in a fire. And... I was there—in another room—as the house collapsed around me. The memories are so vivid still. Pieces of metal and wood crashing down. Smoke billowing through the air. I couldn't breathe. I couldn't see. I had walled myself up in the maintenance closet under a metal shelving unit, and I sat there, weeping until I fainted from smoke inhalation. Help arrived shortly after and resuscitated me."

I wiped a stream of tears from my face with both palms and heaved a sigh, embarrassed by my outburst.

"My sister had already enlisted with Celestial Galaxy and left Earth, but I was home from pre-academy training for the season break. I survived, somehow, and our parents didn't. I enlisted shortly after the incident, boarded a recruitment ship, and never looked back."

"I understand now why you are at odds with your element," Kinasetsu replied. "But there is something you must learn about elemental energy, Valhara." He took a step back and turned my attention to a twig he had plucked from the ground. "Vagrant energy has no allegiance or agenda. It is neutral; neither dark nor light. This branch, for example..." He lifted it in front of me and withdrew his other hand from a pocket in his cloak. There was a small red speck of light between his fingers. He flicked the sparkling dust at the branch and it caught fire, ablaze with cascading waves of blue, violet, and orange. "Energy does not, by default, choose to be destructive."

The twig continued to burn brightly, but the fire did not so much as catch fire to, or wither the remaining dead leaves that had twisted around the stalk. It stayed encapsulated by flame, but untouched by the heat.

Kinasetsu removed another flake of glowing dust from his pocket and dropped it onto the stick. With a flash of white, the entire twig turned black and crumbled to ash in his hand.

"The fire inside you is only as destructive as you will it to be," he continued, tossing the ashes onto the ground. "It will not burn unless you will it to burn. You have nothing to fear, Valhara. Despite what may have happened in your past, you are in control of your fate now. You survived for a reason. The energy protected you."

"Then why didn't it protect my parents!? Why couldn't I protect them?"

"If you accept your training and discontinue dwelling on the past, you *will* be able to protect those you care about. As a child, you did not know how to control your powers. Guardians must be shaped by a master—someone who understands the behaviors and effects of loose energy."

Surviving the accident didn't mean I was to blame for my parents' deaths. It was beyond my control.

I didn't start that fire, but I also couldn't stop it.

"I'll try again, Kinasetsu." I raised my hand and flattened it, palm out, toward the distant field. My eyes closed and I focused.

He had told me to think of myself as fire. To envision every detail of it.

Heat. Color. Movement.

I began to form the shape in my mind—a spire of red-hot flames radiating heat.

"See the fire pouring through your blood," Kinasetsu

said. "Watch as it weaves through the forks and bends of each vein. From the soles of your feet, to your legs, to your torso. Watch as golden light seeps through the heart and is forced back out into the rest of your body, its warmth and life releasing through your skin. Calm. Free. Under your control."

A subtle tingling feeling flitted over my skin and the palm of my hand felt cold, as if I were grasping a chunk of ice. Only, it wasn't uncomfortably cold. Just cold. I remembered the flickering candlelight in the hallways at night—the friendly, soft auras guiding me through the winding castle walls of Kinasetsu's palace.

Then I thought of my wonderful new acquaintance, Firagia, and how the beautiful firelight of his colorful wings had kept me pleasantly warm in the cool desert night, but how it did not singe my hair, though it was mere inches from it.

"Ask it to listen," he continued. "Speak to it in your mind and will it to be what it is you wish for it to be."

I didn't know what I had wanted it to be, but I tried to think of something.

A flower? Yes. The beautiful flower Firagia had given me earlier. It was a lovely shade of peach and magenta. Vibrant. Graceful. Just like the dragon who had gifted it to me.

Pressure built in my hand and I flexed my fingers against discomfort and tightness. I flinched, gritting my teeth and letting out a soft grunt as a deep force pushed against the inside of my palm like something trying to escape from beneath the skin.

I opened my eyes and turned my hand over, watching a glimmer of scarlet light quickly vanish. I began to lower my arm, defeated and frustrated that I had come so far only to release it so quickly.

"Do not lose focus." Kinasetsu lifted my arm again and pressed his hand under my elbow to brace it. "Focus again."

I heaved a sigh and decided to keep my eyes open this time so I could see what was happening. I turned my palm over and brought my hand in slightly nearer to my chest.

Visualize what I want from it...

I want to protect the people I love. I want to have the power to keep myself, my sister, and... and...

When the mahora spider had attacked us, I'd blacked out, in a way... forcing the memories of what had occurred out of my mind. Because of fear? Perhaps. Anger? I didn't know exactly, but I *did* know that what I did saved Mattheia's life. That thing would have slaughtered us both had I not done whatever it was I had done. My fireproof sword had been singed by remnants of the mahora's prickly hide—evidence. Without that fire, there would have been no way to defeat it.

My jaw tightened as I vividly recalled the nasty, bloodthirsty crimson eyes galloping toward me, staggering on bloodied stumps of what legs remained, yet eager to end me like it had the poor pegasus moments before.

When the fire took over, my body had felt lighter, as if I were floating.

I'd lifted my sword up and it had caught fire, burning so hot, it turned bluish-white. Then a red glaze flushed across my vision and...

My attention shifting back to the present, a spark ignited in my palm and I gasped. A ring of soft orange and yellow light sprouted from my palm, twirling in place like a cyclone.

"Push the negative thoughts out," Kinasetsu instructed, removing his hand from my arm. "Remember, the energy is neutral. It has no will other than your own. You choose the shape it takes."

Thinking about the mahora spider had angered me enough to cause the fire to resurface, but Kinasetsu was right. If I had the power to control the consequences of the fire I wielded, then I needed to be careful, and I needed to stay collected.

Then I remembered...

I'd done this before—back when I had been tested for my promotion to Lieutenant. A firearms exam required me to stay calm during a simulated war zone. We weren't allowed to wear noise-dampeners, and we had to fire shots as the lights kicked on and off at random intervals. It was stressful—infuriating, to say the least—but we were forced to do it because it mirrored reality. It is absolutely vital to keep a level-head in a loud, strenuous environment. If you don't, you can die.

Preparing for the test was tiring. Frustrating. Even depressing, at times, because I couldn't imagine what it would be like to fail and be left behind while friends moved through the ranks without me. But I succeeded because I worked hard. I studied day and night, and I cleared my mind and focused.

The coils of color in my palm swirled and pinched together, lifting and twisting as they folded over themselves, forming what vaguely resembled the rose Firagia had given me. I grinned, the smile stretching so far, it kind of hurt my cheeks. A lightness and joy filled my chest and tears came to my eyes again. Good ones, this time. Happy ones.

"Excellent," the cleric said. "Now close your hand and release it back to the earth."

My fingers curled inward and the flames licked at my skin, feeling cool—almost damp. The fiery rose crumbled to amber ashes which were swiftly carried off by the wind.

I had passed my Lieutenant's test... and I would pass Emerald's, too.

I lay draped across my bed inside Kinasetsu's castle, mulling over the events of the past week.

The cleric didn't know how long it would be before Emerald attacked.

Weeks.

Days.

Hours.

I trained from dawn to dusk, because every sedentary moment could cost me my life. And for the first few days, it was excruciating—acclimating to the intense sensations that coursed through me every time I summoned fire. Cold. Pressure. Pain, even—depending upon the size of the flames emblazoning my hands. Over time, the color changed from pale yellow to shades of indigo and violet, lines of deep ember-orange accenting the vibrant wisps of wild light.

Levitation was a subtle side-effect of full-on envelopment and I became accustomed to the phenomenon of my feet barely coming up off the ground whenever I fully accepted the energy into my body.

Heat rises.

It was terrifying at first, while I was fully conscious of what was happening. Back when I'd fought the mahora spider, I didn't realize what I was doing because everything came and went in a flash of fragmented memories.

Would I be strong enough to take on Emerald—the ancient Guardian with enough magic to defeat numerous Guardians before me?

How could I compare to great historical martyrs like Joan of Arc? I'd never done anything that astonishing.

Would I ever?

Kinasetsu had told me I could use my powers to protect others, and he was right. I had protected Mattheia from that creature. Maybe I didn't understand what was happening back then, but I did now.

My abilities would mature over time, and the old cleric admitted he did not know the true extent of a Guardian's control over vagrant energy. It was for me to discover as I moved forward in my journey.

But the more I thought about it, the worse I felt. Deep, unforgiving sorrow disturbed my sleep, cutting into my dreams at night and then terrorizing my waking thoughts. Every hour of lost rest made the next day more difficult. How long could I hide the fatigue from Kinasetsu?

I wrapped my fingers around the edge of my pillow and wrinkled the cool, satiny fabric. The weight of everything to come had my stomach in knots, but it was thoughts of Mattheia that kept me awake long into the night.

Having the ability to draw fire from energy made me an Elemental Guardian, but it didn't define me as a human. What good would the ability to protect others be without anyone to protect? My sister would leave C.G. to marry and live with Captain Ventresca. Jacksiun would transfer to Aquarius (if he hadn't already). And I'd slammed the door on a relationship with a man who had risked everything to find me the cure for mahora poison. A man I... fell in love with.

There were so many more important things to be thinking about right now, but I couldn't keep my mind off him. The way the sun cast a staggered shadow over his brow, across his brilliant blue eyes when he smiled in the sunlight. How light danced across the natural, yellow-gold tones of his hair when the breeze caressed his face.

Sitting in Kinasetsu's garden with Firagia in the evenings after training revived pleasant thoughts of Mattheia and me on the roof of Silver Diamond. The stars taunted me from above, illustrating how small and insignificant I was in the vastness of our galaxy and the universe.

Every meal alone in the castle starkly contrasted the engaging conversations we had in the empty cafeteria on days when he worked late.

My throat tensed and twisted and I pushed back against the growing sadness. My cheeks felt warm and flushed, and my face tightened as stifled tears escaped my eyes. No matter how hard I squeezed them shut, my eyes wouldn't stop pouring.

Who was I really fighting for?

My friends? My family? Mattheia?

Kinasetsu said I needed to be confident and true to myself, and that I had to face Emerald with no reservations about my abilities or the lengths I would go to defend those in need.

How could I be true to myself when I'd been lying this entire time?

I wiped tears from my face and sniffled, using the edge of my pillow to dab my cheeks.

A brilliant red glow radiated from the hallway, just outside the threshold to my room. I sat up on my bed and looked toward the archway, unafraid, curious. It wasn't like Firagia to visit me late at night.

"You can come in," I said.

The tall, graceful dragon slipped into my room and

approached my bedside quietly, a serene, comforting smile curling his lips. The vibrant fire of his wings lit the room with cozy, warm umber shades.

I opened my mouth to speak, but paused as he reached a long, slender hand out toward my face.

"Why do you torment yourself with these thoughts, my dear?" he said, brushing a lock of hair away from my face with a gentle swipe of one of his claws.

"I don't know," I replied. My head dropped down and I closed my eyes as I let out a huff of defeat.

"I believe you do." He lifted my chin with his warm, scaled finger and gazed at me; his endearing green dragon eyes were easy to confide in. "If you care so deeply about the young commander, then you must accept your feelings for him and push aside apprehensions."

"But I can't go back there. After this... *If* I even survive—"

"You will, Valhara." His gaze intensified. "Do not say such things."

"Alright. Assuming I do survive, I have to return to Celestial Galaxy until my service term ends in a few years. Trying to keep a long-distance relationship like that wouldn't be easy for either of us. I don't want to commit to something I can't commit to." I wiped my face again and sucked in a congested breath, a faint whimper reverberating in my throat. "Please stay out of this, Firagia." I glanced into his eyes and reached up to stroke the bridge of his muzzle. "You're kind and compassionate, but you don't know what I'm going through and you can't possibly understand how complicated things are."

"Could you love him?" he asked, raising his head slightly.

"Wh-what?" I scoffed at the audacity of his question.

"It is a simple question, Valhara." He shrugged. "I see no reason why it cannot be asked."

Could I love Mattheia?

The memory of us sitting together at night on the roof flashed across my mind and—for a fleeting moment—the exhilarating sensation of our first kiss fluttered through my heart, bringing a brief smile to my lips.

Could I love him? Or... *did I?* I didn't know anymore. I had spent so much time and energy pushing him away—telling myself to stay detached even though I wanted him in my life.

"I had to let him go," I replied to Firagia, sighing. "It had nothing to do with my feelings for him and everything to do with our responsibilities to our academies. I'm not at liberty to be involved in a relationship that could impair my judgment while I'm working."

"And what if he were a commander at your own academy? What then?" Firagia's eyes narrowed slightly, but not judgingly.

I didn't want to think about it anymore. It was already hurting, even more than it had the night before. Firagia's prying questions opened old wounds, forcing me to confront the feelings I'd swept beneath the veil of responsibility.

"The reality is he's not. Pretending he is won't change things." I crossed my arms.

"Very well, Valhara," Firagia said with a defeated nod. "I am only trying to help you. Fate has its reasons for all things. It brought us together, and it moves the fabric of time with deft hands. Goodnight and sleep well, my dear."

I forced a smile at him and then he turned and left my room.

I did sleep better that night, actually.

Perhaps it was the kind voice of Firagia that helped me find some peace. Regardless, I slept soundly for the first time in several days. The next morning, I was able to train with greater concentration and stamina than I'd had in the previous sessions, and I felt that I had made real progress. The virulent coppers and violet hues danced in wild patterns across my fingertips, the pain that once accompanied them now seemed nonexistent. The pressure was subtle—barely noticeable at all.

I lifted my arms up over my head and brought in my hands until they were a few inches apart. The tingle of light energy tickled my fingers and a riveting jolt of adrenaline coursed through me, lighting a spark between my hands which morphed into a colorful, lifelike flock of miniaturized birds. They mirrored exotic songbirds that frequented Kinasetsu's garden in the mornings. The cleric had challenged me to capture their essence in flame.

I lifted my gaze and lowered my hands out in front of me to watch the small versions of the gigantic, long-tailed birds flapping and dashing in a circular formation, ablaze. I smiled big, proud of myself for the amazing work I had done. The birds were so lifelike—small, but perfect reflections of the real things, all the way down to their elaborate head plumage. It was like my own personal menagerie— right there between my hands.

Kinasetsu backed away from me and turned toward the castle.

"What is it?" I asked, glancing at him. The fiery visage began to flicker as I lost focus.

"You may stop," he said, raising a flattened hand.

I released the energy back into the air and watched, saddened, as beautiful crimson plumage faded to ash.

"But I was doing so well today," I said with a sigh. "Are you not happy with my progress?"

"We are finished," he replied. "That is all the training I require from you today."

What?

It was barely lunchtime and I'd only been in the garden

for, at most, an hour. Typically we were there until dusk, when Firagia would join us briefly and then I would have dinner and head to bed.

"Is everything okay?" I asked, to make doubly sure we were finished.

"Yes. However, you should remain here for a few moments longer."

Why?

I squinted at him and shrugged. "Alright. I hope you're not upset with me in any way. Kinasetsu?" He had already turned and was scuttling off.

"You are progressing adequately," he said without turning to face me, then he disappeared into the greenery and, presumably, back into the castle.

I found a patch of soft grass and sat down cross-legged, plucking a tiny yellow flower from nearby to bring up to my nose. Everything smelled pleasant in Kinasetsu's garden, and I hadn't found a flower I didn't like. This sunlight-yellow one resembled a daisy, only the center was magenta instead of yellow or brown.

Why did he want me to stay where I was? Would he return?

But he said I was done training for the day, so...

I lifted my head to look around. An eerie stillness blanketed my surroundings and it instantly turned unnaturally quiet. The birds had hushed and the wind had calmed.

Something was off.

"H-hello?" I scrambled to my feet. "Who's there?" My pulse quickened and I clenched my fists. Cool energy trickled down my arms and into my twitching fingers.

"Valhara?" A voice shattered the silence.

I swerved around and gasped. The energy drained from my hands.

"Mattheia!?" I separated a row of hedges and wedged through to reach him on the other side. "What are you doing here?" I asked, sweeping leaves from my pants. "How did you—"

"I needed to see you again," he said, locking eyes with me as he approached. The Pegasus Sword hung from a scabbard near his hip. "We need to talk, and I think you owe it to me to listen because..." He brushed a hand through his hair and heaved a sigh, the metallic silver accents of his dress uniform reflecting sunlight as he moved. "I-I don't think I'll have the strength to do this again if you say no."

"I'll listen, Mattheia. Please, speak freely." His presence made my heart flutter. I hadn't expected our paths to cross ever again, but I *was* unexpectedly happy to see him.

"Valhara." He took a step closer and reached to take my hand, but then decided against it. "I didn't want to let you go, but you gave me no choice. You walked away and you shut me out. End of story. And... as angry and hurt as I was, I accepted it as just that—the end. Because you can't force a person to feel something they don't feel. I accepted the fact that I had misinterpreted our relationship and... your willingness to fight for it. And that was the end of it for me. I stopped trying to put the pieces back together in my mind and stopped wondering where we took a wrong turn."

He swallowed hard and closed the space between us, finally taking one of my hands into his and cupping it. "But then something I can only describe as *incredible* happened. An apparition came to me last night and told me the truth about you. Why you ran. Why you let go even when you didn't want to."

An apparition?

"I don't completely understand what's happened, or what an Elemental Guardian is, but if that's what you are, then I want to learn everything I can about you. And if being associated with you means putting myself in the line of fire, then I'll stand with you against whatever darkness comes. All I ask from you in return is for you to look me in the eye, and tell me—without factoring in any long-distance, different academy excuses—that you're willing to try this again. Valhara." He squeezed my hand lightly. "Will you give *us* a second chance?"

Mattheia's patient, trusting blue eyes implored me to answer honestly. He'd come all this way to ask me one last time if I'd take him back.

I didn't want him to see it, but my lip quivered as I tried

to hide the painful truth.

I sucked in an anxious breath, reaching up to sweep a tear from my cheek. Then he closed the space between us and lifted an open hand to press his palm against the damp skin there.

"Valhara?" he whispered, tipping his head inquisitively as his thumb stroked away a second tear.

I glanced shyly up and nodded, a frown still weighing down my lips. "Yes. I'd like to have a second chance at this."

He smiled and wrapped his other arm around me to pull me into an embrace. I hugged him back and sighed with relief.

I never wanted to let him go. Knowing that he cared enough to come back for me after I'd hurt him so much, meant something amazing.

He stroked a hand down the back of my head and clutched me tightly, all of our anguish and worry melting away from the heat of our embrace. We stood there in silence, just holding each other for several moments. And it felt nice. Nicer than it ever had before. Like the shadow of doubt had lifted from my soul and I didn't know or care why.

It felt as if things were going to be okay now.

It just did.

"Thank you for giving *us* a chance," Mattheia whispered.

"No." I pulled away slightly and gazed up at him. He raised an eyebrow. "Thank *you* for coming back for me."

"Of course." He pressed his thumb and forefinger to my chin and lifted my face. A rush of joy flooded my body and I came up off my heels and kissed him. He stumbled back a half-step and then planted his feet to steady himself, his hands clasping me at the waist.

New energy and strength filled me and—for a moment in time—I knew I was making the right choice. Mattheia was meant to be there with me. I knew it, now more than ever.

Why did I let him go? Why couldn't I see it before?

He slid his fingers up my sides and carefully took my face into his hands, withdrawing from our kiss to gaze into my eyes. His smile was serene and thankful as he spent some time focused intently on me. He swept my loose hair over my ear, his fingertips rising to playfully adjust the cherry blossom hair clip.

He leaned in and pressed his lips to my forehead, the soft, comforting kiss making my eyes close.

"Valhara?"

A subtle jingling noise drew my attention and my eyes reeled open.

"I want to give you something," he said, lifting a silver chain up over his head and lowering it into his hand. Two silver-tone rings hung from it.

"What are those?" I narrowed my eyes. Both rings had engravings along the bands and I could just make out a hint of faceted, blue sparkles coming from them.

"These... were my parents'," he said, unclasping the chain and sliding both rings off and into his palm. "I want you to have one as a reminder that I'll always be thinking about you no matter where you are, and to symbolize that we still have each other no matter how many hours, days, or light-years separate us."

"Oh, Mattheia, I couldn't." I shook my head. "They must be priceless."

"I love you, Valhara." His gaze pierced mine. "Maybe it's too soon to say it, but I've felt this way for some time. And... if things change and we don't work out, then we'll deal with it then. For now, I'd like you to have this." He separated the rings, slid one onto his own finger, and took my hand and set the other ring in it, curling my fingers closed around it. "Please take it. I... don't know if it will fit you, but..."

I slid it onto my ring finger, hoping for the best. "It does." I smiled, surprised it seemed to fit just right.

"Oh?" He dropped the chain into his pocket. "Well, that's even better."

"Thank you," I said, spinning the band gently around my finger. I'd never worn a ring before today, but it felt nice—like it belonged there.

Then my heart sank.

Gazing at my hands reminded me of the secret I'd yet to explain... The truth about what I was.

"How much do you know?" I asked, looking up at him.

"About?"

"About what I am and what I can do."

He shrugged. "Not much. The apparition told me you have the ability to conjure fire and that someone is trying to hurt you because of it."

Thinking the visage may have been Emerald, I had to ask. "Was it a woman? The entity that visited you?"

"No." He shook his head. "It was a creature of some kind, but it was too blurry to see. Bright red with orange and yellow waves of light circling it. It all occurred fairly quickly so I don't remember many details. I do recall its eyes, though, because they were an otherworldly shade of green."

Firagia?

No.

What reason would he have to confront Mattheia?

Unless...

Mattheia took my hand. "You can tell me anything, Valhara. This starts with us trusting each other from now on." His grasp tightened gently and a warm grin curled his lips. "I mean that."

He did mean it. I could tell from the look in his eyes.

"I need to show you something. Please don't be alarmed." I backed away and he watched. "Do you want to know why I'm staying here on this island?"

"The apparition mentioned some kind of training, and it said you were having trouble focusing because of your concerns about... me."

Who else knew about my feelings for Mattheia?

"I assume Kinasetsu is teaching you how to use your powers, right?"

"I can show you what I've learned if—"

"Yes." He nodded excitedly. "Please."

I lifted my arms out to the sides and raised them slowly, willing the fire inside to come to the surface and bind with the free energy in the air. The heat within my core erupted and grew until a glow emerged from beneath my skin, igniting around me like a fuse; a radiant purple and orange glow swallowed me whole.

Mattheia's eyes widened and his jaw eased open as he watched, but he remained calm.

I brought my hands in toward my chest, curling a plume of indigo flames around my fingers. "I can bend loose energy to my will. Conjure, control, and resist fire."

My necklace floated up and drifted in the air as my feet lifted a few inches off the ground. Sparks of yellow and orange fire licked up, seeping from my skin and encapsulating me in waves of color-shifting light.

A whoosh of air gushed through me and then Firagia burst from my necklace, shooting toward the sky, followed by a trail of sparking colors. Then he slowly descended until he landed beside me, lifting up off his front legs to stand and allowing his wings to extinguish.

Mattheia's brow wrinkled, but he wasn't nearly as shocked as I'd thought he'd be.

I turned my head to look at Firagia and allowed my fire to fade, my feet hitting the ground at the same time. Firagia smiled, his smooth, scaly cheeks rising with his toothy grin. He sauntered closer, lowered his head to investigate my hand, and then reached for it and lifted it into view.

"I see you two have put your differences aside," he said, examining the ring on my finger. His head came back up and he winked, a flicker of golden light flashing through his green eyes.

"Yes." I narrowed my eyes suspiciously.

Mattheia gasped. "You!?"

Firagia twisted toward him.

"You're the one who came to me. I recognize your voice."

"Firagia?" I glared at him, awaiting an answer.

He bowed.

"*I sought only truth.*" His voice reverberated through my head, though he did not speak out loud. "*I feel your pain, your hopes, and your fears, Valhara. Mattheia's affections are chaste; you must give him the chance you have promised.*"

Had I been subconsciously manipulated?

"*I have not manipulated you. I allowed you to see truth without bias.*"

The truth?

Truthfully, I liked Mattheia. I wanted to believe things could work out—that he and I might—

The earth shook beneath my feet.

"Valhara?" Mattheia lunged for my arm. "What was that?"

"I-I don't know."

Firagia came down onto all fours and arched his back defensively, snarling and baring his fangs as his wings burst into bright waves of heated flame.

The ground rumbled again and I reached behind my back for my sword, snapping it off the magnetic mount. Out of the corner of my eye, I noticed Mattheia flexing a hand toward the Pegasus Sword.

"You don't know how to use that," I said out of one side of my mouth. "It will be a liability if you draw it here."

"Right," he whispered. He relaxed his fingers and then reached diagonally across his chest to slip his gun from its holster.

Firagia continued to search our surroundings, his nails plowing into the grass as he rotated in place, his tail whipping through the air anxiously.

Dirt fired out of the ground, and a row of long, barbed vines shot up through the grass, towering high overhead, bending and twirling like angry snakes. I grabbed Mattheia by the sleeve and bolted to the side as one of the flailing things crashed down nearby.

Firagia dodged the next two vines that lashed after him but was struck by the third. It wrapped around his hind leg and squeezed, sending him into a panic.

Mattheia aimed and took a shot at a coil spiraling our way. I couldn't help Firagia from where I stood, but he wound his body around until he could snap his jaws onto the thorny vine and rip it off with a crushing bite, spitting the thrashing remains at the ground. It squirmed away and burrowed into the dirt. Then the remaining vines withdrew and vanished.

Another tremor rippled below and a thunderous crack sounded from behind a tall line of brush.

"It came from over there," Mattheia shouted, pointing. Firagia charged in that direction, leaping through the shrubbery and disappearing into the green.

Everything went quiet. I grasped my sword until my knuckles went white. Mattheia held steadfast to his gun. We stood in silence and I held my breath while I listened carefully. I couldn't hear Firagia... or anything else, for that matter.

No birds.

Not even the wind.

A subdued crackling sound reverberated from behind the greenery, followed by an ear-splitting snap. Firagia exploded through the wall of plants, sending a cloud of fire and burnt leaves up into the air, surrounding us with smoke and ash. He landed with a hard thud and then a massive figure came barging through behind him.

"Morgan!" Firagia howled, scrambling to his feet and standing up on his hind legs.

As the name flitted from his mouth, a picture of the enchantress, Morgan Le Fay, darted through my mind, planted there by Firagia's own thoughts. I looked up at the thing made of twisted green and brown—trees and vines that had come together to create the shape of a woman in a long, flowing dress with bell sleeves and a sash of thorny roses entwined at its waist. It towered several feet above us and lumbered our way, tearing earth open with each dragging step. Its head bent to the side with an unnerving pop. Wooden eyes, glazed over with smoldering white light, glowed and pulsed behind withering green.

"Guardian..." seethed from its mouth, branches moving like lips.

My heart raced and I flexed my fingers, willing a coil of yellow and blue firelight to spiral up both arms. Mattheia looked over at me and gasped.

"Valhara!? What are you going to do?"

"I don't know," I replied. "Whatever it takes to keep you safe. Back up!"

I jammed my sword into the grass to keep it within reach, and then squeezed both hands into fists; golden-sapphire ripples cascaded over my skin, radiating intense heat.

"Don't come any closer!" I raised a flattened hand and conjured a focused ball of energy around my fingers. With my pulse thumping through me, the light began to flicker sporadically, dimming and brightening as fear infected me.

"You are unworthy of your gift." The haunting mess of nature jerked its head up and then to the side, mechanically. "I will not allow another Guardian to soil my land."

A white-hot blast buzzed past me and struck the thing in the face, igniting a patch of twigs making up its cheek. Mattheia had impeccable aim, but the shot wasn't enough.

The thing resembling Morgan hissed at the fleeting damage and then began to whisper something in a language I didn't understand. A deep crack tore through each side of its body and a row of thick branches peeled back from the sides of its dress, splintering into rigid, erect quills pointing our way. The frays curled outward and then launched at us, whizzing through the air across the garden.

I plucked my sword from the ground. "Duck!" The heat of my fire dissipated and I took Mattheia's arm and tugged him down. Firagia leapt into the air and flew in front of us, catching fire to the entire row of deadly thorns before they could make contact.

"You are a coward!" Morgan hissed, sweeping a hand down to tug its skirt in so it would reform.

"How did you get here, Morgan?" Firagia asked. "Why have you attacked my Guardian?"

"Do not side with her," the creature replied with a rustle of its leafy lips. It continued to close the space between us. "She is not pure of heart. She must die."

"No." Firagia withdrew a few steps and his body began to emit a subtle red glow. "She will not die. Not at your hands or anyone's. Not while I am her Spirit. Reconsider your target, Morgan. Please."

"After all I did to preserve you? Ungrateful dragon!" The thing bent forward and opened its mouth wide to release a chilling screech that made a sick feeling swell in my stomach. Mattheia and I covered our ears.

Firagia shook his head and scampered to my side. "The Morgan I knew sought only to preserve life, not take it away!"

It was clear to me now that Emerald had assumed Morgan's image to confuse the poor dragon.

"I gave you a choice, beast!" it continued. "You have chosen incorrectly. Now you will die with the unworthy one."

"Stay back, Mattheia!" I glared at him. He was reluctant to move, at first, but understood the severity of the situation and backed off several feet.

Holding my sword firmly between my hands, I called the fire again. A bolt of blue and yellow light jolted through the blade, igniting it with red and fringing the metal with swirls of violet.

The thing watched me, following my every move as I circled it. I kept a close eye on the freshly formed splinters peeling up on its skirt, careful to stay just shy of their aim. A second wave burst from it and I dodged as many as I could, swinging my sword to deflect them. A handful grazed my leg and I grunted as quills shredded a hole in my slacks, nicking the skin. A riveting burning sensation erupted from the scratch, spreading out in every direction until my entire calf twinged.

"You are weak!" the monstrosity roared and let out a spine-tingling cackle.

"There's nothing funny about this!" I clenched my jaw. A rush of color flushed through my vision and I removed one hand from my sword and thrust it out in front of me, sending a tremor of heat and light at Morgan. Fire consumed the thing, leaving all the details and edges smoldering with brilliant orange.

It cried out and hunched over, wailing as plumes of smoke wafted from its body. I used the moment to lunge at it. The Azure Phoenix came down swiftly and firmly, hacking into the statue's right hand, dismembering it. A pile of leaves and vines fell to the ground and shriveled.

The wretched wail coming from its mouth made my ears ache and a stabbing pain dart through my brain. My knees weakened and I doubled over on the ground, struggling to grasp my sword while shielding my ears from the sound. A burst of fire whizzed past and I looked up; Firagia had taken to the air. He swooped in, head first, and plunged into the creature, sending it tumbling to the ground with a trail of burning embers sizzling up the length of its body.

"Try again!" Firagia shouted, taking off for a second strike.

I approached the now silenced figure and raised my sword. Just as I did, the thing shot up from the ground, a thousand thin, scraggly roots sprouting from its back, helping to right it on its base.

Morgan shook out her arm. Dark brown stems sprung from the plant creature's gnarled wrist and stretched out, twisting and bending until they had reformed the missing hand.

Instinctively, I looked back at Mattheia to make sure he was safe.

He was gone!

"Mattheia!"

The monster turned, bent over, and slammed both hands against the ground. Its arms merged together into one gigantic, twisted vine that then came coiling toward me.

Firagia lunged for it, but Morgan jerked her shoulders to the side, whipping the vine up to deflect his attack and throw him off balance.

The burning sensation continued working up my legs and was now in my thighs and hips, still tingling with unsettling pain. I had to get through it. I had to muster the strength to carry on. Where had Mattheia gone? It was hard to focus with him missing.

The dirt beneath me trembled and I lost my footing, tumbling onto my back with a thump. The Azure Phoenix fell from my hands. The breath knocked from me, it took a moment to gather my senses. I covered my eyes against a dusting of dirt and rocks as the newly-formed double-vine exploded out of the ground. I rolled onto my stomach and stretched out an arm to reach for my sword.

The searing pain of a thousand needles piercing my skin shot through my body. The vine had grabbed me by my feet and quickly twirled around my legs, twisting and turning, swirling and squeezing me as it snaked up past my waist toward my arms. I flailed in the dirt, fighting back even though the struggle made the thorns embed more deeply into my flesh. I made the mistake of grabbing at it with my hands and screamed in pain, recoiling, my hands now bleeding.

"Firagia!" My voice broke and the air was forced from my lungs. I gasped—ribs compressed by vines—suffocating.

I tried to conjure the fire again, but it wouldn't come.

I couldn't...

My strength had...

"Back!" a voice boomed.

I couldn't tell whose it was.

The thing released me in an instant, uncoiling from my body and slithering off. I took in a breath of air and coughed, rolling onto my side and cringing as every inch of me felt as if it had been scuffed raw. Burning. Stinging. Pressure and pain. Sickness in my stomach. A massive headache.

I lifted my head to look around, but everything was a blur of colors sifting across my vision.

"I'm here!" I heard Mattheia say just as he crouched down beside me and rested a hand on my shoulder. I grimaced and bit down. "Everything's going to be okay."

How could everything be okay when every inch of me felt like a thousand needles had become lodged beneath my skin?

I squinted. All I could see was light and all I could hear were distorted screams and thrashing sounds. Bright blue light flashed across my field of view and then everything went quiet.

"What happened?" I asked weakly.

A warm, friendly presence neared—Firagia. I couldn't see him very well, but I sensed him approach.

"Can you help her!?" Mattheia asked with panic in his voice.

"The wounds are deep," a different voice replied— Kinasetsu.

"I can," Firagia replied, coming down low to the ground as he reached out a gentle hand to brush my shin. I let out a shriek as the subtle pressure made the piercing ache rip through me again. "I am sorry, my dear," the dragon said quietly. "There is something you should know about our connection." He wrapped a hand around my leg and I sucked in a sharp breath, holding back another outburst.

Cold swept over my leg and all of the stinging suddenly dampened. I regained enough strength to push up onto my elbows and watch Firagia as he knelt at my feet, grasping my leg now with both hands. My vision began to clear and I watched as he closed his eyes and concentrated, his grasp tightening on the wounds.

I squinted, unsure of what I was seeing.

It appeared as if tiny marks were opening up across Firagia's scales, revealing the delicate pink skin underneath. He gritted his teeth and scowled, snarling beneath his breath as his lips wrinkled.

"Dragons can absorb wounds from other living things," he said, breathless, his voice cracking. "As your Spirit, it is my responsibility to protect you. I failed. I must endure the consequences." All of my pain had dissipated, just as a row of pierce marks dotted his sides and he released my leg.

He cowered and let out a deep, beastly growl. My body no longer roiling with ache, I sat up and reached out to touch him. My fingertips brushed against his scales and he jerked away from me with an abrupt hiss.

"I apologize," he said, ashamed. "I will heal soon, but..." He bore down again and stifled a groan. "Not quickly enough, I am afraid." He forced an uncomfortable grin.

I looked down at my blood-soaked clothes and tugged a pant leg up several inches. The skin was smooth and intact.

"Thank you," I said, releasing the fabric.

Firagia sat a little straighter now, as if some of the wounds were fading, and then bowed his head. "Anything for you, Valhara," he said with an earnest, exhausted smile.

I dried my hair and changed into clean clothes. Washing so much blood off my skin was gut wrenching. There were holes everywhere from the thorns that had pierced me. Now my skin looked as if nothing had ever happened. I didn't know Firagia could do such a thing, but I was grateful he could, and that he would sacrifice his comfort for a girl he'd only met recently.

"Valhara?" Mattheia called from just outside the threshold of my room.

"Come in," I said as I buttoned the second to the last button on my shirt.

He came through the archway and paused there to look

at me. A look of relief and thankfulness came across his face.

"I'm... glad you're okay," he said as he approached. He swept his fingertips across my brow and cupped my cheek with his palm, an air of sadness about him. "I wanted to help you. I did. But I couldn't, so I had to get help. I would have done anything but—"

"It might be like this for a while," I replied, forking a hand through his fair, golden hair. "You're going to have to get used to it. I'm sorry."

He took a deep breath. "I'm second in command at Silver Diamond. If something happens to Captain Lansfora, I'll be the head of over twenty thousand personnel. *Twenty thousand.* And when you were in danger, all I could do was run for help. I felt like a fool not being able to stand beside you. But..."

"We aren't fighting standard military-grade battles, Mattheia," I said. "Nothing either of us learned in academy training could have helped when that thing attacked. It's not your fault. You did what you could and I think you made the right decision."

"You're lucky to have him," he said, looking down at my necklace.

"Who?" I cocked my head and then realized what he'd meant.

"Firagia. He's otherworldly, to say the least. If it weren't for him, I don't know how you would have fared with all of those wounds. That thing... it—"

"I would have been okay," I said, smiling encouragingly. "You came all this way to ask me if I'd like to try being with you again; I wouldn't let you down on the first day."

His sweet smile made my heart a little lighter.

"He clearly cares about you, Valhara. As much as I do, if not more, somehow. That dragon is unlike any living thing I've ever come across."

"Because he's not a living thing. Not any more."

"Wh-what? But..."

"He's a life force—a manifestation of his former self created by energy. He knew who Morgan was because she was the enchantress who preserved his soul in crystal." I fidgeted with my necklace.

"Well, it's because of him that I'm here today. It's like he knows me better than I know myself. When he came to me as an apparition of firelight, he asked questions regarding how I felt about you. And... I was compelled to tell him the truth. There's something very special about him. When he looks into your eyes, you—"

"Feel safe?"

"Yes."

Firagia had warmth about him that could be likened to the presence of a parent or loved one, and even though we'd met recently, I was beginning to cherish him like family.

"You make me feel safe, too," I said, taking Mattheia's

hand.

"I'm glad to hear that, Valhara." His smile was bitter-sweet.

"You are not safe here anymore," Kinasetsu said, tossing a shriveled-up, dead rose branch onto the floor in front of us—remains of the monstrous thing that had attacked in the garden. He brought his box of sparkling lights over to the throne and sat with it, propping up the lid. He leaned over and sorted through various twinkling colors with his long fingers. "I have no power to stop her now that she has broken through the barrier and found my castle. You must not let down your guard, Valhara. Emerald will strike again."

"When?" I asked, shifting the leather strap on my shoulder to make my sword more comfortable on my back. I hadn't parted with it since the attack.

"I do not know," Kinasetsu replied. He lifted a handful of fuchsia stars from the box. "I can attempt to cast another spell to cloak your energy, but it will be fleeting."

"She will come for you regardless," Firagia spoke up as he entered the throne room from the hall, his soft red aura bouncing off the walls.

"How do we protect her?" Mattheia asked, turning to face the dragon.

"You cannot," he replied somberly. "But... perhaps *I* can reason with Emerald. Her half-sister, Morgan, preserved my soul in hopes of providing guidance and support for an upcoming Guardian who might find themselves in Emerald's wake. She could see into the future and knew terrible things awaited every Elemental Guardian born after her death. Morgan and Emerald had both been cast out by their brother, the king, and thus shared an enemy. Perhaps I can use that as a means of negotiating the terms upon which she seeks to challenge you." Firagia looked at me. "You and Arthur are very different, Valhara. As an intuitive dragon with the ability to intimately connect with your thoughts, I know this to be true." He bowed. "Please allow me to go to her. I am familiar with Alyssia and where her soul likely resides. If I can find her burial ground, I can follow the remaining energy trail to her, plead your innocence, and then try to make her see who you really are."

"Is that even possible?" I glanced at Kinasetsu who sat with his head resting on a fist.

"I cannot say," he replied. The white sparkles in his eyes appeared brighter than usual. "Every Guardian's experiences differ. I am unable to predict exactly what is to come."

Firagia could make it back to me in a flash if need be. Our link allowed him to teleport whenever I summoned him, my amulet acting as the portal. I wasn't afraid of being without him for very long.

"Go." I stroked Firagia's head gently. "Be safe, my friend."

"I will do my best," he replied with a toothy grin. "Have faith." Firagia got down onto all fours and then bounded into the air, his amber and scarlet wings ablaze as he soared up toward the ceiling and vanished, like a ghost, through the masonry.

"He'll do his best," Mattheia said, taking my hand.

"I know he will," I replied with a sigh. "But will she? Will Emerald listen to him?"

"If anyone can convince her that you're worthy of your powers, it's him."

"*I will...*"

Firagia's voice echoed through my head and I gasped.

"Valhara!?" Mattheia's hand squeezed mine.

"It's him. It's Firagia."

Blue and white flooded my vision and I was suddenly soaring across the horizon. Fluffy white clouds tumbled by beneath me.

I lost my balance and fell forward. Mattheia grabbed me and held firmly as I quivered, my body feeling weightless as I dove through an endless sea of sky.

"*Do not fear,*" Firagia said. "*You are seeing what I see. I can release your mind if—*"

"No. Don't. Keep showing me."

If Firagia would face Emerald, I wanted to be there with him for support in any way possible.

"Is everything okay, Valhara? What's going on?" Mattheia's voice trembled.

"I'm fine. I can see through his eyes. Through Firagia's eyes. Brace me so I don't fall."

"I will, Valhara. You're safe."

The stunning, iridescent dragon dashed across the evening horizon with an aura that lit the sky like a comet. We flew through cloudbursts and over miles of ocean and mountain ranges. Past an active volcano spewing puffs of dark grey. Up and over a monstrous storm crying curtains of rain and clashing thunder and sparks of white. He ascended back into the clouds and carried on, shooting like a star as fast as his energy could take him.

Then he slowed and descended, passing a massive, ancient castle—eroded by time—and a long span of tumultuous lakes where the powerful breeze swayed the trees as if they were blades of grass.

He came down near the side of a mountain and landed as softly as a mouse. Firagia's muzzle rose and he sniffed the air a few times.

Cedar.

I smelled it, too.

He followed the scent up the mountain and around the side until he came to a large rock formation—a cave entrance.

"Be careful," I said.

"Of course," he replied, only in my head.

"Where is he?" Mattheia asked anxiously. He couldn't see what I was seeing.

"He found a cave. Somewhere in Alyssia."

I returned my attention to Firagia's vision and watched as the dragon cautiously entered the dank, dark place. He jerked his head, listening in various directions as it was difficult to see in the shadows. Hollow vibrations. Water dripping in the distance. The scent of petrichor filled my nostrils.

He drew energy from the air and fueled his wings to burn more brightly until the walls farther ahead flickered with bright yellow light.

He narrowed his eyes and gazed into the blackness that went on forever.

"Show yourself!" Firagia called into the abyss.

Our hearts raced in unison as we waited in silence.

"Why have you come, dragon?" a hoarse, eerie echo replied.

"I have come to defend my Guardian—to plead her case to you so that you may not harm her."

Green and blue lights glistened up ahead, twinkling on and off as they twirled in random spirals. I couldn't tell what they were, but they frightened me with their strange formations.

"Why has she not come to defend herself?" the voice continued. "Does she send you in her place? Are you her slave?"

"I am her Spirit and her friend," Firagia retorted, planting his claws into the gravel. "Now stop your foolishness and face me civilly, please!"

"I am no fool!" the voice roared, and in a flash of white-hot light, Emerald appeared before Firagia, her vivid purple velvet gown dotted with the magic lights.

"I lost my Spirit to my ignorant brother. My poor, dear Malachite. And you..." She bared her teeth in a snarl. "You come and dare claim that your Guardian deserves mercy? If she should deserve such... she should have come and asked me herself!"

My hands felt ice cold.

I-I couldn't breathe all of a sudden.

Firagia panicked, too, and I felt his own consciousness darting back and forth.

"Valhara!" Mattheia grabbed me by the shoulders. "What's happening!?"

My body grew cold and heavy. My eyes burned.

Then I fell, this time, tumbling onto damp, hard earth. Stones scratched against my palms.

I opened my eyes and lifted my face. It was dark all around, except for the raging fire of Firagia's wings blazing in the distance up ahead and the small point of light peeking through the cave entrance in the opposite direction.

Mattheia reached down and pulled me to my feet.

"Oh, no. We're in Emerald's cave!" I looked toward Mattheia. My breaths quickened. "You can't be here, Mattheia. She'll—"

"Save your strength," he interrupted. "Focus on the fight that's coming." He tried to mask the fear in his voice but failed. "Don't worry about me right now."

I couldn't see him very well, but I felt his warm hand come up to touch my face. Then I felt his lips against mine when he kissed me, holding me gently at the back of my head.

"There's no one else like you in the world, Valhara," he whispered, kissing my cheek as I shuddered in fear. "Show her that."

My eyes met his. I could see better in the darkness, now that my light had begun to burn. A soft yellow aura flitted through my clothing.

Mattheia smiled and my fiery glow bounced off his proud expression. "I believe in you," he said. "I always have."

I inhaled a deep breath. "I'll do my best," I said, and then took off running toward Firagia.

Wet rocks rolled beneath my shoes and I slipped a few times, quick to catch my balance or I'd risk injury. "I'm not afraid of you!" I said, rushing to the dragon's side and planting my feet as firmly as I could in the slushy dirt.

Firagia veered his head toward me. "I am sorry! I did not know she would bring you here!"

"No time for apologies. Let's focus!"

"Very well!" Firagia grinned. *"We will win this, Valhara,"* his voice softly poured through my mind, filling me with much-needed confidence.

"We will," I responded, without speaking. I was getting accustomed to the mind connection.

"I don't want to fight you, Emerald," I said. "I just want to live and keep the people I love safe. I have no intention of harming anyone with my power."

"Liar!" She scowled, her eyes shimmering with virulent red. "You lie in an effort to save yourself. You have gone so far as to manipulate that poor beast into believing he must sacrifice himself for you."

"I protect her willingly!" Firagia straightened up, puffing his chest proudly. "I am sorry darkness took your dear Spirit from you, but that does not mean I am not worthy of the same respect as he. I am no slave. I fight voluntarily by Valhara's side just as Malachite fought by yours."

Emerald stepped closer, her long, dark hair curtaining the sides of her face. "Then you will die by her side, as well. And... at the claws of your own precious kind!"

Firagia and I glanced at each other, unsure of what she'd meant. Then a series of loud cracking sounds rang out and our focus shot back to her. She'd bent over on the ground, her back arched and her neck bent upward.

Her skin glazed over with icy white and rippled with the

texture of thick, reptilian scales, each one peeling up from her flesh like an iridescent glass leaf. Six horns of graduated sizes pushed out of her head—three on each side—and then curled up into sharp crescents with jagged black designs etched in.

Firagia and I staggered backward as Emerald's body began to grow and lengthen, her bones moving and shifting as her violet dress tore away to reveal more glossy scales. Her face stretched outward, pulling into a long, narrow muzzle, much like that of a horse, except the nostrils were bigger and rounder, and the jaw lined with huge, carnivorous teeth.

I wasn't going to wait for her to get big enough to crush us within the narrow cavern, so I twisted around and ran toward the cave entrance.

"Get out!" I shouted at Mattheia.

We hurried, dodging fragments of debris and stone tumbling from the ceiling as the creature continued to manifest behind us, roaring and unleashing hideous, blood-curdling moans of agony and rage.

Just as we made it out, the ground began to thunder and a heavy clomping sound rose louder and louder until a colossal, shimmering white thing came bursting out of the entryway, bringing with it a downpour of shattered stone. We shielded our eyes.

The air cleared and a gust of cold hit me. "Mattheia, keep your distance," I said, my breath a puff of white. There weren't many places for him to go, but...

We stepped back and craned our necks to look up.

It must have stood twenty feet tall, easily dwarfing the mahora spider. Frosty-blue chevrons ran down its neck like fused plate armor. Jagged edges trimmed the beast's jaw line, chin, the bridge of its nose, elbows, and tail, which was at least as long as the rest of its body combined. Tiger-style black stripes decorated the length of its back, the front of each leg, and embellished all six horns curling from the sides of its head. Along its back, two tall rows of quills protruded in a v-shaped line from the base of its neck down to its muscular rump. It was impossible to miss its tail, which ended in a large, fanned-out appendage of webbed spikes flattened like a wide shovel.

The enormous dragon hunched down as if it were a lion about to pounce, and its terrifyingly large head lowered toward the ground. The glistening white mouth curled into a snarl as it bared its fangs. Droplets of saliva fell from between its jaws, each one instantly freezing as it hit the ground.

"How dare you!" Firagia snapped, clenching his jaw and glaring at the dragon.

I didn't want to start a conversation; all I wanted to do was get out of there, but a quick look around showed no escape route in sight.

"I knew you would recognize me," the thing seethed in a thunderous, deep voice, taking a step closer and flexing its massive, ice-blue claws while scratching lines into the bedrock below. "All dragons know of Emperor Kiva, Lord of the Ice."

"Lord Kiva died trying to save the dragons!" Firagia replied. "How dare you tarnish his image with your villainy!"

"I can take any form I wish," it said, snapping down its teeth. "Now, Guardian." It turned to look at me with glimmering red eyes. "You will die!"

Kiva came at us fast, kicking into a rampant gallop. I'd never fought a dragon before and I didn't know where to begin, but I sensed spitefulness brewing in Firagia's heart, and that triggered the fire in me to ignite almost instantaneously. I forced my hands out in front of me and willed a wall of flame to climb up, blocking the attack and making the dragon paw violently to extinguish a bolt of yellow light nipping its icy brow.

It backed away and flattened a giant clawed hand against the rocks, closing its eyes as its dragon mouth formed words I couldn't decipher. A plume of white essence leached up from below and a line of glossy shine forked from its fingers, covering the ground with a thick sheet of ice which extended past my firewall, putting it out instantly.

"*I will distract him,*" Firagia said to me in my mind. "*Use everything you've learned, Valhara!*" He leapt into the air. A flash of red-amber light zipped over Kiva's head, drawing the attention off me.

Firagia continued to dart back and forth in front of Kiva, instigating it like a red firefly buzzing to and fro. Kiva swatted, but Firagia kept phasing between physical and energy forms so each strike went straight through his body.

Then it started—the familiar pressure and warmth bubbling inside, pushing softly against my ribcage as my feet came up off the ground. Heat grew rapidly and a breath was knocked from my lungs as a massive wave of purple and orange fire erupted from my chest, shooting outwards in a beam of concentrated heat. The ray struck the ice dragon in the side, knocking it off balance and searing a black mark across its scales. It howled angrily and spun around to face me.

The giant mouth opened and Kiva propelled toward me, snapping its jaws wildly. I swung my sword and deflected a bite, knocking into one of its incisors and losing my footing. I stumbled. The sharp ringing in my ears made my head spin. I looked up; it was coming at me again!

I tried to conjure a second wave of fire, but it wouldn't manifest swiftly enough.

Come on. Come on!

I lifted a shaking hand as the white monster charged my way, concentrating on bringing the energy to my fingertips once more.

Kiva came to an abrupt halt and let out a furious growl that shook the earth. It abandoned its focus on me to bend its thick neck to look behind, hissing angrily.

Mattheia had jammed the Pegasus Sword through the end of its tail, anchoring the dragon to the ground. The large yellow stone faceted in the crossbar began to emanate white-hot light and he let go, startled. A flash of yellow shot toward the sky, pulsing like a beacon. Firagia dove down and ushered Mattheia out of the beast's reach while it was distracted.

The dragon tried to pull free, but the blade had become lodged in the thick layer of ice. It contorted its cumbersome body around and frantically worked to dislodge the blade. Its giant claws clumsily tried to grasp it and its frustrations grew.

The silver blade glistened and a soft humming sound filled the air; the noise was melodic and subtle, like a delicate lullaby suspended in time.

Was the blade... singing?

A high-pitched whinny rang out from the clouds and my gaze shot up. Iridescent sorrel brown wings soared over our heads, flanked by a wispy, black tail whipping through the air. The buckskin pegasus galloped across the sky and then came plummeting headfirst toward Kiva like a cannonball. The horse bashed into the dragon's shoulder and pushed it off balance.

The Pegasus Sword continued to beam with white-gold light, just as it had the first time we'd seen it.

"The sword!" I called to Mattheia. "It must have summoned the pegasus!"

Mattheia nodded. "What do we do now!?"

I didn't know.

Kiva and the pegasus fought, tackling each other, though the poor horse was hardly a match in size. Firagia joined in and rose up behind Kiva to cast a fire storm down across its spiny back. With its tail still nailed down, the ice dragon's movements were limited.

The pegasus kicked Kiva in the face and darted off to wind up for a second blow. At that same moment, Kiva let out a deep grunt and tugged its tail forcefully. The sword flew over our heads like a toothpick, whizzing past and disappearing into the distant trees.

Firagia and the pegasus barreled down from both sides and, upon impact, Kiva shattered into thousands of pieces of glittering ice dust that flew up into the air. I coughed as cold fragments stole the breath from of me. Firagia swooped in and ignited a cloud of fire around us both, instantly melting the ice particles. The pegasus neighed loudly and then all I could hear was the fading whistling made by its wings as it disappeared back into the clouds.

"How far will you go, Guardian?" Emerald asked, manifesting from a swirl of the twinkling ice fragments. "How hard will you fight to protect *yourself*?"

Myself? What did she mean by that? Hadn't that been

what I'd been doing all along? Protecting myself? And...

I gasped and cut a glance at Mattheia.

In a flash, Emerald swept him into a ball of white energy, paralyzing him inside an orb of sparking forks of lavender light.

"Let him go!" Firagia roared.

"This is not his fight!" I added, my rapidly-beating heart threatening to burst out of my chest. "He never did anything to you!"

"Loyalty is a fickle thing," Emerald hissed, dropping Mattheia's limp body down at her feet. A flick of her wrist and a thick ice wall formed, separating us. I could barely see through it at all and could make out only a blurry shape moving on the other side.

She started speaking in a tongue I didn't recognize again.

"She's enchanting him!" Firagia's eyes widened. His rising fear crept into my own veins, making my stomach turn. "We must do something before—"

A ferocious howl cut through the ice, sending me to my knees to cover my ears. I squinted as the pain in my eardrums thumped and the ringing disoriented me.

Through cloudy ice, I saw Mattheia hunching over, his body deformed and arched. A series of loud cracking sounds shook the air and he cried out as his bones shifted inside him, growing and lengthening until he was higher off the ground.

A second later, a massive thing stared back at us through the ice. White fur flecked with grey and black. A powerful muzzle decorated with long, sharp fangs, and a hungry crease on its lips. It clawed at the ice with paws the size of a human head, and then stepped back and charged into the wall, sending a large crack up the center. It backed away and charged again, smashing through the ice.

"Mattheia!?"

The bright blue eyes in the thing's head were a dead giveaway. Emerald had transformed him into a grossly oversized mountain wolf.

It snapped its jaws and growled as it approached, its head low and its body poised for an attack.

"He will not recognize you," Emerald announced, rising up above us to land on the arch that remained of the ice wall. "Guardians have the power to protect and destroy. You must decide who lives and who dies."

"I won't hurt him!" I yelled. The sound of my anger provoked the beast and it lunged for me. I dodged to the side and Firagia swooped in to block the attack. The wolf slid across the icy floor and then came back to its feet, shaking its head and snarling again, its muzzle wrinkling fiercely.

"Then you will die," Emerald added with a harsh laugh. "You have no choice."

"We always have a choice!" I reached for my sword but hesitated.

No. I can't...

If I drew my weapon, I'd risk injuring him.

"You must defend yourself," Firagia reminded me.

"How?" I replied, shaking as the enormous white beast trudged closer. Puffs of white breath drifted from its nostrils like smoke.

"Speak to him. Remind him who he is. Try to break her control."

How!?

"Mattheia! You know who I am," I said, withdrawing my hand from my sword.

The wolf lowered its head to ready a second strike and we circled each other.

"We fought the mahora spider together. That's how you got the Pegasus Sword." I pointed but realized it was nowhere in sight. "It called the pegasus that fought by our side moments ago." I spotted a long, tan wing feather on the ground and slowly bent to retrieve it, not breaking eye contact with him. "See?" I held it out toward the wolf; I couldn't stop my hand from trembling.

He stretched his neck out to sniff the feather, taking in a few whiffs of its scent before snorting and then lunging forward to latch onto it and rip it from my grasp. He coughed it back onto the ground and then returned his attention to me, snarling.

"I don't want to fight you!" I inched back and it pursued,

its hungry blue eyes delving into my soul and unearthing new fears from deep within me.

What if I couldn't stop it? Would it... Would *Mattheia* kill me?

The wolf pounced, tearing a line of deep gashes into my shoulder as he passed. Then he jogged up ahead to turn around to refocus his aim, crouching down and waving his giant fluffy tail excitedly.

"Valhara!" Firagia landed beside me and quickly looked over my arm. "You cannot let him destroy you. You *must* fight back!"

"How!?" I tried to cover the wound with my hand. Blood oozed through my fingers and the wolf eyed me up again as I tried to cauterize the gashes. A glow of yellow light poured from my skin and I smelled my own flesh sizzling from the heat.

The bleeding stopped.

"Kill her!" Emerald commanded from her post overhead.

A flurry of white rushed me and I froze in place, refusing to fight back or hurt him. In my defense, Firagia lifted his arms out to the sides and sent a fury of color into a cyclone around us both, igniting a patch of the wolf's hair and making it retreat.

"I will not stand idly by and watch everything you have worked for crumble to ash!" Firagia scowled. "Fight back,

Valhara!"

"No!" I huffed furiously. "It was *your* idea to get us back together. You told him to come for me and now you're asking me to murder him? I won't do it! I can't. I... love him."

"I know," Firagia replied solemnly, the intense sadness in his eyes confirming he understood the dilemma. "But you cannot die, either. Mattheia may be lost to us now and if you die, too, it will all be for naught, my dear." He reached up to press his soft, scaly hand onto my wounded shoulder and closed his eyes briefly, absorbing the pain and acquiring a set of shallow gashes on his own body. "Please, listen." He winced. "As your Spirit, but most importantly, your friend."

Thoughts I'd never anticipated coursed through my brain. Thoughts about how far I was willing to go to try to save myself, and was I willing to die to preserve the love I had for Mattheia? Sickening suggestions of murdering the man who had sacrificed so much for me made me furious.

I wouldn't do it!

Emerald could turn *him* into a beast, but she couldn't make me into one, too.

As those affirmations haunted me, the protective cyclone of colorful fire began to disintegrate and we were confronted, once more, by the hulking white wolf.

He separated his jaws and roared, saliva splashing onto my skin. I gritted my teeth and did the only thing I could think to do.

I closed my eyes.

I closed my eyes, clenched my fists, and stood there, as silently as possible. Holding my breath. Trying hard not to flinch as he moved closer and sniffed, exhaling hot breath onto my skin.

"*What are you doing, Valhara!?*" Firagia's panicked words drifted through my mind.

"*I'm not like the others,*" I replied silently. "*I'll prove it.*"

The wolf rammed me with his head and knocked me onto my back. The rocky floor pressed painfully against my backbone and I groaned, struggling to keep my eyes shut as the wolf proceeded to shove me with his snout.

He growled impatiently and pawed at my arm, tearing open skin. I cried out and covered my face with both hands, my breaths shuddering in my chest.

The wolf came at me again and I tensed up.

Heavy breaths came and went from his powerful lungs. Then he lingered there, his bloodthirsty head inches from my body.

Was he deciding what limb to go for first, or was he awaiting Emerald's command?

I flinched as his cold, wet nose nuzzled me in the side, much more gently than before. He whimpered softly.

"Wh-what?" I uttered, my eyes easing open at the odd sound.

I slowly separated my hands from my face and the animal

backed away, lowering his head.

"Mattheia?" I came to my knees and reached a shaky hand out.

The wolf lay down and rested his head on his outstretched front legs.

"Do you know who I am?" My voice cracked as I forced myself to move closer, fear making my legs heavy.

He whined and crawled across the ground to reach me, lowering his muzzle to nudge my hand and lick it lightly with his large, rough pink tongue.

"Do you remember? Are you in control now?" I asked.

He snorted and pressed his nose to my knuckles, looking at me and then back at my hand, motioning back and forth a few times until I got the message.

The ring?

I lifted my fingers to the light so the sun reflected off the silver band he'd given me.

"This? You remember this?"

He bounded eagerly to his feet and yipped.

"Good! I knew I could trust you!"

The wolf pressed his large forehead against me and I roughed up the thick, white fur with my fingers.

"I did it, Firagia," I said, looking back. A proud smile stretched across his scaly face.

"I am sorry I misled you," he said so only I could hear it.

"You were trying to protect me. It's your job."

Mattheia lifted his mouth toward the sky and howled, making the earth rumble.

"Enough!" Emerald's voice shattered the remaining ice.

Mattheia turned sharply to face her, his fangs bared and a hearty growl resonating from his throat. I took a deep breath and shook out my arms, the sting of my new wound dampened by a rush of fresh adrenaline.

Mattheia darted off after Emerald, climbing the scattered remains of ice and rock to try to get to her, but she vanished and appeared behind him. She continued vaporizing and re-emerging in different locations, making him leap from place to place frantically.

A buzzing sound rattled through my head and large shards of broken ice began to levitate off the ground, commanded by Emerald's hand.

With Firagia by my side, I willed an even stronger, taller wall of colorful fire to come up around us, blocking the deadly spears as she hurled them in our direction. A wave of warm water hit us and the wall died down.

"What is it going to take to stop you!?" I curled my hands into fists, exhausted now but struggling to muster every last shred of might.

Emerald floated closer, the hypnotic blue and green sparkle patterns growing brighter on her flowy dress. She lifted her hands and the lights blazed white as she readied another spell.

I doubled over, panting while trying to catch my breath.

I can't keep doing this.

Mattheia scrambled down the rock formation and came to my aid, pushing his furry nose up against me supportively.

"I'm trying, Mattheia," I huffed, my mouth parched. "I'm... trying so hard." I snapped my sword off my back and held it firmly. Emerald drifted within reach and I bolted after her, the Azure Phoenix igniting in a blaze of red-hot light.

A humming noise saturated the air; I looked up and saw a massive ice crystal spiraling toward me at break-neck speed.

White flashed across my field of vision and I was thrust to the ground, the breath knocked from me. I rolled over onto my side and strained to come to my feet, my ribs aching from the impact. Elbows shaking.

"Mattheia?"

Firagia saw him first and tightness squeezed my gut as I turned.

"Mattheia!?"

No longer a wolf, Mattheia lay stretched across the rocks, his shredded clothes draped over his body. Blood pooled around him and, as I approached, the gaping hole in his side came into view. I gasped and crumbled to my knees, a breath seizing in my lungs.

He'd taken the strike—the giant spear of ice meant for

ME. I lifted his cold, limp hand into mine and squeezed it gently. "Mattheia?"

No response.

"Mattheia, no! What were you thinking!?" Anger billowed inside, fueled by pain and terror. "I did all this to protect *you.* Why would you—" He was cold as ice, and I couldn't hear a heartbeat when I pressed an ear to his chest.

"Can you help him, Firagia?"

Blood continued to color the ground crimson, saturating my uniform.

The dragon came up beside me and furrowed his brow. "No. I-I cannot."

"You healed me! Why can't you heal him!?"

"Well... I *can,* but... You do not understand. I will—"

"I don't care what it takes! Save him," I commanded, glaring. "Do it, please! I'll take care of *her.*"

I came to my feet, drained of all sensations.

"Why did you do that to him!?" My fingers formed fists so tight, my nails pinched the skin. "Was turning him against me not enough!? I thought this ridiculous curse... challenge—whatever it is—was about *me!*"

"The fool cast himself into danger," she replied. "I did not force it."

My body felt cold and hollow and my mind clear and centered. Bright red light flickered through my line of sight as my surroundings dimmed out of focus and only my target remained in view.

"Don't. Call. Him. A fool..."

Before, when I had drawn vagrant energy, I willed it *kindly*, asking with grace and hope in my heart. But now, as red-hot energy poured into me from my surroundings, I *ordered* it to come. I *demanded* its presence and strength.

Emerald exhibited no honor or fairness in her senseless attacks, so I would treat her with the same level of respect.

My body drifted up from the ground, higher than I had in the past. A racing vortex of rocks and ice kicked up around me and spun rapidly, flashing with a mix of fire and ignited earth. The force of the wind tunnel pulled Emerald in and she struggled to break free, but I held on with all my might.

Her body broke through the barrier and floated closer, passing partially through the debris. Warm white and violet light swept over her, searing the edges of her dress and nipping at her skin with fiery orange embers.

"You won't haunt anyone else," I hissed through clenched teeth. "I won't let you."

Emerald's skin blackened and the edges of her dress and hair began to shrivel and burn away to peels of smoldering cinders.

The scent of burning flesh made my lips wrinkle.

I'm not a murderer...

I felt mercy and guilt tugging at my heart.

As spiteful as I was, I didn't want to kill her... or anyone for that matter.

I only wanted to live.

I wanted Mattheia to live.

Perhaps it was too late for him.

Emerald had been murdered by her jealous brother. She'd been devastated by the cruel card of fate dealt to her, and she blindly targeted other Elemental Guardians in her quest for vengeance.

I wouldn't die at her hands, nor would I destroy her by mine.

"I'm not like you!" I released my hold on her and allowed the whirlwind to collapse. Emerald hit the ground and her body burst into a flurry of leaves. The dry, brown flakes flew up and were quickly carried off by a gust of wind.

I fell to my knees and gasped for breath, every ounce of my adrenaline burned; all my muscles stung.

The air was silent.

My Spirit's presence in my mind had been muted. Or had it gone? I couldn't tell.

"Firagia?" I looked around. No warm light flickered in the distance and I felt very alone all of a sudden. My mind was empty and quiet.

On my hands and knees, I crawled over to Mattheia's body. Some color had returned to his skin and... he was breathing!

"Mattheia!?" I rolled him carefully onto his back. The

wound was nowhere to be seen.

He groaned weakly and his eyes fluttered opened. "What... happened?"

"You're alive!" I heaved a breath of relief and smiled, taking his hand into mine. "You're going to be okay."

His head tipped to the side and he went unconscious again.

But I wasn't scared anymore. He was alright and...

I turned my head.

Firagia!?

I screamed.

Firagia lay curled up on the ground a few feet away, as if he were sleeping, except his body had become the same translucent white as frosted glass. I released Mattheia's hand, shuffled over to him, and then pressed my fingers against his ice-cold body. Hard as stone.

"Firagia?" My voice rose and a whimper reverberated in my throat. "Firagia? What's wrong? What happened to you?" I tried to shake the dragon, but I couldn't so much as make him budge.

What had he done!?

He had said something about not being able to heal Mattheia, but then he said he could and...

I didn't know he'd meant it would kill him!

"Ah!" I cried out to nothingness and tears poured out of my eyes and down my cheeks. "It wasn't supposed to be like this!"

No one could hear me.

I bent over and slammed a fist against the dirt, the riveting pain shooting up my arm made me howl.

I raised my hands and tried to bring heat to them again. Maybe... maybe I could warm Firagia back to life? Maybe if I could...

But a spark wouldn't come.

The light wouldn't manifest in my hands.

"No!" I couldn't even force a tiny glimmer of fire to grow in my grasp. I was so tired.

So weak.

Fatigue set in, and it set in quickly. My surroundings began to blur and my head felt heavy.

Help! We needed help.

But... how?

How would they ever find us in the abandoned ruins of Alyssia?

No one knew where we were.

It would take more than luck to get us out of there. It would take...

Luck?

My mom's cherry blossom barrette...

The tracking particle Mattheia had put in it for me back when I was at Silver Diamond. It was still there. Did it still work?

My arm seemed to weigh a thousand pounds, but I strained to bring it up so I could reach the silver clip. I fumbled to clasp onto it, then I slid it from my hair and depressed the sensor affixed to the back.

After expelling my last sliver of strength just to push the button all the way down, my consciousness faded away and I fell.

I awoke in an infirmary. The lights had been dimmed and only the soft beep of nearby monitors sounded. Sterile, unwelcoming air surrounded me.

I sat up and rubbed my head, accidentally tugging the intravenous line and flinching from the uncomfortable sensation. An I.V. drip had been strapped to my wrist. My vision was hazy, but I could focus well enough to make out the logo on the back of the door.

My pulse rose and the monitor began to beep more fervently. Why was I at Silver Diamond again!? Why didn't my captain send someone to take me back home?

"Hello? Is anyone there?" I scooted over on the bed and

set my feet onto the cold, hard tile floor. It sent a shiver up my spine and I cringed, recoiling back onto the bed. There was shuffling outside; someone was coming.

They knocked on the door before entering.

"I'm awake." It hurt to raise my voice and I coughed from the roughness tickling my throat.

A doctor came in and flipped on the lights fully. He came over to the bedside and examined my vitals on the monitor.

"How do you feel, Lieutenant?" he asked, lifting one of those magnifying flashlight things up to peer into my eyes. "Your pupils are responding properly." He pressed the back of his hand to my forehead. "Your fever has definitely gone down, too. Do you know what your name is?"

"Yes." I scoffed. "Of course, I do. I'm Lieutenant Valhara Hawksford of Celestial Galaxy, and I demand to know why I'm being detained."

The doctor chuckled and it made my jaw tighten. I wasn't a child. I wanted to be talked to straight.

"You're not being detained, Lieutenant," he replied with a shake of his head. "Captain Ventresca requested we care for you until you had recovered enough to safely clear the flight back to Celestial Galaxy. We aren't keeping you here by force."

"Then let me go."

"I can't discharge you until I've checked that you're doing well and that you don't have any lasting side effects from the trauma of whatever happened to you on Alyssia. I'd also like you to speak with a physical therapist before you—"

"Doctor." I looked him in the eye. "I'm fine. Please, let me go. Thank you for tending to my injuries, but I need to get back to work at my own academy."

"Let me check with the commander, first. I have strict orders to run your evaluation past him before discharging you." He stood and slipped a small tablet out of his white coat pocket and swiped open an application. He typed in a pass code and pressed his finger to the device screen. It beeped and he then began typing up a message to, presumably, Mattheia.

"Is Commander Draven well?" I asked quietly.

"Yes. He had a few bumps and bruises when he arrived, but they were trivial compared to yours and he was released the same day."

"How long has it been?"

"You were admitted last Friday." He tapped a button and his tablet chirped.

"*Last* Friday?"

"About a week, Lieutenant." His gaze came up from the tablet.

I was supposed to be back at C.G. by now. The captain had only given me three weeks leave.

"I'll let you know as soon as I hear anything," he said. "Press that yellow button on the side of your bed if you need me."

I nodded and the doctor shut the door. I heaved a sigh, pressing my back against the firm but somewhat uncomfortable pillow as I looked up at the ceiling.

I lay there, resting my eyes, wondering what I would say to Mattheia the next time we met. Wondering how we were going to make this relationship work. I'd promised to try, at least, but it seemed daunting still.

Jacksiun had probably left already and was now getting acquainted to Aquarius, while my sister and Captain Ventresca were making plans to leave together soon. And there I was, trying to get my own life in order.

I just wanted to be happy. I wanted to be successful at work and have people who cared about me in my life.

My hands tensed and my lip began to quiver as I thought about Firagia and the sacrifice he'd made. What would a Guardian be without a Spirit? Was Emerald truly finished with me?

What if she—

A dull whirring sound buzzed through my ears and my eyes reeled open.

A ghostly white aura manifested at the end of my bed, surrounded by a subtle blue halo of light.

Emerald!?

But... she appeared very different this time. Her dark velvet dress had faded to a soft, snowy white, and the spirals of piercing-bright color had muted, emitting a less threatening glow.

"What do you want?" My voice wavered. I tried not to be afraid, but the eerie sight made me shudder.

"I have come to ask for forgiveness," she whispered. Her pupils were large and round, childlike. Innocent. She had a changed demeanor to her body language now, and her vehement, angered glare had become calm and forlorn.

"Forgiveness?"

"I misjudged you, Guardian," she continued, "and I pressed you beyond what was necessary to pass proper judgment. Your disdain toward me is understandable and I am sorry for the pain I have caused."

"I did everything I could, but you kept pushing me. Pushing *him*. And then Firagia... he..."

"I did not expect your Spirit to make such a grave sacrifice for you. It was not within my right to force the majestic beast to forfeit his life for the boy."

"His name was Firagia, and he was my friend. But what do you know about friends? You've been punishing Guardians for something your brother did years ago. Guardians who probably didn't deserve to be punished." I looked away from the ghostly apparition and scowled. My chest tightened and I forced myself to hide the sadness growing inside me over my fallen companion.

"You are right, Valhara," Emerald said, looking at me

affectionately. "My challenge was meant to see how far you would go to protect those around you. I wanted to know if you were selfless and worthy of the great gift the earth granted you. But I made a narrow-minded mistake. I did not expect your companions to risk their lives for you, as well."

"Neither did I." I crossed my arms and cleared my tightening throat. I wiped a tear from my cheek.

"You are loved by many, Valhara, and that yields more victories in battle than any weapon. I learned something from you, Guardian, and I cannot ignore what others have given up for you. Please accept my apologies and my request to be forgiven. I want to rest. I want my soul to sleep in peace and I no longer wish to pursue this rage that has long festered inside me."

Emerald glided to my bedside. I gasped and drew back, pressing deeper into the pillows behind me as I had nowhere else to go.

"I offer you this gift." She lifted a hand toward my necklace. "My life force." Her fingers pressed against the crimson stone and it began to glow.

Something stirred in the back of my mind. A presence.

I felt *him* again—Firagia—easing back into my thoughts, our connection being revived.

"Take heed, Guardian, while your Spirit retains his former abilities, I have granted him a physical form which leaves him subject to damage... and even death. Care for your dragon friend, as my sister once did. He is irreplaceable."

"Th-thank you, Emerald." I wiped a second tear from my face, but it wasn't one of sadness anymore. Firagia was there. His mind flickered to life inside my own, his thoughts whirling excitedly with new vigor and joy.

"*Grant her peace, Valhara,*" Firagia's voice resonated in my head.

He was right. She deserved closure now and I was the only person who could grant it to her.

"Thank you," I said, again, smiling. "I forgive you, Emerald."

A warm grin curled her lips and her eyes narrowed with tranquility and happiness.

"Go be with your husband and Malachite now," I added. "I'm sure they miss you."

She faded away into sparkling iridescent white dust.

"*You did the right thing,*" Firagia added. "*Now, allow yourself the same courtesy, Valhara.*"

What did he mean by—?

There was a knock at the door. I sucked in a quick breath.

"Come in." My voice cracked.

The handle twisted and a black sleeve pushed opened the door, its silver trim catching the light.

"Valhara." A bittersweet smile curved Mattheia's lips.

"Hi."

"How are you feeling?" He walked softly across the room.

"Much better. Good. I-I feel good."

"You've been cooped up here for a while. It's late, but would you be okay with taking a short walk with me and getting some fresh air? I know your body's still healing, but I'll help you. The doctor said it would be okay to go out for a bit. If you want."

I glanced at the clock hanging on the wall opposite me and then at the frosted-glass window to my side. It looked dark outside. Likely past student curfew.

That hadn't stopped us before.

"Sure." I scooted closer to the edge of the bed and then grunted as the muscles in my arms ached and tensed.

"Careful!" He braced me as I stepped onto the floor. I wobbled a little as I put weight and pressure on my knees and feet. He made sure I could stand okay on my own before he turned and bent down to retrieve something from the drawer of a nearby cabinet.

"Here," he said, handing me a set of clothes. It was a uniform of some kind—definitely not my own—and it also wasn't a standard-issue from Silver Diamond. It was dark green with brassy-gold trim on the sleeves. "I'll be outside the door if you need help with anything."

"Thanks."

He left my room.

The doctor returned to remove my I.V. and then I cleaned up and changed into the new uniform.

We walked down the quiet hall together, the once familiar motion now surreal. Glass windows passed us by. Security
personnel I'd come to know and see quite often, vigilant at
their posts.

I'd miss this academy.

The amazing new firearms I had been allowed to train
with.

The library archive.

The students I'd befriended.

Even the pizza.

But most of all, I think I'd miss the homey little dinners
I had at Mattheia's house. I'd miss the wonderful fruit cup-
cakes his mom baked whenever I was over. Mattheia told
me she baked them especially for me, even though she pretended it was an everyday thing. Once I'd complimented her
on them, she made it her duty to provide them to me on
every visit.

And that dog of his. Well, of his mother's. Daisy. The little fuzz ball had wanted to eat me the first time we'd met,
but that had faded with time, and she eventually sat on my
lap while Mattheia and I talked on the couch.

I'd miss Wolf, too, the dog that had graciously welcomed
me into Mattheia's office early on in the term. I had gotten to
see him a few more times and he seemed to like me, too.
Mattheia really liked big dogs. I was okay with that because
it made him happy.

I loved to see Mattheia smile. The sweet, charming look of happiness in his eyes made the world less threatening, if only for a few moments. Now I'd be going back to C.G. and had no idea when I'd see him again. Sure, we'd discussed it, but that wouldn't make it any easier.

There was no denying how I felt anymore.

After he'd taken the blow for me as the enchanted wolf, I told him that I loved him and... I meant it.

"Go ahead," Mattheia said, gesturing toward the maintenance ladder. "I'll come up after so I can help in case you slip."

I wrapped my hands around the cold bars and lifted a foot onto the first rung. It took more effort than usual to reach the top, but I did it, and pulled myself up out of the hatch and onto the rooftop.

I crumpled over and panted, trying to catch my breath.

"It wasn't that hard before," I said with a cough.

"I'm sorry."

"I'll... be fine." I exhaled. "I'm just glad I wasn't out for much longer."

"Me, too." He unrolled a thick mat and motioned for me to sit. Then he held out his arm to help me lower myself to the floor without stumbling.

I inhaled deeply and the cool air felt good in my lungs. Mattheia was right; I did need to get out of the infirmary.

He plopped down beside me and reached for my hand,

taking it gently into his lap and cupping it with both of his.

"I-I thought it was over when Emerald attacked us," he said. "I thought... we were all going to die." He squeezed my fingers and his hands started to shake as his breaths became shallow. "When she turned me into that... *thing*... I couldn't think clearly. All I could do was linger in the back of my mind and yell at it to stop. But it wouldn't listen. It just kept going. Kept wanting to hurt you." He looked at my shoulder and brushed it with his other hand. "I'm so sorry, Valhara." His crystal blue eyes looked into mine and he forced a smile. "I'm glad you're okay," he said, swallowing hard and looking down at his lap.

"Thank you for protecting me." I brushed his fair golden hair over his ear and lifted his chin. "You said you'd do anything for me and you've proved that to be true numerous times. I owe it to you to appreciate and trust you more, and... I'd like to start by telling you how I feel." I filled my lungs and exhaled, chuckling to myself at how incredibly difficult something so simple had suddenly become.

The words were there. They had been there before and they were there again.

I just had to say them.

"I love you, Mattheia." They finally came out, though my heart was racing now.

His smile cracked wider, his thumb massaged my hand, and he spun the silver ring on my finger.

But he didn't say anything in return.

He just stared at the ring, silently.

It wasn't like him to bite his tongue.

"What?" I cocked an eyebrow and leaned closer. "Wh- what is it, Mattheia?"

"Will you marry me?" He lifted his face and his gaze pierced mine.

I gasped. A row of goose bumps swept across my skin and my hair prickled on the back of my neck. "Oh," I exhaled the word. "Uh..."

He lifted a hand and silver gleamed. "We've already got the rings." His adoring smile made my heart flutter.

We had, hadn't we?

"I know how I feel," he continued, "you know how you feel and... well, we've proven we'll do anything for each other. We've been through things no one else has." His forehead wrinkled. "We fought a dragon together, Valhara."

"And a mahora spider."

He laughed. "Exactly! The fact that we're still together— that we still have each other and *want* each other—that's something, right?"

"Yes."

"Then what do you say?" He shifted his weight, facing me head-on. "Lieutenant Valhara Hawksford, will you marry me?"

I nodded. "I already said yes."

"Oh!" His eyes lit up joyfully and his smile couldn't have gotten any bigger. "I... don't know what to say, then. Uh..."

"Then don't say anything," I whispered playfully, looking up through my lashes at him.

He released my fingers, took my face into his hands, and pulled me into a kiss.

It was wonderfully warm and I felt his heart thumping excitedly in his chest as my hand settled near his shoulder, wrinkling the fabric of his uniform.

When he released me, he swept his hand across my brow and rested his palm at the side of my neck, his thumb caressing my jawbone.

"I do, however, have one question," I started. "How is this going to work?"

"Glad you asked," he replied. "Now, before you start freaking out about the whole being-light-years-apart thing, I actually have something else I need to discuss with you." He cleared his throat. "In the past few weeks, there's been discussion and planning to create an entirely new sector of this academy. It's been named the Citrine Exploration Division and will focus on the attainment, study, and preservation of rare and unique weaponry and artifacts from around the world. As a newly minted branch of Silver Diamond Academy, we felt—we being the captain and I—that it should have some new, fresh ideas. Ones we haven't been running on for the last decade."

I looked down at the brass-colored trim on my uniform.

"You came with very high recommendations from Captain Ventresca. As high commander of Silver Diamond, on behalf of our academy, I'd like to offer you the position of Voyage Admiral with the Citrine Sector. Your rank will go up and Celestial Galaxy will deliver your original contract over to us, making you a member of our full-time elite personnel."

"I..." A breath caught in my throat. I didn't know how to respond to that.

Technicalities started darting through my brain as I considered his second proposal.

I suppose, if we were married, it wouldn't necessarily be a conflict of interest, right? Not if we worked in different departments. Had he really thought this out that thoroughly, or was it all just a coincidence?

"Did you make this happen? Is it because—"

"Valhara?" He pressed his hand onto my shoulder. "We would have offered it to you anyway, but... you were leaving to go back to Celestial Galaxy and you were adamant about returning. Captain Lansfora contacted Captain Ventresca and discussed your qualifications just before you went home." He paused. "Okay, so maybe this had a *little* to do with my suggestions, and your own, but it wasn't *all* my doing. Please don't think about it like that. You're more than qualified and you deserve recognition for your skills and expertise. Please consider it."

With Jacksiun having transferred to Aquarius and Atira returning to Earth to marry Captain Ventresca, there wasn't much left for me at Celestial Galaxy.

I only wanted to go home, wherever that was. Be it in space, or... with Mattheia. I wanted to belong.

And I kind of liked how the new uniform looked on me, too.

"I accept your offer," I replied.

Mattheia puffed out his cheeks and huffed a breath. "Oh, good."

"You seem relieved."

"Yes. Well, I may or may not have told Captain Lansfora," he lowered his voice, "and a few other people," he cleared his throat, "that you already accepted the position."

"What!?" I shoved him firmly in the arm, but teasingly. "Why would you—"

"You said yes!"

"Yes, but..." I sighed. Okay. I did say yes. "Alright. You win. But don't go about making decisions for me. I can stand on my own, thank you very much."

"I know, Valhara. You've made that crystal clear with your actions."

"Admiral, huh? That's new."

"I think it works for you. Admiral Hawksford. Or... will that be Draven?"

I shrugged and shook my head. "I haven't thought about

that, yet. One thing at a time, please."

"Of course, Admiral."

I looked up at the sky. "I don't know how long it will take for me to get used to that, but... it has a nice ring to it. I worked hard for everything I have today, and I'm glad *someone* noticed it."

Mattheia's hand brushed my chin and he tipped my face toward his.

"*A lot* of people noticed," he said softly, looking me in the eye.

A buzzing startled us and Mattheia's fingers slipped from my chin to reach into his pocket for his phone. There was a red text alert I couldn't quite read from where I sat.

"Hmm." He grimaced, swiped away the message, and then started tapping a reply.

"What is it? What's happened?" I leaned closer, but he tipped the phone out of view.

"Something to do with Alyssia. I can't discuss it all with you because it's classified, but it involves your department. I *can* get you immediate clearance *if* you request it." He tapped the send button and the message went through.

Alyssia? That was Jacksiun's homeland. His parents lived there.

"Yes! Please." I straightened up. "Jacksiun's from there. If it involves his country, I need to know about it."

"Then you'll find out soon. Do you feel well enough to

get briefed tonight? It's fairly time sensitive and—"

"Yes."

"Alright. Let's go." He stood and helped pull me to my feet. "I'll walk with you to the new sector." He reached into his pocket and slid out a keycard of some kind, which he then passed to me. "You'll need this, Admiral." He grinned.

The sliding glass doors were striking, dark yellow—the type of yellow used in flight goggles and visors to help one focus. Mattheia demonstrated how to use my keycard in the newly re-designed door lock and then stepped off to the side.

"You're on your own for now," he said with a nod of encouragement. "I believe in you." He winked and it made me feel, only slightly, less apprehensive.

I walked into the room and looked around. A giant unmanned computer system stretched across the entire room and huge projection systems hung overhead, bringing to life three-dimensional models of Earth and its continents.

A door whooshed open nearby and I swerved around. "Jacksiun!?"

"Hello, Valhara," he said, tipping his head as he approached.

"What are you doing here? I thought you were at Aquarius?"

He took in a deep breath and rolled his shoulders back. "I haven't exactly been honest with you about a few things." He reached a hand toward his glasses and grasped the frame between his fingers. He slid them down off his nose, folded in the arms, and tucked them into his shirt pocket.

"What are you doing?" I raised an eyebrow.

"I need to tell you the truth about who I am."

My heart felt like it was beating a thousand pulses a minute and a lump formed in my throat. What could he possibly have been hiding from me all these years!?

"You remember where I'm from, right?"

I nodded because I was too stunned to get a word out.

"I'm here at Silver Diamond because I need your help and I came here because I wanted to ask you to come with me when I go home to my... parents."

"Why? I have work to do. I don't know if Mattheia told you, but... I have a new position now. Here."

"And that's exactly why I came to you, Valhara. The commander told me what you are—that you have the power to control energy and conjure fire. We *need* your help."

"Who is 'we' and why did *they* send you!? What's this classified information I couldn't be told earlier?"

"What's my name, Valhara?"

"What!?" I scowled. "Don't play games with me. You're my friend. At least, I thought you were. Why are you messing with my head? Tell me whatever it is you need to tell me. Now!"

A flicker of orange light shot through my vision and Jacksiun's eyes widened. "Ah!" He gasped and stumbled back a step.

"Tell me the truth, Lieutenant Ray." I emphasized every word sternly.

"I'm..." He cleared his throat and sighed. "I was born in Alyssia, but transferred to the Mainlands as a child to enlist and remain under the protection of Celestial Galaxy."

"The protection? What?"

"Ray is a truncated form of Rayvenstar. My proper title was removed for my own protection."

Jacksiun Rayvenstar of Alyssia? His 'proper' title?

My jaw dropped. I wanted to knock him in the shoulder for the cruel joke, but... it wasn't like him to ruffle my feathers for his own entertainment, so I had to stay calm.

"As in... *King* Vincent Rayvenstar's heir?" My voice trembled. "The heir of the Alyssian throne?"

He nodded.

Jacksiun was a prince!?

I stared at him, dumbfounded. What could I say?

What was left for me to ask him?

All these years… he'd been hiding his identity from me.

"Who else knows?" I growled. "Who else has been lying to me?"

"Only Captain Ventresca, Captain Lansfora, and—as of this week—Commander Draven. And, of course, a handful of others at C.G. Valhara, please understand I had nothing to do with this. I didn't want to keep it a secret, but I had to for your own safety."

"My safety?"

"Did you really think they'd let a *lieutenant* command the Goliath?"

Maybe?

"It's C.G.'s strongest, fastest ship. They let me take it because they knew I'd be safe onboard and I offered to chaperone *you* because… I knew it would keep you safe, too."

"Then how did you end up on the Mainlands?"

"My father wanted me to live a normal life and grow up around peers, not subjects. So he sent me to a school on the Mainlands and that's where we met. He thought it would help me see the world how it really is. Something outside the confines of castle walls." He stretched an arm toward me. "Please don't be angry."

"So you're Prince Jacksiun?" I pulled back from his touch. "And your father, King Vincent, sent you here to ask for *my* help? Why? What on earth can I do that his esteemed army can't?"

"Do you know what a bloodmane is? They're—"

"Ancient creatures. I'm familiar with them." I recalled the dream about Emerald's past—how she had shape-shifted into one of the nightmarish things. Massive, part-lion, part-serpent creatures with a rampant thirst for blood.

"My father was excavating an old temple site near the palace and the workers struck the entrance of a bloodmane hive. It awakened the pack from their hibernation and they..." He paused and chewed his lip. "Hundreds of people have been killed already and more will die with each passing day if we can't stop the creatures from rampaging. My father's armies don't have the technology or strength to pierce bloodmane armor. Maybe... you can help us." His soft blue eyes gazed into mine and sadness grew in me. "Please, Valhara."

It wasn't like Jacksiun to beg for anything. Ever.

He looked slightly different without his glasses, but as I stared into his gentle irises, I knew he was the same person I'd befriended as a child—the same man who had helped Mattheia save my life when I had been poisoned by the ma-hora. But now there was so much pain and worry in them. Sorrow twisted his face and his eyes shimmered with des-peration. Jacksiun didn't show weakness easily. In fact, I'd known him to always be the kind of person who would hide his pain instead of talking about it, no matter how much it hurt to do so.

He was a lot like me...

"I'll do whatever I can," I said quietly, avoiding looking into his eyes because I felt uncomfortable and unsure of how to address him now. He was a prince, after all.

"Thank you, Valhara." He rested his hand on my forearm. "I knew I could rely on you."

"How could I say no? You're my friend. I don't let friends down and I don't lie to them, either."

"It won't happen again, I promise you."

"I appreciate that."

"That being said, is there anything you want to tell me?" I caught him glancing at my hand. "Anything at all?"

"Only that you were right about Mattheia," I replied, a smile creeping across my face. "And... if I'm allowed to have the Prince of Alyssia at my wedding, he *will* get an invitation." I smirked.

Jacksiun chuckled.

"Now, *Your Highness*, let's talk about saving your father's kingdom."

"Please don't call me that," Jacksiun groaned, shaking his head. "It *really* doesn't sound right coming from you." He withdrew his phone from his pocket and began messaging someone. "I'll let them know we're ready to start working. Please excuse me while I make some calls."

I nodded and turned away from him, lifting my hand to touch my necklace. I brushed a thumb across the warm, polished stone.

"I don't think the journey ahead will be a smooth one, my friend," I whispered, too low for Jacksiun to hear as he spoke on his phone.

Firagia's reply echoed softly through my mind. "*It never is,*" he said. "*It never is.*"

Get the coloring book and see all your favorite characters and scenes come to life!

Available at most online retailers

ISBN 978-0-9974485-2-8

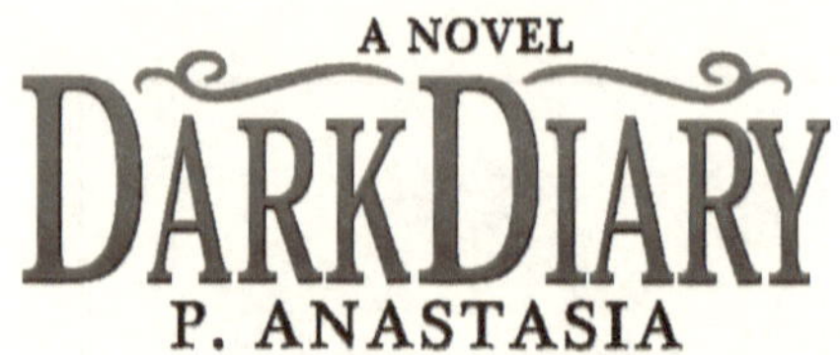

A young woman with a dark past encounters a young man with an even darker one. More human than vampire, *Dark Diary* is a quaint, sophisticated romance detailing the accounts of two lovers who have paid **the *ultimate price*...**

This timeless, standalone, genre-crossing love story with supernatural undertones and a flourish of historical romance, will capture your heart and never let go.

Forbidden romance in the vein of classics like *Wuthering Heights*, frosted with the seductive allure of immortality, *Dark Diary* documents a pair torn apart by time. The story is told by a 400-year-old immortal and a 21-year-old modern-day artist.

He's trapped in a never-ending circle of guilt over the loss of a friend and lover.

She's haunted nightly by visions of her own untimely death.

Together, they find solace by sharing secrets beneath the light of the moon.

Fluorescence

**My name's Alice Green.
I hope, for your sake, you *never* meet me.**

A riveting paranormal romance, *Fluorescence* is engaging and unabashed—a coming-of-age urban science fiction unlike any other.

It lives in her bloodstream. It's unpredictable and could flare up any time, exposing her secret. Alice was a normal teenager, until a dying race of aliens chose her and a handful of others to preserve bio-luminescent DNA known as Fluorescence. Now, she and the others must hide their condition from the rest of the world, while trying to learn the truth behind the living light.

In a unique genre, *Fluorescence* is a striking blend of audacious young love, fantasy, and science fiction.

Each full-length novel in the complete tetralogy is narrated by a different character, driving the story forward in a new and exciting way. It evolves from a quiet beginning into a gripping saga, exploring the real-life limitations encountered while harboring a volatile secret.

P. ANASTASIA'S fresh take on storytelling resonates with darkness, charm, and passion—the embodiment of her unique writing style. With origins tracing back to the late nineties, the creative fire that became Fates Aflame was drawn from P.'s love of role-playing games, mythology, and all things magical.

Drawn to the craft in childhood, she began attempting to produce her first book at age 11. While working toward her college degree, she wrote news and editorial columns for two campus newspapers. After graduating with a degree in Communications and spending a year studying abroad in Kofu, Japan, she followed her heart to her publishing aspirations. She currently resides in the beautiful, green state of Kentucky with her husband and her ever-inspiring fur-babies. On the side, she serves as a professional voice talent for radio, television, and audio books.

P. Anastasia is the author of nine novels: *Exile of the Sky God*, the *Fluorescence* series, *Fates Aflame, Fates Awoken,* and *Dark Diary*.

Thank you for reading!
If you enjoyed this story, please support the author's writing journey by posting a review on Amazon or social media. Share your thoughts with friends, other readers, and book clubs.

More books at:

PANASTASIA.COM

www.ingramcontent.com/pod-product-compliance
Lightning Source LLC
Chambersburg PA
CBHW020624120726

47905CB00003B/937